THE HELLION

ALSO BY S. A. HUNT

Burn the Dark

I Come with Knives

S. A. HUNT

THE HELLION

A TOM DOHERTY ASSOCIATES BOOK
NEW YORK

This is a work of fiction. All of the characters, organizations, and events portrayed in this novel are either products of the author's imagination or are used fictitiously.

THE HELLION

A Tor Book
Published by Tom Doherty Associates
120 Broadway
New York, NY 10271

www.tor-forge.com

Tor® is a registered trademark of Macmillan Publishing Group, LLC.

The Library of Congress Cataloging-in-Publication Data is available upon request.

ISBN 978-1-250-30651-7 (trade paperback)
ISBN 978-1-250-30650-0 (hardcover)
ISBN 978-1-250-30649-4 (ebook)

Our books may be purchased in bulk for promotional, educational, or business use. Please contact your local bookseller or the Macmillan Corporate and Premium Sales Department at 1-800-221-7945, extension 5442, or by email at MacmillanSpecialMarkets@macmillan.com.

First Edition: September 2020

Printed in the United States of America

0 9 8 7 6 5 4 3 2 1

This one's for you, firebrands and hellions out there, women that fought and scratched and bit like demons and lived to tell the tale. The first one I ever met was my mother Kathy, and she set a standard.

SSDGM, y'all.

CONTENT WARNING

Intense Scenes

Domestic Violence

Self-Harm

Abuse and Misogyny

The beast in me is caged by frail and fragile bars
Restless by day and by night rants and rages at the stars
God help the beast in me

—Johnny Cash, "The Beast in Me"

Time is the substance from which I am made.
Time is a river which carries me along, but I am the river;
it is a tiger that devours me, but I am the tiger;
it is a fire that consumes me, but I am the fire.

—Jorge Luis Borges

THE HELLION

INTRO

Then

Her first night in Heinrich's compound was a long one. The teenager lay under a wool military blanket in the deepening twilight, listening to the silence of the desert and rain drumming on the tin roof. The man slept hard, his breath a steady susurration barely audible under the rattle of the rain. Occasionally, heat lightning flashed across the ceiling, throwing her makeshift bedroom into ghastly ghost-story detail.

An incredible crash of thunder shook the room.

Terrified, Robin sat bolt upright and threw the curtain aside, preparing to run for the door.

"Good morning," said Heinrich.

As always, he wore all black—jeans, boots, a thermal henley draped on his broad shoulders. The witch-hunter sat on a stool at the kitchen island, tall and lanky, with an expressive mouth and hard eyes, and his skin was the cold, steely kind of black, like he'd been carved from the night itself.

One of the many things she would pick up from him: the paranoid gunslinger tendency to sit against the wall, so she couldn't be shot in the back. Or have her throat cut, how the witches liked to get you when your guard was down. Simple and effective.

"What time is it?" She put on a pair of the fresh new socks she'd bought on the way through Mississippi. Reaching under the cot, she dragged out her new boots and wriggled into them.

"About six." Heinrich beckoned her over. "Come on, I made food."

The teenager joined him at the kitchen island, where he'd made omelets and bacon on a big plug-in griddle. French press half-full of coffee. A cookie sheet rested on a towel, loaded with several flaky biscuits. Nearby, a radio quietly played a morning drive-time show.

"Boy howdy, you know how to do breakfast." Robin poured a big cup of coffee, dipped a spoonful of sugar into it, and made herself stir it before gulping half the cup in one go.

He watched her. "Most important meal of the day."

Caffeine clawed the sleepiness from her brain. "Been so long since I had a good cup of coffee," she said, downing the other half. She poured another cup and took an omelet, along with bacon and a biscuit, and ate ravenously. "Don't let you have it in the psych ward."

"We'll need the energy." The man peeled open a biscuit and spooned jam into it. "Today you start your training. Sleep okay?"

"Slept like shit." She ground the back of her wrist into one grainy eye, her fingers shiny with grease. "Thanks for asking."

"Yeah," he said into his coffee cup, "I know the feeling." He grinned. "You gonna sleep good tonight."

• • •

According to the man, the building they lived in had been used by the Killeen Fire Department as a training structure. The lower floors were devoid of furniture or decoration—just bare cinderblock walls and cement floors. Heinrich led her all the way down and around the back of the bottom staircase to a rusty steel door.

This he opened, and he shined a flashlight into a closet full of junk: two sawhorses on which hung a pair of flak jackets, a plastic trunk, and leaning in the corner was an assortment of PVC pipes pushed through foam pool noodles and wrapped in duct tape.

"Here, put this on." He took one of the flak jackets and handed it to her.

The instant she took it from him, the heavy jacket hit the floor. She gathered her arms inside and lifted it over her head. Two slabs of armor in the front and the back, and one pressed against each hip. Heinrich meticulously fastened all the buckles and straps, pulling them tight until the vest fit her like a turtle shell. He rapped his knuckles on her chest, the flashlight shining in her face. "This is called an IOTV. It's a military—"

"Flak jacket?"

"A flak jacket is something different. Vietnam gear. This is desert shit. I don't remember what IOTV stands for, but the ceramic plates can repel small arms fire. It's current military issue. Weighs about forty pounds."

Robin's face went cold. "You ain't gonna be shooting at me, are you?"

"Lord, no." Heinrich smiled. "This is just for weight training. Bought 'em for emergencies, but they make good weight vests." He didn't specify what constituted an "emergency." Instead, he opened the plastic trunk and dug out a pair of things like icepacks. Velcro ripped open and he slipped them around Robin's ankles. "Ankle weights."

"What is all this for?" Her feet felt like they were made of lead.

"Like I said, weight training. Come on." He grabbed one of the pool-noodle swords and a burlap sack, and led her back upstairs. "Want you to wear 'em for three hours today, and every day from now on. Toughen you up, get you used to carrying extra weight.

Trust me, you'll see where I'm going with this after that three hours."

By the time she had climbed back up the three flights of stairs, the teenager was huffing and puffing. "Jesus," she wheezed, leaning against the wall of their den as Heinrich stepped over to the record player and put on a Fugees album. The speakers banged out "Ready or Not," and Lauryn Hill sang about playing her enemies like a game of chess.

"Tired already?"

"No," she sighed.

"Good," said the man, and he threw her a padded stick. She barely caught it, almost fumbling, and when she looked back up, he had heavy pads strapped to his hands. "Let's work off that breakfast, kiddo."

• • •

The rain worsened into a downpour—bad enough Heinrich had to let down the tin-sheet awnings covering the windows. They spent the entire time in the "lair," as he called it, beating each other with the pads and the boffer. Plenty of room there, an open space some thirty or forty feet square, the furniture pushed out of the way, with that dusty Oriental rug in the middle of it.

Their sparring session was soundtracked by everything from Ray Charles to Ol' Dirty Bastard to James Brown to twenty different heavy metal bands. "Nine times out of ten, once you're face-to-face, they gonna try to claw you with their fingernails," he said. "Like fightin' a wildcat." She tried to bat his padded hands aside, but somehow he kept managing to shrug past it and deliver a volley of body blows. "But it's a last-ditch effort. They'll try to keep you from even getting close in the first place."

Frustration twisted around her chest, binding her even tighter than the IOTV. She couldn't seem to move fast enough to get through his hands. "They'll use tricks, try to appeal to your empathy. Lie to you. Offer you riches, immortality. They'll make you see things. Terrible things. Wonderful things. Things that make no goddamn sense. They'll make familiars, like they did with your daddy, send those after you. When all else fails, they fall back on the claws."

He slapped her across the face. "You paying attention?"

Heat and ice surged across her skin as a shot of adrenaline hit her, pissed her off, made her see red. Santa Esmeralda crooned in the background, *I'm just a soul whose intentions are good.* She swung the boffer overhead—"Urrgh!"—and caught him across the wrist.

"Good one," said Heinrich. "Time to come down. Get out of that vest and go get some water."

Dropping the boffer, Robin staggered toward the kitchenette, clawing at the IOTV's straps. Clutching the counter, she used her foot to hook a stool and drag it over to sit on. As soon as she got the armor off and let it slam to the floor at her feet, every muscle in her body screamed out in relief.

• • •

December in Texas. Humidity made it unbearably chilly outside, cold right down to the bone, but their lair was heated from underneath by a furnace.

In hindsight, the structure and exertion were probably what cured Robin of her torpor and cleared her head, focused the thoughts scattered by the death of her mother and the breaking of her spell, and fended off her depression, more than the psych medication. First thing every morning, they got up and ate breakfast, then sparred each other until lunch whether they felt like it or not. Heinrich went out to chop some wood while Robin made lunch, then they ate together and spent a few hours poring over old books. Case studies about witches, occult encyclopedias, language trainers, German, French, Chinese, and Icelandic magic tomes, books of hieroglyphs and runes, and other esoterica.

This is where she learned more about the ways and methods of how witches were able to use cats to scry and to control people. She learned the radius from which a *nag shi* dryad could draw life-force, what factors could alter that reach, and the properties of its accretion disk, such as how running water could dampen it; she learned fire was just about the only thing that could kill a witch older than at least forty years, and bullets were useless other than for slowing them down. She learned the various forms witches who held the Gift of Transfiguration could choose to take—beasts and self-augmentation only, no doppelgängers or inanimate objects; she learned how elaborate witches could make their illusions, from simple visions of insects to artificial realities; she learned the range and strength and dexterity of the Gift of Manipulation, which you might know as *telekinesis,* and ways to defeat it, such as blinding the witch, because they could only manipulate objects they could see.

After study time, Robin went outside in her vest and brought firewood up the two flights of stairs to the third floor, whether they needed it or not. By Christmas, she had filled the entire eastern wall of the furnace room with chunks of oak and pine, and Heinrich had to cut the loads from five to two per day.

Then it was suppertime. The weekends were downtime, and they made big, heavy meals on Saturday and Sunday like slow-cooker Italian meatball soup, chicken enchiladas, steaks and baked potatoes, and pizzas of all shapes and kinds, and during the week, they nibbled the leftovers for supper.

After dinner, they crashed on the couch with a little bowl of ice cream or a soda float and watched TV or a movie out of Heinrich's collection. DVDs and VHS tapes covered one entire wall of his den. Robin lost count of the number of times she fell asleep on the couch watching Zatoichi annihilate a gang of troublemakers.

"Wherever I go," said the blind swordsman, "I'm the god of calamity."

• • •

By that summer, their sparring looked like something out of one of those movies. The teenager worked him around the den with the boffer, and he juked and jitterbugged out of the way like Sinatra, the both of them swashbuckling up and down the stairs, from the window and through the kitchenette. Whenever he managed to parry the boffer and go in for the kill, either he'd get kicked in the leg and staggered, or Robin would twirl the boffer over her head and down across his forehead.

One day, she backed him into the kitchen and he managed to pin the boffer with a cabinet door. Out of some kind of instinct, Robin snatched a barbecue fork out of the dish drain and tried to stab him with it, but Heinrich shielded his face with his free hand, and the fork jammed deep into the hard foam of the punch pad.

Pulling out the fork with a wince, he tossed it in the sink, then slid his hand out of the pad. Two neat puncture wounds vampired the back of his fist.

She gasped. "I'm—"

Heinrich gathered himself, standing. "It's okay."

"I'm so sorry."

"I said it's okay." Blood dripped on the kitchen floor between their feet. "The apprentice has become the master," he said, backing away to the first-aid drawer. He dug out a roll of gauze and wrapped it around his injured hand. "Maybe," he began, as the girl ripped a handful of paper towels off of a nearby roll and wiped up the blood, "maybe it's time to finally show you something."

She gave him a confused look.

"Come with me," he said, grabbing a combat knife off his bed and clipping it to his belt.

They clomped down the stairs to the bottom floor of the fire tower and into the closet where he kept the pads and boffers. In the back of the room was a steel rack with cardboard boxes. In one of them was an orange case, and inside the case was a flare gun. He handed it to Robin.

"What do I do with this?"

"Stick it up your ass? I don't care. Just don't lose it."

She shrugged and jammed it into the back of her jeans.

Outside, Robin followed him through the broad main avenue running through the middle of Hammertown. Spaghetti-western shopfronts loomed over them on either side, their façades welcoming them inside with signs in Arabic. He stepped down one of the side alleys, cutting between a tin shack and a two-story building. Left, around a corner, through a chain-link gate with a *Beware of Dog* sign in Arabic.

Brazen sunshine baked the dirt under their feet. Before them spanned a seemingly infinite vista of Texas desert and, in the distance, a backbone of vague gray mountains.

Between here and there was a lone bur oak, with a short thick trunk and branches stretching in every direction. This tree draped shade over a dilapidated barn with a high, pitched roof and a broad door. Strung through the handles was a strong new chain, secured with three padlocks. The man took out a keychain and unlocked all three, tossing the chain aside. Then he opened the door, pulling both panels aside.

Inside, a ragged, filthy woman in a tattered dress stood tied to one of the support posts under the hay loft, her tangled hair over her face. Ripe body odor hung in the air, along with some pungent, fruity undercurrent Robin couldn't quite identify.

"Oh, my God!" she cried, pushing past into the room.

Before she could free the man's captive, one hand shot out and grabbed the drag-handle of her vest, stopping her in her tracks. Heinrich pulled her gently backward, pointing at the ground.

"Icelandic containment ward."

On the dirt under her feet was an enormous circle etched with salt, an elaborate runic diagram comprised of a dozen concentric circles. Between each circle was an unbroken sentence of hundreds of sigils. With his bandaged hand, Heinrich directed Robin's attention to the walls and ceiling, where dozens of *algiz* protection runes had been painted on every visible surface. Then he pointed at the woman tied to the support beam in the center of the runic bullseye. Glinting in the woman's chest was the handle of a dagger. "Is that a witch?" Robin struggled to make sense of the scene.

Nothing witchlike stood out about this scrawny woman, whose face was pale with abject terror and exhaustion and misery. The woman peered at them through a curtain of matted hair. "Oh, God." Her voice was kitten-weak. "Are you here to save me? This man has had me trapped here for months."

A burst of anger gave Robin the words she needed. "You mean you've had a witch out here the entire time? Like eighty feet from where we sleep? Are you high?"

"Please help me," said the woman. The silvery dagger was buried in her chest right up to the cross guard, and a stain ran down her belly in a banner of dull brown. "I think I might be dying."

"You ain't dyin', Tilda," Heinrich said mildly.

Writhing in her bonds, Tilda stared at him with wild, baleful eyes. The man stepped across the outermost circle of the containment ward toward her, taking care to disrupt the runes with his foot.

"What are you doing?" asked Robin, her heart beating a little faster.

"Been a couple of months since I been around to see my good friend here." Heinrich stepped inside another of the concentric circles. Dry dirt gritted under his boot as he disturbed another ring of symbols. "Thought we could stop in and say hi before lunch." The woman's eyes didn't leave Heinrich's face. Terrible eyes, the washed-out blue high beams of a dope fiend, glaring from under thick eyebrows. Heinrich stepped into another of the circles and a slow smile spread across her face, revealing jagged teeth in ink-black gums.

"I don't think that's a good idea," said Robin.

Fear gripped her. Shivers ran through her like a stampede of wild horses, and her face and hands became cold. The sound of her mother's last words, echoing in the back of her mind as Annie

Martine lay broken on the floor—*Cutty. Witch.* The sight of her father writhing on his back next to her, blood gushing out of his mouth and nose. *Witches aren't real witches aren't real witches aren't real*—but they were, weren't they? They were real. And here was one, right in front of her, large as life and dark as death, glaring at the both of them as her mentor crept closer and closer.

"Nothing is a good idea, except in hindsight." Heinrich stepped into another circle, scuffing the diagram again. "Every decision we make is a Schrödinger's Box. D'you know what that is, Robin Hood?"

"Sure. Yeah. The cat in the box."

"The cat in the closed box, both alive and dead until you open it and find out which it is. Every decision we make is a Schrödinger's Box—both good and bad. We never know which until after we make it."

The woman's breathing came quick and fast, blowing streamers of her hair out in front of her face, *huff huff huff huff* like birthing breaths in a Lamaze class. She laughed under her breath, casting all pretense aside. "You're a pretty little one," she croaked, her cheek meeting her shoulder in a bashful sort of way. "A little older than I like, but that just means I'll have to cook you a little longer. You're still ripe."

"Cook me?"

"Yeah, Robin Hood," said Heinrich. "They eat virgins, remember? They're pedophages? Didn't your mother ever read you the story of Hansel and Gretel?"

"You mean that's *real*?"

"Yeah, it's real. We been reading the same books up there in that tower, ain't we?" The man took another step into a smaller circle, dragging his foot through the salt symbols. "Remember that one I made you read about witches in medieval Russia?"

She winced. "I'm sorry. It was long-winded as shit and really badly translated. I only made it about halfway through."

Dust shook out of the witch's clothes, hanging in the sunbeams coming through the hayloft, as she thrashed violently in her bindings. Rope bound her wrists and elbows behind the pole; rope kept her neck pinned. "It's been so long since I've eaten," said Tilda, grinning with those gnarly brown teeth.

"Anyway, who the hell said I was a virgin?" asked the teenager.

Halfway through scuffing another of the circles, Heinrich shot her an incredulous look. "You were involuntarily committed in your sophomore year, and you've been in there ever since. Your mother was about as religious as you can get in the South without mailing your paycheck to Billy Graham. You trying to tell me you got laid in the nuthouse?"

"Well, you did just call it the 'nut' house."

If he'd been wearing glasses, he would have peered over them at her.

"No, I didn't get laid." Robin scowled. "I was too busy going through the Ludovico technique, sleeping through HGTV reruns, and eating spaghetti with a plastic spoon to care about sexual intercourse. Besides, antidepressants make it hard to orgasm, apparently."

"TMI, kiddo."

At this point, the man was only a few feet away from the witch. Her mouth opened, and kept opening, and her tongue uncoiled, fattening, lolling from between her teeth like a purple python. Lengthening, sharpening, Tilda's teeth bristled in her cavernous mouth. "Come a little closer, Heinie," she said, grinning.

"Heinie?"

Despite herself, Robin couldn't help but laugh.

The man stepped inside the last circle, a ring of runes some six feet across. Reaching out with her serpentine tongue, Tilda could almost reach him—close enough, in fact, for Heinrich to lean backward to avoid getting licked in the face. As he did, he moved around the witch, sidling around the inside of the innermost rune ring.

"What are you doing?" asked Robin.

"Oh, nothing." Heinrich's hands rose in that *don't mind me* way.

The witch watched him, her tongue curling around her own upper arm. "What *are* you doing?" she asked, as if she couldn't believe what she was seeing either.

Then Tilda looked down at her feet. Robin looked down as well, and realized the Icelandic containment circle had been disturbed in a straight line from her own toes to directly in front of the witch. The witch's eyes came back up to Robin's face, grin widening. In one swift motion, Heinrich slid the combat knife out of its sheath and cut the ropes.

Looking back and forth between the two of them, Tilda seemed to be indecisive about who to go after first, but she turned toward Robin and lunged forward, reaching—

—the teenager flinched in terror, falling—

—but Tilda was immediately halted by the silver dagger in her chest, doubling over around it. *"Gurk—!"*

"What the hell, dude?" said Robin, sitting on her ass in the dirt. She reached behind her back and pulled out the flare gun he'd given her earlier, pointing it at Tilda.

"The Osdathregar." Heinrich stepped away from the witch, standing by the innermost rune ring. "In the Vatican Archives, documents call it the Godsdagger. Secret verses of ancient Hindu texts refer to it as the Ratna Maru." Tilda reached up and grasped the hilt of the Osdathregar, trying to wrench it loose. The man paced around the perimeter of the ring, his hands clasped behind his back. "Nobody knows who made it; nobody knows where it came from. All we know is that it's powerful enough to stop a witch cold in her tracks."

Hollywood had conditioned Robin to expect the eldritch and the ornate: a wavy flambergé with a pewter-skull hilt, cord-wrapped handle, and a spike for a pommel, a Gil Hibben monstrosity from a mall kiosk. But the real Osdathregar was a simple main gauche with a gently tapering blade a little wider than a stiletto. The guard was a diamond shape, the handle was wrapped in leather, and the pommel was only an unadorned onion bulb. The diamond of the guard contained a small hollow, and engraved inside the hollow was a sinuous scribble.

"See that symbol there?" Heinrich pointed at the hilt. "That means *purifier* in Enochian, the language of the angels. Regardless of where it came from, this is a holy weapon. Which means even if it can't outright kill a witch, she can't remove it from where it's embedded. Deep magic, baby. You stake her into the floor, or a wall, wherever, she'll be there until the end of time, or until you come along and pull it out."

With the flare gun's muzzle, the teenager gestured to the diagram that filled the barn floor. "What about this, then? And the ropes?"

Heinrich shrugged. "In my line of work, I've learned to appreciate redundancy."

"What *can* kill a witch, then?"

A wry smirk. "Come on, Robin Hood. That's Mickey Mouse kindergarten shit. You *know* what kills a witch."

". . . Fire?"

"Ding ding ding!" cried Heinrich. "We have a winner! Now, listen—I've brought the anger out in you, Robin. Made a fighter out of you. You finally cut me. Now I need to get rid of the fear. A knife ain't nothin' but a worthless piece of steel unless you're willing to use it!"

With that, he pulled out the dagger.

Now nothing stood between them.

"Guns can't stop me, child," said the witch, marching resolutely through the gaps in the ward and out of the barn. In broad daylight, she was even more disgusting, a crusty ghost wrapped in shit and rotten fabric. Blood running down her chin looked like hot black tar, dribbling all over the ground. Her fingernails were yellowed spades. Her hair was the woolly, filthy mane of a lion, and her eyes were fiery red and yellow, with pinprick pupils.

A shout from the man in the barn: *"Fire, you idiot!"*

The flare gun in her hand. Robin pointed it at the witch and pulled the trigger, but the safety was on.

Tilda didn't even flinch. "Nice shootin', Tex," she cackled, and charged, tongue snaking, harpy talons extended.

"Fuck!"

Panic made a live wire out of every nerve in Robin's body. Stones dug into her knees. She aimed the flare gun with both hands and fired. The flare hit center mass.

Waves of incredible heat washed over the little barnyard as the creature erupted into flames ten feet tall, a tornado of smoke and light. Tilda shrieked madly, staggering toward the teenager, flaming hands outstretched.

"Grain alcohol," said Heinrich, coming outside to join them.

Blackened fingers combed through dim orange whorls of light, cupping and clawing, searching. The rest of her was obscured by the column of fire. The teenager shuffled sideways along the fence, trying to keep the flaming witch from grabbing her. "I see you burning, Robin Martine," gurgled the thing in the flames. Collapsing on her knees, and then kneeling prostrate in the shade of the giant bur oak, Tilda laughed through a mouthful of fire. "One day, your enemies will trap you, and you will burn just like me." She fell over and lay motionless, a black wraith shrouded in light. "You will burn," she said in a strained hiss. "You will die."

The last syllable seemed to stretch on forever, becoming the soft rustle of the bur oak's leaves, until it faded into silence, broken only by the warp and woof of the flames biting at the wind.

They stood there and watched her burn until she was a coal sculpture, twisted into a fetal position in the dust.

"That wasn't pleasant," said Heinrich.

"Wasn't a fucking birthday party, that's for sure."

He looked over at her, genuinely surprised. "It's your birthday?"

"Yeah," said the teenager, and she walked away, still gripping the flare gun in one trembling hand.

"Happy birthday," he called after her.

"Stick it up your ass."

SIDE A

Frail and Fragile Bars

Track 1

Now

The lonesome notes of the Eagles' "Hotel California" wailed into the sweltering stillness. But no warm smell of colitas rising up through the air, just the pickle-brine stink of an unshowered woman who'd spent the last several hours in a hot-box.

Penny-colored grass punched through the desert around them, and the sun was a merciless diadem on the blue brow of a cloudless sky. A river of asphalt ran straight out to the horizon in both directions, coming from nowhere and going nowhere. She stood next to the Winnebago, swearing at the top of her lungs, sweat soaking into her clothes, her ringlet Mohawk plastered to the side of her head. If this had been her usual Kool-Aid dye job, Robin Martine's wavy dimetrodon sail of hair would be staining her neck with a dark lilac purple. Her underwear felt like a snot-rag.

Around her chest was a nylon harness, with a camera mounted on her chest. As it always had, the GoPro recorded her trials and tribulations for her YouTube channel *MalusDomestica,* this time bearing witness to one of her rare outbursts of anger.

Their air conditioner gave out hours ago and the Winnebago was a sweat lodge. If the tire hadn't popped like a shotgun shell and started flapping around inside the wheel well, she might have passed out at the wheel and driven them into the desert. She tugged at her T-shirt to air out her sweat. A thing jutted from the tire, something like a pull-start or maybe a meat hook, a plastic T-shaped handle with a pointy metal bit sticking out of the middle.

"A hundred thousand miles of hot sand and lizard shit, and you just happen to find the only whatever-the-hell-this-is in Texas!" Robin gave the Winnebago a ferocious punch, *clank!*

The aluminum body was hot enough to burn and left red scrapes on her knuckles. She winced, massaging her hand.

The Winnebago's door opened and Kenway stepped out, carrying a little Coleman cooler. "What'd Willy do to *you*?" He dropped the cooler in the shadow of the RV. He wasn't wearing a shirt, and he'd developed quite a tan on their tour down the American west coast this spring. Six months of fighting supernatural hags and their minions had trimmed the weight he'd gained moping around in Blackfield. His belly had slimmed to a wall of blond-frosted sandstone, and his hips narrowed to a V of muscle. Under his dock shorts, his prosthetic leg glinted in the sun. After the events of the last Halloween—a battle against four of the hardest of hard-core witches and a newly resurrected Mesopotamian death-goddess—Kenway had tagged along and made himself the big brawny Short Round to her Indiana Jones.

"Ironically, you ran over a tire tool." He wrenched it out of the tire. The remainder of the air hissed out in a tired, resentful sigh. "Tire guys use it for patching or something." He shrugged. "I wouldn't know; I'm not a tire guy."

Robin caught herself staring at him. "Just grab the jack, beef-cake."

He tied his hair back out of his eyes and opened the hatch in the side of the Winnebago. Hauling out the jack, he shoved it underneath the right fender and was about to start pumping when Robin stopped him.

"I got this," she said, grasping the jack handle. "Go get me the spare and the lug wrench."

"You got it."

He went around to the back of the RV, leaving her to deal with the jack. The first couple of pumps were easy, a quick squeaky-squeaky, but on the third pump, the rod stopped short in midair. Robin gripped the handle with both hands and threw herself onto it with everything she had. It screamed and gave a few inches, almost dumping her over onto her face. *What I wouldn't give to be able to*

(hulk out whenever you want?)

do whatever it was I did back in that house, she thought. *Whatever that monster was that Andras turned me into that night.* Her memory showed her a portrait of herself in the silvered glass of a mirror, her skin a latticework of shadows, her heart shining inside. Nothing like the woman she was now: short, sinewy, tanned, with coalsmoke eyes and a thin, expressive mouth. *That girl-shaped effigy, that wicker-wire sculpture with the bottle-rocket soul.*

Cambion.

She stared at the dirty steel staff in her hands as if it were a bloody sword. Blue paint flaked off to reveal rust red, polished by decades of hands. *Cambion. Crooked.* She threw herself on top of the jack handle again with a tortured squeak and the Winnebago started to tilt. *Devil-girl.*

Laughter. She rounded on the comedian.

"You all right?" Kenway stood there stifling a grin, the massive spare drooping from one hip.

"Yes, thanks."

Sweat beaded in his beard, his forehead glittering. He set the tire down on the roadside with a basketball *pung-pung* and shoved at the side of the RV, rocking it. "I'll push, you pump. This should make it easier." He shoved again, and she pushed down on the handle. Him shoving and her pumping, she was able to raise the flat tire off the dirt.

While Kenway made sandwiches with the stuff in the Coleman cooler, Robin changed the tire with much sweating and cursing and kicking. She crouched down and cupped her arms underneath it, lifting the spare like a sumo wrestler, and heaved it onto the axle with a grunt. After screwing on the lug nuts, she let the Winnebago down on all fours with a *thud* and armed sweat from her forehead, leaving a gray smear.

After washing her hands, she sat with Kenway, eating turkey-and-salami sandwiches, sharing a big bag of Doritos, and drinking Blue Moon in the shade of the RV, listening to music. Aerosmith. *Janie's got a gun.*

He finished his lunch first and carried the flat tire around back, heaving it into the spare compartment. Robin pushed the last bite of her sandwich into her mouth and carried the cooler into the RV.

Bladed weapons glinted from their mounts on the interior walls—swords, knives, tomahawks. All the windows were open and a breeze struggled through, trying to dilute the stuffy air. She unbuckled the GoPro harness and tossed it onto the bed. Her T-shirt clung to her like shrink wrap on ground beef. She pulled it off and tossed it in the hamper.

Since she wasn't wearing a bra, when Kenway turned around his eyebrows bobbed straight up. "Well, okay."

The wind stiffened her nipples. She shot him a guarded look that dissolved into a smirk, and she held up a fist. "Rock, paper, scissors. Winner gets the shower first." They shook fists at each other, and on the fourth beat, she held up the two-finger peace sign of scissors, but he pointed at her with an accusing finger.

Puzzled, she asked, "What is *that*? This ain't rock-paper-pistol."

He made an A-OK sign with his other hand and stuck the pointer finger through the loop of his forefinger and thumb. Then he sawed it in and out of the hole.

"Ohh." A slow smile spread across Robin's face. "We both win, then."

She turned off the GoPro, hid it in a dresser drawer, and unbuckled his belt.

• • •

WELCOME TO KEYHOLE HILLS,
WHERE ROUTINE ENDS AND ADVENTURE BEGINS!
POPULATION 2,849
ORIGIN OF THE MA'IITSOH HIKING TRAIL

Thank God, no witch graffiti.

Most graffiti is an unintelligible mess, but if you know what you're looking for, you can find special runes hidden in the design that tell you there's a witch living nearby. They use runes to passively communicate with each other, same way hobos did back in the *Andy Griffith* train-jumper days.

The highway led up a hill and through a gap between two sandstone bluffs. Time and weather had punched a space as big as a house through the stone, creating a keyhole-shaped wedge of indigo air.

On the other side of the pass was a low sprawl of houses, businesses, and fast-food signs. There wasn't a two-story building in sight that Robin could see, and the squatness of Keyhole Hills made the sky look heavy and oppressive. The town seemed to melt down an enormous sagebrush slope that reminded her of a Skee-Ball game, as if the highway lowballed tourists into one of the motels and shops littering the grade. *The City Visitors' Center, 10 points! Roger's Gas-N'-Go, 25 points! The Best Western, 50 points!*

They hobbled into a shade tree at the edge of town, a white cinderblock garage surrounded by desolate old cars and stacks of tires.

To Robin's surprise, the transaction was painless—the tubby, grease-handed man with the Teddy Roosevelt face actually had the right kind of tire for a 1974 Winnebago Brave, and he was more than willing to mount it on their rim for the right price. Robin bought an extra just in case, and she and Kenway wandered into town on foot.

Gravel grumbled under her Converses as they walked through a neighborhood of bungalows, tract houses, and mobile homes, divvied up by sidewalks and chain-link fences into a lockstep grid. Most of the grass looked like loose hay. Dead as hell. Fortunately, unlike Georgia, the humidity was low and every breeze scraped a little sweat off.

A figure fell into step with them. "Hi, love," Annie Martine's spirit murmured in her sketchy-AM-radio voice.

"Hi, Mom," said Robin. Annie still popped in from time to time ever since her daughter rescued her out of the witches' soul-sucking apple tree. Evidently, her daughter was the only one that could see her, because no one else ever seemed to react.

"Is she here?" Kenway's eyes searched the empty space around his girlfriend.

"Yeah."

"Tell her I said hi."

Speaking to ghosts no one else can see tends to freak people out, but he seemed to handle it admirably well. She wasn't sure if he was just humoring her or if he actually believed her mother was there, but she was grateful for his cavalier attitude.

The ghost grinned. Annie liked Kenway.

"She says hi back."

Occasionally, she wondered where Annie went when she wasn't visible. Was she hanging out in some afterlife waiting room? Chilling in some discreet room in the mansion of Robin's head? She pulled up her T-shirt to wipe her face, flashing her belly. "Gendreau said they wanted to meet at a lunch café."

"You nervous?" Her self-appointed "cameraman" wore a Margaritaville T-shirt with the sleeves cut off to show off his new tan and the tattoos on his shoulders: Army Air Assault on one side and a rampant gryphon on the other, clutching a spear and a clawful of olive branches. Shitty and blue, they looked like icons on a fifteenth-century map.

"Hell yeah, I'm nervous."

"He said they were gonna be cool."

"I dunno." She smiled tightly, trying to make a face to telegraph "anxiety." It was probably more like "constipation." "If they were cool, wouldn't they want to meet me at their home base in Michigan instead of the middle of nowhere?"

"We were already out here—maybe they just wanted to meet us halfway."

"Maybe." Almost three thousand people in town, according to the city limits sign. That sounded like a lot, until you considered the alternative—Blackfield alone was probably twice that, and nearby Houston had two million people. "They probably think I'm going to flip out and go on a rampage or something." Robin flourished a hand around them. "Not much out here. They're probably like, 'If we talk to her in public, she'll be more at ease, but we don't want to endanger a Houston amount of people.'" She frowned. "Been months since I went into Beast Mode. We've been in dozens of fights. It ain't happened again."

He didn't say anything for a little while. She flashbacked on the memory of tearing open her father, the cacodemon Andras, the tickling-brushing of all those insidious spiders spilling out of his hollow body and coursing up her arm like a lacy black sleeve. "Maybe I need a demon to touch me again—to infect me—to make it happen."

Am I full of spiders?

Jesus Christ, what kind of a question is *that?*

"I think you're reading too much into it," Kenway finally muttered.

A bird circled high overhead on some invisible thermal. Robin said, "Gendreau didn't tell 'em right away that I was working for them now."

"What'd he tell them?"

"That I drove away into the sunset after the fight with Cutty. I think he was trying to protect me. Feeding me leads under the table like I was his secret James Bond and he was my M."

"Maybe G wasn't counting on you making more videos, and for the Dogs of Odysseus to see them and realize you still had the Osdathregar."

"Well, I did kind of tell him that I was going to close my channel down." Which would have been a lark. She made way too much money on that thing to give it up. Besides . . . in the three years that she'd been running her YouTube channel, she'd grown to like the attention. The fans.

Attention whore, said the psych-ward nurse in her head.

No, Robin thought. *They're the family I never had. That's why I love them.*

Kenway shook his head. He didn't say anything, but the accusation was there: *You lied and got G in trouble.*

"He must have done it because of what I did in the Lazenbury," said Robin. "Saving his life. Guess he felt like he owed me. But they don't *sound* pissed off about being left out of the loop, from what G told me." She stopped at an intersection and peered up and down the road. "They sound like they just want to meet me and get a feel for me. Ugh, I don't see this café anywhere."

A little dog barked at them from behind a fence. Beyond the dog was a mobile home, and a scrubby, pot-bellied old Hunter S. Thompson look-alike in a T-shirt and jeans sat on a warped deck porch with a glass of iced tea. Homespun knickknacks hung from his eaves: twisty blue blown-glass tadpoles, bamboo wind chimes, dreamcatchers.

The dog stopped barking all of a sudden, as if he'd fulfilled his quota for the day. Annie's ghost stopped to poke a silvery finger through the fence, and the dog sniffed it. Robin blinked, startled.

The old fella waved at them. His eyes twinkled even through his rosy bug-eyed bifocals. "Welcome to the Hole," he said, tossing a hand like a symphony conductor giving his final bow.

"Excuse me, sir," said Robin, leaning on the old man's fence. The dog—some kind of scotty-dog schnauzer or something—sniffed her through the chain link. "Do you know where we can find Uncle Joe's Diner?"

"Uncle *Mac's*?"

"Yeah, Mac's, that's what I meant. I must have been thinking of Joe's Crab Shack or something."

"What I wouldn't give for a good crab joint." The toothpick rattled around in the man's teeth. He pointed one gnarled finger over their shoulders. "Mac's just yonder ways, about three blocks down and one up. If y'all havin' dinner there, get the chili. They do somethin' wonderful with black beans. Best I ever had."

"Thanks."

"What brought yuns out this way? We don't get many visitors out here. At least, ones that ain't here to get lost out on the Ma'iitsoh. Y'all hikers?"

"You could say that." Overgrown grass brushed against the titanium gleaming under the cuff of Kenway's shorts as he leaned against the fence. "She runs a video channel on the internet, driving around the country. Kinda like a travelogue."

The old man grunted. "Like them shows on TV? Travel Channel? The chunky kid with the frosted hair and the bowling shirts?"

"Sorta like that." Robin squinted. The sun lurked directly behind the trailer, throwing hot sunshine in her face. "We're just passing through and wanted to stop and grab dinner with some friends. Said to meet 'em at Uncle Mac's."

"Tell 'em Gil sent you." He hesitated. "On second thought, don't do that."

Laughter. "Thanks."

Gil's grin faded. "Just behave yourself while you're in the Hole, aight? Try to stay on this end of town." He jerked a thumb over his shoulder at his trailer, even glancing in that direction, as if they could all see straight through it to some distant point. "Don't wander past the Conoco up on Fifth. There's . . ." Took off his glasses to knuckle one eye. "Well, let's just say there's *folks*. Folks you don't want to run into."

"Message received."

Gil put his rose-colored glasses back on. "Enjoy your dinner. You two want to give an old man some company and put away a few beers before you take off again, I'll be up all night."

• • •

Uncle Mac's was done up in retro soda-jerk—pastel colors, lots of jagged, futuristic Atomic Age angles. Big metal sign out front that looked like a Nike swoosh. Sketched out with neon in the middle of the swoosh was a ten-foot-tall football player, and three footballs traced an arc from one outstretched leg. Underneath this was TOUCHDOWN GRILL, and if the sign still worked, the neon figure would've been kicking an animated football—but by the time Robin and Kenway saw it, the sign was out of commission, and that extended leg just looked like a tremendous jagged penis, ejaculating footballs in a machine-gun stream.

Stepping onto the curb in front of Uncle Mac's Diner, she was overcome by sudden apprehension—*Is this a trap? Is it going to be the third degree? Are they going to lull me into a false sense of security and throw a bag over my head?* Surely, Gendreau wasn't going to do that to her. If he was there and going along with the whole thing, he had to be cool with it, right?

The healer-magician had been keeping her a secret since September, dear weird quiet Anders Gendreau, with his vulpine good looks and taste for svelte yet outdated clothes. He'd been the one to approach her after losing her arm to the witch Theresa LaQuices, and, other than her childhood friend Joel, he'd helped her acclimate to her new existence as a cambion.

Cambion. Half-girl, half-demon. Half Netflix devotee, half abyssal monstrosity. An image of the bloodworm popped into her mind: that wriggling red appendage creeping out of her amputation scar that had turned out to be her arm growing back.

She shuddered at a sense-memory of the bloodworm curling against her hip.

"You okay?" asked Kenway, his blue shadow draping over her.

She squinted up at him. "Yeah."

"You're untouchable, hon," he reminded her. "You can *eat* those motherfuckers if this thing goes pear-shaped. You're a half-demon, witch-eatin', goddess-killin' badass. Go in there and own 'em. If they ask for an arm and a leg, give it to 'em, and then grow 'em back."

The man was actually *proud* of her eccentricities.

She grinned crookedly. "It's not that easy, and you know that."

Track 2

Carly Valenzuela was at the mall again, and it was because the power bill came.

Her mother raced down the Valenzuelas' driveway as the post office's Ford Taurus with its British passenger-side steering column backed out into the road and pulled away with its payload of mail, amber beacon flashing from the roof. As soon as she saw the number inside the envelope, Marina got her purse, locked the front door of their doublewide, and went straight to Keyhole Hills High School.

Their ancient Blazer sat in the parking lot. Carly had come out of the school, chatting with her friends, and heat blossomed in her face when she recognized it, and Marina inside, staring at her in barely veiled fear. Carly got into the Blazer and tossed her bookbag in the backseat—didn't ask questions, didn't ask why her mother was picking her up.

This wasn't her first surprise pickup.

Taking a blue top off the clothing rack, Carly held it against her chest to appraise it, looking at herself in a nearby mirror. A band of silver shredded its way from one shoulder to the waist. Fifteen-year-old Carly was pretty and petite, like her mother, with dusky skin and rich black-brown hair. She was noodle-skinny, cervine, almost all leg, with a gazelle neck; sometimes, her friend Patrick would grab the plastic skeleton in Biology class and puppeteer it at her, teasing her in a Pepe Le Pew accent. *Oh ho, heh heh, oui oui, eez a sexy skeleton just like me, eh hey?*

She caught her own eyes in the mirror, bright jade stones shining with need.

Disgusted, Carly returned it to the rack.

Her mother sat stiffly on a bench by the dressing rooms, her purse clenched under one arm. Marina Valenzuela had always been a bit of a firebrand, a coltish woman with a mane of springy tresses and a narrow, classically beautiful face. But these days, an insidious gray crept across her temples and her face was lined, her eyes those of a wounded hawk, haunted but alert. The fire had gone out, replaced by a frantic quiet that hummed underneath like a live wire. She had gone from buxom to willowy, almost gaunt, and when she walked her elbows sawed subtly at her sides, hands always worrying at each other.

Haggard, thought Carly, an intrusive thought. Felt horrible, felt hateful, but if the shoe fit. . . .

"It would look lovely on you," said Marina.

The blue shirt. Carly experienced a stab of shame. "Yeah. It would." She raked aside a cluster of clothes and spotted an even nicer shirt, a baby doll peasant blouse even her grandmother would have liked, with poofy shoulders and flowers embroidered along the hem. She almost took it out, but an icicle—of fear, of regret, of resentment—slid into the pit of her belly, a cold sword into a warm scabbard, and she left it on the rack. She stood there staring at the clothes, thinking.

Suddenly, she rounded on her mother and suggested, "Why don't we go to the food court? That sandwich place has smoothies now. I've been wanting to try their blueberry-pineapple."

Marina looked at the floor and then at her watch. "We give it a little while longer."

"How long?"

"About an hour. He went into work at two and he didn't get his lunch break until at least five."

Fury bubbled up in Carly's chest. She folded her arms. "We can't hang out in La Rue all day, Mom. There are only so many clothes to look at. We've been in here for, like, forty-five minutes. Besides, this is just cruel. I hate looking at clothes I can't buy."

Marina thought it over and stood, hitching her purse up on her shoulder. "Okay," she said in defeat.

Feeling like a spy sneaking through Nazi territory, Carly led her mother out of the clothing store and they hesitated in the corridor, standing between a sunglasses kiosk and a hurricane-simulator booth. Then she spotted the toy store down one of the wings and headed that way.

As is de rigueur in the twenty-first century, the toy store was all but abandoned. Carly and Marina wandered into the back and browsed the action figures and board games. "Why didn't you ever teach me chess, Mom?" asked Carly, holding up a box. Regal figures marched across a checkered surface. She never had video games, but the Valenzuelas always had board games and card games. Checkers, Clue, Chutes & Ladders, Sorry!, Scrabble, and of course Monopoly. Poker, Go Fish, craps dice, dominos, Jenga. Her father liked teaching her poker.

Her father used to like a lot of things.

"I don't know how to play either," said Marina. "Maybe you could look it up at the library and we can learn how to play it together." Her eyes trickled listlessly across the board games, and then she checked her watch again and said, "This was a good idea, I guess. Santi, he would not expect to find us in a toy store."

"We always come here. Sooner or later, he's going to find us. Why can't we go somewhere else for a change?"

"You know we can't go to my sister. Elisa's girlfriend is one of Santi's bunch. He'd go straight there as soon as he got home. Probably there right now, wanting to know where we are." Marina pulled out a game box, stared at it without reading it. "Besides, if we run into him here, there's not much he can do." She made a sweeping gesture. "Too many people, eh?"

They were alone there in the toy store. If Santiago Valenzuela caught them back here, it would be perfectly private.

But he didn't. Carly and her mother hung around in the toy store, gradually relaxing, the knot inside the girl's chest loosening, until the two of them were chatting coquettishly like a couple of girls, snapping at each other with hand puppets. In front of a display of collectors' Barbies in glittery dresses and gauzy white gowns, Marina gave her a mini-lesson in Latin Hollywood history.

Eventually, Carly migrated to the bookstore in the east wing, her mother in tow, and this time wasn't like the last—this time, it felt like Carly was in charge. Less of a hideout than just a trip to the mall with the woman who raised her. They browsed the bookshelves with studious eyes. *Do you ever read Nora Roberts? Have you read* Tommyknockers? *Do you remember when you would read this to me when I was little? Do you think you could cook some of the stuff in this cookbook?* Time turned back a few years and Carly forgot she was a teenager, and Marina lost a little of that wrung-out look. She even smiled.

A couple of hours later, Marina finally drummed up the courage to follow her into the food court, and they got smoothies—Carly blueberry, her mother piña colada—and Chinese food for an early supper. The meal was halfway over when Carly looked up, knuckled a bit of cabbage into the corner of her mouth, and said, "Why don't we stop by that cop store on the way home?"

"Cop store?" Marina asked. She ate everything with a fork, including the egg rolls, drizzled generously in duck sauce; her hands stayed impeccable, ornate rings inherited from Carly's grandmother on every finger.

"Yeah. The law enforcement shop on the highway. Like, PX Sports and Tactical, or something. Went in there once with Renee. They have stun guns and pepper spray—"

Marina erupted into a gush of near-incomprehensible Spanish. "Are you out of your mind? If I pepper-spray Santi, he will kill us both and then burn the house down with us in it."

Carly grit her teeth. "He's going to kill us anyway, one day. You might as—"

"Do not say that. Do not go there. Santi is not actually going to *kill* me. Do not be ridiculous." Where a tooth used to sit in her mother's mouth, one of her canines, was now a dark gap. The rest of them were tall, the pale purple gums receded, with the white-brown sheen of a seashell. "I was using a figure of speech. Santi wouldn't kill a fly. He's all bark and no bite."

"He bites, Mom. He bites and you know it."

Marina abandoned her meal and took out a cigarette.

"You can't smoke that in here, Mom."

Marina paused, pincering the cigarette to her lips, the lighter already in her hand. "What are they going to do—throw me out of the mall?"

• • •

"We should be getting back." Code for *Your father should be back to work by now.* Marina stubbed out her Marlboro Light in a half-cup of sweet-and-sour sauce. Carly dropped her dinner trash into a waste bin and the two of them headed for the food court exit.

"This was nice, for a change," said Carly. "You should go to the library with me sometime when I go do my homework. You said in the bookstore you liked cookbooks and mystery novels. And you and me can, like, look at stuff on the internet? I can make you a Facebook account and all kinds of stuff. Did you know that Gabriela Herrera is on there? Didn't you go to school with her?"

"Sounds very familiar, yes. I think so."

"She said she went to school with you back when you lived in Houston. I think it was maybe late middle school? High school?" Carly and her mother walked through the entranceway toward the curb, the parking lot gaping black before them. Wasn't hot enough yet to make the asphalt feel soft like cold peanut butter, but give it a few weeks.

Parked in a handicap slot some eight hundred feet away, in front of the J. C. Penney back entrance, was an olive-green motorcycle.

"Oh yes! I remember her! She was going out with Joseph Mireles. Does she have pictures on this Facebook?"

"Yeah?" Carly said in that *uh-doyyy, of course* way. "She's tiny and cute and, like, she wears these big black eyeglasses that make her look nerdy."

"I might go to the library with you, then."

"Mind if I come too?" asked Santiago behind them.

All of the blood in Carly's face and hands ran into her feet, and a match-head flared in her heart. Her entire body felt like she'd been splashed with ice water. Marina twitched in shock and did an ungainly about-face, stumbling down from the curb onto the crosswalk.

"Been meaning to catch up on my reading." Carly's father stood up from where he'd been sitting on a marble bench, out of the way. Santiago Valenzuela was tall and broad like a pit fighter gone to seed, with a Lorenzo Lamas mullet that grayed in racing-stripe arcs over his ears. The sleeves of his chambray shirt were fold-rolled to his armpits to display the riot of tattoos on his arms. He ground his cigarette out on the bench and flicked it into the wood chips. "What brought you to the mall, my lovely ladies?" he asked, his eyes lurking behind a pair of black tactical sunglasses. Santiago gave his wife a peck on the temple and put his arms around their necks, walking between them in his easy, bowlegged cowboy stride.

On top of the work-shirt was an unseasonably warm leather vest. Tab patches over his heart said LOS CAMBIANTES and ROAD

CAPTAIN, and they encircled the stylized face of a wolf. The same feral wolf-face occupied his back, a silvery-blue patch the size of a dinner plate. Carly tried to think of something to tell her father, but she took too long and Marina came up with something first. "I wanted to come and price swimsuits, Santi. It's *summer,* honey, time to think about swimming!"

Glancing at his daughter, Santiago took off his glasses and his eyes bounced off the ground at her feet as if he were visualizing her in a bikini. He chuckled darkly, shaking his head, *that ain't happening,* and opened the Blazer door for his wife.

As Marina sat down, Carly recognized a subtle fear on her mother's face. Dad was being nice. *Friendly,* even. Not that this in itself was cause for alarm—they wouldn't be a family if Santiago were violent a hundred percent of the time. But in this situation, having caught them being scarce and telling obvious lies, Carly expected anger, swearing, exaggerated gestures like slamming the car door . . . but he closed it easily, softly, and stood there with his hands on the windowsill, looking in at Marina. It was unsettling. "I'm here instead of work because I got laid off today," he said, and paused—for emphasis, for drama, to test their reactions? His eyes were hard and bright, but his voice was grim velvet and his mouth was set in a crooked, regretful slash. "Almost a hundred of us, for the next two or three weeks."

"Toyota laid you off?" asked Marina. "Que chingados pasa con esta gente? They can't *do* that. They can't. Who do they think they *are*?"

"It happens." Santiago shrugged. "Slow sales? Recalls? Who gives a shit?" He leaned over, looking at his daughter in the passenger seat. "Guessin' you two already ate dinner. You smell like Chinese." He smiled. "Reckon I'll dig up something at the house. Sure we've got something I can nuke." Never mind the fact he had money. Could have marched right into that food court and gotten his own damn dinner. Carly *hated* this wounded-bird act. *Woe is me, you are so unfair to me, I do so much for you.* Story was always the same. He reached in and gently plucked the smoothie out of his wife's hand, sucking at the straw. "Mmm, piña colada. You got good taste, baby—but that's why I married you, ain't it?"

Marina smiled, a humoring, humorless smile, almost demure. "You can come swimming *with* us." He handed the cup back to her. Styrofoam rasped as Marina slid it into the cup holder. "Look at this layoff as a vacation, yeah? You deserve one. You work *so hard*."

He stared at Marina's face until he finally looked down at his feet and back up at her. "Yeah. I reckon." He reached in and pulled her into a kiss on the mouth, a long, full kiss that released with a satisfying *smack*. "I'll see you at the house," he said, and clapped the windowsill once before he walked away, which to Carly was code for *Go straight home and I'll be watching to make sure you get there.*

She waited for the throaty tiger-snarl of Santiago's motorcycle to burst into the afternoon air to ask her mother, "Why didn't we just *keep driving*?" but the radio was too loud (Taylor Swift exhorting them to shake it off, shake it off) and Marina didn't hear her, or maybe she just didn't want to.

Nestled against Carly's left foot was her purse. Rattling softly against the tube of ChapStick inside was a can of pepper spray.

Track 3

As she opened the door, the diner's air conditioner chilled the sweat running down Robin's back. Health Department certificate by the door boasted a score of 96. Jukebox was crankin' out the hits: Johnny Cash, Shania Twain, Blondie, Rolling Stones. Right then, Bob Seger sang "Turn the Page," and for some reason it made her think of musty tweed seat covers and cold dawns under a rust-orange streetlight. *You walk into a restaurant, strung out from the road.* How could anything bad happen in a clean restaurant with dirty music?

Accoutrements and pictures were nailed to wood paneling: framed photos of sportsmen (tee-ball teams in orange uniforms, a golfer holding a trophy over his head), pieces of antique farm equipment, hand-painted advertisements for local businesses. The center of the diner was a counter lined with stools where men sat quietly grinding up dinner—truckers, mostly, in chambray shirts and jeans, the backs of their necks like cooked hams.

Staring at the truckers' broad backs, she considered, *When you're a teenager, you wonder if people like you. When you're an adult, you wonder if you like people.*

"Think that's them," said Kenway.

Three people quietly browsed menus in the corner. A dark, handsome Indian guy with coiffed hair and a trim beard. Gendreau, who'd had his hair cut short in a choppy shock of platinum blond; he looked less like a Slytherin alumni and more like David Bowie's Thin White Duke. The other occupant of the table was an Asian woman graying around the temples.

Gendreau waved. "Hello, Miss Martine."

His smile was light, but his brilliant eyes seemed tired. The curandero wasn't wearing his Willy Wonka frock coat in the Texas heat, but a simple dress shirt and a pinstripe vest and trousers, both in raincloud colors. His silk tie was done up in some kind of elaborate knot. The scar across his throat was a puckered pink crescent.

The Indian man wore a T-shirt and jeans; the Asian woman was dressed in a white tank top, a droop of chintzy necklaces and bracelets, and a long skirt. Made her look like a beatnik schoolteacher.

A strange feeling came over Robin when she caught a knowing glint in the woman's eye. She seemed familiar, like someone she'd known in middle school.

Where do I know you?

"Didn't know you were going to be bringing your pet bear," said the handsome Indian, pointing his chin at Kenway. British accent, a sleek and cozy *guv, luv,* and *bruv* brogue that made Robin think of dark cobblestone streets, the BBC, the London Underground. "Asha Navathe," he said, shaking her hand. He indicated the older Asian woman. "This is Rook."

"Asha Navathe to you, too," said Kenway, shaking his hand.

"That's—" Navathe blinked, confused, and then he shook it off and smiled. "Nice to meet you, mate."

"Pleased to meet you," said Rook. "I am an Origo."

"The folks that handle artifacts?" asked Robin, recalling the conversation she'd had with Leon Parkin and Heinrich Hammer in the kitchen of her childhood home.

"Yes," said Rook. "Sort of a cross between a museum curator and an armorer."

"She's our Q." Navathe reached over to pound her heartily on the back. "Well, one of them, at least. She's sort of middle management. Strong enough for an away team, but pH-balanced for administrative paperwork."

"As long as I'm not a redshirt."

Navathe smiled. "You'll always be my Spock."

Shaking her head, Robin said, "If this conversation gets any geekier, I might have to cut bait and run." She looked around, tried to see if she could pick out any tinfoil-hatters, conspiracy theorists, or other wack jobs that might be listening to their conversation.

"There's no one here to hear," said Gendreau. "You probably wonder why we chose to meet you here. That's why. Totally random. No chance of being overheard by an unsavory third party."

"I figured you were . . . I don't know, trying to make me feel at ease by meeting in public," said Robin, "but in a place with minimum collateral casualties. A small, rural, out-of-the-way Podunk to mitigate damage in case I were to . . . Dia-blow." She smirked at her own pun.

"You think we don't trust you?" asked Rook. "Or are you afraid there's a legitimate reason for that?"

"No, I—" Even though her teeth were well taken care of, Robin thoughtfully rubbed her face, subconsciously trying to conceal her mouth. The anxiety there in this well-lighted restaurant, surrounded by strangers, was all too real. Made her feel like a Little Girl surrounded by Adults.

Incredibly frustrating. Alone, she was totally confident and in control of herself; she could talk to the millions of people on the other side of her camera without anxiety. But if you put her in a roomful of people, a roomful of eyes and faces, an invisible hand tightened around her throat. This was why she'd never been to any of those conventions they hold for YouTube creators, like VidCon. She dearly loved her viewers, but if she had to face a crowd of real people, she would probably curl up in a ball. Kind of thing that develops when you grow up living in the woods with no friends and then spend several years in a psych ward.

She thought back to the Top Dollar Gentlemen's Club and wondered how she'd ever gotten through it.

Anger. That was how. Anger.

Well, that and liquor.

I can make you do anything, said Heinrich's voice from the well of her memory. *All I gotta do is piss you off.*

"She hasn't had any incidents since Blackfield," said Gendreau. A ring on his left hand shimmered in the sinking sunlight, a square-cut ruby set in a Celtic knot of silver.

"You've said as much." Rook's stiff affect softened. "Look, I think we're getting off on the wrong foot here." Her hands were on the table, holding each other lightly, nonconfrontationally. "You probably think we're some kind of shadowy, elitist cabal, don't you?"

A waitress appeared from nowhere and took their drink orders. Robin eyed each of their faces in turn as they spoke to her. She felt like a cornered, feral animal, and hoped it didn't show on her face. "I honestly don't know what to think," Robin said. "Don't know much about you. Ain't much on the internet about the Dogs of Odysseus."

"As it should be," said Navathe.

"We're not the Illuminati," said Rook. "After the old guard was pushed out of the order—the right-wing fogies that still believed in Crowley's ways, the robe-wearers, the pyramid-heads, the bloodletters, the *real* Skull and Bones types—we're all that's left."

Navathe injected, "We're basically like a bunch of old college pals. A pack of pub mates that just happen to know how to do magic. We're the underdogs, really. There *are* Illuminati types out there—"

"The old men that Frank ran out of the Order in the sixties and seventies went out to join other groups and companies, and found their own," said Gendreau. The waitress returned with their drinks, handing him a water with three lemon wedges. "*Those* are the *real* cabals. They're why I wanted you to keep quiet about what you were doing and discontinue your YouTube channel."

After she left with their dinner orders, Navathe leaned in. "Some of those shady crews actually want to *recruit* you."

"Recruit me?" asked Robin.

"A cambion is top dollar in occult circles. You're the first known cambion since old times. If magic was football, there'd be scouts lining up around the block to sign you up for big-league teams."

"But I don't even know how to do that again. To . . . make myself demon again. I don't even think it was me that did it the first time."

"We know that," said Navathe.

Robin relaxed. "So, you're not afraid of me, then?"

The magicians glanced at each other. "No," responded Navathe. "We're not afraid of you." He grinned and cupped Gendreau's shoulder with a hand. "Papa G here has been quite persuasive as to your erstwhile harmlessness."

Gendreau paused. "I don't think that word means—"

Navathe pinched the curandero's cheek. "You're so cute when you correct my grammar."

"I'm . . . I'm glad to hear that." Robin relaxed so much she slumped down in the seat. She could have cried. "I've been worried ever since. *I'm* the one that's afraid, then."

"What do you mean?" asked Rook.

"You weren't there when my demon father, Andras, changed me into that wire-sculpture demon thing, the same thing that he was. He corrupted me. I saw myself in a mirror. It was fuckin' scary."

"I'm partial to *fucking terrifying,* myself," Gendreau noted, but then something on Robin's face made him quail. "Oh, I'm so sorry."

"I have nightmares about it."

"She wakes up covered in sweat and goes into the bathroom for hours," said Kenway. "Stares at herself in the mirror. Won't let me touch her for a week afterward. Sometimes, she can't sleep. Stays up for days at a time. Those days, we don't do much traveling, and if we do, I do all the driving."

"I know it's still there. Still *inside* me, forever. Like herpes."

Disgust passed across Navathe's face. Robin studied her hands, the right hand with its scars and veins and wrinkles, and the unblemished left hand that looked ten years younger. The hand the witch Theresa bit off last Halloween, the hand that Robin inadvertently grew back with the power of transfiguration she absorbed from Theresa. The fingernails grew faster on that hand, as if the nail beds were more fertile, but the nails were soft and brittle and sharp, like a baby's. She'd cut her face and the insides of her nostrils numerous times with those toddler razors. Woken up with scratches on her cheek. She had to keep them bitten down. They were painted, but she'd chewed them until only the quicks were black. "I may not *look* demon anymore," she said, looking up, "ever since I pulled my mother out of that *nag shi* dryad tree and evidently earned my humanity back, but I can still absorb powers from witches and relics."

"Even after burning the reborn Ereshkigal?" asked Navathe.

Rook shook her head. "All heart-roads lead back to the death-goddess. All those teratomas are a piece of her, a seed of reincarnation. So, if the magic still works, she's still alive . . . somewhere there in the After. Or Before. Or whatever the hell you want to call it. All you did was slam the door in her face."

"Ghost soup," said Navathe.

"The huh?"

"Phantom fondue. Spook bisque. The primordial supernatural minestrone from whence we all came, and to whence we all eventually go back."

"*Anyway,*" said Robin, "if you aren't afraid of me or what I'm capable of, and you didn't want to see how long my horns are, why did you want to meet me in person? We could have just as easily had this conversation over email or Facebook or something."

Navathe smiled. "We didn't want to see how Satanic you are, love. Just the opposite. We wanted to see what kind of a person you are. Off-camera, you know."

"She's a damn good person," said Kenway. "An amazing human being, and an outstanding friend. I could have told you that."

"Well," grinned Gendreau, "you're a bit biased."

"Human being." Rook reached over and clasped Robin's fingers in gentle solidarity. Tattooed on the back of the woman's hand was the *algiz,* the rune that protected them against baser forms of magic like the spell that made minions of the cats of Blackfield. Looked like a Y with an extra arm in the middle, and almost seemed to trace the blue veins under her skin. "That's what we wanted to see. We didn't want to see how much demon is in you—we wanted to see how much *human* is in you. Could have done without the secrecy and tall tales from G here, but it's good to see mad old Heinrich didn't rub off on you."

Oh, he definitely rubbed off on me.

Gendreau dipped his head, his eyes flicking to the table in guilt. "Yes, well, I . . . I wanted to stave off this confrontation for as long as possible, because I didn't know what you were all going to do once she was in arms' reach."

"You know us better than that," said Rook. "It's not that you didn't trust *us;* it's that you didn't trust your *grandfather,* isn't it?"

The curandero nodded. "Yes, I suppose that's it."

Navathe told Robin, "Francis Gendreau is the one that threw Heinrich out of the Dogs. He's the most vocal of everybody about demons, being a demonologist himself, and he's been the most opposed to contacting you since we learned what Heinrich did to you and your mother."

"Frank and Heinrich's father, Moses Atterberry, were in seminary together," said Rook. "Moses became pastor over Walker

Memorial Church there in Blackfield, and Frank went on to Italy to continue his education in demonology and . . ."

"Exorcism," finished Navathe.

Ice rushed down Robin's scalp as she made a connection. "Do you think it's possible that he could exorcise the demon part out of me?"

Navathe winced. "Afraid not, love. That is an integral part of you. It's in your spiritual DNA, so to speak. It's not *in* you; it *is* you. Might as well try to exorcise the color of your skin. Or your hair." He raised an eyebrow at her purple-and-black mohawk. "What *is* the original color of your hair, anyway?"

"Dark chestnut," said Robin. "Okay. It's my turn to ask a question."

The Origo smiled. "We're an open book."

"Yes," said Navathe, smirking, "and just like a book, I am full of good sex and big words."

Rook quipped, "You're also going to have a bad ending."

"I'm assuming you guys are magicians like Doc G here," Robin said, tucking one foot under her leg and hunching over the table, speaking low. "He can heal people . . . What can *you* guys do? What are *your* relics?"

The Dogs of Odysseus seemed hesitant. Navathe sat back and folded his arms. It was probably meant to seem authoritative, but to Robin it looked more like a protective gesture, as if the temperature in the room had gone down ten degrees. "You're . . . you're not going to suck the powers out of them, are you?"

Robin echoed his earlier smirk. *Come on, you already know me better than that.*

Reaching into her purse, Rook brought out a Zippo and flicked it open. "Mine is the Gift of Manipulation, psychokinesis. This lighter shell contains a lock of hair from a teratoma extracted from a Czech witch in 1909."

"Like Marilyn Cutty?" asked Robin, her arm-hairs prickling.

"Aye."

"And then there's mine," said Navathe, opening the messenger bag sitting on the floor by his chair. He took out a snow globe and placed it on the table. Inside, a cartoon alligator stood on a popsicle-stick surfboard in a drift of Styrofoam snowflakes. Around the rim of the globe's base it read: I SPENT CHRISTMAS 1988 ON DAYTONA BEACH!

"Let me guess," Robin said, "you can make it snow?"

Navathe shook his head. "Nope."

"Control an army of surfing alligators?"

". . . Nada."

"Capture people in a glass ball?"

"What—? No, I can't capture people in a glass ball." The look of bemusement on Navathe's face evaporated. "It controls fire, mate. Pyromancy," he said, flourishing the last word in a *duh, what else would it be* way. "The Gift of Wrath."

"Fire?" Robin pointed at Rook. "She's the one with the Zippo lighter, but *you're* the firestarter?"

"*Twisted* firestarter." Navathe asided, "I'd keep going, but I was never really into the Prodigy—more of a Chemical Brothers man, myself."

"No one ever said magic had to make sense." Rook put her lighter away. "The artifacts serve as conduits for the teratomas' power. We can't channel the raw magic the same way you or the witches can. Magic is all about metaphors, you know. Connotations. A lot of it is channeled by inscriptions and moving parts. Frank claims there are relics that can perform necromancy. An egg timer, namely."

"Necromancy?" asked Kenway. "Bringing the dead back to life?"

"Aye. Well, not so much back to life, you know. . . . Well, you wind the egg timer backward and it'd bring someone back. For a little while, at least. While the timer was running. Not the same as resurrection, according to the records; they were more like golems, dumb dead brutes with nothing but violence in their heads. That's what the records claim, anyway."

"Speaking of relics," said Gendreau, "do you still have that watch I gave you?"

The watch with the hidden power that lent Robin telekinesis and provided the secret weapon she needed to defeat Marilyn Cutty. "I do." Robin jerked a thumb in the general direction of the garage where they'd parked Willy. "In my stuff back in the RV, but the heart-road inside is closed. If you want to use it again, you'll have to put another teratoma in it. Had to devour the power inside to be able to use it."

"Devour the power," said Navathe, clenching his fist at her. "That would make a magnificent tagline."

"That will take years, perhaps decades, of re-bonding, re-augmenting, re-training," said Rook. "I wish you'd spoken to us before you ruined a relic, Robin."

"I didn't exactly have your number. Not to mention I was pinned to a wall and trying not to be killed by a witch at the time."

The magician had no response to that.

After the waitress returned with their food, the next few minutes passed in a quiet interlude of scraping forks and slurping drinks. Robin couldn't help but watch the magicians' faces, wondering what they were thinking. "So, what happens now?" she asked, wiping her lips with a napkin. "Am I in the order, or, I don't know, *consulting* for the order? Or did Doc G make a fatal oopsie by being my under-the-table Judi Dench?"

Gendreau crowed laughter at the ceiling.

"Bond got you pegged, M," said Navathe.

"For real, though"—Robin centered the conversation again—"are we cool? Is this a new-employee orientation, or are you sizing me up for a cell?"

Rook licked her lips thoughtfully. "It's taken a lot of coaxing to talk Frank Gendreau into letting you work with the Dogs as opposed to containing you, or eliminating you outright. For what it's worth, the three of us have all been convinced of your humanity since we first laid eyes on your video series, as well as the rest of the subordinate Dogs."

"We like to call ourselves the Underdogs," asided Navathe.

"G here has been fighting for you ever since he came back to Michigan," continued Rook. "Whatever transgressions Heinrich committed, *you're* not at fault here. That award goes to the dead guy."

The iron ball that'd been sitting in Robin's bowels lost a little of its heft. "That's good."

"Not that we honestly stand a chance even if we *did* decide that you were too dangerous to ignore," said Gendreau. He carved off a piece of ham (he was eating ham and eggs, which surprised her, as she'd had him pegged as a rabbit-food-eater), and then he added, "You're a girl wrapped around an atom bomb. I'm only glad you're on our side."

"I don't know." Robin mopped up the last of her ranch with the end of a chicken finger. "I'm not *that* bad."

Rook shook her head. "You are powerful. We feel"—and here the magician glanced at the others, and then back at Robin—"that with training, and the right preparations, that you can learn to harness, bring out, and more fully utilize that side of you, that latent demon inside of—"

"No," Robin interjected, "I don't *want* it to come out. I like it where it is: where I can't see it."

"But—"

"You don't know what it's like to look down at your hands and see hollow claws made out of wires, and . . . like the demon you just tore apart, you wonder if you're full of spiders, too."

"Full of spiders?" Navathe and Gendreau said in unison.

"Yes. When I pulled the demon apart, there was nothing inside of him but spiders. That's how he changed me in my mother's house—he infected me with those spiders." A familiar tingling sensation crawled up Robin's scalp as she remembered that black night in the Hell-annexed Victorian. When she looked up after clawing at her head, the magicians were staring at her as if she'd gone mad. The diner seemed ten degrees colder.

"*Real* spiders?" asked Navathe.

"I don't think they were 'real' spiders," said Robin. "When they touched me, it was like being molested by the ghosts of perverts and psychos. The spiders were wicked thoughts, black cravings with legs. Abstract. Crawling, violating metaphors."

Navathe winced. "That sounds horrible."

"Not as horrible as seeing them chew away my humanity and turn me into the same kind of monster as Andras." Robin's appetite was at the door, threatening to leave. "I think I can live like I am now. But . . . I don't think I ever want to be that thing that I was, ever again."

"So . . . what?" asked Rook, "does it require coming into contact with a demon to cause a full transformation?"

"As far as I know."

What does it take to change me? she wondered. *Do I have to get hurt to do it? Will it happen every time I get seriously hurt? What if I'm in a car accident and I demon it up in the hospital?*

Maybe if I let them help me, I can learn how to control it. Not to be able to Hulk out whenever—

(Were you about to say "whenever you want"?)

Maybe if I let them help me, I can learn how to keep it from happening again. She looked at her hands, the one that was just old enough to hold a beer and the other one that looked like a high schooler's. She flexed the younger hand. She could still imagine the texture of her demon hand, like a combination of driftwood and vulcanized rubber. Twice as large as her human right hand, a green-black eagle foot big enough to squeeze a volleyball flat.

Her fingers had scraped against each other hollowly, like bird bone. She could remember feeling it resonate in her teeth.

Are you sure you want to give that up?

I want to control it. I want to put a leash on it.

Track 4

Astride the Royal Enfield, Santiago Valenzuela felt like a god—one of those Greek gods, perhaps the god of war, a mountain-legged giant full of piss and lightning. He didn't remember their names, or perhaps he never knew, but that didn't stop him from sitting ramrod-straight on the motorcycle's leather spring-seat, his hands clenching the grips as if they were axe handles. Wind beat and howled against his bare face. He didn't wear a helmet, so his hair was a rippling charcoal mane. He caught a glimpse of himself in the windows of a Wendy's on the way out of Lockwood and thought he looked like a lion tearing ass across the bushlands.

La Reina wasn't your average biker ride. She wasn't a sleek road machine painted in sparkly red, with chrome and flames. She looked more like something Indiana Jones would escape from Nazi stormtroopers on: a primitive but powerful Tinkertoy with one cyclopean floodlight and toothy bicycle spokes. The exhaust and the engine were gunmetal gray, but everything else was powder-coated olive green: classic Army power.

Got her three years before in a police auction. He'd been there looking for another car to go with Marina's Blazer, something Carly could learn to drive when she was old enough, but something about the powder-green motorcycle spoke to him, reached right out of that impound lot and grabbed him by the balls and refused to let go. He sat there on those folding chairs on that brisk Saturday morning in November and the auctioneer's voice just sailed right over his head. The only voice he could hear clearly was a pregnant, beckoning sound in the middle of his head like the slow tearing of long strips of paper.

At first, he thought it was his imagination. Santiago looked over his shoulder and his eyes danced across the faces around him, but everyone was sitting as still as mannequins, a few of them with their hands up.

Don't they hear it? he squinted. *Don't they hear that? What the hell* is *that?*

"Two thou, two thou, do I hear two fitty?" droned the auctioneer, a small bald man in a plaid shirt. He stood behind a lectern borrowed from the Lockwood PD conference room.

The gray sky was the lid of a lead-lined coffin. Santiago stared at the powder-green motorcycle. Something was trapped inside the machine, eager to escape. *Scrrrrrrrratch.* The sound scrawled down the slopes of his skull until he couldn't take it anymore—he could almost *see* the sound rolling down the corner of his eye, a fuzzy gliding bruise like a finger pushing against his eyeball.

"Two thou, I hear two thou, do I hear two fitty?"

Santi jabbed a peace sign at him.

"Two thou fitty . . . do I hear two-sanny-five?"

Scrrrrrrrrrrratch. His fingers remained skyward as the price climbed. *Let me out,* the sound seemed to plead, a talon being raked down the inside of a cardboard box, a shard of bone sliding down the inside of a helmet. *Take me back to the road. Take me. I belong on the road.*

"No more takers? No more takers. Last chance, last chance. Four thousand." The auctioneer smacked the edge of the lectern with a ball-peen hammer. Flowers were painted on the handle. Santiago would always remember those flowers, tiny blue ones with white centers. "*Sold,* to the man in the black vest."

Two weeks later, he sold his original bike, a 1974 Harley shovelhead he'd inherited from his father, Emiliano.

He hadn't heard that strange phantom scratching since.

The boys at the clubhouse asked him why he'd given up the heirloom bike, teased him for weeks about it, asked him if the bike was a welcome gift for joining the Army. All he could tell them was that it was love at first sight. And it was, in a way. Over time he more and more often referred to the bike as his "Queen"—La Reina, which drew comparisons to Lorena Bobbitt and comments about getting his dick burned while he was fucking the exhaust pipe, which he quickly put a stop to.

When he first bought her, there was a sidecar attached. For a while, he left it on. Several times (who are we kidding, *many* times) he filled the sidecar with ice and used it as a rolling beer chest. Sometimes, back in "the old days" in the weeks and months after he bought her, he gave Carly a ride in it. Nothing quite like seeing that lovable little stick figure sitting in the sidecar like a prairie dog peeking up out of a hole, the wind whipping her silky hair across the sides of her helmet.

Then she officially blossomed into a real teenager and grew out of her evening rides, a flower too big for its pot, and Santi went to fewer and fewer shindigs with the boys (that's what he called 'em on the good days, "shindigs"; when he was feeling his oats, they were "fuckarees"), until finally one hot summer evening, like casting aside a crutch, he took off the sidecar.

Took hours, and he never could seem to find all the bolts affixing it to the Enfield's frame—there seemed to always be *one more to take off*—and he'd had to give up and cut the damn thing off with a Sawzall, like an arm trapped under a rock. These days, the sidecar sat in a tangle of weeds by the woodshed behind their trailer, a green husk rusting in the shadow of a stand of hickory. Unlike the bike, which never seemed to deteriorate at all, the sidecar had steadily slipped into a twilight zone of corrosion, the floor rusted out in big buckshot holes.

He could still remember the terrible, rending squeal of the reciprocating blade chewing through the support rods. Even then, a dark corner of his mind wondered if it was the power saw screaming or the bike itself.

Until he cut off the sidecar, he hadn't done any maintenance on the bike at all, outside of keeping the fluids topped off. They say a Harley ain't a Harley unless it leaks, but the Enfield was as mint as the day he bought it—which is to say that it wasn't exactly princess-pretty even then, very obviously "pre-owned," but that it never really got any worse than that. Never visibly depreciated prior to the sidecar amputation, other than the random nick and dent. Santiago had smacked her with a rock one Saturday while mowing the lawn and knocked out her headlight. It stayed broken until he fetched a new bulb and ordered a fresh lens.

You better believe he cursed up a storm when he broke that light. He turned the air blue. That was the week Marina lost her tooth for dropping breakfast on the floor. Santi slept on the couch for a while. (Their marriage might not have fared so well if he knew she'd tearfully gathered the scrambled eggs off the floor while he was outside smoking and blowing off steam, and put it back in the pan and served it to him anyway.)

For several months after he cut off the sidecar, the Queen turned into a real bitch. The morning after Santi performed his laborious amputation, he dragged himself out of bed exhausted and sore, and went outside to discover a huge patch of greasy darkness under her pendulous gray belly.

At first, he thought he might have accidentally cut a line or something, but there didn't seem to be any damage to the engine. He'd even thought to disconnect the electrical lines that ran out to the sidecar's taillight before he cut through the strut, yet, no, everything was intact. But she continued to drop every quart of oil he put in her, as if she'd come down with some kind of mechanical Montezuma's Revenge. And for months, whenever he started her up, La Reina would only weakly cough to life and sputter like Archie's old jalopy, as if to spite him for what he'd done.

Ultimately, she got better. She learned to live without the crutch, got stronger, learned to lean into the turns the way she couldn't with the sidecar, a sinuous steel snake. She evolved past the dowdy World War II image and became something new and strong.

The white Army star stenciled onto the gas tank glowed as solidly as the day of the auction. Santiago's gloved hand caressed the star, untouchably hot in the livid Texas sun, and he followed Marina's Blazer through the city-limits pass and into Keyhole Hills. The tiny town declined the deeper they went, front lawns getting grayer and more strewn with toys and junk, until the Blazer trundled into the real beating heart of the Keyhole, where the only homes were dust-beaten mobile homes and the grass no longer grew except in breathless patches of brown stubble.

Marina parked the Blazer in its customary bald patch in front of the trailer, and Santiago grumbled past to the woodshed at the back corner of the lot, where the amputated sidecar languished in rattling bone-colored weeds. The "woodshed" was little more than a lean-to of splintery gray wood, three walls and an A-frame roof to keep the Queen out of a rain that hardly ever fell. He turned her around to face the trailer and walked her into the lean-to backward. The engine cut off with a final series of stuttering reports. Santi's leg swung up and off in a roundhouse arc like John Wayne climbing down off a horse, and he gave La Reina's flank an affectionate clap.

Keys were in the Blazer's visor. He pushed them into his pocket.

Inside the trailer, it was sweltering, even though Marina was going around opening all the windows. Sweat already rolled down his back and collected on his upper lip. Air conditioner hadn't been on all day. The light in the stove hood was on, throwing a soft glow over the oven, and that dug at his mind as wasteful, but he wordlessly turned it off. He wandered from room to room, opening windows and turning off lights. The night-light in the bathroom was plugged in. He unplugged it. Still enough daylight to see. The fan in the bedroom window was going, a rattletrap piece of shit sucking hot air out of the backyard. He turned it off. A Glade plug-in in the bedroom smelled cloyingly like birthday cake. He unplugged it and, after resisting the urge to throw it out the window, dropped it in the wastebasket in the bathroom. The DVD player under their bedroom TV flashed *12:00*. He unplugged it too, and decided to unplug the TV as well.

So much shit in this house sucking up power for no good reason, plugged in and unused.

This made him think of the girls. They were hiding at the mall because of the power bill, he knew. He usually let them hide. But he was so pissed about being laid off when he came home—a bright, hot, shaking, petulant anger—that by the time he'd doubled back and walked around the mall for a while, it had sublimated, burned itself out into a low simmer, the kind of dewy born-again clarity you have when you climb out of a sweat lodge. It was a pretty day. Lots of pretty girls out. How can you stay mad with the wind in your face and the Queen between your knees?

He found the power bill slipped into a stack of junk mail on the kitchen table. Marina stood at the sink drinking a glass of water. Carly sat on the couch, watching some inane bullshit on TV. $179.45. Last month, it was $152.72. *What the hell are we using so much power on?* He tried to remember how often they used the air conditioner the previous month.

"It's that security light outside, love," said Marina, over her shoulder. She hugged herself with one arm, talking into her glass as the rim rested against her lower lip. "It's old as Jesus himself and runs all day and night." Santi leaned over the table to peer through the blinds into the front yard. Mounted on a power pole by the fence was a stark blue lamp that hummed and shimmered venomously. It was there when they moved into the trailer twelve years before.

"That can't be it," he said, letting the power bill plop onto the table. "It's just one light. Besides, ain't that a city light? How are *we* paying for it?"

"It's on our property, baby."

He wanted to turn the TV off, but he knew it was one of the few things that kept Carly from wandering the streets like a cat in heat, and the last thing he needed was a litter of kittens.

The crap that his daughter watched astounded him with its inanity. Shows about people that compulsively ate paint and collected their toenails in jars. Wop teenagers in New Jersey with bleached hair and Cheeto-orange tans. Fat white trash from the Midwest. A family of midgets. He snorted laughter, an airless scoff. *It's all so stupid.* A slow flash of adrenaline rippled across his chest. Marina finished off the water and washed the glass out in the sink, and put it in the dish drain to dry.

When she turned around, Santiago was standing directly behind her. She twitched but said nothing. "I love you," he said, his big hands sliding into place over the knobs of her shoulders.

A subdued, vulnerable affection came into her eyes. "I love you too, Santi."

His Kegel muscles twitched. He was getting an erection. He could feel the blood pooling in his penis, hardening it like an overinflated tire, tightening the crotch of his Wranglers. "We'll get through this," he said reassuringly. His smile was tight, and it didn't reach his eyes. "We always do."

"Yes," said Marina. She was relaxing.

"My love."

". . . Yes?"

"You weren't at the mall to buy bikinis, were you?"

Scccrrrrrrrratch. Fingernail on a coffin lid.

"No, Santi." Marina looked down at his chest. "We weren't. I'm—"

"Why did you lie to me?"

"I'm sorry." The corners of her mouth drew down deeply. "I knew you would be mad at me when you saw the power bill, and I didn't want to be home for that."

"I don't care," he told her. "I don't care you were at the mall."

She gazed up at him, confused.

"I know why you were there. I don't care. I've always known where you were going. It's human nature to run away from pain. Can't blame you for that. Part that pisses me off is that you lied about it."

"I wanted—" She glanced away, breaking eye contact. "Well, I wanted to—"

"You wanted to what?"

"I was afraid you would—"

Santiago glanced over at Carly. Her eyes were glued to the TV screen. She was completely oblivious.

Turning back to his wife, his hands glided softly up the slopes of her shoulders to cup the hinge of her delicate jawbone. The lobes of her ears rested on his index fingers. *Sccrrrrrrratch.*He kissed her, a reaching, gulping kiss. His dick was a hot, pounding iron bar.

To his mild surprise, her hands found their way to his hips, and she kissed him back. His tongue flicked across the back of her teeth. He pulled away, the echo of her soft, pillowy lips still on his. He could smell the powdery candy-like scent of her foundation, and the bacon-grease feel of her lipstick lingered on his mouth.

"Afraid I would what?" he asked.

". . . Afraid you would hurt me."

"Amor, if I wanted to hurt you, I would hurt you any old time. I don't need a crazy power bill to do that." His thumbs caressed the blade of her jaw and settled across her trachea, thumbtips against each other. He squeezed gently and the affectionate look in Marina's eyes immediately fled, replaced by mild alarm.

"Santi?" she asked, but it was the last word she could manage as his hands tightened around her throat.

Her face faded to a rich red. *Sccrrrrrrratch.*

The sensation of choking Marina was so invasive, it was almost sexual. His penis twitched again, an involuntary, convulsive movement. His heartbeat drummed in it, a hot slim pulsation against his zipper. He reveled in the exquisite quality of her face, the curves of her cheeks and jaw soft and brittle and transient, dark liquid sloe-eyes staring at him in confused horror. Her heart struggled to push rhythmic blood past the pads of his thumbs.

Marina's hands bunched his shirt into fists. She gulped for breath. He interrupted it, pressing his mouth against hers, and he kissed her again. No wind came from her nose.

She tried to twist away, but his hands locked her in place. Marina's hands fluttered around the countertop behind her—her ass was jammed hard against it—feeling the edge of the cupboard behind her head, knuckles rapping against the toaster—but there was nothing in reach. She found a dishtowel and whipped it against the side of his head, but it had no effect. Santi was squeezing so hard, his biceps were trembling. Marina's mouth was wide open in a terrified O, her eyes glassy and huge, the only sound coming from that black pit a thready rattle: *kkuuuhhkkk, kkuuuhhkkk.*

"I'm so tired," he told her darkening, almost-purple face. The gap where that one canine tooth used to be was filled with her pink tongue. "I give and I give and I give, and all you do is take." His lips drew back in a rictus of fury. "Well, I don't have anything to give you today. What are you going to take *now*?"

"Daddy?" asked Carly.

His daughter stood behind him, her purse in one hand.

"What are you doing?" Carly's posture was low, knees bent, fight-or-flight, eyes huge, mouth slack. He could smell the fear rolling off of her in coils of girlsweat. It smelled like snakes and Magic Markers.

"Nothing," he told her. His erection pressed hard into Marina's belly. "Go watch TV."

"L-Let go of Mama," Carly told him.

"Go watch your goddamn TV."

"I'm telling you, Daddy. Let go of Mama."

Scccrrrratch. Santiago did just that. His hands sank slowly to his sides and Marina gasped air as if she'd just come up from a pearl dive. She doubled over, barking great ragged croup-coughs.

"You're *telling* me?" He stepped toward Carly. "Or what?" he asked, voice rising. "How about you just do what the hell I tell you for once?" Out of the corner of his eye, he saw his own right hand float up and point imperiously at Carly's face. "Go watch your stupid-ass shows and mind your own business."

She pulled something out of her purse. A can of Axe body spray?

He took another step toward her and she abandoned the purse on the table, clutching the aerosol can in both hands like a pitcher getting ready to hurl a fastball.

Marina recognized the can in her hand. *"No, Carlita!"*

"What are you g—" he started to ask, and the can came up at the apex of her extended arms. Carly sprayed him in the face, a clabbery stream that ripped wetly across his hairline.

Shock was his first reaction, followed by confusion. It didn't *smell* like Axe body spray. What it *smelled* like was cheap salsa, or maybe sriracha. His nose burned. "What the hell?" he asked, his forearm coming up to slick some of it away. Instead of clearing his eyes, however, he only painted a streak of feverish pain across his forehead. His hands were rust-orange. Orange juice? *Battery acid?* The liquid trickled downward, breaching the walls of his eyebrows, and when it seeped into the sensitive flesh of his eyelids, he understood what it was: pepper spray.

BEAR SPRAY, he read on the black can in his daughter's hand, six seconds too late.

2 MILLION SCOVILLE UNITS.

Dear sweet titty-fucking Jesus!

A foul cloud of pepper fog filled the kitchen with choking heat. Carly and Marina both started coughing, her mother's purple face greasy with sweat, Marina dry-heaving and gasping. Santiago didn't notice, because his head was full of pitchfork-toting devils from the hottest alleys of Hell. As soon as the Mace reached his eyes, razor blades sliced across the whites of his eyeballs. The scream that burst out of him was an atavistic, unfiltered expression of terrified agony, a shriek from a dying pterodactyl. He collapsed on his knees, covering his eyes with both hands. *"Fuuuuuck!"* he bellowed in a broken, high-pitched howl, his forehead pressing his knuckles into the linoleum floor. *"Fuuuuck!"*

"God oh God," his wife chanted frantically. She poured water from the tap, gagging. "Here, Santi"—*cough, cough*—"roll over."

He did so. Marina poured the water on his eyes. It didn't help. The water spread the Mace to every corner of his face and made things worse. It was in his ears. The superheated screws being driven through his eyeballs didn't let up; they kept winding deeper until he could feel them penetrating his brain. His eyeballs were chestnuts being roasted over a roaring bonfire, and any second they were going to explode, *crack-crack* like M-80s. Sizzling eye-goo all over the kitchen.

Rolling over onto his hands and knees, Santiago pounded his head on the floor in a panic, *bump, bump, bump,* skull against linoleum. His brain felt like Jell-O bouncing flaccidly inside his skull, but nothing compared to the cosmic glory of the torture in his face. Maybe if he knocked himself out, he could sleep through the pain.

"Milk!" said Carly, coughing.

"What do we need milk for?" Marina wrenched the refrigerator door open. "We don't *have* any milk!"

"The guy at the cop store"—Carly wheezed, coughing—"said milk would help. Here!" She snatched up the last of her smoothie, pulled off the lid, and flung it into her father's face.

The relief was immediate, but it wasn't enough, only tepid calamine on a radiation burn. Santiago tasted blueberries. He crawled across the floor and scaled the cabinet to the sink. Opening the sink tap, he stuck his face under the cold flow, but all it did was wash off the smoothie. The pain remained and only intensified.

Infuriated, Santi grabbed the microwave in both fists and hurled it across the room. Both women screamed. A window shattered and the microwave hit the kitchen table with an incredible *BOOM!*, sliding off onto the floor. Santiago's hands crabbed across the counter until he found something else: the toaster. He jerked the cord, ripping the wires out of the plug in a burst of sparks, and fired the toaster in the direction of a woman's voice.

A hollow metallic noise. Carly grunted.

Whipping a drawer open, Santi rummaged through a pile of utensils. The first thing he did was run a finger down the blade of a filet knife and cut it open. He swore incoherently, grabbed something else, and threw an ice cream scoop, knocked the corkboard off the wall. Coupons and takeout menus scuffled through the air. He threw the pizza cutter. More glass broke. The front door opened and he heard his wife and child run outside. Santi pushed away from the counter, rammed his hip into the table and knocked over a chair, and walked into the edge of the half-open door, a hammer-blow to the eyebrow. Stars fizzled in his head.

As he shoved the screen door out of the way and staggered onto the front porch, he heard the Blazer's doors clap shut, and even through the pain he couldn't help but giggle madly.

"I got the keys, bitch!" Santiago shouted. "You ain't goin' *nowhere*!"

With no rails to stop him, he walked off the edge of the porch and flopped facedown on hard, dry clay like Wile E. Coyote, winding himself.

Every square inch of his head felt like it'd been dipped in lava. Santiago belly-crawled across the dusty yard toward the side of the trailer and made his way along the underpinning until his groping hands found the garden hose spigot. He twisted it, the tap opened, and the hose fattened. He followed the hose out to the pistol sprayer, leaving a trail of curse words, and lay on his back, blasting himself in the face. Ice-cold rubber-smelling water ran up his nose, choked him, gushed under his eyelids. He held his nose and tried to keep his eyes open to flush them out.

That familiar scrape down the bowl of his skull. *Scrrratch.*

Take me out on the road, Santi.

He released the sprayer handle and the water stopped. He gasped for breath and the heat came right back, causing his eyes to reflexively lock shut again.

Take me. Let's go.

"Urrrgh! I'm gonna kill both of you!" He wrestled his shirt off and continued to spray himself in the face. A slow lightning bolt spread throughout his sinuses, like his brain was getting too big for his head, pushing his eyeballs out, and he couldn't help but open them.

First thing he saw through the haze was Carly's terrified face. His wife and daughter got out of the useless Blazer and fled on foot. He let out a hoarse roar and blood trickled out of his nose, salty copper on his tongue.

Snow-white hair shagged virulently across the back of his hand like bread mold growing in a time-lapse video. That same cracking feeling in his head, a walnut in a vise, now spread through his arms as if they were getting longer, the bones telescoping. His knuckles crunched. Veins under his skin rolled as the muscle behind them rippled. His fingernails were longer, sharpening into points.

What the hell?

Strange, horrifying, this phenomenon—yet somehow familiar. *God, it hurts so much . . . it hurts even more than the Mace. Is this happening again?*

(Again? It's happened before?)

—Yes, baby boy, I'm in here waiting. We'll run the ridge again, haha, hoho—

Faint memories flickered in the dark behind his eyelids, of standing in the desert with other men. Yellow eyes glinted in the night. Someone kicked off a pair of underwear and *they're all naked—*

Disgusted and frightened, he opened his eyes again to get away from it, just in time to see Marina pull Carly away, mesmerized horror on their faces. Santiago screamed—or perhaps he thought he screamed; the scraping noise in his head occluded even the constant snore of traffic out on the highway.

Sunlight rekindled the heat in his cheeks and eyes. Soundtracked by the sound of a claw being dragged down a blackboard, he went back to spraying himself in the face with the hose.

—They're getting away, Santi. You can catch them if you just get up! Catch as catch can!—

Been a few times when Santiago wondered if the voice talking in his head, the voice coming from the motorcycle, was the Virgin Mary. Impossible—the Virgin Mary wouldn't be having him do things that left him covered in blood when he came back to his senses. Would she? The shapes he saw in his dreams, the beasts he ran with now, was that part of God and the Holy Mother's plan?

No, not possible.

Sometimes he wanted to tell her to shove off, whoever she was. But her voice was a fine wine, silky and hot and slick, the atavistic taste of some blind primal urge, like masturbation or the purest fury—sang to you in the moment, and when you opened your eyes again, it was all over with, leaving you with a sense of bewilderment, shame, and sometimes awe at what you'd just watched your other self do. Nights spent in the sweaty skin of another were just nightmares in the cold light of the morning, half-remembered, spliced-together film reels that played in hiccups and jumps. Memories drifted across the floor of his mind like leaves, like pieces of a horror movie he'd seen a long time ago.

Talons he'd seen curling out of his fingertips were nothing but a trick of light, right?

Right?

Every time he fell under her spell, it punched a hole in his brain.

And that motherfucker was straight-up Swiss cheese these days. PTSD from a war he'd never fought in. Ever since the first time this happened, on a jaunt out into the desert on some kind of deranged vision quest.

Peyote had unlocked these weird sensations, these fleeting glimpses of savagery. Not long after buying the Royal Enfield, he'd been talked into some shrooms by one of the boys, and he didn't remember anything else of that first night except getting on the motorcycle and leaving the clubhouse. Woke up the next morning naked next to a campfire on windswept hardpan, the motorcycle standing guard over him like a horse in some old-timey Marlboro ad.

What he did remember was being badly frightened by the sight of giant pawprints, claws twice the size of his hands, in the sand around his improvised camp. At the time, he'd convinced himself that a mountain lion had come to investigate him during the night.

He flexed his aching hands now, studying them through the tears.

Let's go find those whores, those tramps that hurt you, La Reina whispered in his head. *Run them down. Grind them up in our gears. Burn them in our engines. They belong to us. This house belongs to us.*

"Yes, Mother Mary," Santiago said, lips brushed by dead gray grass. "Hallowed be thy name."

The road belongs to us.

Track 5

"What do you mean, we won't get the Winnebago back until morning? It was just a busted tire!" Robin had cornered the mechanic in his garage, her fists on her hips, and Jake, as his shirt said, was pressed against the wall, clutching a clipboard in both hands in a shielding manner. Some charcoal-and-rotten-eggs smell overpowered the sweat-and-motor-oil funk soaked into the cement.

"Well, you see, ma'am," he said, taking the pen out from behind his ear. He fumbled it onto the floor.

Robin stared at him. Jake abandoned the pen.

"You see," he began again, "when you put on the spare and let the Winnebago down off the jack, you—you did it too fast and bent the rim. So, it's gonna need a new one . . . but these old 'Bagos, they got different rims, so I had to order you a new one. Got a guy comin' out from San Antonio tomorrow with some parts, I asked him to bring one of those rims down with him, so I can put it on in the morning."

First time the Smell happened—road rage at an Arizona traffic light just before Thanksgiving—she was mortified; she thought maybe there was a rotten egg in the RV, or God forbid, she'd shit her pants. Is it actually possible to be so angry you shit your pants? But after talking to Kenway about it, she realized it was her breath. When she was pissed off, her breath smelled like sulfur.

Brimstone.

In the dark garage, her eyes were luminescent. Only faintly so, almost a trick of the light, a suggestion of luster. Mechanic Jake's eyes darted from her face to the GoPro camera on her chest and back to her face. It was turned off at the moment, but people still regarded the camera with suspicion.

"That okay?" he asked.

Robin sighed and relented, walking away. "Yeah, whatever."

"Ain't gonna be a whole lot more cost-wise, but it's—"

"I'm not worried about the money," she told him, walking backward a few paces. "I just want it done. And no fooling around in the engine, please. I don't want any surprise nickel-and-diming. Tire and rim."

"Yes, ma'am," he said, coolly.

Felt like she was being too hard on him, but she'd been taken by mechanics before, back when she was driving the Conlin Plumbing van. *He'll probably tack on a little extra labor for the attitude, but better that than digging up extra engine problems like shitty little potatoes.* Maybe she should send Kenway in to address the bill later. Just because she was a woman, they acted like they had all the leeway in the world to run over her, like she was some kind of bimbo that didn't know what was going on when they talked about how it was gonna take three weeks to order a new part from China or God knows where. But discovering that you're half-demon has a marvelous effect on one's confidence, and she just didn't have the patience for the runaround anymore. Better, she found, to let them think she's a bitch and get shit done than to pussyfoot around and be forced to haggle for days over irrelevant engine issues. *I checked your transmission fluid and found some other stuff wrong while I was in there.* No, you didn't, you lying prick. You changed my oil for no reason, even though I just did it myself two months ago. *One of your other tires wasn't holding air either, so I went ahead and replaced that one, too.* Gee, thanks.

Not the best tactic at a restaurant, where people can spit in your food, but situations like this? Fair game.

An ancient bulldog stood out in the garage driveway, a scruffy little monster with the watery bloodshot eyes of an old pothead. He hobbled around, muttering and soliciting affection from the two men. Gendreau's immaculate hands were crammed in his immaculate pockets; he wouldn't have anything to do with the dog, so Kenway was doing all the petting. An airport pull-along sat on the oil-stained gravel next to the magician's foot. His pinstripe vest was matched with a pair of tactically aged gray skinny jeans, making him look like a banker from Tombstone. Early-evening sun turned the scar on his neck pearlescent pink.

"So, what's news, Miss Martine?" the magician asked dourly. Robin manhandled the dog while she imparted Jake's tale of woe.

"Tryin' to give you a rim job," said Kenway.

"What?" asked Gendreau.

"Bent rim. Giving you the runaround. Rim job. Bent rim. Get it?"

Robin rolled her eyes and turned the GoPro on. "I get it, but I'm not sure I want it."

"I ain't complaining," Kenway continued. "We can get a motel room for the night. Be nice to sleep on a real bed for a change, one with plenty of room to stretch out, and, God willing, a bathtub."

All of the irritation drained from Robin's face. The relief was so palpable, she almost fell over. "Oooh. Yes. *A bathtub.* Okay." She went back into the RV and scooped some toiletries and clean clothes into a Walmart bag. She also grabbed her MacBook bag and the Osdathregar from its customary place—hidden under the mattress—and locked the Winnebago up.

After locking up, she opened the window over the kitchen sink to keep it from getting too stuffy in the Winnebago.

It would be safe there in the garage.

• • •

Earlier that afternoon at the Diner of the Ejaculating Footballs, they were polishing off their last few bites when Navathe had mentioned something about getting dessert, but Robin's heart just wasn't in it. Not in the mood for one of those dried-out-looking pieces of pie in the counter case. Not after a conversation about the hell-spiders that might or might not be inside her.

"So," Robin said to Rook, trying to change the uncomfortable subject, "you said you were an Oreo."

"An Origo, but, yes."

"So, what does an Origo *do*? You never really elaborated."

With a thoughtful sigh, Rook searched her mind for the words. "These relic objects and the teratoma elements don't just fit together like puzzle pieces, or chocolate and peanut butter. They're more like *pickles* and peanut butter. They have a strange affinity for each other in the end, but you have to make them play nice to tease that synergy out."

"Wait," said Kenway, "go back a bit."

"What confused you?"

"The pickles-and-peanut-butter part. What? What is that?"

"Never had a pickle-and-peanut-butter sandwich?" asked Rook, disbelief flashing over her face.

"Uhh, no."

Robin waved all this away. "We'll talk about gross sandwiches later; right now, I want to know more about Orlando."

"Origo?" asked Rook.

"That's what I said."

Navathe burst out laughing.

"We Origo are artificers," continued Rook, with a disapproving head-shake. "We are editors of magic, singularly talented at 'conductive semantics,' or what we call *shadow grammar,* the rhythms, the rituals, and the syntax needed to pair heart-roads with items, imbue them with meaning, and to pair the completed relics with their potential users. You have to find just the right host object that will most efficiently, most powerfully, and most compatibly house that teratomatic matter." She pointed to Navathe's snow globe. "This took several years of trial and error with a dozen objects before we could find one that would respond to the rituals, accept the teratoma, and output an acceptable level of energy. But it only took three months for Navathe to attune to it." Gesturing to Gendreau's ring, she said, "This, however, only required three objects to find one that would receive the lock of hair embedded in it. But it took a year and a half to find someone it resonated with and teach them how to channel the energy coming through the relic's heart-road. It takes a lot of time and finesse."

"So, why do you implant the teratoma matter into a conduit? Why don't you just surgically insert the matter into the user?"

Giving a *woof* of horror, Gendreau interjected. "Incredibly dangerous. The teratoma would infect the person and turn them into a witch of Ereshkigal."

"By the time the teratoma had set up enough to start channeling energy into the user, you'd have to kill them to get it back out," said Rook. "It would start generating another avatar of Ereshkigal herself, just like Marilyn Cutty's coven, their matron Yee-Tho-Rah, or any of the other witches you've hunted."

"Something men don't usually survive," said Gendreau. "As for your other question, Miss Martine, about whether this is a new-employee orientation or a noose-fitting? Well, let's just say it's the next phase of your probationary period."

Robin's head tilted like a curious dog. "Probationary?"

"Frank didn't fully trust the idea of relying on your YouTube videos for assessment," said Navathe. "He wants a firsthand vantage point. Says it's too easy to doctor the videos to exclude violent incidents and loss of control. The camera is too friendly."

"But I've never *lost* control," said Robin.

Kenway stepped in. "She hasn't, that I've seen. Hell, she's got more control than I do. Don't ever let *me* get near a box of Fudge Rounds. Retirement has made me a fool for pogey bait."

She poked the hulking veteran in the belly. "I try to keep the old man on the nutritional straight and narrow. I can't hunt witches if my partner gets winded putting on his seat belt."

"Hey, it was the *one time,* all right?"

"Well, there's a difference between scarfing down junk food and losing your mind and killing people. So, Frank's appointed someone to be your auditor," said Rook, speaking over them, and she flicked a finger at Gendreau. "And he says that since Andy here has taken it upon himself to be your secret liaison, *he* can fill that role."

Gendreau had been grinning at Robin and Kenway, but then his face fell. "What? Wait, *me*? You want *me* to go with them?"

"Not me, I don't. Your grandfather. I guess since you're the one that knows her the best, you're the one most suited for the task. Personally, I think it's him punishing you for hiding her over the winter."

The curandero tugged down his shirt collar to fully reveal the scar from Karen Weaver's knife. "Last time I rode into battle with Robin Martine, I got my throat cut. I almost died. If it's all the same to you, I'd like to sit this one out. Watch from the sidelines."

Rook rubbed her forehead, chagrined. "It's not up to me. This is from Frank."

"Yeah, well," said Gendreau, getting fired up. He stiffened, as if he were about to get out of his chair. "Grandpa Frank can come stick *his* dick in the fire if he wants to. I'm a lover, not a fighter." Robin was surprised; it had been the first time she'd ever really seen him lose his cool. One of the men sitting at the diner counter looked over his shoulder at them. "I *know* why he's doing this, and it's not funny. It's not funny *at all.*"

"You know that's not true." Rook shook her head. "He loves you. He loves you for who you are. He's not putting this on you to punish you for that. He's assigning you to this because he believes in you."

"Please excuse me," said Gendreau, "if I think that's horseshit."

• • •

Rook and Navathe had departed to head for Killeen, where they would spend the night and catch a morning flight back to Michigan. Gendreau remained with Robin, and the magicians' absence left him aloof and sulky. The self-appointed third wheel walked behind her and Kenway as they marched through Keyhole Hills. Everyone had retreated inside for dinner and evening TV, so they walked through a quiet postapocalyptic twilight of jack-o'-lantern windows. Dogs *wurf*ed quiet warnings at them from the shadows. "So dry and dusty here," he muttered to himself. The tiny pull-along luggage rattled and thumped along behind him. "Starting to miss Petoskey already."

Robin slowed to match his pace and slipped her hand under his elbow so they walked with linked arms. "You don't have to be afraid to ride with me," she told him. He was almost a foot taller, so she had to look up at his pale, fine-featured face. "We're not going to let anything happen to you."

His chin subconsciously dipped to hide his scar.

"That night in the Lazenbury really messed you up, didn't it?"

"I almost died." The corners of his mouth twitched downward. "If you'd asked me a year ago if I cared about living or dying, why, I'd have to give it legitimate consideration. For a long time, I've never been the most . . . vibrant soul. I've had a long, strange, hard life. But after lying on that parquet floor, frantically trying to remember how to knit flesh back together as my life's blood pumped through my fingers, I . . ."

He trailed off.

"You're not carrying your bull-pizzle cane," said Robin.

"You destroyed the relic that was in it." Wasn't said accusingly, only a droll statement of fact.

"To save your life."

Gendreau finally looked at her. His mouth was set in a firm line, but his eyes were glazed with distant fear. "And I overflow with gratitude for it."

They continued to walk. Eventually he said, "I traded the cane for a ring." He extended a hand to display the gaudy fixture on his left index finger. The ruby darkled in the evening light with red depth. Something was lodged inside like a piece of fruit in cherry Jell-O. "Certainly more convenient than carrying around a three-foot bull penis. But I'm still learning how to use it. I carried the cane around for eight years. Only had the ring since Thanksgiving."

"So, it took time?"

"Yes. Like Rook said, the relics serve as conduits for the teratomas, and it took time to attune to the relic, to learn how the conduit works—how to work the power inside. It's sort of like being a soldier with a gun. He has to be trained in how to use it accurately, and to familiarize himself with it, to be effective."

"Why do you need the conduit, anyway?" Robin asked. "I mean, I know the teratoma can't be implanted into you. But why can't you just hold the matter?"

"Unlike you, Miss Martine, we human mages can't utilize the raw power inside the teratoma. We don't have any natural function or limb or organ for that. Going back to that soldier, it'd be like giving him a handful of bullets with no gun and asking him to go out and do his job. Sure, he could probably fetch up a pair of pliers and a hammer and make it work, but it wouldn't be very useful or accurate—and he would probably hurt himself in the process. I don't think we can even do *that*."

The three of them paused at a Wendy's to let a Range Rover trundle out onto the highway.

"You've also got to consider compatibility." Gendreau loosened the elaborate knot in his necktie. "The magician's mental fortitude must be up to the task for harnessing the power in the relic, or bad things can happen. As you well know, the teratomas are all pieces of the death-goddess Ereshkigal, and all the relics derive their power from her."

"With you so far."

"If the relic is too strong for the magician, it will corrupt them. She can't reincarnate herself through a relic—the teratomas must be embedded in organic tissue to mature and metastasize—but she can still reach you here," he said, tapping his head. "She can get to your mind. She can manipulate you."

"Sounds like you folks walk a razor's edge."

"We do, we do. Dangerous dance, Miss Martine."

A dry breeze shifted up the street, blowing a paper bag along the gutter. The scent of hamburgers washed over them in a warm, fragrant wave. "You can call me Robin, you know."

"I know."

"Do you feel more comfortable calling me Miss Martine?"

"I do. For now."

"Okay." She thought for a moment as they walked. "So, are there artifacts too powerful for any of you to use?"

"I'm sure there are, but the Origo keep a pretty tight lock on them. Rumor has it there's one for resurrection, one that can manipulate time. One that can kill with a glance. But I've never seen them. They're all kept in a big warded vault in our place in Michigan."

The motel was a horseshoe-shaped collection of suites with a Tommy Bahama theme. She paid extra for the "El Presidente," which was what passed for a deluxe suite in a motel where a third of the rooms were occupied by full-time residents. The room was done up in tasteful shades of ecru and blue; the curtains were white linen and looked like sails. The bathroom was tiny, a pass-through they shared with Gendreau, who took the suite next door. A rear corner was occupied by a great big oval bathtub with jets in the bottom.

"Hell yeah," said Kenway, taking off his shirt and shoes.

The TV was a tube television probably a decade old. Robin flipped through channels until she stopped seeing commercials. "Animal Planet," she said into the GoPro's all-seeing eye. "Good enough." She turned it off.

"Saw a frozen yogurt place down the street," Gendreau said, peeking in. "I'm craving chocolate. You two want me to bring you back anything?"

"Surprise me," said Robin.

The magician gave them a thumbs-up and disappeared into his suite.

Wasn't long before both of them had stripped and were sitting in lukewarm water, jets going full blast. Water gurgled and foamed like fresh champagne. Kenway dunked his face and slicked his hair out of his eyes. "Tell you what, there ain't nothin' like a cold bath on a hot day."

"Like a tropical pool," said Robin, her head resting on the edge. She closed her eyes.

"Well."

"Well what?" she asked.

"What do you think?"

"About what?"

"The magicians. You gonna keep working with 'em?"

She didn't open her eyes, speaking to the ceiling. "Don't guess I have a choice. I imagine I'm either with them or against them. And I don't want to be against them when I don't know their full capabilities."

"Can't be *that* black-and-white. They didn't know you and G were working together, and they never mobilized a hunter-killer death squad to take you out, did they? Nobody showed up to turn you into a toad."

"Maybe that's what Sara and Lucas were. Maybe they came out here as a team to catch me, and G let me go because he saw how cool I am after we took out Cutty's coven."

"Maybe! They seem like good people. Maybe they were like a

lot of us soldiers—good people coerced into doing questionable things."

She got up and moved across the tub, straddling his thighs. "I don't like talking about it," she said, kissing him. A half-truth—really, she was just tired of the topic and wanted to get laid. "Can we do something else?"

"Fine by me."

When she was perfectly still and silent, she could feel his heartbeat. He kissed her again. She reached under the water and guided him into herself, then sat astride him, surrounding him, appreciating the feeling of fullness he gave her. It wasn't the dumb animal sex they had in the Winnebago after changing the tire, but a tidal, thoughtful exercise that barely rippled the water. She didn't finish earlier—it was too damn sweaty and muggy in the RV—but she did now, a flash-burn of pleasure that coiled in the pit of her belly and rose along her spine. Muscles in her thighs shuddered, and her body hardened, trapping the air in her lungs. Then the coil shredded brightly and her breath escaped in a blast of euphoria.

Then his stomach tensed and she knew he was there, too, climaxing; she let him stay and spend himself inside her. Always had, since they started sleeping together, and this was how she knew she was genetically incompatible with other people.

She stared down at him, each breathing in the other's face, and wondered if it would be any different if he were part demon, too.

"What you thinkin' about?" he asked.

"Nothing." It didn't bear discussing. Robin kissed him.

"I know that look. That ain't 'nothing.' There's gears turning in that skull of yours. Penny for your thoughts?"

She sighed, reading his face. "The one magician chick. The Asian."

"Rook?"

"Yeah. Does she seem familiar to you? Like . . ."

"Like, you get a friend request on Facebook from somebody, and you creep on their pictures, and you recognize some of the people in them as old classmates, so you figure, *I went to school with this person, and—*"

"*Rook* is a weird name, too, ain't it?"

"Yeah," said Kenway. "Like a code name or something."

A knock at the bathroom door. She slipped off of him and retreated to the other end of the tub, sinking low and peering over the edge. "Come on in."

Gendreau's muffled voice: "Are you decent?"

"No, but is *anyone* decent, really?"

A sigh. "Can I come in? This stuff is melting."

"Velcome," Robin said in a bad Lugosi accent. "Come een, come een."

The magician eased the door open, peeking through his fingers. His other hand carried a carton with cups of frozen yogurt. "I'll put it in the mini-fridge for later," said Gendreau, putting it away. He crept back out through the bathroom.

A moment of floating later, Kenway said, "How can you be afraid of a dude that buys you frozen yogurt? That guy's on your side."

Track 6

Then

"Now put it back together," said Heinrich Hammer, resetting the stopwatch.

Strains of Red Hot Chili Peppers murmured from the distant tower, yelling about sabretooth horses and paisley dragons. Lying on the picnic table in front of the girl were the component pieces of an assault rifle. The adobe wall behind her looked as if it had been blown out by a grenade, revealing an eternity of desolate Texas scrubland where buzzards circled on distant thermals.

"Still don't understand why I need to know about guns like this," the teenager said, glaring insolently. "Thought you said the only thing that can stop a witch is the dagger, and the only thing that can kill her is fire."

"You won't always be fighting witches."

"Like what? Vampires? Werewolves?"

"Don't be a smart-ass. Vampires and werewolves don't exist

and you know it." More pepper than salt back then, his hair glittered in the sunlight that filtered through the holes in the canvas awning.

She sneered. "Didn't think *witches* existed either."

"You're gonna be fighting people."

"People?"

"Like I told you," said the big Black man, pacing in front of the table. "Like what happened to your daddy. The witches and their cat-people familiars. Got to be willin' to put them down before they can kill you."

"So, I *shoot* them?" she asked, incredulous.

"If the witch had time to build an army of familiars, yes. You'll be out there all by your lonesome, Robin Hood. One word from the old woman and the townies will come pourin' out of the woodwork like a swarm of cockroaches, tryin' to rip your kidneys out." He paused, his eyes blazing. "Is *that* the way you wanna die? Crawlin' across the floor, tryin' to push"—he clutched imaginary intestines—"your guts back in with bloody hands?"

Robin grimaced. She was pale and puffy from living the last two years in a psych ward, with the dark-circled, suspicious eyes of a little girl who's spent that whole time plotting and mourning in the lucid hours between doses of antipsychotics and antidepressants.

"Knives for the witches, guns for the bitches."

"Okay," she said, bracing herself. "I get the picture."

He clicked the stopwatch. "Go on, then."

Her hands fluttered across the table from part to part—first, the bolt went into the bolt carrier, then the bolt carrier slid into the upper receiver along with the charging handle. Then, the handle and trigger assembly bolted onto the bottom of the upper receiver. She pushed the recoil spring into the buttstock and attached it to the upper receiver and handle.

Flipping it up and standing it on the stock, she fit the handguard pieces back onto the barrel and laid the rifle down on the tablecloth.

Click. "One minute, seven seconds. Six seconds faster than yesterday."

Reluctant pride burst in her chest. Heinrich sat across from her, digging in his pocket. She thought he was going to come up with another one of his coconut cigars and light it, but he took out something that looked like a tiny fencing sabre made for action figures. "You forgot something, though."

"The firing pin. God *damn* it."

"Attention to detail, honey," he said, dropping the pin on the table. He did, then, take out a cigar and light it. "Those crazy cat-people ain't gonna be the only thing comin' atcha." He squinted, blowing smoke over their heads that smelled like burning leaves, reminding her of autumn. "Them witches can turn into things. Monsters. *Big* monsters."

"Monsters?"

"Transfiguration. You'll see—makes them vampires and werewolves in them old Universal movies look like Fisher Price–level shit. And no, guns like this won't *kill* 'em, but it'll slow 'em down. And when you're buttin' heads with a seven-hundred-year-old priestess of the god of death, every second counts." Reaching into the collar of his ratty henley shirt, Heinrich took out a necklace and opened the pendant to sneak a peek at the cameo inside.

"What is that?" Robin muttered, fidgeting with the firing pin in a desultory fashion.

He showed her a delicately carved picture of a woman's face in profile, like the head on a nickel. "Belonged to my daddy, Moses. Picture of my mama. She gave him this when he went to Vietnam. He was a chaplain in the Army. Caught some shrapnel and they sent him home; he took up with the church there in Blackfield. Hell, I reckon he's still there."

"She's pretty."

He grunted and put the pendant away.

Drawing deep on the cigar, he took it out of his mouth, picking up the stopwatch and blowing smoke over her head. "Arright, now I want you to take it back apart, and this time don't forget the firing pin. If you wanna eat supper tonight, you better beat your disassembly time."

Time resumed with a *click*.

Track 7

Now

Red numerals hovering over the nightstand flipped to 12:04 and Robin sat bolt upright in the bed, waking up from another dream of the desert, and training with Heinrich. *Got to be willin' to put them down before they can kill you,* echoed his phantom voice from across the years, like sitcom laugh tracks from a long-dead studio audience.

Gray light flickered across sinuous shapes. They'd fallen asleep with the TV on, turned down low, whispering nonsense.

Infomercial. Robin flipped through the channels until she found some kind of cartoon and slid out of bed, slipping into a T-shirt. She got a cup of frozen yogurt (turned out to be peanut butter fudge) out of the mini-fridge and sat on the floor at the foot of the bed, staring up at the TV and not really paying attention, eating yogurt with a plastic spoon and occasionally wiping her eyes with the back of her wrist.

When she finished it, she gently placed the empty cup in the wastebasket so as not to wake up Kenway and lay back down, staring up at the ceiling as the TV pushed strange shades across the smooth plaster. She got up again and thought about going outside—maybe go for a smoke or something. Cigarette right about then sounded pretty good, but they'd both quit smoking ages ago. No turning back now.

Maybe some water. Some water would make her feel better. Yeah. It always did after she'd eaten too much sugar.

The bathroom light was on but the door was almost closed, just a bare crack of yellow hanging in the darkness. This wasn't odd, since she'd left the light on as a night-light so she could still see if she got up in the middle of the night, as she'd been doing lately. She opened the door and discovered someone standing in the shared bathroom.

Leaning over the sink was a pale, willowy woman in a towel, inspecting her face in a foggy mirror with her fingers, maybe pinching a zit. Feminine hips but broad shoulders and big, delicate hands. On the flat of her shoulder like a cattle brand was an *algiz* tattoo, a Y with an extra arm in the middle.

Blazing sea-glass eyes. The woman's reflection looked at her in surprise.

"Oh!" blurted Robin, and she whipped the door shut.

Her heart banged. "I'm sorry," she said, suddenly very aware of the smell of the fresh paint on the bathroom door. "I didn't know anybody was in there."

The stranger had been exceedingly familiar. That brief glimpse of her burned in Robin's mind for a moment, a stark, too-bright image, and she realized that the woman's throat had been a ragged pink smile. And only once the door was closed did she retroactively notice the ruby ring on the left index finger.

Wait, what . . .

"It's okay, Miss Martine," a soft voice said from inside. "I just got out of the shower. Should have locked the door, but I thought you were asleep." The door eased open of its own accord to reveal

Anders Gendreau in an old T-shirt and jogging shorts. All Robin could do was stand there, silently hunched over her folded arms as if she were standing in the snow at someone's front door. Gendreau stared at the carpet. "I always wait until late at night to take a shower, so nobody will, ehh . . ."

They stared at each other for several seconds, the magician silhouetted by the bathroom light. He let his hands wander awkwardly down to his sides, as if he wasn't quite sure what to do with them.

Mastectomy scars peeked out of the cut-off sleeves of his t-shirt, pink lines across the bottom of his chest. Robin didn't know what to say or do. The thought occurred to her to hug him, or compliment him, or, in a wild fit of pique, tell him that she loved him (and she *did,* she supposed, there in that instant, even if only platonically—how can you *not* love such a gentle, stuffy, important scarecrow?), but all of them seemed inappropriate, so she did the first thing that popped into her head and apologized again.

"I'm sorry."

"It's okay." Gendreau stepped back into the bathroom and went back to inspecting his face.

"Thank you for the frozen yogurt."

Gendreau gave her a wan smile. "You're welcome."

She pointed at the sink. "Do you mind if I get some water?"

"Go right ahead."

Robin stepped into the bathroom and slurped it straight from the faucet.

When she straightened, Gendreau's face went soft. "Have you been crying?" In the mirror, Robin could see that her eyes were rimmed with red, the whites turned pink.

"It's nothing."

"No, it's *not* nothing." One of Gendreau's long, nimble hands found its way to her shoulder, and he glared past Robin at the sleeping figure on the bed.

"It's absolutely not *him,*" said Robin. "Kenny's a teddy bear."

"Oh. Was it the dreams he told us about?"

"Yeah."

Gendreau twitched, as if he were about to remove his hand, but left it there. They remained this way for several seconds, until he glanced down at himself as if checking to see if his body was still there.

"Will he wake up if we talk too loud?"

"Kenway?" The shape on the bed was motionless, the big veteran's soft respiration a whistly ebb and flow. "No," said Robin. "That man could sleep through a rolling gun battle in a hurricane full of snare drums."

The curandero brushed his teeth. He finished, shaking the water out of his toothbrush, then rinsed his mouth out and awkwardly smiled at her. "This is where we part ways. Good night, Miss Martine. I hope you feel better, and I hope you have better dreams. You know where I am if you need to talk."

"Probably not falling asleep again tonight."

"That's a shame, but fair, I suppose," said Gendreau. "You gonna be all right tomorrow?"

"Me and coffee are old pals." Robin held her hands out and shook them as if she had the jitters. "I'm probably eighty percent bean at this point. Besides, I am not unaccustomed to operating on a bare minimum of sleep. This is not unusual for me."

The magician shrugged. "Want me to slap you if I see you nodding off?"

"Sure."

Gendreau laughed. "Sleep good."

"You too."

Gendreau paused in the doorway.

"My deadname, my birth name, is Irene," he said, closing his eyes. "Only my grandfather Francis, Asha, and Ha—" He corrected himself. "—perhaps only one other knows . . . and now *you* know. I had it legally changed to Anders as soon as I turned eighteen. I started testosterone about five years ago." His eyes opened again, and he glanced at himself in the mirror. "I mean, I don't really keep my transition a secret, but I don't go around advertising it, either."

"I won't say anything." *Ha?* Robin thought. *Ha-who?*

The magician stepped into his suite and closed the door.

All right, then, Gandalf, keep your secrets.

As soon as he left, Robin leaned on the counter, alone in the bathroom, and allowed herself to take off her emotional mask, let down her shields. She leaned on the counter, her face inches from the faucet. Ran cold water and gulped some of it straight from the tap.

She faced herself in the bathroom mirror as the water ran hot and steam climbed out of the sink. Wiping a swath of fog from the mirror, she revealed her face—sweaty hair, pale skin, Pepto-pink eyes. For a brief second, the stream of condensation running down the left side made it look as if her left arm had been amputated again, and she reflexively gasped.

"Goddammit," she said in a strained whisper. She ran a hand down the mirror, wiping the mirage away.

Her reflection, peering through the foggy gap, said nothing for a change.

Something gripped her system—terror? Relief? She wasn't quite sure. As she straightened, she was racked by real tremors—a tectonic quaking that started in her knees, tensing her abs, compressing her lungs, driving the breath out of her. She pressed fists into her eyes until she saw stars. Gritted her teeth until they ached. *You got this,* said something inside her. *Stand up. Shake it off. Rub some dirt on it.*

Her heart hammered in her tightening chest, demanding to be let out. She was suddenly too big for her own skin. Felt like the slightest cut and she would explode into a thousand little screaming starlings.

Adrenaline drip-fed into her system. Robin gripped the counter, breathing deeply and smoothly through her nose.

When the water got as piping hot as it was going to get, she plunged both hands into it. Immediate and enlightening, the scalding sink-water felt as if it were eating straight through both hands, slowly and excruciatingly, like acid. The pain infuriated her, emboldened her, dampened the fear, chased away the memories of hags in the dark with embers for eyes that chased her through filthy houses, raving and slobbering and threatening to tear her in half and eat her. Mental images of her own face, made of wire and twine, flaming green in the bowels of the Darkhouse. Sensations of the hog-monster breaking bone, ripping muscle, swallowing her arm whole. Blood running. People running.

She stood there, running hot water over her hands until they were raw and sore, then she backed away, dazed, and sat on the edge of the bathtub, flexing her biceps and squeezing her thighs until the agony in her hands began to subside.

I can get you to do anything in the world, climb any mountain, swim any sea, said a phantom Heinrich in her head; *all I gotta do is piss you off.*

Pain. Pain pissed her off.

“Kill them all,” she growled under her breath, staring into her own dark runny-mascara eyes in the bathroom mirror. “Kill ’em all. Burn ’em to the ground. All them witches. You’re gonna fucking do it, ain’t you? You’re not gonna run, you coward. Are you?”

“No,” whispered the girl in the mirror, her face stark white.

The raccoon-eyed valkyrie punched herself in the chest, a single gorilla-beat, with her new arm. Dull pain welled across her pectoral muscle. She did it again. “You’re not gonna run, are you?”

“No, ma’am,” the girl in the mirror said a little more confidently.

She punched herself again, leaving a bruise.

“Good.” Robin stood up and scowled at her reflection. “Then let’s do this,” she said, scraped tears off her face, and turned off the water.

• • •

As she left, Gendreau sighed. He'd been leaning against the door in his own suite, listening intently. Tossing his T-shirt into his open luggage, he stood in front of his own mirror, the one on top of the desk, and studied the occult tattoos covering his torso.

Whispering a litany of words in Icelandic, he caressed the surface of the bathroom door, and light glimmered briefly across the new paint. Then he did the same to the front door. His protective sigils installed, the magician glanced toward the suite next door and climbed into bed.

In the fabric darkness of Robin's computer bag, the Osdathregar grew warm.

Track 8

They roamed the midnight streets, looking for refuge, slipping in and out of the blue-white glow of buzzing streetlamps. Subtle thunder grumbled on the horizon as the sky grew darker and darker.

The first place Carly and Marina fled to was Elisa Valenzuela's house. Marina's sister-in-law.

Since she was the overnight stocking manager at the Lockwood Walmart, Elisa had been asleep—but her girlfriend Isabella Talamantes was there and awake, and she'd let them in easily enough, unaware of the pepper-spray incident other than a stray remark about how they smelled like cayenne. Even after she'd noticed the finger bruises materializing on Marina's neck, Isabella hadn't overreacted. She'd been concerned, but she was growing accustomed to seeing the bruises Santi left on his wife. Isabella was an RN at the Keyhole Hills assisted-living center, so she was prone to administering medical help and advice herself, but she didn't say anything.

Not my circus, not my monkeys.

But as soon as they explained the events that led to them fleeing the house—Santi choking Marina, Carly spraying him with bear Mace—Isabella did a one-eighty on them and ran them out of the house. "I don't want him in here pitching a fit," she'd said, ushering them back outside as gently as she could. "I love you as much as a person in my position can, Marina. But you know how Santi is these days."

"Elisa would not stand for-for"—Carly thought her mother was going to say *cowardice*—"this; she would stand up to her brother and—"

"Well, he's not *my* brother," said Isabella.

"He's as good as—"

By then, the three of them were on the front porch. Isabella backed into the house and spoke to them through the screen door. "I'm afraid of him. We *all* are. He's *mean*. He's getting to be like he used to be back in the day. And it's that damn motorcycle. Ever since he bought that stupid Enfield, it's like the damn thing's taken over his life. He grinds you two into the dirt over the bills and spends all his disposable income taking care of that bike."

"Where are we supposed to go?" Carly had asked.

"I don't care, as long as it's not here."

"Some sister *you* are," Marina spat.

Isabella stared at them for a long time through the screen. "I don't want Santiago in my house in a hysterical state." She sighed and seemed to deflate. "Why don't you go talk to Gil? Gil has a shotgun. Santi will listen to Gil, and if he don't listen to Gil, then by God he will listen to two pipes of Ave fuckin' Maria."

So, they went to Guillermo Delgado's house.

Gil's windows were dark, his doors were locked, and his motorcycle was gone. Probably down at Heroes drinking away his demons. They kept moving, hustling down the sidewalk as the day grew shorter, listening for the demonic belch of La Reina's engine, and ended up sitting on the sidewalk behind the Conoco until her mother began to complain about how her ass hurt.

Gil still wasn't home when they checked again, so they started walking to Lockwood, taking the secondary street parallel to the main drag so Santi wouldn't catch them out on the surface road.

"Where are we going?" asked Carly.

Her former scared-rabbit pace had slowed to a desultory walk. Marina forged forward, her steps stilted and weary like a robot that's forgotten its purpose but is still full of drive. "I don't know," replied her mother. "Maybe the county police." Which would be a better idea than the Keyhole PD, an institution everyone knew was under the thumb of Los Cambiantes. A couple of the gang's members were officers themselves, clean-shaven gestapo on black-and-white motorcycles. "Maybe we'll just keep walking right out of Texas. Put down roots somewhere else."

Unrealistic, Carly knew, but it was a comforting thought.

A familiar blatting rumble resonated in the distance. Marina stopped short in the orange warmth of a sodium lamp, abject terror on her face.

La Reina.

They were caught on a weird stretch of road with nowhere to hide, a straight two-lane funnel flanked on both sides by a wall and a fence. Their north was a tall, nameless aluminum warehouse that ran the length of the block, and their south was a chain-link fence containing a crowd of cars in various states of disrepair.

Carly opted for the fence and cars. A dumpster stood at the edge of the orange light. She scrambled up on top of it and then climbed atop the fence and picked her way over the barbed wire, earning a painful scratch. She tumbled over and landed in a crouch, falling over on her arm.

The sound of the Enfield's engine ripped against the valley of houses, a hollow snore. Sounded like he was maybe three blocks north, cruising low, looking for them. Marina grenade-lobbed her purse over into the car yard and clambered on top of the dumpster like a baby climbing onto a couch, stiff and awkward. One of the plastic hatches made a thumping-cracking noise, threatening to cave under her weight.

"Come on, Mama!" Carly pleaded.

Marina fussed back at her in Spanish, picking her way over the barbed wire like a spider crawling across the strings of a guitar.

"Come on! *He's coming!*"

"I'm trying!"

Just as Carly saw La Reina's one Sauronic headlight appear at the stop sign two blocks down, Marina jumped over the fence. Her jean jacket snagged on the barbed wire and she only made it nine-tenths of the way down, suspended from the tail of her jacket like a baby, her shoulders hiked up to her ears.

"Shit!" hissed Marina, lapsing into more Spanish cursing, her toes scratching at the gravel. "Help me, Carlita!"

A distant star, the headlight-eye paused at the intersection. La Reina cruised across the asphalt at a jogging pace, just fast enough to stay upright. Carly grabbed the waistband of her mother's jeans and pulled at her hard, but she just sprang up and down on the twangling wire.

"You'll have to take off your jacket," she said. Marina wriggled and bucked like a fish on a line.

The headlight approached the four-way at the end of the block. Marina slid out of her jacket and fell onto her knees inside the fence, leaving her jacket hanging from the wires. Dry weeds rustled against their legs as Carly hurried her into the labyrinth of cars, and the flat bluster of Santiago's motorcycle drummed in their chests as he motored past, either not seeing or not recognizing the jacket hanging from the fence. The splash of his headlight washed past them.

Minutes passed as Carly and her mother crouched behind a white Hyundai on flat tires. Some insidious voice in Carly's head kept telling her: *He can see your feet under the car, he can see the top of your head, he can hear you breathing, he's gonna find you he's gonna GET YOU HE'S COMING HE'S COMING.*

La Reina's engine faded into the distance, heading east.

"Maldita sea," Marina said, cursing in Spanish, snagging her jean jacket. "My only good jacket. Stupid, stupid."

"You'll be fine, Mom." Carly hooked her fingers into the fence and looked down the street, almost in disbelief that her father was really gone, untrusting of the sound of his engine shrinking into the night. She half-expected him to double back on a dead engine and no lights, gliding silently down the road like a ghost.

Marina's fussing wound down and she joined her daughter at the fence. "I'm sorry, honey."

"For what?"

"I don't know." She threw her hands up, face twisted in frustration and despair. She was out of breath and sweaty, disheveled by her flight over the fence. "For all of this. For—"

"Not your fault, Mama. You—"

"I married him."

"If you hadn't married him, you wouldn't have *me*." Carly gave her mother a tight hug. As she backed out of the embrace, she glimpsed a finger bruise on her mother's neck. "You aren't the one that bought that motorcycle, either. None of this is your fault. Okay?"

"Do you—" Marina brushed away a tear with the palm of her hand. "Do you really think it is the bike?"

"Sometimes, Dad looks at La Reina like it's talking and he's the only one that hears it. You ever notice him doing that? Like a dog when you make noises at it. He even . . . he even kinda turns his head sideways."

Marina let go of the fence and paced around Carly, gesticulating. "Now you're talking nonsense. Next thing I know you're going to be seeing chupacabra and such. Bigfoot." She wagged a finger. "Stop calling it 'La Reina' like it's a woman, Carlita. It's not a woman; it's a motorcycle." Her admonishment ended on an uncertain, doubtful note. "*Anyway!* What do we do now that we're *in* here?"

The girl examined the cars parked around them at haphazard angles.

"We hide."

They pulled door handles, trying to get into a dozen, two dozen, three dozen cars, but they were all locked. She considered breaking one of their windows with a brick she found under one of their tires, but the noise might attract unwanted attention, and some part of her wanted at least one layer of protection from Santiago besides the fence, if he came back.

Toward the front end of the lot, a Winnebago silhouetted against the late night skyglow of Keyhole Hills. Carly tried the door, but it was locked—all three of them, driver, passenger, living compartment.

"The window is open," Marina said, pointing at the side of the RV.

One of the windows was partially open, about six inches. "Pick me up and I'll climb through it and open the door from the inside," said Carly. "We can spend the night in there and figure out what to do in the morning."

Her mother gaped at her for a second with a shocked look, but also somehow admiring. "All right then, mi pequeña ladrona."

Searching through her mother's purse, Carly found a pair of fingernail clippers. Attached to the swivel was a nail file with a cuticle hook on the end. Marina linked her hands together and her daughter stepped into them. She stood, carrying the girl's foot against her belly, wobbling. Carly pierced the window-screen with the cuticle hook and sawed it open from the top, tearing a slit down one side. Then she cut from right to left across the bottom, making an L-shaped hole.

Tossing the nail clippers aside, Carly clutched the edge of the window and let it take her weight, bracing her feet against the wall. "Okay," she said, trying to do an awkward chin-up. Marina pushed Carly's butt with both hands. Carly lifted herself inside, belly on the windowsill.

Inside, it was stiflingly hot. Carly lay on top of a kitchen sink like a mermaid looking for water, on her belly with her legs scorpioned behind her. She dragged herself in and lowered her feet to the floor.

Streetlights outside threw a fevered light through red curtains, turning the interior into a boudoir. Objects hung on braces nailed to the walls, and at first Carly thought they were huge, ornate crosses—this ingrained by a childhood spent in a Catholic household—until her eyes adjusted to the darkness.

Blades. Swords, daggers, a few axes. Tomahawks.

"What the hell?" she murmured, taking one down, an exotic three-pronged weapon that looked a bit like a pitchfork with a sword handle.

"Carlita?" a voice chirped from outside.

Carly let her mother into the RV, then closed and locked it again. "What is this?" asked Marina, gawking at the weapons hanging on the walls. "Conan the Barbarian's Winnebago?"

"Who is that?"

Marina winced. "Oh, you make me feel *so old.*"

Sweat beaded on her forehead and rolled down Carly's back. "I feel like I've been here before," she said, plopping down in the nook. Even the table's Formica surface was warm. Her mother went into the front, where the lights of the commercial district were a dazzling play of blue and silver, and squatted behind the console.

"Damn, no keys."

"Wasn't planning on stealing it, Mama. Just spending the night here. Then we can figure things out in the morning."

Carly went into the back and opened the window over the bed. A cool night breeze immediately slid in, drying her sweat. She lay down on the bed—made with a precision neatness—and closed her exhausted eyes. The duvet smelled like a man: brisk, dark, sharp. She briefly wondered what the man's name was and what he was like, and then she was asleep.

"Carlita."

Another furtive whisper. Someone shook her. "Carlita."

She turned over and looked blearily at her mother. Marina sat cross-legged on the cramped bed next to her. She was a silhouette, a black head and shoulders against yellow stripes where a streetlight cast itself through the blinds.

"Yeah?"

Marina didn't speak for what felt like a full minute. Carly could feel her mother's eyes searching her face. When she finally spoke: "You saw what I saw?"

Now Carly's turn to look for words. "Dad?"

As if her mother had to pry her words out of the mud of her thoughts, Marina spoke softly, almost whispering. "Yeah. Did I see . . ."

A chill skittered down Carly's spine. "I didn't want to say anything, in case I was seeing—" She wanted to say *in case I was seeing things,* but only crazy people "see things," don't they? She mumbled something about a trick of the light and Santi having Mace-foam on his arms. *His arm-hair had turned white and gotten longer, like the fur on the Abominable Snowman or something.*

"That scream there, just before we left," said Marina. "That did not sound

(human?)

like my husband."

And maybe it wasn't just her imagination that led her to believe that Santi's eyes had turned yellow, dark golden irises. Carly's hands found each other and she lay in the darkness of the Winnebago, picking her fingernails and staring in baffled fear at her mother.

Rain began to rattle on the roof.

Track 9

"Wake up!" sang Kenway, shoving the mattress and bouncing her up and down. "Wake up!"

"Who gave you meth?" Robin's eyes were grainy and achy. Sunlight seeping in around the curtains shot hot bolts of lead into them. Felt like she'd been asleep for about fifteen minutes.

He shook the bed some more and raked open the curtains, flooding the suite with morning sun. "Nobody. Just got a good night's sleep in a real bed after an evening in a hot tub. Better than any meth. Now get your cute butt out of bed and let's go get Willy and find some breakfast."

She slid her head under her pillow and growled again.

"Coffeeeee," he said in a low, haunted whisper.

Reluctantly, she slithered out of the sheets and into a pair of jeans.

• • •

The rims had just arrived when the three of them got to the garage about nine. "It'll probably be lunchtime you can come pick 'er up," said Jake, and that was fine, but when Robin stepped into the RV to deposit yesterday's clothes in the hamper, she saw that someone had cut the screen open in the window over the sink.

"What is *this* shit?" she demanded, storming out the door.

"What shit?"

"*That* shit!" She pointed at the window, where a flap of gray mesh flagged in the breeze. "Who cut my window up?"

The mechanic checked his clipboard as if he was going to find the answer there. *7pm, another oil change. 8pm, turtle wax. 9pm, slash a window open.* "Ah, I have no idea, ma'am. Wasn't like that when you brought it in?"

"Hell no!" Robin turned to Kenway. "Baby, will you go in there and look to see if anything's been stolen?"

"Yeah, sure."

She threw her hands out in an astonished shrug like *What the hell?* and looked up at the sky as if perhaps she'd see meaning written in the clouds. That's when she noticed a security camera mounted to a power pole in the corner of the lot.

"That camera!" she said, pointing.

Jake squinted up at it.

"Ain't hooked up to nothing," he said. "Been there for what, ten years now? *Used* to work, until somebody throwed a rock up there and busted the lens out of it." He drummed his pen on the clipboard. "Damn kids, you know? Ain't had nobody come down and fix it, never really had the money to bother. Nobody ever breaks in anyway. Just a bunch of junk cars on flat tires. About the only thing you'd wanna steal are my tools, and I lock them up in a tool cabinet in a locked closet. If you—"

Glancing over Jake's shoulder, Robin caught her reflection in the mirror over the garage sink, and at first, she thought she saw a pair of ivory horns curving up out of her own skull,

(we wanted to see how human you are)

but she shifted her weight and realized she was standing in front of an antique aluminum Coors bar poster. A bas-relief of a silver bull loomed over a snowy mountain range, horns wide and pointy. "Whatever!" she snapped, angry that she'd startled herself over something so stupid. "I'll find a place in Houston or somewhere that does screens."

Kenway emerged from the Winnebago. "Everything's where it should be, as far as I can tell." He halfheartedly waved a hand in front of his face, as if waving away a pesky fly. "You gonna file a police report?"

He smells it, thought Robin. *The brimstone.*

"No point, really," she told him. "Even if they show up, and even if they give a damn, they won't find any clues, and there's nothing stolen. So, they won't do anything." She stormed out of the lot, the men in tow. "Let's just go get something to eat and something cold to drink before I kill somebody with my bare hands."

They found a Waffle House six hot blocks away and drowned some eggs and bacon with a load of coffee.

"Why do you two call your RV 'Willy,' anyway?" asked Gendreau. He looked trim and slim in an impeccable white blouse with the sleeves neatly fold-rolled.

"Braveheart," she said.

"That Mel Gibson movie?"

"It's a 1974 Winnebago Brave. We caught *Braveheart* on late-night cable up in Oregon and started calling it the Brave William Wallace. It stuck. Sort of evolved into Willy, I guess."

Across the street they found a mom-and-pop coffee shop with Wi-Fi, where they all got iced frappuccinos to gird them against the day's rising temperature and Robin spent the rest of the morning editing videos for YouTube. Thousands of comments on Malus Domestica videos to read as her footage struggled to force itself through the coffee shop's modem, and she only made it through about three hundred of them before her eyes tried to cross.

Around lunchtime, they wandered into the shopping center next door and discovered a pawn shop. No witch-relics, thank God.

A small tube television sat on a shelf, unplugged. Sadness and loneliness emanated from the speaker-holes like the frost vapors curling out of a chest freezer. Robin touched it, and for a brief moment the screen blinked on an image of Fred Astaire dancing with Grace Kelly. She sensed a floral pattern, stark fluorescent light, the squeak of shoes on tile, the smell of industrial antiseptics.

Ever since the events of last October, she had developed a sort of sixth sense about old things. Psychic sense of smell, maybe. Probably a by-product of developing a sensitivity to teratoma relics. Or maybe it was bullshit. She hadn't told anyone about it. Possibly just her overactive imagination. Probably.

Antiques are haunted by memories, echoes of usage; they give off an aura, like the sun's heat resting in the frame of a car. Most people can feel this, to some degree. When you look at an old violin on a pawn shop shelf, you can see its carewornness, imagine the passion of the person that originally owned it: practicing music every night, driving her parents crazy. You see an old VCR and wonder who owned it, and picture a band of teenage friends spending a sultry summer night watching *Friday the 13th* on cassette tape. Robin, though, she could lay a hand on an antique or pawn shop trinket and tell you things about it that no one should know. Never specific names, only fleeting, faint sentiments—a wedding band might whisper *I hope it's a girl,* or a knife might conjure up auditory hallucinations of the *rip* and *squelch* of its previous owner field-dressing a deer.

A blue-and-cream six-string guitar hung from pegs on the wall behind the sales counter.

"Mind if I hold this?"

The clerk smiled. "Sure."

As she held it, an image flashed in her mind: feminine hands with black fingernails, sliding up and down the neck, tickling a Motley Crüe arpeggio.

A girl's guitar. She bought it.

• • •

As soon as the mechanic smelled the whiff of sulphur still clinging to her clothes, he had trouble making eye contact with her. "Extra rim's in the compartment with the spare."

"Figure out what happened to my window?"

He shook his head. "'Fraid not. But I glued it back together for ya. Had a hot glue gun layin' around. Should be dry by now. Just a little temporary thing until you can get to Houston, I guess. It'll keep the bugs out."

"Thanks."

They hashed out the invoice. Everything was aboveboard. She paid with cash she'd pulled out at an ATM outside the pawn shop. "You did good, gipper," she told him. "Other than the random vandalism, if I ever have car trouble out this way again, I'll have to come back here." She raised a fist and he hesitantly fistbumped it.

Back inside the RV, the air was a mouthful of hot cotton. Kenway climbed into the driver's seat and cranked it up, turning up the AC and flooding the compartment with cool air. As he pulled out of the parking lot, Robin deposited her new guitar in the bedroom and went around, closing all the windows.

"On the road again," Gendreau sang in his best Willie Nelson impression. He parked his narrow butt in the breakfast nook. "So, where we headed, Miss Martine?"

"I was hoping you could answer that, Mr. Auditor."

Ever since Robin had started doing witch-killing gigs for him, Gendreau had her looking for teratomatic relics on the side. Only one that year, an antique bell jar clock with a toe bone inside.

Before the Dogs of Odysseus used teratomas to create new relics, the only people who made them were magicians contemporary to Aleister Crowley—Black and Red magic practitioners, namely. When Gendreau's grandfather Francis took over in the sixties, those old-school magicians destroyed or stole many of the relics before White magicians could get their hands on them.

When a magician with an old relic died alone, it would usually be passed down to their descendants and next of kin, who were none the wiser about the relic's abilities. Gendreau was alerted to the clock through a newspaper article about a "haunted heirloom." The family that inherited the clock claimed it was haunted by the ghost of the wife's grandfather, because the day they brought it into their house and put it on the mantel, strange occurrences began to happen: papers would blow off the living room coffee table, doors would slam shut. One evening during an argument, the family dog was thrown out of a window by an invisible force and a hellacious wind had blown around the room for several minutes.

Robin knew what was up the instant she laid hands on the clock: a witch teratoma, imbued with the Gift of Mind. The family accidentally channeled the psychokinetic power in the relic through their emotions. A man-made poltergeist.

According to Gendreau, relics were usually to blame for strange paranormal phenomena such as, for example:

poltergeists
Spontaneous Human Combustion
time-slips
objects falling from the sky such as fish, buttons, coins, or stones
out-of-body experiences
accidental dimensional jumps.

Those unaccustomed to relics often aren't aware of what's happening. If they even notice the insidious effects of a relic, they blame it on ghosts, or bad dreams, or carbon monoxide. Ignorance is bliss, as they say, and the ignorant will do the most intricate mental gymnastics to explain away the strangest phenomena. Anything to maintain that bliss, that thin membrane between their everyday world and the unknowable.

Sometimes, a mental break will force them to acknowledge what's happening to them, and their experiences will converge. They'll have a car accident. Go into a coma. Wake up in the hospital with clairvoyance. They'll get beat up, or mugged, or raped, or bullied at school, lose a loved one, and suddenly develop telekinesis or pyrokinesis—not even realizing in all these cases the paranormal energy was there all along, suppressed by their need to maintain that all-important bliss, waiting in the wings, feeding them little tidbits of evidence: blips of insight, mysterious fires, poltergeist activity, rats or snakes that follow you wherever you go.

Complacency, and the hunger for normalcy and safety, can camouflage a lot of strange shit.

Self-aware relic owners—those were the dangerous ones. They had internalized their experiences, processed the phenomena; they understood what they had, and they would fight you tooth and nail to keep it. Luckily, she hadn't encountered any of those yet.

Gendreau took out his phone. "I'll see if I have any emails."

"I'll be in there," said Robin, pointing at the bathroom. She toddled in place as the floor tilted with the sway of the RV. "Need a minute to myself." She stepped inside and opened the tiny window, letting in a gust of road breeze.

Rummaging through a tub under the sink, she found a bottle of nail polish. Midnight Black. She put a foot against the opposite wall to steady herself and leaned back. Dabbed a bit of the black paint on her left index nail and held it up. *That'll work.* She got this way sometimes, wanting to do things like paint her nails like the girl that had once owned the guitar. Just like she siphoned off the teratomas' power, she "got a little bit of the memories on her" from hand-me-downs, like soot from handling charcoal.

Wonder if I could somehow find the girl and give her the guitar back. Wouldn't that be fine?

Smelled a little like charcoal in there, actually.

Sweat, too. Gym sweat. Feet and ass. Robin flicked the switch for the bathroom air cycler. A fan rattled to life. *"Look out, fucker!"* shouted Kenway from the front of the Brave, stomping the brakes.

The tires barked with a seal-like tremolo, and the whole Winnebago lurched forward, pressing Robin against the wall behind the toilet. A heavy figure behind the shower curtain leaned toward her, threatening to fall in her lap, and Robin gasped, her eyes widening, adrenaline rocketing into her system. *Oh god it's a dead body there's a killer on the loose and he left a dead body in my shower!* And then a hand thrust out to brace against the wall over her head. A feminine squeal of surprise came from the cramped shower. The Winnebago swooped hard starboard, a shudder rolling through the floor as Kenway slewed into a parking lot.

Her heart fighting to get out of her chest, Robin snatched the curtain aside and found two women standing in the shower, squeezed together.

Awkward silence. Robin stared at them, holding the curtain aside with paint-wet fingernails. The taller one was a scrawny, dewy Disney-channel teenager. The other was an older lady, mid-forties maybe. Both rolling with sheets of sweat, and Mom's makeup was coming off in maudlin streaks.

The teenager grinned apologetically.

"Who the fuck are *you*?" Robin stood up in indignation and shoved the older woman back into the shower. The girl bumped her head on the shower's plastic wall and a bar of soap clattered to the floor. "The hell you doing in my bathroom?"

"Hiding?" asked the teenager.

"What's going on in there?" asked the magician.

"You the ones that cut my window open?" Robin demanded. She felt a warm shape at her back and saw Gendreau in the mirror, standing behind her.

"Yeah." The teenager gazed at Robin with the squinty, suspicious eyes of someone that's trying to remember your face. "I'm—I'm sorry. I cut it open with a nail file so we could hide in here. Th-The doors were locked."

"*No shit, Shirley!* I wonder why they were locked. Did I wander into fucking Canada, where nobody locks their cars up and the milkman gives you a kiss hello in the morning?"

The teenager fought a smile in spite of herself.

"Do you think this is funny?" Robin was talking as much with her hands as her mouth, almost yelling. "Breaking into people's cars? Hell, *homes*? You realize I *live* in here, yeah?"

"We were hiding from my husband," said the older woman, in a thick accent. Mom sat up straighter, prouder, looking Robin in the eye. Her neck was ringed with a collar of faint purple bruises, soft tiger-stripes that lined the edge of her jawbone.

Knocked off-balance by the woman's face, Robin relented. She had seen that mama-bear look before.

"Your husband?" asked Gendreau, concerned.

"Santiago." Mama Bear cupped one hand at her throat as if she were choking; a few more words almost made their way out of her, but not quite—as if she wanted to explain but the words were too big to push out.

"Y'all scared the living shit out of me." Robin's eyes ricocheted back and forth between their faces. She finally stepped back out of the room with a sigh, defeated. "Come on out and get some air; you're both sweating like priests at a playground. What are your names, at least?"

"I'm Carly." The stowaways sat elbow-to-elbow in the kitchen nook. The teenager's eyes flitted starrily between Robin's amethyst mohawk and Gendreau's Willy Wonka–David Bowie look. The girl's clothes were relatively upscale, a green baby doll blouse and jeans, but they were old, threadbare, almost too small. Someone bought her nice school clothes last year and she was outgrowing them.

"I know you from somewhere," she said. "You look so familiar."

"I get that a lot." Robin plopped down across the table.

"This is my moth—"

Mama Bear interrupted. "Marina. Marina Valenzuela."

Robin blinked. She picked up her messenger bag and dug through it, taking out the GoPro camera and turning it on, and she pressed the camera into a little wall mount so that it aimed down the length of the table.

"*That's* where I know you from!" Carly stiffened. "That YouTube channel about hunting witches!"

"*Witches?*" asked Marina.

"Something's been nagging me about this RV all morning, like I've been here before, and now I know what it is. This is Robin Martina—"

"Martine," Robin corrected.

"—and she makes a TV show about hunting witches across the US."

"It's not a TV show; it's on YouTube."

By that time, Kenway had wallowed out of the driver's seat, climbing into the living compartment. Carly twisted in her seat, miming with her hands, aiming a camera with one hand, the other stabbing with a dagger. "It's called Malice Something-or-other. I don't subscribe to it, but I've seen it before."

"Look," said Robin, waving her hands, "I hate to get mixed up in this kind of shit these days. I been playing Nancy Drew the last couple of years, sticking my nose into screwed-up families when I happen to run into them like this, but I don't know if I can keep doing it. I've done things I'm not proud of. There's a child molester in a cemetery down in Clearwater that's there because of me."

Both Kenway and Gendreau met her eyes. Only Kenway's held any real surprise. "Wait, you *killed* a guy? Like, not a witch or a monster? Just a normal, everyday dude?"

"It was him or me!" Robin almost shouted. "He came home from work early before I could get out of his house, and he caught me hiding in a closet. Luckily, it was the closet where he kept his golf gear. We had a fencing session with nine irons and he broke two of my ribs. And a picture that was hanging on the wall. And a vase of flowers that was sitting on the kitchen table. I broke the TV and smashed the front out of a china cabinet. He almost broke my arm." She folded her arms defensively and stared out the window at some distant point. "Hit the guy in the head a little harder than I meant to. And . . . probably too many times. I guess I shoulda stopped after the third one."

"Jesus."

"His wife helped me get rid of it. *Him.*" Robin heaved a deep, soul-searching sigh. "She went to the police before I ever showed up, but they didn't have enough evidence to do anything, and when her husband found out what she did, he beat the shit out of her."

Suddenly, everything came out in a rapid, nervous over-explanation. Lot of bad blood on her hands. The rapists, child molesters, wifebeaters she'd intimidated and . . . just say it, *say it out loud,* okay, the assholes she'd *killed*. "They were pieces of shit, begging for an ass-kicking." Felt like an asshole, hated admitting the things she'd done in the past, hated having done it, hated defending it. "But when Kenway came along, I stopped letting people pressure me into this vigilante stuff." Before that, really—several months before going home to Blackfield to confront Marilyn Cutty's coven. She stared at the unimpressed Gendreau. "You *knew*, didn't you?"

The magician shrugged vaguely. "We do our homework, Miss Martine. You've left a trail of newspaper stories as long as my arm. We've been watching your progress since Neva Chandler. That's when we knew Heinrich had taken you under his wing. We've been putting two and two together for quite a while."

"Jesus," Kenway said again, softly, staring at nothing in particular. He sounded lost, absorbed. The big man trundled away back to the front of the RV and dropped into the driver's seat, and the Foghat pouring out of the stereo climbed a couple notches.

What's his problem, anyway? thought Robin. *He was a soldier.*

Like he's got room to talk. She glowered at the back of his head, then at Carly Valenzuela. Kenway. Carly. Kenway. Carly.

"He doesn't know?" asked Gendreau.

"He does now. Thanks, bud!"

The magician winced.

Throwing herself into the passenger seat next to her boyfriend, Robin leaned in and murmured, "What's your beef, Han Solo?"

He looked at her from the corner of his eye. "I don't know." Those baby blues wandered slowly all over the dash, the wheel, the radio. "Guess it just made me see you differently. Only ever seen you kill witches. I didn't know you—"

"He was a child molester."

"Do you know that for sure?"

"Yeah." Robin nodded sternly. "I had evidence."

"Still, that doesn't give you the right to play judge, jury, and executioner. Look, if Afghanistan taught me anything, it's that not everybody deserves to die."

"No, but sometimes they ask for it, don't they?"

Kenway stared at her face.

"They stomp right up to you and demand it," she said. "Them or you."

"I guess. But there's a difference between some insurgent jumping your shit with an AK-47, and Joe Bob from Accounting who's just being an asshole. That's war. This is just Tuesday."

"If anything, the child molester deserved it more than some goat farmer that's just shooting at you so the Taliban doesn't kill his family."

He sighed. "You ain't gonna kill this guy, too, are you? This woman's husband. He's full human, ain't he?" His hands curled over the steering wheel and he kneaded it tightly. "I hate a wife-beater as much as the next guy, and I'll bust him in the goddamn mouth for hittin' a woman, but I ain't Dexter fuckin' Morgan. I'll do the Buffy thing and fight monsters all day long, but if that's your jam, count me out."

"I'm not going to do it that way," she said decisively. "No more humans. Monsters only. I made that decision a long time ago." She leaned in to kiss him on the forehead, but he leaned away. A beat passed as she stared at the side of his head. He glanced at her, distrust on his face. *Seems like the more he learns about me, the less he likes me,* she thought, her heart slowly sinking like quicksand.

To her surprise, Annie Martine stood in the hallway, only visible by the veneer of light on her spectral skin as if she'd been stenciled onto reality. As usual, neither Gendreau nor the two women noticed the ghost.

"They need your help, baby," her dead mother said with her hollow telephone voice. "You can't leave them here to face this man all alone, ethics be damned."

Dammit. Robin sighed.

"All right," she said, addressing the Valenzuelas, "you're coming with us up north."

Carly sat up. "What?"

"I'm assuming there's a battered-women shelter in Michigan near your granddad's secret volcano lair, isn't there, G?"

"Yeah, sure." The magician leaned against the counter, examining his impeccable nails. "I know of a couple. Heard about them volunteering at the soup kitchens. And Francis does not live in a volcano, thank you. There are no volcanoes in Michigan. Not anymore, anyway."

"You? Volunteering at a soup kitchen?"

"Yeah? What's wrong with that? Don't think I'm the kind of person that does things like that?"

Everybody gave him a dry stare, even the Valenzuelas.

"Okay, yeah, I don't exactly stand behind the line and ladle it out, but I donate on a regular basis and do a little driving . . . and I've been known to show off a little in the kitchen from time to time. You don't grow up in Frank Gendreau's house without learning a thing or two about Creole cooking." His smile faded. "How come we're taking them to Michigan? Why not Houston?"

"Houston isn't far enough." Robin studied Marina's and Carly's faces. "How you feel about that? I'm sure there's good schools there you can finish out high school in. You're a pretty kid; it should be easy to make new friends."

Something nonverbal passed between the Valenzuelas in a glance.

"I don't know," said Marina. "We have a life here, you know? How can we just leave it behind?"

"*This* life?" As she said it, Robin rubbed her neck. "I'll take care of you two," she said, with perhaps a little more exasperation than she meant. "I . . . I promise. Just try not to cut open any more of my windows, okay?"

This harried woman must not have heard anything like that in a very long time, because Marina's eyes instantly filled up with tears of relief.

Track 10

After he'd wallowed on the front lawn for a while, Santiago gave up on the water and went into the house to look for milk. Someone—Carly?—had said something about milk, and he vaguely remembered hearing about a Klan shindig where one of the boys' father-in-law got pepper-sprayed by a cop. According to what they said, the proteins in milk break down the oils in the spray. *Oleoresin capsicum* was the word he'd used. He wasn't a big fan of having something with the word "cum" in it on his face.

He didn't find any milk, but a cup of expired yogurt lurked in the crisper. He dipped it out with his hands and smeared it all over his face, and the cold Yoplait felt so good, he almost pissed his pants.

After he washed off the yogurt and had a quick beer, Santiago got on La Reina and canvassed the entire neighborhood, and then cruised down the highway going out of town at a stately pace, watching for his wife and daughter walking along the roadside. Traffic backed up behind him, honking irritably. He threw them the finger until it turned into a chore and he ignored them. "Go the fuck around!" he bellowed into the night wind.

After riding all over town and not finding a damn thing, he came home and crashed on the couch.

When he woke up early the next morning feeling like Rip Van Winkle, he called his brother, Alvaro, and told him to get the guys together and come out to the house. "Marina and Carly ran off," he said, his voice low and hoarse from screaming. "Running around the neighborhood somewhere. Hiding, probably. All I know is, I can't find 'em. Kid Maced me in the middle of an argument between me and her mother, and I guess I kinda overreacted. They took off on foot because I had the keys to the Blazer."

Alvaro paused for a second. "Yeah, okay," he said, his own voice muted by the long grip of sleep. "Let me get a shit and a shower and I'll be down there as soon as I can."

The morning wind felt good on his still-throbbing face as Santiago sat on the front porch.

What happened to me yesterday?

He was lucid and clear-headed, but his eye sockets radiated dumb, thick heat as if he'd spent all night fighting a fever. He put down his beer and looked at his hands, expecting to see that bizarre white shag draping from the outer edge of his wrist like Liberace's shirtsleeves.

Are my fingernails longer? Is that my imagination?

He bit them, cutting them off one by one with his teeth and spitting the ragged little crescent moons onto the barren front lawn.

El Tigre, said Grandmother.

Abuelita had been dead for going on twenty years or more. Dropped dead in San Jose when he was in middle school. Never did an autopsy that he knew of, but he remembered his mother saying she'd had a blood clot in her brain.

El Tigre.

She used to tell him stories about the tiger that lived in a cave in the desert and ate bad little boys. "If you don't behave and eat your vegetables and go to church, little Santi," she'd say in her sweet, articulate Spanish, "El Tigre gonna catch you asleep in the middle of the night and eat you up." Her pursed, weathered lips were like a leather wallet, full of false teeth instead of money. She would punctuate the warnings by raking a handful of fingers at him and uttering a fey "Rowr."

This boogeyman was born out of their nightly ritual, a bedtime story that consisted of selections from a Spanish-language edition of Rudyard Kipling's *The Jungle Book* printed in the '70s, a double-sided book, twice as thick as it ought to have been; if you flipped it over you could read *Rikki-Tikki-Tavi.* But he didn't care about an Indian mongoose; he was all about Mowgli's adventures in the jungle with Baloo the bear and Bagheera the panther. Abuelita didn't want to use their names, though, because she thought giving them Spanish names made them more relatable, so she just called them Oso Papá and Gato Negro. Bear Daddy and Black Cat. Shere Khan the tiger was the antagonist of that story, the skulking-prowling villain that wanted to eat Mowgli the wolf-boy. Abuelita didn't want to use his name, either, so she just called him the Tiger.

What made him think of that? It'd been so long.

He went into the trailer, where he stood in the kitchen, his eyes traveling slowly around the cabinets and cupboards.

Two boxes, one brown and one blue: Carly's Cocoa Pebbles and Marina's Frosted Flakes. He took down the Frosted Flakes and poured a bowl of it, dropped a clean spoon in it, remembered too late there was no milk in the house. "You got to be kidding me," he said to himself in the quiet trailer.

He looked at the beer in his hand.

Santi poured it out into the cereal, then sat and ate it, disconsolate but calm. Tasted like sweet foul horror, like a diabetic's piss. Tony the cartoon Tiger gawped at him from the front of the box with his cheery, confident, idiot grin. He ate beer and cereal until the rip-roar of motorcycles rumbled into the driveway.

• • •

Three motorcycles, four riders: Tuco, Maximo, and Santiago's brother and sister, Alvaro and Elisa. Elisa rode bitch with her brother, wearing her Walmart shirt; she must have just come from work. The rest of them were wearing colors: leather Los Cambiantes vests like his own, with the big wolf head on the back.

"Morning, Santi," said his brother. Alvaro was a shorter, slimmer, slightly more handsome version of Santiago. With their long hair and lean figures, they both looked like failures from an Antonio Banderas cloning project, though Santi drew the short end of the genetic stick there.

"Mornin', Alfie."

Kid sister Elisa had that suspicious look in her eye—*What did you do this time?*—but she didn't say anything.

The second one off his bike was Maximo, the biggest goddamn half-Mexican any of them ever saw: six feet of pure muscle, his face masked by a Captain Haddock beard. Max ran a gym in Keyhole Hills, a country club for meatheads in a former five-and-dime, with a ragged-out boxing ring and just enough weights for a handful of people.

Last of them to walk over was secretary Tuco, a spindly little hipster Cuban with a rat face and tortoiseshell sunglasses that made him look like he just stepped out of a remake of *The Breakfast Club.* Looked like a useless dweeb, but Santi knew Tuco used to work for the cartel as the kind of guy that knew his way around a car battery and a pair of nipple clamps.

"Lost my temper." Santi glanced over his shoulder at the broken window. "Carlita Maced me and I kinda . . . kinda lost my shit. Scared both of 'em right outta the house." He chuckled stiffly. "Hurt like hell. Can said *bear spray* on it. Stuff could take the paint off a Cadillac."

"Where the hell did she get *bear spray*?"

"Probably the internet," said Tuco. "You can get that shit on Amazon, man. You can get just about anything online, if you know where to look."

"Don't matter where she got it." Santiago headed for La Reina and threw a leg over her saddle. "What matters is where they went. You guys help me look for 'em."

"Know what direction she went in?" asked Tuco.

"No. I was too busy giving myself a hooker bath in the front yard."

Alvaro rubbed his face. "They could be anywhere, man. Got a night's head start."

"Can't have gone far," said Santi. "They don't have a *whole* lot of runnin' money. Ain't gonna be buying a plane ticket anytime soon. They're still in town, unless they hitchhiked out, and I don't see that happening. People don't pick up hitchhikers anymore."

"Carly by herself, maybe," Tuco said, hitching his glasses up on his nose with a knuckle.

"That's my little girl, Tuc."

Maximo grunted. "Goddamn pervert."

Tuco shrugged. "Hey, I'm just sayin', yo."

"Yeah, you just sayin'. Hell outta here with that."

"Where are *you* assholes going?" asked Isabella Talamantes, scuffing down the sidewalk in flip-flops, a big fast-food cup sloshing with crushed ice in one hand. She shuffled into Santi's yard and gave Elisa a kiss. "Goin' out to look for Marina and Carly?"

"Yeah," said Maximo. "How'd you know?"

"She came by the house yesterday while Elisa was asleep, looking for a place to spend the night."

Elisa blinked. "You didn't let her in?"

"If she hadn't pissed off Santi, I might have." Isabella looked Santi up and down. "I didn't want *this* bull in my china shop throwin' a bitch fit, tearin' shit up," she said, and sipped at her melted ice.

"That's my sister-in-law, Bella," said Elisa. "You can't just turn her away."

Isabella subtly recoiled from the growing anger on Santiago's face. "Baby, I love all three of you girls," she said, "but, I—uhhh, I just didn't—"

"You didn't what?" said Santi, putting his kickstand back down.

"I didn't want to get involved." Isabella made a half step behind Alvaro, subconsciously shielding herself. "I've had all the drama I can handle, you know?"

Santiago casually walked toward her. Isabella held her cup behind her leg and Alvaro stepped aside out of morbid curiosity, maybe, or perhaps just because he didn't expect what was coming. "Why didn't you let my wife stick around?" He didn't talk with his hands like he usually does, but they were tensing, tightening. *"Why didn't you stop them?"*

"I just—"

Santi punched her once in the face, a meaty, soundless jab that popped her head backward. Isabella's feet slipped out from under her and she fell on her ass.

"Whoa!" hooted Alvaro. "Hey."

Elisa flew to Isabella's side, clutching her girlfriend's face. "Ohhh *my God*!"

All three of the other men stepped in to separate them, but Santiago didn't keep coming. He hovered on the other side of his fellow bikers, Maximo's beefy hand holding one shoulder. Tuco paced back and forth in an invisible cordon like a hockey goalie from a video game.

"*You* let her go, Isabella," Santi fumed, "now they're out there, God knows *where,* probably dead in a gutter for all I know."

Blood streamed down Isabella's lips from her busted nose. Elisa took a napkin out of her purse and dabbed it against her girlfriend's face, tilting Isabella's head back. "Si no la golpeó, ella todavía estaría aquí, pedazo de mierda," she growled, muffled by the fabric. *If you didn't beat her up, she'd still be here, you piece of shit.*

Santiago twitched, but Maximo squeezed him. Santi gave him a death-look, then turned and stalked over to his motorcycle, heeling up the stand again and heaving himself onto the kickstart. It didn't start with the first kick.

Before he could try it again, Max came over. "Hey."

Santiago met his eyes.

"Listen, I'm going to help you find your wife and little girl, Santi," said the barrel-chested biker. "But you got to ease up, man. You gotta *chill*. How you gon—"

"Yeah," Santi said curtly, interrupting him. He flicked his eyes down at La Reina's gas tank, then back up at Maximo. Max said nothing, but the look on his face carried a grim concern. "Look, what happens in my house is my business, yeah?"

"A man's home is his castle, I guess."

"I'll work on it. Arright? I got a temper. I know." The motorcycle underneath him seemed to thrum even though the engine wasn't running, a subtle throb, an aftershock of an aftershock. Santiago felt better astride La Reina, centered, like it was home base in a game of tag. A rolling sanctuary. Safe, more in control. "Maybe if I quit drinking or something." *Or maybe if that bitch quits sneaking around behind my back.* That creeping insidious fingertip dragged down the inside of his skull. Santi chuckled. "Maybe start doin' yoga."

Max paused. "You feelin' all right? You look like you passed out in a hill of pissants."

"I got bear-Maced, you meatball. That stuff is supposed to drive away a six-hundred-pound bear. And I ain't talkin' about Yogi Bear, 'ey Booboo." Jumping on the kickstarter again, Santi got the bike cranked and La Reina snarled to life. "Don't worry about me," Santi smiled, shouting over the engine. "I feel *grrrrrrrreat*."

• • •

Elisa glared at Santiago's back until he rounded the corner and disappeared.

Isabella looked at the wad of blood soaking into the Walmart vest. "Sorry I messed up your thing."

"Sorry my brother is such an asshole. He wasn't always like this."

"I doe, you say it every dibe he gets pissy. Like that barbeque last Fourth of July when he spanked by little boy? I could have lost custody for that. He told be I should beat the gay out of hib for playing with baby dolls." Isabella took the vest away. Her nostrils were plugged with blood. "Be! Can you *beliebe* that shit?"

Elisa didn't know what to say.

"It's that fugging bike," said Isabella.

"The bike?"

"That green piece of shit he drives. He's been getting bore assholish ever since he cabe hobe frob the auction with that thing."

"What? What are you talking about?"

Isabella dropped her cup of ice when Santiago popped her in the face, and it now melted in a puddle on his patchy lawn. She halfheartedly kicked it into a healthier patch of grass. Maybe it would help the lawn grow. "Sobething about it. You haven't ever seen hib cock his head like a dog and sneak a peek at the boatercycle sometimes?"

"Can't say that I have."

"I *ain't* crazy," said Isabella, beginning the long plod back to their apartment a few blocks away. She spat a glob of blood into the weeds next to the Valenzuelas' leaning mailbox. Falling into step behind her, Elisa clutched her hands behind her back, stooped like a miser on the verge of financial ruin. As she walked, she dreamt up cruel and elaborate punishments for her brother. Punch him back. Eye for an eye.

Track 11

A half hour west of Keyhole Hills, Kenway decided he was thirsty and the Valenzuelas needed to eat, so they pulled into a tavern at the city limits of Almudena: a tall neon sign outside depicted a spread-winged eagle and the word HEROES. A series of overcompensating pickup trucks lined the sidewalk, alongside a Harley Davidson in mint condition and a Jeep Liberty plastered in bumper stickers that said *Long days and pleasant nights* and *Strangers by birth, ka-tet by choice.*

Inserts standing on each table boasted a military discount, along with something called "Mangorita Chicken." Place was dark but clean, with a karaoke stage in one corner and a herd of rednecks nursing beers at the bar, all glued to a baseball game on the flatscreen mounted to the ceiling.

"A sports bar for vets?" asked Kenway.

"Pretty much," said the waitress, a tiny, athletic Hispanic woman in a T-shirt and black Lululemons. As soon as Robin saw her, she knew who the Liberty belonged to. Her nametag read MONICA. "We're the unofficial neighborhood VFW."

One of the men at the bar was *not* watching the game. A short Hispanic guy with an undercut and big fishy eyes glared at their table, studying the Valenzuelas as if trying to recognize them. Another man from the other end of the bar slid off his stool and carried his beer over to their table.

"Hey there," said Gil.

Robin almost didn't recognize him without the Hunter S. Thompson glasses. "Hi."

Gil wore an ancient Molly Hatchet T-shirt under a black leather vest with a LOS CAMBIANTES patch over the heart. On the other side: VIETNAM VETERAN. The dim fluorescents made him look leathery and dignified, like the Most Interesting Man in the World from the Dos Equis commercials. When she saw that he was actually drinking Dos Equis, she couldn't help but snort. "Fancy runnin' inta you out here," he said. "Awfully far out from the Hills for lunch, ain't it?" He gestured to an empty seat with his beer bottle. "Mind if join you?"

"Not at all," Robin said.

Marina Valenzuela watched him with anxiety. Carly could have been looking at a rattlesnake; the girl's dewy complexion turned a little gray.

Gil sat down, his old-man pot belly straining at his T-shirt. "Hey, soldier."

"Hey . . . Gil?" Kenway said, brightening.

"Ayup."

"Nice to see you again."

"Likewise. So, they built this place back in '82, when the airbase between here and Keyhole was still running," said Gil, as if he were resuming a conversation. "South Gate comes out half a mile from here. They got a lot of business from the Air Force guys, but then there was some kinda downsizing initiative a few years ago—can't rightly remember the acronym now, BRAC, I think—and they closed the base. Sold the land to developers. Now they're just the unofficial neighborhood VFW." He peered through his eyebrows at Carly and Marina. A wry, chiding look. "Hi there, Marina."

"Hey, Gil." Marina produced a cigarette, and she obviously wanted to smoke it but no smoking in Heroes. Instead, she twiddled it in her fingers like a pen. "You having a good day? Weather's nice."

Gil shrugged. "Can't beat it."

Marina gazed at the cigarette in her hands so intently, it was as if she were trying to light it with her eyes.

Unable to abide the awkwardness, Gendreau said, "I take it you two know each other."

"Used to run around with her husband," said Gil. "Didn't know you folks knew each other. You friends visiting from out of town?"

Before Robin could launch into a lie, Marina said, "No."

Silence hung over them for a moment. Gil sighed and took a drink of his beer. "What are you doin', hon?"

"Getting lunch, Gil," said Marina. "It's lunchtime." She hesitated as Gil's question lingered in front of them, and then she lifted her chin to advertise the bruises on her throat, quietly letting the evidence of Santi's subtle brutality speak for itself.

Perhaps she was afraid that if she spoke, she'd break down. That was the impression Robin got.

A few moments of quiet company passed, and then Gil spoke up again, pointing at Marina and her choked neck with his beer hand. "You know he's going to do worse than that when he catches up to you, yeah?" The old man swirled his Dos Equis and took a sip. "He's been goin' over the Hills with a fine-toothed comb, Marina. His sister said he's got Tuco, Alfie, and Max with him. He's pissed."

"Well, he can *be* pissed," said Marina. "I'm done."

"Broke Isabella's nose for letting you leave."

Marina turned red.

Gil leveled a tired eye at Robin and absently stroked his beard. "Hon, I don't know you from Eve, but . . . can I give you a piece of unsolicited advice?"

"Only kind of advice I'm familiar with."

He blew through his nose in ugly amusement. "Get Monica to put your lunches in doggie bags and hit the road. Leave Marina and Carly here. You don't want to be on the premises when Santi and Max show up."

"Why's that?" asked Robin.

Gendreau's head tilted in confusion. "How does he even know they're here?"

Twisting stiffly in his seat, Gil gestured toward the bar. The creepy guy with the Innsmouth Look and undercut eyed them, his face underlit by the screen of his smartphone. "See that guy right there?" Gil asked. "That's Joaquin Oropeda. One of them Los Cambiantes. Bet you a cool grand he's texting Santiago right now to tell him you're here with his wife and daughter."

Leaning forward confidentially, Kenway asked, "The hell is goin' on?"

"Just givin' you and your girlfriend some friendly guidance."

Robin growled, "I ain't afraid of some bag-of-dicks wife-beater. I don't care if he shows up with the Hell's Angels and the ghost of Adolf Hitler, I've put down worse than *his* ass."

Gil took out a toothpick, unwrapped it contemplatively, and stuck it into his mouth. Then he stared at Robin as if he were reading a menu. "Hon, I doubt that very highly. Can you not see I'm trying to save your life? If Santi shows up and you're still here, he's goin' to drag you all out by the hair of the head, take you into the dark of the desert, and straight-up *kill* your ass, and there ain't a soul here that's gonna do shit-all about it." He scanned the rednecks at the bar. "Everybody *in* this place is scared of Los Cambiantes. And the Cambies ain't scared of Joan Jett, Peg-Leg Pete, and a queer with a three-hundred-dollar haircut."

Gendreau darkened.

"Why are *you* in here, then?" Robin jabbed a finger at the wolf patch on Gil's vest. "You're evidently one *of* 'em."

"I *founded* Los Cambiantes. I'm the old man. Pops. Lame-duck president, you know? Started it when I got home from the war. Santiago was just a baby back then. He was V-Z's boy. V-Z probably knocked up Santi's mama the day he stepped off the bus."

"What does *Los Cambiantes* mean?"

"The Changelings," said Gil. "I started the bike club for myself and the other local vets that came back from the war. Came home to a country that'd moved on without us. We didn't belong here anymore. We wun't Texans anymore—hell, we barely rated as Americans. We just wun't part of this world no more. We was ghosts."

"Yeh," Kenway grunted, his face pinching. He folded his arms in what was ostensibly supposed to be a grim, authoritative posture, but he was hugging himself.

"*You* know what I'm talkin' about, son," said Gil.

"Wolves in a land of dogs," Kenway said, softly, monotonously, as if in a trance.

"So, what'd you do, anyhow? Baghdad?"

"A couple tours in Afghanistan. The first one was a year, but I only got about seven months into the sandbox before I got hurt and had to fly to Germany."

"Hate to hear that."

Kenway shrugged: *It is what it is.*

"Anyway," continued Gil, "I wanted a symbol of our fish-out-of-water state of existence. Something that would stand for our newfound displacement. So, I run across the word 'changeling.' Friend of mine up at the church, Father—" He paused to search his mind. "—Castellanos, he told me about it, he was in the theological seminary or . . . something. A changeling is when a mother believes her baby's been stolen by fairies and replaced."

"Right," said Robin. "It's got a second meaning, too. *Los Cambiantes,* that's also a phrase in Spanish meaning *money-changers,* or *money-lenders,* or something like that, ain't it?"

"Did your homework. We been known to do a little loaning and laundering on the side. I'd be lying if that wun't the second reason why I chose that name. Guess I'm a sucker for names with a lot of meaning. When Father Castellanos told me about it, I was just wild over it. Don't reckon the youngbloods know about the changeling idea—they think it's about the money thing."

Marina exploded into hysterical laughter.

Gil blinked. "The hell *you* laughing at?"

She couldn't answer; she was laughing too hard, *haw-haw-haw*ing at the ceiling, her head tilting back. "It's just—it's just—" Her sunglasses slid down the top of her head and she caught them before they could fall off. "If only those *pendejos* knew they're all a bunch of fairy babies."

Everybody at the table erupted, all of them laughing so loud, the guys at the bar turned to shoot dark looks.

Joaquin Oropeda got off his bar stool and went outside.

"Anyway, I reckon I'm startin' to age out, ch'know?" said Gil. "Half the boys I started the club with are dead—two of 'em ate a gun, one of them took too many pills, one of 'em died of a heart attack. That only left four others, and the youngbloods muscled *them* out eventually. Now it's just Santi and his friends. Technically, Maximo outranks him by seniority; Max is Lonnie Cabral's boy, Lonnie's the one's ticker went out on him, too much steroids, too much chorizo, who the hell knows? Man had bigger tits than his old lady. But Santi's the kind of kid that's so good at bein' an asshole, he makes *you* wanna be a asshole, too."

Gil checked his watch, a brushed-steel piece of Walmart shit. This did not escape Robin's notice.

"I'm still not afraid of him," she said.

"She's *killed* bigger guys than Daddy," blurted Carly, but then she seemed ashamed of what she said and withdrew.

Gil's watery yellow eyes searched Robin's face, and he seemed impressed by what he saw. "Maybe there's a little steel in you, hon. But it ain't gonna save you when Santi gets his claws into you.

'Cause I'm here to tell you, he's got claws. And they are *long and sharp,* amiga. They've *all* got claws. And teeth." He finished his beer. "What did I tell you when you walked past my house?"

"Not to go to the other end of town. There's folks—"

"Folks you don't wanna run inta. Well, that's who I was talkin' about. Santi and his boys. They're . . . *weird.*"

"Weird?" asked Robin. "Weird how?"

As if he'd rather run away than talk about it, Gil took a sharp draw of breath and looked around like a trapped animal. He leaned forward and dropped his hands on the table as if he'd presented her with an invisible shoebox. "Mega weird. Weird with a capital W."

"Like, *cannibal* weird?" asked Kenway.

Gil stared at Kenway and wiped his mouth with his hand. "Around Valentine's Day this year, about . . . one in the mornin'— I'm an old man, y'know, never did sleep good, 'specially after the war. Went for a walk and ended up down at the dump. Part of the river goes by the dump, so there's a lot of trees growin' down there that can't really take root up here in the highlands 'cause it's all dry and shitty." He went to take a drink of beer and remembered the bottle was empty. "Been down there probably a thousand times in the last ten years. Ain't but a fifteen-minute walk from my trailer. Like to go down there when I can't sleep and just sit on one of them sandstone rocks in the moonlight and listen to the river talk. Soothes me. Helps me settle down in a way this moose piss can't. Helps me sleep.

"Well, I went down there that night, and I'll be damned if Santi and six of his boys wun't down there by the water, butt-ass naked in the dark."

Track 12

The entire table fell quiet, as still as a painting of dogs playing poker. "When you said *weird*," noted Gendreau, "that's not quite what I was expecting."

"Didn't say they was porkin' each other in the butthole; I ain't sayin' that at all. Santiago and Tuco and probably half 'em kids are as warped as wax windows, but as far as I know, they don't play hide-the-pickle. Nuh, well, I'll tell you, Santiago had his old Royal Enfield down there, and he was sittin' naked on that thing like he was Lady Godiva. Pecker everywhere, sausage fest if I ever saw one. But that wasn't even the weirdest thing about it." He licked his lips. Not a lascivious gesture but the nervous habit of a man with secrets. "They had on these headdresses." Gil mimed a giant helmet with his hands. "Big-ass headdresses, like animal heads, like some kind of Indian ritual, you know? All of 'em had on wolf heads 'cept for Santiago. He had on a tiger head. Most realistic damn mask I ever saw."

Ice slid down Robin's spine. "Wolves? Tigers? The hell were they doing?"

"Search me. Didn't get to find out either, 'cause one of 'em musta saw me back there in the trees watchin', 'cause all of a sudden, every damn one of 'em turned to look in my direction. I about-faced and hauled ass out of there. Ran the whole two or three miles home. Ain't ran like that since my days with the outfit. My leg was fuckin' screamin' at me, and my heart was doin' barrel rolls, but I ran 'til I thought I would *die*. I could *hear* them kids comin after me, the whole way—laughing, snapping, their bare feet on the road behind me." Gil took a deep breath and let it out with his words. "When I got home, I went straight into my trailer, locked the door, and fished my old Mossberg out of the closet. Sat up and watched old westerns on cable and drank coffee 'til the sun came out."

"Wild story," said Gendreau. "That why you don't have anything else to do with them? Because of . . . whatever they were doing?"

"That, and I don't really know any of 'em. Not no more."

"Do you think it's Santeria, Gil?" asked Marina.

He shrugged. "Santeria? Voodoo? Deal with the devil? Halloween masks? Who knows? What I know is, they're crazy, and they're dangerous." Gil sighed, and took the toothpick out of his mouth. "Glad to see you get out of there, Marina, but . . . shit." He looked around as if he'd just realized where he was sitting, and pushed his chair back, standing. "If you're gonna get out of here, y'all go. *Get.*" He spoke with an exasperated resolve. "I'll do what I can to stall Santi."

Carly spoke up. "Robin's fought witches. *Killed* witches. She can handle those guys. I *know* you have, haven't you? I've watched the videos."

"Witches, yes," said Robin. "Biker gangs, no. There's a certain protocol and expectation that go with fighting the supernatural, but I have no idea what to do about these guys. Bikers that run around naked in headdresses? Sounds more like they need psychiatric help."

"Don't matter if they hang bells from their ears and paint their assholes blue," said Gil. "There's a whole society of them sons-a-bitches, and they're packin' heat."

At that, Gendreau stood up and gulped down his Dr. Pepper like he was in a drinking contest. He put the cup down on the table and belched so loudly and deeply, the men sitting at the bar stared at him. One of them took the Lord's name in vain. "I agree with Mr. Gil," he said, wincing as he fished a fiver out of his wallet and tossed it on the table. "We need to split. We'll worry about getting the Valenzuelas something to eat once we're out of the county, at least."

"Smart man," said Gil.

"Dammit," fussed Robin, and she stood up as well. Kenway and the girls took this as their cue to get up too.

Monica came out of the kitchen as they headed for the door. "Where you-all going?" she asked, confused. "Food's only got a couple more minutes."

Gil jerked a thumb over his shoulder. "That's Santi's old lady. They gon' get her somewhere safe, I suspect."

"Oh," said Monica, peering over at them. "*Ohh.* Does he know?"

"Thanks to Joaquin, he does. Probably on his way here."

"Oh, *shit.*" All of a sudden, she was as enthusiastic as Gil, if not more so, sweeping them out the door with her order notepad. "Yeah, go. Y'all better get out of here while the getting is good."

• • •

When they stepped into the oppressive Texas heat, Robin was pleasantly surprised to not hear the approaching snarl of motorcycle engines. Gil followed them outside, putting on his rosy *Fear and Loathing* sunglasses.

"Ay," someone said in a thick accent, stepping out from behind one of the pickup trucks. "Where you goin'?" Joaquin Oropeda, a smartphone in his hand. "You gonna wait right here." His other hand had a pistol in it, a boxy little black thing—a Glock, maybe?

Intense eyes protruded from his ruddy face. "Santiago gonna be here any minute, puta. You gonna be right here waitin' on him. Uh-*uh*," Joaquin said, pointing the Glock at Gil. He'd been slowly reaching for the 1911 he'd put in his waistband. "Don't even think about it, old man. Give it here." Gil swore. He lifted the 1911 out with a pincer grip and put it on the ground.

While they were all focused on the drama of Gil's surrender, Kenway punched Joaquin in the face.

This had the unexpected consequence of causing the biker to fire the Glock under the veteran's arms. The pistol's report sounded like a hand grenade going off in the dry stillness of the Texas afternoon.

Kenway doubled over. "*Urrgh!*"

"*You shot my boy!*" screamed Robin, heart thudding.

As if in reflex, she kicked off from the pickup's rear tire and launched a Superman punch into the man's eyebrow.

The impact threw Joaquin flat on his back, and the Glock clattered across the ground. He scrambled to his hands and knees, started to run for the gun, but Robin was already on top of him—she locked her legs around his waist and hooked an arm under his chin, tightening it around his throat. Rear naked choke. "Bitch—?" Joaquin grunted, saliva spattering her forearm. He rolled over and slammed her against the parking lot.

Sun-baked pavement stung through her shirt. Sweat rolled down her face. Joaquin coughed. Robin tangled the fist of her choking arm in her shirt to anchor it, freeing her other arm to punch him savagely in the ear. Joaquin shouted, bucking and wriggling.

Ka-chak!

Sound of a pistol's slide being pulled. "Let's be copacetic, hon," said Gil, pointing the 1911 at them.

"Call me 'hon' again and you're gettin' some of this, too," Robin told Gil, her mouth muffled by her shirt sleeve. She let go of Joaquin and shoved him off. Asphalt burned her hands as she scrambled up.

The fish-eyed biker glared at them, reaching up to touch his ear. His fingertips came away bloody. "Busted my eardrum, *puta*."

Robin ignored him, going straight to Kenway's side. He sat next to the truck, his back against the tire, cupping a hand over his stomach. Blood ran down his side, dripping on the hot pavement. The smell of it cooking was like a fuse-box fire doused in barbecue sauce, sweet, salty, metallic, electric. Dizziness came over her—not at the sight of blood itself but to see so much come out of this man.

The magician was there. "Come on, let's go."

• • •

Marina romped the Winnebago as hard as she could, doing seventy up a two-lane highway, right up until they got into Almudena, a tiny pitstop of a town with a handful of red lights. Kenway lay on the bed in the back, turning the duvet red with blood. Red light swirled out of Gendreau's ruby ring and orbited his hands in flitting pulses like electrons around an atom as he worked on the veteran's wound.

Sifting through her bathroom drawers, Carly came up with something wrapped in plastic. "Need a tampon?"

The curandero glanced at it, then up at her. "Not today, thanks."

She mimed sticking it into Kenway's entry wound as if she were dipping a french fry into ketchup. "Mr. Tuco says you can plug a bullet wound with a tampon."

"Oh. I must regretfully decline."

Stop-and-go traffic whipped Robin into a fury of panic. She paced up and down the length of the RV, out of her mind.

First thing she said when they got Kenway into the motorhome was "Where's the nearest hospital?" but the Valenzuelas didn't say anything. Carly looked shell-shocked. Marina seemed to know where she was going, so Robin didn't ask about it any further—but as they came out the other side of Almudena, they emerged onto another two-lane that stretched to the horizon.

"Where are you going?"

Marina glanced over her shoulder. "Killeen."

Robin blinked. "*Killeen?* That's two hours out! He could bleed to death before we ever get there! *Are you fucking bananas?*"

"I'm not going back to Lockwood," Marina said, glaring over her shoulder with steel in her eyes. "Not with Santi behind us."

"There's a hospital in Lockwood?"

"Yes, but—"

"Take us back to Lockwood. I'll burn your husband's bridge when we get to it. Right now, I have a man back there with a bullet hole in him. Bullet hole that's *your* goddamn fault."

Saying nothing, Marina didn't slow down or stop, just drove. Drove and drove, her eyes fixed on the road.

Mental gears grinding, Robin watched the front of the Winnebago eat up the road. Then she stormed back to the breakfast nook and lifted one of the bench seats. Inside was a sawed-off shotgun, five shells strapped to the stock. She carried it up front and pressed the double barrel against Marina's ear.

"Turn the RV around. *Now.*"

"What the hell?" Carly, by her side. The teenager grabbed her elbow and pulled the shotgun away, but Robin jerked her arm out of Carly's hands.

"She's not going to shoot me," Marina said, calmly. "Not while I'm driving."

"Good point," said Robin, and she put the shotgun on the floor. Then she reached over the seat, grabbed a double handful of Marina's shirt, and hauled her off her feet by her neck. The Winnebago immediately veered toward the middle of the road, reflectors thumping under their left-hand tires.

"Let go of my mom!" Carly beat on Robin, slapping and punching her.

Grabbing the teenager's face, Robin cornered her in the door well, squishing her mouth into a goofy duck pout. Marina dropped back into the seat, coughing, taking control of the RV again. "Hit me again and I'll zip-tie you to the front of the RV. You can eat bugs all the way to Michigan."

"Miss Martine," called Gendreau. "Come here."

"Wish I'd thrown your ass out the minute I found you." Robin picked up the shotgun, heading into the bedroom. *"What?"* she asked, annoyed at being interrupted.

Motes of red light still swirled around. The healer looked up with a vaguely offended expression, arms filthy with sticky blood. "Look, I'm working on closing off vessels and getting him stabilized so I can get to the bullet. Halfway there already. If I can get at least that far, we won't *need* a hospital. Bullet went in about three inches to the left of his navel, hit his pelvis, and now it's on the other side, just under the skin. Have to get to it through his back." He pointed to the closet. "Pair of forceps in my bag, and a bottle of alcohol. I need them."

Kenway grunted. "Do I get workman's comp for this?"

Track 13

Santiago arrived with the Los Cambiantes in tow—a couple dozen men, some of them riding double. Shotguns bristled from saddle-bag scabbards, and half of them were wearing pistols.

Monica didn't bother to approach him. Thomas behind the bar didn't say a word as Santi checked the bathrooms and kitchen, and then the back office. The owner, Aaron Fuentes, had already been by for his morning managerial rituals, but even if he were there, he wouldn't challenge Santi either. Not while the Los Cambiantes charged them a protection fee.

"Where is he?" Santiago growled softly to the waitress.

"Gil?"

"No, *Waldo,* you fuckin' blowup doll. Gil Delgado—where'd he run off to?"

Monica clutched her clipboard to her chest as if it was a shield. "Went out with those folks that were here earlier. They ordered food, but as soon as Gil talked to 'em, they left without eating it."

"What about Joaquin?"

"He left before they did."

"Did they have my wife and daughter with them?"

No point in lying. Santi had her dead to rights. Monica's hands scrunched into protective fists. "I thought they were friends from out of town or something. Are they not?"

"See what they were driving?"

"No, I haven't been outside."

Santiago resisted the urge to judo-flip her over the bar and headed back out into the midday heat. He wore a white T-shirt with the sleeves ripped off to bare his brown shoulders. The leering Texas sun draped across his neck like molten gold.

Tuco and Maximo stood by the entrance, their fingers in their hip pockets.

"Which way'd they go?" asked Tuco.

Which way'd they go, boss, which way'd they go? Santiago had to swallow a crazed laugh at the mental image of a Looney Tunes character. "Gil took them outside after Joaquin called me. I don't know if they did something to Joaquin or what, but I know Gil didn't go with them, because his bike is still here."

Their eyes cut over to the mint-condition motorcycle at the end of the parking lot.

"That means he's still here somewhere," said Tuco. "And he ain't gonna get far with that 'Nam shrapnel in his leg."

Panic built inside of him as Santiago paced in frustration. *They have my wife and daughter,* he thought, his fists on his hips. Barely aware of the heat now. *God almighty, I'll forgive them for everything, just don't take them away from me. They're all I have.*

You know where Gil went, said a voice.

A brightly colored bird perched on La Reina's handlebars.

A toucan.

The bird's beak clattered like bamboo wind chimes. At the same time, Santi could feel that long banana-boat beak scraping the inside of his skull in long, languorous, excruciating strokes. He could almost *hear* it.

Sccccccratch.

Black stains ran in rivulets down the corners of his eyesight, pulsing in time with his heartbeat. Santi stared. *Follow your nose,* said the voice inside the motorcycle.

The toucan flew away in slow motion.

Invisible currents flowed into his sinuses as Santiago's nostrils flared, so cold it made his teeth hurt, like icy mountain air. The atmosphere there in the secluded, open desert—the middle of nowhere, really—was so clean and clear, he could smell fucking *everything.* Broiling sunlight softened the pavement into the consistency of a granola bar. The exhaust from their bikes was a noxious swamp of dirty poison. Breath from the men standing around him puffed out in raunchy volumes: Tuco had had a liquid lunch but Maximo had eaten a hamburger. Santiago could smell the mustard and onions somewhere in that beefy miasma.

"Jesus Christ." Tuco backed away from Santiago, eyes locked on his face. "You see that, Max?"

Men made alarmed noises. Everyone watched him with wide-eyed expressions—some of them a baffled sort of amusement (*Is this some sort of elaborate prank?*), and some of them outright fear. Santi ignored them, pushing through the throng. Something else, something behind their combined sweat-musk and the funk of asphalt and halitosis . . . to the east-northeast, he sensed the astringent undertone of Gil's aftershave, Pinaud Clubman—citrus, jasmine, lavender, rubbing alcohol.

Also a thready, milky odor. Fear.

He started toward the end of the parking lot, where a side road went past Heroes into a subdivision sprawling across the desert. The men followed.

"What's up with his face?" someone asked.

"Cap, no offense," said Tuco, "but you look like a gorilla got face-fucked by a bag of Cheetos."

They don't remember, said the voice in the back of Santiago's head. His teeth ached. Pain rimmed the orbital bones framing his eyes. *They've been at the edge of humanity with us, but they don't remember, do they? They've danced with us out here, but they don't remember the steps.* That voice diminished as he walked away from his motorcycle. The feeling that La Reina was home base in a game of tag or second base in a ball game got stronger and stronger; the farther he strayed from it, the weaker the signal got, and the more anxious he became. Sooner or later, someone's going to put the ball on him and then he's *OUT. OUT LIKE GOUT, OUT LIKE TROUT, OUT LIKE—*

"You okay, Cap?" asked Maximo. "Where are you going?"

They don't remember the dance, thought Santiago, or perhaps it came from somewhere deeper, somewhere darker. *They don't remember the wild, the nights when we made them like me, and we ran under the full moon for the first time. They don't know their secret desert hearts. They don't know how they can rip and tear like El Tigre.*

"I'm fine."

El Tigre? The sun beat on him.

Do you remember, Santiago? Do you remember, El Tigre, how it was to rip and tear and dance?

Their road captain walked around the corner of the sports bar and started down the street, following his nose. Turning his head was like dialing an FM radio up and down the band: every angle introduced him to a new smell, and if he stayed tuned into a specific station, he could follow it to its source.

Men lagged behind and dropped away, heading back to Heroes. A few minutes later, he only had Tuco, Max, and a handful of other guys. Fine. He didn't need many, if any at all. *You'll remind them,* said a voice that might not have been Santi's own. *You'll give them back their claws and teeth, and we'll ride a merry chase. Tonight, we'll dance again, and we won't let them forget this time.*

Claws? Teeth?

Gil's fear-stink and citrusy aftershave slowly came into focus as Santiago traveled into the neighborhood behind Heroes, down a dusty, patchy street that hadn't seen a fresh paving in decades (Santi, in fact, stepped into a rather deep pothole and almost fell). It carried them into an arrangement of ranch homes on patchy brown lawns. Many of them sported FOR SALE signs in the yard or FORECLOSURE NOTICE taped to the front door. Santi followed the scent-trail to the end of the block, took a right, to the end of *that* block, then crossed the street. The house he found there—a Brady Bunch kinda place with yuccas out front—was foreclosed as well.

Outside the crusty old dog turds studding the dead grass, the property *reeked* of Gil and Joaquin.

The front door was kicked in.

Tuco headed in that direction, but Santiago stopped him. "He's not in there. Thought he could outsmart us."

Smell Radio led Santi around the side of the house where stairs curled down to a basement door set in the exterior wall. Santi went to open it but Max put a hand on his broad chest.

"Hold up." He directed Santi to the side and pressed his back to the wall.

Reaching over his shoulder with a Miyagi backhand, he knocked on the basement door. Several gunshots rang out from inside and bullets punched through the door with the hard knocking of a judge's gavel, spraying splinters out into the brown grass.

A moment of silence.

Max knocked again. *Pock, pock, pock*—more bullets tore holes in the wood.

"What you doin' with that peashooter, *vato*?" asked Max, talking out of the corner of his mouth. "You ain't got enough bullets for all of us. We can wait you out."

"No, we can't," said Santiago. "I ain't got time for that."

Gil shouted from inside the cellar, "I ain't tellin' you where they went, Santiago. Not giving you a chance to beat that woman again. She ain't done nothing to deserve that shit. Ain't neither one of 'em have."

"I'll decide what she deserves. I'm her goddamn husband."

"What kinda man—" Gil started to say.

"She's my *wife,* old man," said Santiago. Anger swelled in him, anger at the situation, anger at Gil for withholding information, anger at Marina for running off, anger at whoever these people were that took her.

Tuco gave him a weird look.

"Got something on my face, Tuc?" Santiago accidentally bit the inside of his mouth as he spoke, and a bolt of pain flickered down his neck. Saliva flooded his mouth.

Tuco's eyebrows jumped. "No. No, man. Ain't nothin' on your face."

Santiago grunted. Teeth felt funny. Sinus headache getting worse, spreading to his cheeks and eyes. Mental note to hunt down some Tylenol when he got back to the house. "Old bastard only got the one mag on him," said Joaquin Oropeda from inside the cellar. "If you're quick, you can—"

"Did I say you could talk?" asked Gil. "You ain't *shit,* son. I killed Viet Congs that was more man than you. One more word and I'll paint the ceiling—you got me?"

"Yeah, yeah."

"Brought this on yourself. If you'd just kept your mouth shut—"

While Gil was distracted, Santi took the opportunity to go for the door. But when his hand hit the doorknob, the knob snapped off as if it were made of chocolate. Gouges across the front of the cellar door—four claw-marks separated by Gil's bullet holes. He examined his hand. Seemed . . . bigger? *Longer,* somehow. The palm looked larger than it ought to, and his fingers tensed unnaturally, the tendons standing out. Both hands had developed this weird, strained tetanus appearance. Fingernails were *definitely* longer, two inches long, maybe, hooking forward in pointed spikes.

Claws, he thought.

Claws, thought the deeper mind.

On top of all that, the snowy white arm hair was back. This time, it was frosted with orange.

Santiago eyed Maximo. The slab of beef was looking at him with open concern. "Man—" he started to say, but Gil unleashed another volley of bullets through the door. Two of them missed by inches, but the third one tore Santiago's ear to shreds. All the rage came to a head and Santiago's body welled with a searing internal light. Euphoria and pain rippled down his arms and his skin seemed to tighten. Stitches popped in his jeans. He threw himself at the cellar door and it imploded around him, caving in and disintegrating as if it were little more than balsa wood.

As he entered the cellar, something roared in the darkness—a dragon? *It sounds like a dragon; what the hell is that?*

Both Gil and Joaquin screamed. Gil pushed Joaquin and Santi shoved him out of the way, his fingernails catching in the man's clothing.

Blood spattered across the cellar wall.

"*Jesus shit!*" cried Gil Delgado, running for his life. He scrambled to pull open a casement window in the back so he could climb out, and Santi caught him, snatching his leg and dragging him out of the shadows. The road captain turned and flung Gil across the cellar as if he were nothing but a bag of trash.

The old man smashed into a pegboard, and a collection of tools fell off the wall in a cascade of junk. Santi was immediately on him, slapped the 1911 out of his hand before he could fire and lifted him up, holding him against the wall. The pistol clattered underneath a worktable.

"WHERE ARE THEY?" bellowed Santiago. Rich, cloying, saline, like popcorn butter, a smell told him that Gil had pissed his pants. "WHERE DID THEY GO?" The white-orange arm hair was now a fin of shag the color of mango-flesh, hanging from Santi's arms. The agony in his face was intense, as if his nose was broken. Salty blood filled his mouth.

"Santi." Gil writhed in fear and pain, his Hunter S. Thompson glasses hanging off his face. "What's *happening* to you? What *is* this?"

"What is *what*?"

"*Look* at you, man! What the hell *are* you?"

Santi bounced Gil's head off the wall. *"Tell me who has my wife and where they went!"*

"Some chick with a Mohawk and a vet! Big blond guy!"

"What are—" Santi began, but then he caught sight of his reflection in Gil's sunglasses.

Two tiny monsters gawked back at him. In just five minutes, he'd grown a beard, eggshell-white, cropped, silky. His eyes were bleeding, running down his face in twin harlequin trails. Yellow teeth jutted from his bloody mouth: too big, too many, all of them pointed. Black pinstripes rippled outward from his lips and eye sockets in a dozen concentric half circles. His face was a tiki mask of feral rage.

Teeth.

"Jesus," Santi said in shock, backing away.

Do you remember now?

Collapsing to the floor, Gil scrambled around for purchase on some kind of weapon. Snatching up a hacksaw, he held it at port arms, shaking with the palsy of terror.

Do you remember the dance?

No one else was in the cellar with them. The thin sour-milk smell of fear drifted around the room on a lazy breeze, and Santi realized the gangbangers outside were all afraid to come in. "What is wrong with me?" The orange-white hair had climbed onto his knuckles and hung like a dandy's lace sleeves.

Nothing wrong with you, said the voice from far away, a weak signal, almost just a current in the air. *Do you remember the dance? Do you remember the night?*

"What am I?" Santiago asked, reeling around the cellar. He found a tall red tool chest and jerked drawers open, rummaging through tools. The third drawer had a pair of pliers in it. Santi used it to grip one of his demonic-looking fingernail-hooks and pulled.

Pain shot up his finger. He cried out.

"That goddamn Enfield." Urine made a dark stain on the front of Gil's Wranglers. "It's doin' something to you, kid. Got the damn devil in it, maybe. Got its claws in you."

"Got the *devil* in it?" said Santi, throwing the pliers at him.

Gil flinched; the pliers went wide.

"Do you know how stupid that sounds?" Santi paced. His own voice sounded exhausted, bewitched.

"Yeah, yeah, it sounds stupid, yeah."

Scrrrrratch. Santi pulled open a drawer and found a pair of scissors. "It's that bitch," he grumbled, cutting off the strange hair growing out of his arms in a horrified frenzy. Locks of Creamsicle-colored hair littered the floor. "*She's* doing this to me, you know? My nerves. She's got me so stressed out, I'm losing my mind, Gil. I'm seeing shit." Tears spilled down his cheeks, mingling with the blood to make red tracks. The words were almost sobs. "Got laid off, man. Laid off. I'm fuckin' broke. My daughter hates me. She turned my little girl against me. What am I gonna do?"

"We'll figure s-something out." Gil was in full-on negotiator mode, hands up, speaking in an ingratiating tone. "I know you don't like it, and I don't either, but, hey, maybe we can get Bobby back out here and we can push again. Move some product east, for a little while. Just to get you back on your feet—"

Santiago rounded on him with the scissors. "Told you I wasn't goin' back to that shit. I don't want my daughter anywhere near it. Heroin, cocaine, meth, I don't—I don't want her near that. *I'm done.* I told you." Then, as he paced around the basement, he seemed to come out of a trance. "My daughter." His beastly face darkened. "What are they driving?"

"Driving?" asked Gil.

"*The people that took my family,*" Santiago snarled, and went at him. Gil yelped and stumbled back; Santi caught him by the throat and pinned him to the wall again. He held the scissors against Gil's cheek, pointed at his eye. "What are they driving?"

"A-a-a wuh, a Winnebago," stuttered Gil. "Shitty old brown Winnebago. Looks like an ice cream truck."

Standing there holding the scissors to Gil's face, Santiago just breathed. He finally spoke again. The first several words were muddled because his lips were dry and stuck together. "How d'you like being president, Guillermo? Noticed you don't wear the rank patch on your vest anymore. You ashamed of being president of Los Cambiantes?"

Gil glanced down at where his PRESIDENT tab used to be and shook his head. The scissors poked a dot of blood out of his cheek. "No, not at all. It's just a, a security th—"

Hooking Gil's glasses off with the scissors, Santiago tossed them aside. "High time you retired, grandpa. Been thinking I'd make a pretty good president. What you think? I'll give road captain to Maximo. Max'll make a great rocap."

Do you remember, El Tigre? Do you remember the night?

"Sounds g-good to me," Gil smiled nervously. Tears rolled down his face. "M-maybe I'll even move out to the beach. Get out of you guys' way. Yeah, I think I like that." The soon-to-be-former president of the Los Cambiantes still had his hands up in surrender. Santiago braced Gil's wrist against the pegboard and slammed the blades into the palm of his hand, nailing him to the wall with a scissor stigmata.

I remember.

• • •

Noises came out of that cellar like Maximo had never heard outside of a horror movie. Screaming, growling, crushing, rending, tearing, splattering. The Mexican Mountain winced, his eyes cutting over to Tuco. Slimy bastard stood there with a placid, lizard-like expression on his face, eyes inscrutable behind his Kadeem Hardison flip-shades.

Five or six men stared at the doorway with cold anxiety. "What the *hell* is going on in there?" one of them asked.

He was answered by the sight of Santiago Valenzuela coming out of the cellar. Their road captain was plastered in gore, his hair stringy and lank. Gobbets of flesh speckled his shirt, and his teeth—normal, chisel-edged human teeth instead of the pointy goblin teeth he'd had a few minutes ago—were stained red. He looked like a pot of marinara had exploded in his face.

"Congratulations," said Santi, clapping Maximo on the shoulder. "You just got a promotion." He ripped the Velcro ROAD CAPTAIN tab off of his vest and affixed it to Maximo's. "Enough of this goat-rope. Let's roll out."

Maximo looked down at his new rank tab (noticing the bloody handprint Santiago left on his shirt) and then up at Tuco's easy reptilian grin.

"Congrats, big guy," said Tuco, and he followed after their new president.

Maximo watched them all funnel out of the foreclosed property in a loose crowd of dazed, fearful expressions. Faces of men who had been dragged into a strange but not wholly unwelcome darkness.

On legs that didn't feel like his own, Max wandered into the cellar and into the green stink of deep shit.

Hanging from a scissor plunged through one hand was a mauled corpse. The marionette that used to be Gil was unrecognizable. His face—and hell, *the front of his skull*—was gone, leaving nothing but the bottom rim of teeth and a pulped cavity. His sinuses were a pink pit under the white cauliflower of his ripped brain. His throat was torn out and so were his guts, intestines draping over his lap in wet gray loops.

Max stared at the dead man, his hands trembling. Nothing *ever* made this behemoth shake.

He wasn't disturbed so much by the fact that he was looking at a mangled dead guy. Wasn't the first time he'd seen one. Neither was it that one of his closest and oldest friends apparently *ate* the parts that weren't here. *Yeah, that's messed up,* he admitted, but when he looked at the corpse, it felt as if his brain was packed in a box of Styrofoam peanuts, insulated from the enormity of the tableau in front of him. He could feel the terror and disgust, but it was outside of him, like looking out at a burning-hot sun from inside an air-conditioned house. Something had put down a wall between him and reality, it seemed like—something wanted him divorced from what he saw, what he did.

An invisible thought-finger dragged a jagged nail down the inside of his skull.

Ay, Boo-Boo! I see a pic-a-nic basket!

One eye twitched.

No. Max tracked bloody boot-prints back into the sunshine. *Part that disturbs me,* he thought, as he stumbled across the crunchy grass, *is that it's makin me fuckin' hungry.*

SIDE B

I Am the Fire

Track 14

From time to time, a faint Tibetan-singing-bowl drone emanated from the bedroom: Gendreau's magic fingers, dutifully sealing Kenway's gunshot wound. Doc G had gotten the big vet stabilized a little while back; Robin wasn't sure when. Could have been ten minutes before; it could have been half an hour. When you're on pins and needles like this, every minute feels like a day.

All she could do was sit still and wait for the all-clear, trying not to glare at the kid. Robin and Carly sat in the breakfast nook, the sawed-off shotgun on the table between them like Spin the Bottle. The RV's radio belted out some scratchy classic rock. Bad Company. *Six-gun sound is our claim to fame.*

"Sorry I dragged you into this." Carly touched the shotgun with tentative fingertips. "It was my idea to hide in here."

Robin grunted.

"So, is it true?" she asked. "You really kill witches, for real?"

"Yes."

More uncomfortable silence.

"How many?"

"Too many. Not enough." She was covered in scars, but it didn't seem like the time to tell stories.

Prying herself out of the nook, Robin finally realized that her hands were bloody and so was her shirt. She pulled it off and deposited it into the garbage, then washed her hands in the kitchen sink. Her bra smelled like hot-dog water. She changed into a fresh one and a black *My Favorite Murder* T-shirt.

When she sat back down, Carly said, "You throwing that bloody shirt away made me think of something."

Robin stared expectantly.

"Couple of months ago," Carly continued, "a mountain lion got into Keyhole Hills for a while and it was, like, tearing peoples' garbage open until Animal Control came out from Lockwood. Took it out east or something. *Anyway,* I was heading to school one morning and it, like, tore open our garbage and pulled it all over the yard. That *really* pissed Dad off, but Mom and me picked it all up before he got home, so it wasn't that bad. But I found something in the garbage when we were picking it up that I put in my bag before Mom could see it."

"A bloody shirt?"

"Yeah. And bloody jeans."

"Well, your dad *is* an outlaw biker." Robin stared out the window at the evening. The sun was a giant doubloon in a dusky indigo swell, chewed at the bottom by a sawband of black desert hills. Stars dusted a glittering arc overhead. "I would imagine he comes home with blood on his clothes once in a while."

Evident by the quietly stricken expression on her face, Carly hated to think about that. "Yeah, but . . . not like this." She mimed pulling something apart. "Those clothes were, like, ripped to pieces. Like the Incredible Hulk tore 'em up. The butt was blown out, the legs were split, the button was gone, the fly was broken. The shirt was *completely* messed up. They were, like, just rags, you know?"

Robin's nail polish stood at the back end of the table with a dirty coffee mug, a newspaper's comics section, and a bottle of ketchup. She picked it up. Vampire Red, a deep bloody mahogany. Wasn't black, but it might as well have been. She went back to painting her nails, as she'd been doing when Marina so unceremoniously surprised her by falling out of the shower.

"So, where did you learn those moves?" asked Carly. "Like, when you punched Wacky in the face."

Wacky Joaquin. Robin scoffed.

"My old boss, Heinrich, taught me. Said it would come in handy, fighting familiars."

"Familiars?"

"Witches can sacrifice housecats and 'send' their souls into people, turning them into feral maniacs. Basically, they turn into the zombies from that movie *28 Days Later*, except if you leave them alone for a while, they'll start licking their nuts."

"Wow," said Carly. "All this time, I thought your videos were fake."

"Nope. But that's the point."

Bad Company became Kansas. *Carry on, my wayward son*. Robin finished repainting her left hand's nails and held it up to assess them. "I imagine those bloody clothes you saw have something to do with what Gil said about seeing your father in the woods."

"The animal masks?"

"I don't think they were wearing masks."

Strained horror cast a shadow over Carly's face. "You mean . . . their *heads* changed? Is that what you're saying?"

"More than *that* changed." Robin blew on her nails. "Seen a witch turn into a one-ton hog monster with her tits hanging on the ground. Saw another one climb across a ceiling and through a hole the size of a baseball."

"Like *werewolves*?" Carly asked, incredulous. "Are you saying my dad and his friends are *werewolves*?"

"Werewolves don't exist."

"Then what the hell is happening?"

"I think it's a relic of Ereshkigal turning them into something else with the Gift of Transfiguration."

Carly gave her a dumbfounded look.

"Witches derive their powers from a tumor inside their bodies called a 'teratoma.' When a witch-hunter kills a witch, a specialist called an Origo is able to extract this teratoma from the witch's body and use it to craft a magical weapon." As she continued on to explain relics, she quietly offered Carly the nail brush. Perhaps if she could occupy her mind with something as mundane as painting someone's nails, she might calm down. With practiced strokes that looked better than Robin's splotchy mess, the teenager took her right hand and proceeded to do just that. "Witches were created by an ancient death-goddess named Ereshkigal. Ever since she was banished to the afterlife, she's been trying to resurrect herself here on Earth through our bodies. Teratomas are usually made of hair, or bone, and sometimes you'll find a whole body part in there like a finger or an eyeball. That's a part of Ereshkigal's body. We're all doorways that she's continuously trying to come through."

"My dad has one of these, these . . . relics?"

"I believe so." Robin blew on her nails again. "Does your dad have any family heirlooms? Anything around the house he's really attached to?"

The girl swallowed. The polish brush trembled in the air just above Robin's finger. "He does, actually. He bought a bike a couple of years ago at a police auction. Calls it La Reina."

"Lorena?"

"No, La Reina—*the Queen.*" She started painting again, and Robin could feel her gathering up more words. "Sometimes, he looks at it funny, like when I make a weird noise at Mr. Delgado's dog and it turns its head sideways."

Got to be it, Robin thought, blowing on her fingers. She let Carly finish painting her nails. A soothing, meditative task, and it went a long way toward calming them both down. *Never seen a relic that big. Wonder where the teratoma is?*

While her nails dried, she stepped into the bedroom to check on Kenway and talk to Gendreau.

"How's he doing?"

"Just in time, Miss Martine." The curandero brushed sweat away from his forehead with his arm, leaving a smear of blood. "Help me roll him over so I can get to the bullet in his back." The gunshot wound looked like it had been cauterized with fire-heated steel wool; whorls of angry red flesh marked the place where the quarter-sized entry hole had been.

"Shit on *me*! Goddamn!" cried Kenway. "Can't we just leave it in? Pretty please?"

"Could get infected. Or travel into a vital organ. Pretty close to one of your kidneys as it is, and as far away from a hospital as we are, we could do without renal failure, friendo. That's something I can't necessarily treat."

The vet sighed. "All right, all right."

He raised himself up onto his elbows with a wince. Gendreau grabbed the leg of Kenway's shorts and hooked a hand under his arm. "You take his hand and pull him, and I'll push. One, two, three," Gendreau chanted, and they flipped him over.

"Aaarrrggh," Kenway groaned into one of the rare patches of duvet not soaked in blood.

"There it is." A smudge halfway up Kenway's back, so faint it could have been a trick of the light. Gendreau's eyes slipped closed, and his head tipped back. "Right there, about three inches deep. Carried a chip of bone from his pelvis along with it." Massaging the area with light, graceful movements, the magician muttered under his breath. The skin underneath his hands grew paler and took on a waxy cast.

"What are you doing?"

"Closing off blood to the area so I can cut into it and take out the bullet." Gendreau pointed at his satchel. "Nurse, could you get me a scalpel out of my bag and sterilize it for me with that bottle of alcohol? And those forceps, too?" Robin dug out a scalpel and wiped the tools down. The magician took the scalpel in one hand as one would hold an ink pen and braced his other hand against the skin. As the blade pressed in, the skin split cleanly open like a sausage casing. No blood spilled out, but the tissue inside was a dainty salmon-pink.

"Ah, *sssssshhhit*," Kenway complained into the duvet.

"Be even worse if I hadn't deadened your nerves when I closed off the blood vessels. Quit wiggling, man." Picking up the forceps, Gendreau held the incision open with his fingers, inserting the tiny cupped tips.

"Figured out why Gil saw that shitlord Santiago and his buddies out in the woods wearing wolf masks," said Robin. "One of them has a Transfiguration relic. I'd say it's his motorcycle. But I've never heard of a relic that big before."

"Rare, but they do happen," said Gendreau, glancing at her. "There was a car relic in California in 1938—a Wolseley Hornet, I think—that caused the owner to hallucinate the future whenever he drove it. When my dad was a teenager, a 1958 Plymouth Fury was used in a bunch of murders up around Maine. People said the car itself was possessed, but it was demolished in a car-crusher before the Dogs could study it."

He paused, staring into space.

"What is it?" asked Robin.

"Do you hear that?"

She strained to listen.

Under the constant rumble of tires on asphalt and the throaty hiss of the ancient air conditioner, she heard it.

Motorcycle engines.

Track 15

Out of the darkness they roared, dragging a long convoy down the highway in a spear formation. Robin watched them through a narrow gap in the back curtain. Their bikes bristled with weapons. The Royal Enfield she'd heard so much about led the procession, and sitting on it, as ramrod-straight and dark-eyed as Genghis Khan on his war horse, was Santiago Valenzuela.

"Just keep driving," she shouted to Marina. She urged Carly out of the breakfast nook and opened the bench seat to reveal a foam bed arrayed with gun parts. She took out a black plastic stock, an upper receiver, another part that looked like a vacuum cleaner attachment, and a box of smaller parts, and laid them out on the table. Also a box of what looked like cartoon bullets as big as salt shakers.

Hanging on the wall was a vinyl scabbard and webbing harness. She put it on. Taking a short sword off the wall, she slipped it into the scabbard. Finally, she pointed a remote control at each of the cameras mounted on the walls. Tiny red on-air lights winked on.

"If this is going down," she told Carly, "might as well get some footage."

Santiago blasted around them, passing on the left. *"Hey!"* he shouted at his wife. "Hey!" He shouted again. "Fuckin' *talkin'* to you! Roll that window down!"

The matriarch of the Valenzuela family obliged, filling the cabin with wind, but she didn't say anything at first. "Keep him busy for a minute," Robin told her. She sat in the breakfast nook and started putting gun parts together. In her head, Heinrich's stopwatch chirped. *Let's see how fast you can break this rifle down and put it back together. Tick-tock.*

"Pull over!" Santiago bellowed.

Firing pin into bolt, retaining pin and can pin into bolt, *tick tick tick—"No!"* answered Marina. "I'm not going back!"

"Pull this thing over! We can talk this out!"

Bolt and charging handle into star chamber. *Tick tick tick*. "Oh, my God," breathed Carly, "is that a machine gun?" Her face paled. "Are you going to shoot my dad?"

"Marina!" shouted Santiago. *"Pull over!"*

Marina did the opposite. The Winnebago sped up.

"Long as he's civil, no," said Robin. Trigger assembly into upper receiver, upper receiver front pin to stock, *tick tick tick*. "I'd like to avoid that outcome if possible."

After the briefest of pauses to assess the danger level of what she was about to do, Carly snatched up the remote control for the cameras and pressed buttons at them.

Two of them turned off. Robin looked up. "Hell are you doing?"

"This isn't going on your YouTube channel, lady."

"What?"

"I'm not your YouTube show. My family isn't." Carly turned off the other two cameras. "And if my dad gets hurt, it's not going on the internet like all those body-cam tapes where people get killed by the cops. You're not turning my daddy into a circus."

"I just—" Robin began, but Carly stormed away.

Stumbling into the front of the RV, the girl leaned over the steering wheel and shouted out the window. "Daddy!"

"Give me that remote," said Robin.

"Sweetheart!" said Santiago. "They ain't hurt you, have they?"

Carly shot Robin a glare, and then yelled out the window, "No! But please go away! Stop chasing—"

"The hell you mean, *go away*?"

"She's got a machine gun, and I think she's going to use it on you if you don't stop chasing us."

Tick tick tick. Robin pushed the recoil spring in and closed the AR-15, pinning it together in the back. She banged a magazine against the side of her head to seat the rounds and shoved it into the mag well—*Time. Good work, girl.* Chambering a round, Robin opened the window over the table and pressed her forehead and the muzzle of the rifle against the screen. The man on the bike noticed her immediately.

"No," she told Santiago, "I said as long as you stay civil."

"What do you consider 'civil,' ma'am?" he asked her with a sneer.

"Going your ass away. Far away."

"You have my wife and my daughter." Santiago's hair streamered in the wind like a lion's mane. "What makes you think I'm just going to let that go?"

"This," Robin said, prodding the screen with the assault rifle.

Santiago frowned. "That really the way you wanna play it, lady?"

"No, but it's a game I got a hell of a winning streak in."

His eyes burned with a diabolic anger and he bit down on a frown as he said, "You don't want to play a home game with me. Believe that."

"Go fuck yourself, San Diego."

Kneeling on the bench, Robin angled the rifle, flicked the safety to SEMI, and fired a round through the screen. Past Santiago's head. The ensuing *BOOM!* filled the RV with noise and a shell casing tinkled across the table. At the same time, Santiago ducked and the Enfield wobbled, almost laying down.

"No!" screamed Carly.

She began to charge Robin, but the witch-hunter gave her the Crazy Eyes over the carrying handle of the AR. "Sit down," Robin warned, her voice muffled in her own report-deafened ears. "That was just a warning shot."

"Fuck," spat Santi, slowing until he was out of sight.

"Now get in the bathroom." Robin sat on the table so she could get an angle on Santi behind them. "Lay on the floor."

The girl hesitated.

"Now!" Robin grabbed the newspaper off the table and threw it at her. Carly flinched and the paper opened in midair, scattering itself all over the RV.

Giving Robin an angry look, she jammed the camera remote into the kitchen-sink drain and flipped the switch behind the counter to turn on the garbage disposal. The light over her head came on as if she'd had an idea.

"Sorry, no garbage disposal," Robin said wryly.

Annoyed, the girl stormed into the bathroom and shut the door, and the lock engaged with a *thunk*.

"Good," said Robin, "and stay in there." She went into the bedroom and peered through the back curtains again. Santiago had rejoined the convoy and reassembled into a wedge formation.

"Get on the floor," she told Kenway and Gendreau.

"Don't have to tell *me* twice." The curandero went down like a sack of bricks and squeezed between the bed and the wall, lying on his back. All she could see of him was his Italian shoes. From the front of the RV, she could hear the radio still pounding out classic rock. AC/DC's "Thunderstruck." *The thunder of guns tore me apart,* screamed Brian Johnson.

"Give me a gun," grunted Kenway. Blood trickled out of the incision in his back as he slid painfully onto the floor.

"What I need is for Doc G to finish getting that bullet out of you."

"—Aw, piss," said the magician from behind the bed. He sat up, wriggling around to the big veteran. "Lie down," he said, grabbing his forceps.

"Gun!" demanded Kenway.

She fetched the sawed-off shotgun and handed it to him. He loaded a couple of shells and whipped the shotgun shut.

"Just hang—" Robin started to say, but the rear window imploded, showering them all with glass. Bullets battered the wall behind her. She dropped into a crouch and sidled around the bed, peering around the curtain again. All the men riding bitch were pointing pistols.

"No!" Santiago shouted. "My little girl's in there!"

Then something strange happened.

One of the men behind him screamed, followed by another one. Santiago's face was animated by a vivid black rage. His eyes flickered with amber light. The wind combed blood out of his eyes and mouth and blew it across his temples. Even from here, his terror and fear were obvious, but underpinning it was an almost-orgasmic look of surrender. Bikers to his left and right distorted; hair spent from their scalps, becoming shaggy, and their mouths lengthened, teeth bristling.

"Gil and the kid were right," Robin said. "Werewolves."

"Are you serious?" Gendreau smeared blood across his face again, wiping away sweat. "Well, what are you waiting for, you silly woman? Shoot them, *shoot them all you can*!"

"Why didn't I think of that?"

AC/DC's "Thunderstruck" became Queen's "Bohemian Rhapsody." Robin rested the AR's handguard on the windowsill and the scope settled over the forehead of one of the men. Muscles under his skin rippled and changed shape. Halfway between wolf and man, he looked like some kind of horrendous fetal dog, misshapen and livid purple, face bulging, veins throbbing.

Is this real life? Is this just fantasy?

The formation surged forward and she fired.

Blood and shredded scalp misted the air. The snarling homunculus stiffened as if having a seizure and, teetering backward, he fell onto the road, and another biker swerved to avoid hitting him. She sighted down the scope again as the bikers continued to close in on them.

As soon as she fired, the man at the handlebars leaned forward and the bullet whirred through his streaming hair.

Motorcycles flanked them, passing on the left. Engines reverberated through the Winnebago's floor. Robin turned to shoot at them again, but no window in the bedroom's starboard wall afforded her a functional view.

"Shit," she cursed, heading up front.

Bohemian Rhapsody rang throughout the RV. *Mamma mia, mamma mia, mamma mia, let me go.*

Something heavy hit the roof.

Robin paused in the kitchen, looking at the ceiling. She raised the rifle and prepared to blow a hole in it, but a great hairy arm shattered the window over the sink and palmed her face. The werewolf's oil-stinking claw dragged her backward over the sink, banging her skull against the window frame.

With a kicked-puppy squeal, the werewolf let go of Robin and disappeared into the darkness outside.

Someone had pulled the short sword from Robin's scabbard and jammed the tip in the werewolf's eye. Eyes wide and mouth agape, Carly held the bloody sword with a trembling hand.

"Thanks," grunted Robin. She took the sword and slid it back into its scabbard. "Get back in the bathroom."

"I can help you," said Carly, frantic. "Give me a gun."

"No!"

The skylight hauled out of its hatch with a scream of tearing metal and a monstrous, misshapen canine looked in at them. *"Have you accepted Wolf Jesus into your heart?"* snarled the creature. Strings of saliva drooled into the cabin.

"Accept this bullet into your heart." Robin popped a round in his chest.

Blood spattered across the ceiling and the wolf-man screamed, slithering out of sight. Robin closed the window and pulled the curtain shut, glancing at a camera. "Shit, I coulda made a joke about dogma."

"God, that's so *loud,*" Carly complained, jamming her fingers in her ears.

"Guns usually are."

A hairy arm hooked under Robin's chin, jerking her off her feet. Her head slammed against the ceiling and the werewolf reaching in through the skylight lost his grip, dropping her into the kitchen.

Bouncing off its buttstock, the rifle fired a burst into the ceiling over her shoulder. Blood sprayed out of a hole in the paneling.

I'm just a poor boy, sang Freddie Mercury.

Picking up the rifle, Robin shouted, *"Get off my roof,"* and just for good measure hip-fired a couple of three-round bursts through the ceiling like Yosemite Sam on New Year's Eve, punching holes in the aluminum, *B-B-BANG!, B-B-BANG!*

Terror etched on her face, Carly squared up in the hallway, gripping a tactical tomahawk in both hands like a Templar knight with a broadsword.

The sound of shrieking came from the front seat.

A werewolf clung to the driver door, reaching in through the window, trying to steer them onto the shoulder. Marina threw elbow after elbow into its jaw, fighting with the wheel. "Let go! *¡Hijo de puta! Stop!"*

Gravity turned on its side and Robin and Carly stumbled against the table. Kitchen cabinets opened, spilling cans of food; some of them cracked open, leaking juice all over the floor. *Beelzebub has a devil put aside for me,* sang Freddie. Robin lifted the rifle, aiming toward the front, hunkering into the shot just the way Heinrich and Kenway taught her, and pulled the trigger. The bullet blew through the beast's snout, leaving an aerosol splatter of thick blood all over the windshield, and the werewolf fell out the window. Marina tried to wipe the blood off the glass with some fast-food napkins from the console but only succeeded in smearing it around.

Glass shattered in the back. *BOOM,* the sawed-off shotgun barked.

One of the wolf-men crouched on the bed in a three-point stance, the bloody duvet tangled in one fist. Robin marched toward him firing burst after burst, *RAKKA-TAKKA-RAKKA-TAKKA,* dozens of bullets punching into the monster. *Just gotta get out, just gotta get right outta hee-aaah!*

With one last snarl, the werewolf collapsed and died on the bed.

"Thanks," said Kenway, loading fresh buckshot shells.

Gendreau pushed his patient back down. "Stop moving!"

A motorcycle blatted past, overtaking the Winnebago, and then another. "They're trying to cut us off!" shouted Marina.

"Stay alive, please." Robin left.

From the kitchen, she could see through the windshield. Red taillights glowed ahead of them: two motorcycles, and they were slowing down, trying to force them off the road. "Bohemian Rhapsody" trailed off, becoming Journey's "Separate Ways," that familiar synth reverberating through the room.

Looking for the black rifle attachment, Robin scanned the room and spotted it lying in the door well, rattling around on the bottom step.

"There you are," she muttered, kneeling to reach for it.

As she did, the exterior door flew open and the wind slapped it against the side of the RV, filling the room with a torrent of hot desert air.

Outside: werewolf in a leather vest, clinging to the side of the Winnebago. Robin snatched up the rifle attachment, but the monster tore through the screen door and grabbed her wrist, pulling her halfway through the door frame. Bent double through the screen door, suspended over the highway at breakneck speeds, she screamed, swinging out of the RV. Darkness rocketed past her face in stuttering red images of sagebrush and sand.

"It's over, puta," snarled the werewolf, and it raked claws down the small of her back, grabbing the waist of her jeans.

Stinging pain swelled along her spine. He was trying to pull her out of the door and throw her aside, but all he managed to do was almost drag her jeans off, baring her ass to the buffeting wind.

"Leggo!" she shouted, upside down.

Claws fought to keep their grip on her ass, tearing holes in her underwear. She grabbed the doorframe and aimed the rifle between her knees. *TAK-TAK-TAK!*

Bullets ripped into the werewolf's crotch and it let go of the Winnebago with a wail, tumbling into the road in a cloud of dust. A motorcycle coming up on their starboard side fishtailed around him, almost sliding into the desert.

Carly grabbed her ankle and pulled her back inside. Robin slammed the M-203 attachment onto the rifle's Picatinny rail and screwed the clamp down, then cracked open the attachment and fumbled in the kitchen sink for the giant cartoon bullets she'd put there earlier. "What is that?" Carly asked, as Robin slid one of them into the back of the attachment tube and racked the breech shut.

"Cure for assholes."

In the open door, purple Mohawk whipping in the wind, Robin eyed the biker coming up on their flank.

"Hello!" she shouted into the gale, smiling.

Both men glared at her with glowing eyes. The one riding on the back was a werewolf and his mouth hung open, his long tongue flagging. A silky spider-string of drool trailed on the air.

Someday, love will find you, sang Steve Perry through a curtain of howling guitars and pulsing synths. Robin fired the AR with a noise like pulling a cork out of a giant bottle of wine. *FOONK!* The high-explosive grenade round erupted with a flash directly in front of the motorcycle, followed by an almost-instant report.

Dissolving between the werewolves' legs in a ball of light and chaos, the Harley became a dazzling bottle-rocket, a cloud of flaming parts across the night. Robin squinted against the heat.

"Holy shit!" screamed Carly behind her.

The motorcycle crashed to the ground and somersaulted over the werewolves' bodies, throwing up plumes of sand and fire. Robin ducked back into the RV and grabbed another grenade round from the box in the sink, loading it. "Now to take care of the boys trying to cut us off." She stepped back into the door well and leaned outside into the night, straight-arming the rifle one-handed toward the front of the RV. The barrel swung up.

Could only hold it up pistol-fashion for a couple of seconds, but that's all she needed. Robin pulled the trigger and the rifle coughed, almost kicking out of her hand.

FOONK! The grenade spiraled out and gouged the air with one immense hammerblow. The cop bike exploded into a galaxy of hellfire, but the other wobbled maniacally and fell over, spilling both men underneath the Winnebago.

THUD-THUD. Marina steamrolled a body.

The black-and-white patrol bike cartwheeled over a pool of flame and Marina peeled back the other way, juking right.

Orange light flashed in the RV's port-side windows as the motorcycle slammed against the ground. Robin loaded another grenade and headed for the bedroom where the curtains whipped like Superman's cape, giving her ragged glimpses of the men chasing them. She marched over and ripped them down from their rails so she could see. Taking a knee to steady herself, she fired a grenade out the back window. *FOONK!*

Instead of sailing neatly through, the grenade hit the windowsill and bounced straight up.

For one heart-stopping moment, she thought it was going to explode in her face, and Robin threw herself on top of Kenway, knocking the forceps out of Gendreau's hand. Bouncing once more like a basketball on the edge of a hoop rim, the silver grenade disappeared into the night. One second later, it exploded directly behind the Winnebago and the rear wall *crunched* under the blast's onslaught, a single hard thunder-strike *BOOM* of sound and light.

Shrapnel peppered the bedroom wall.

Blood streamed down Gendreau's face. Robin sat up. He was saying something, but the only sound coming out of his mouth was the electric whistle of tinnitus.

"Whut," Robin asked, dazed.

"I said, *stop with the damn explosives*!" Gendreau said, palming some of the blood away and looking at it. Red fireflies of energy flitted around his head as he pressed his fingertips against his skull. Robin pulled herself over the edge of the bed to look through the rear window. The biker gang's headlights were dwindling into the distance.

"They're giving up." She staggered out of the room, the AR on her shoulder like a baseball bat. "No balls," she said, and tripped over a can of Spaghetti-Os.

Bark at the moon, sang Ozzy Osbourne from the RV's speakers.

Track 16

They drove and drove and then drove some more. Night pressed against the windows like the silk fur of some immense black cat. Reaching under the werewolf's corpse, Robin levered the heavy bastard out into the night. A piece of the trim went with it.

"That's littering," said Gendreau, sitting on the floor as he packed his tools back into his doctor's bag.

"Write me a ticket."

She headed up front and stood between the front seats, leaning on them as if she were a starship captain. Claw marks on her face and ass had been healed by the curandero, but the blood had dried in long painted strands. Kenway and Carly sat in the breakfast nook, a belt of gauze wrapped around the veteran's middle.

Gendreau shuffled out of the bedroom, pushing fallen food cans with his feet. He raked them down the door well and out into the night.

"Hey," said Robin. "I was going to eat that."

"Be my guest, Rambo."

Licking her lips thoughtfully, she showed him her middle finger.

The curandero shook his head and went back to pushing the cans outside. "You *like* it, don't you?" he asked. "It's why you agreed to help the Valenzuelas."

"Like what?"

"Fighting!" Gendreau toed a can of beans into the darkness. Cleaned of cans, the carpet was soiled with leaking food. "The vigilante thing! You're like a Viking battle maiden or something, addicted to war. Look at you; you're all dewy and cranked up now. You love it. You were out here gunning down werewolves to AC/DC and Queen. *You love it.*"

"I guess I do."

Gendreau sighed wearily.

"What do you expect?" she added. "*You* know what my father is. Heinrich raised me to be a weapon, didn't he? The perfect witch-killing machine." Robin shook her head and stared out the windshield. "Other than YouTube, it's all I know."

"Oh, get off your own dick, Billy Badass," said Gendreau. He reached outside and shut the door, cutting off the blustering wind. "One of the things I liked about you when I met you was how even after all the shit you went through, you weren't one of these angsty suffering-hero emo types." Gendreau searched through cabinets. "Yeah, you wear a lot of black, but you didn't feel sorry for yourself. You had rage, but it was a happy rage, a *purposeful* rage."

She shrugged with a pinched smile.

"It's taking you over and you're enjoying it."

"The broom is in the bathroom closet," said Kenway.

"Thanks." Gendreau fetched the broom, which he swept the kitchen floor with. "I dunno," he said. "Guess I just can't help but notice a difference ever since you found out about your father, Andras, and it's worrying, is all. I don't want you becoming self-destructive."

"Your concern is duly noted," Robin replied, perhaps a bit colder than she intended it to be.

The curandero said nothing.

"What does he mean about your father?" asked Carly.

"My dad is an owl-headed demon named Andras." Robin sat next to Kenway in the nook. "It's on my YouTube channel. I thought you watched my videos."

"Only a few of them." Carly stared. "Your dad is a *demon*?"

"Yup."

The girl stared at her hands. "Guess we've got something in common, then."

"No." Robin took Carly's hands and squeezed them. "You can't change a demon. They're pure fuckin' evil. But your dad—something's taken him over. Something in that motorcycle."

Hope gleamed in Carly's eyes. "Does that mean you can save him?" She smiled. "You can make him the way he used to be, before he bought that motorcycle?"

"Maybe."

"Please don't kill him," said Carly, her voice breaking. "He's not a bad guy, I promise. I'm sorry about what I said earlier . . . I didn't mean it." She clutched Robin's hands. "I don't want you to hurt him. The bike. We need to get rid of the bike. You said it's the bike causing this, right?"

"That's my theory." Robin's hands slipped away. "But if he comes at me like those assholes back there, I can't make any promises." They drew up into fists. "My throat doesn't bruise as easily as your mother's."

"It's not the bike," said Marina.

"What?"

Gendreau took out his cell phone. "Calling Rook. Hopefully, they're still in Killeen. Their plane was supposed to take off from Killeen–Fort Hood Airport twenty minutes ago." He pressed the phone to his ear. "Santiago isn't backing off, and we're going to need help. And if we confiscate the relic, the Dogs will want to take possession of it." He paced back and forth. "Hey. It's Andy." He put it on speakerphone. "Wanted to see if you'd taken off yet."

"No," said the Origo, her voice thin and metallic. "Flight got delayed. Tropical depression rolling off the Gulf, and it's got all flights grounded tonight."

"Well, we've got a little problem."

"Not sure I like the way you're saying that."

"Being chased by a biker gang called the Los Cambiantes. Their leader's wife stowed away on the RV trying to get away from him; now he's on the warpath. And he's riding a relic motorcycle. Transfiguration. Using it to turn himself and his friends into werewolves."

"*A gang of werewolves?* Are you shitting me?"

"What?" asked Navathe in the background. "*Werewolves?* Who are you talking to?"

Gendreau put his cell phone on the table. "We might need your help. These guys are tough customers. We have a couple of guns and enough swords to give He-Man a hard-on—oh, and a *grenade launcher*—and we barely got away from them alive."

"Are you still in Keyhole Hills?"

"No, we left this afternoon. On the other side of Almudena, heading toward Killeen right now. We're still an hour or so out."

"We'll head that way now and meet you." The rustle and zip of bags being opened and packed. Navathe's voice came back as he picked up Rook's phone. "You say you had a *grenade launcher*? Where the bloody hell did you get a grenade launcher?"

"Facebook," said Robin. "I know a guy."

"Very cool."

"And very legal." Robin eyed Marina. "What did you mean when you said it's not the motorcycle?"

"Santiago," said Carly's mother, gesturing with her hands as she drove. "There has always been a side to him. Another side, something mean. And, well, the motorcycle, it—como se dice, magnify that side, it strengthen him, work him up. You know?"

"Yeah, I would say turning him into a werewolf definitely exacerbates his more violent tendencies."

"Guess I didn't want to admit it before."

"Dad's not that bad," said Carly.

"You didn't know him before." Marina glanced over her shoulder. "When he was young, before he made road captain, when we first met. His pasion por la vida, his lust for life, was part of why I fell for him in the first place—he was the take-charge kind of man, a leader, I think. Or at least I thought he was. When we had you, he—what's the word?—mellowed out."

"Settled down?" offered Gendreau.

"Yes, settled down. Becoming a father took a little of the heat out of him. That's the Santi *you* know."

"Maybe you mistook a bully for a man with confidence and assertiveness," said Robin. "Wouldn't be the first time that mistake has been made, and it won't remotely be the last."

"Maybe. And now that stupid motorcycle brought it all roaring back. Made it ten times worse."

"I still think he's savable," said Carly.

"We'll see, I guess," said Robin. "The ball's in his court there."

Staring straight ahead, Marina said nothing. A weary sort of determination came off her in waves, like she'd had the veil torn from her eyes and she was seeing the world as it truly was for the first time in perhaps decades. Hard darkness crept into her eyes, as if a sliver of her soul had evaporated, and, like Howard Beale, it gave her the aspect of someone who was mad as hell and wasn't going to take it anymore.

Something fell through the busted skylight and clattered across the floor. Gendreau picked it up.

Pair of glasses. Flip-up sunglasses lens.

Carly stared. "Those are Tuco's glasses."

"Who is Tuco?"

"One of my dad's frien—"

Before she could finish the sentence, the window over the table exploded in a hail of glass and a creature thrust itself into the kitchen.

Flashing teeth like knives, a scaly green monster with a whip tail, like a raptor, a goddamn *velociraptor,* a devil-eyed chupacabra the size of a man. Robin snatched up the rifle and tried to shoot it in the face, but the chupacabra slapped it out of her hands. The pin in the stock broke, the AR cracked in half like a shotgun, and the recoil spring popped out, flinging itself across the room like a snake from a can of peanuts.

While he was distracted, Kenway snatched the tomahawk out of Carly's hands and chopped Tuco's tail off with one hard executioner *thunk!*

Red blood squirted out of the chopped-off tail lying on the table like an obscene Thanksgiving dinner. With an ear-splitting screech, Tuco threw himself into the back hallway in an attempt to escape.

Drawing the short sword out of its scabbard, Robin followed Tuco into the bedroom. The chupacabra was on his way out the back window, skidding in the bloody bedclothes. She grabbed his foot and he wheeled around to bite her. She flinched.

Jaws snapped shut inches from her face. Tuco's breath was a foul fog of dead things and Bud Light. She retaliated with a sword to the chest, and the scales of his skin were so hard that it skated to the side.

Serrated steel agony flashed up her shoulder as a claw raked the back of her arm. *"Aarrgh!"* She swung the sword at his big green face and it bounced off bone, leaving a red gash across his eye socket. Tuco's cavernous mouth opened and a forked tongue slid out of a pore in the floor of his jaw.

"Keel youuuu."

"Go to—"

Talons caught in her ear and cheek, flaying them open, as Tuco slapped her across the face.

Knees buckling, Robin let go of him. She barely made it to the other side of the bed before he flew at her, jaws open and ready to kill. An explosion tore the air in half and Tuco cartwheeled out the window, knocking broken glass out of the frame.

Kenway opened the sawed-off shotgun. "Suck on *that,* chupacabron."

Enormous pain throbbed alongside of her head like a hungry hawk, sharp beak tearing into her with every heartbeat. She touched her ear and winced. Her fingers were sleeved in thick, vivid red blood.

Glass broke up front. Marina loosed a shriek that would make Hitchcock proud. Pushing past Kenway, Robin ran into the kitchen. The windshield was smashed in and Tuco hung over the roof, clutching the steering wheel.

"Let go!" Marina wrenched at the creature's wrists.

Storming through the Winnebago with a purpose, Robin almost made it, but Tuco pulled the wheel to port, throwing her to starboard, and she fell into the door well, slamming against the door and knocking it open. The night tried to claim her.

Barely catching the frame with her fingertips, she dropped the sword and it clattered across the highway, kicking up sparks.

The RV yawed back and forth like a pirate ship on storm-tossed seas, swerving across the yellow line and back again. Carly's mother didn't let go of the wheel, kept fighting the chupacabra for control. But she was losing it. Robin braced herself between the table and the counter. Carly clutched the table, screaming.

Tires barked out long, warbling howls; dishes and cups fell out of the cabinets; the fridge opened and disgorged leftovers onto the floor. The scene was a swinging chaos of noise, a kitchen possessed by howling poltergeists. Kenway staggered up and pointed the shotgun over Robin's shoulder.

She shoved it away. "You can't; you'll hit Marina!"

One particularly deep swerve and a tire exploded with a thunderous slam. The entire Winnebago lurched to that side and dipped in a pendulous bow, and Robin thought—she *hoped*—it was going to right itself, but it kept tilting, tilting, nodding like a drunk. The Tuco-thing slid across the hole where the windshield used to be, screeching helplessly, raking glass out of the frame.

When the Winnebago crashed over onto its side, everybody was thrown against the starboard wall; cans and dishes followed, battering against their heads and backs.

Lizard-gore rocketed across the pavement, Tuco shrieking as his legs were turned into meat crayons under the sliding vehicle. The cabin door was sheared off in a dazzling display of light, and blood sprayed a hot geyser through the open hole. They passed the shoulder and the blood became a choking plume of dirt.

THUD! The guardrail of a bridge slammed into the hood, killing the engine and plunging them into darkness.

• • •

The only light came from the front of the RV, where the headlights projected cones of mist into empty space. One of them was painted in blood, creating a chilling red glow.

Pieces of the cabin's furniture, empty soda cans, very painfully full cans of food, broken dishes, garbage from the bin, medieval weaponry. Robin lay submerged in a pile of debris. "Everybody okay?" she asked, her words slurred by a fat lip. She struggled to sit up. A dozen bruises and cuts blanketed her in three different types of pain. Her face felt like she'd gone a dozen rounds with Muhammad Ali.

One of the swords lay next to her. Miracle she wasn't impaled on it. Kenway grunted somewhere to her left.

"Doc?" she asked.

"Think my fucking arm is broken." The curandero shifted and debris fell over with a clatter. "My ring. Where's my ring?"

"Mamaaaaaa!"

Carly screaming.

Rolling over, Robin clambered to her feet and made her way around the front seat. The teenager was bent double through the remains of the windshield, holding something up.

The only thing between Marina and a long plunge into a rocky crevice was her daughter Carly, their hands clutching each other.

A lightless void yawned beneath them as if they stood at the edge of the world.

Here there be monsters.

"Hold on, Mama," said Carly. "Somebody help me! *Please!*"

Robin crouched over Carly's back and reached for Marina. "Here, give me your other hand," she said, grabbing meaningfully at the air. The woman grasped Robin's wrist, and Robin grasped hers.

Something stirred just to their left.

Pinned between the end of the guardrail and the Winnebago's grille, jammed into the engine, was the scaly chupacabra. The transfigured biker was ruined, hanging half out of the tangle of metal, only his hideous raptor face and one arm free. Tuco realized they were within reach and he reached slowly, languidly, for Robin's face.

Wicked sickle-claws scraped down the hood as he tried to find purchase and pull himself closer. Fresh blood poured across the crinkled metal. He coughed and the sound deteriorated into a bestial hiss. Robin hunkered lower, straining to lift Marina, and the talons came up a few inches short.

Safety glass crackled under her knee. Robin grabbed Marina with both hands and tried to deadlift the woman, trembling, her biceps burning.

Hooks dug into her shoulder. Tuco had her. Sharp points pierced her skin. Too much, too sharp. Her skin gave like wet paper and his claws clapped uselessly against the hood. He pulled himself closer, rib-bones grinding audibly.

Blood from the holes in her shoulder ran down her arm, greasing her hands. Marina started to slip.

"No, *no-no-no!*" Robin shouted.

Carly knotted a hand in her mother's shirt, grabbing the waist of her jeans. Tuco reached out again, one talon inches from Robin's eye.

"Got youuu," he rasped proudly.

A giant blond-haired fist reached in and took hold of the lizard-thing's wrist. "You ain't got shit, son." Kenway straddled Robin's back, pulling Tuco's arm. The monster screamed in pain as bones broke and muscles tore. New blood rushed down the sidelong hood, spraying the women. Kenway dragged what was left of Tuco out of the guardrail and let him fall.

The scaly torso dropped away, dwindling into the shadows, and hit the rocks three full seconds later. *Splat.*

"Here." Kenway reached over Robin.

This caused him to put his weight on her. She felt her center of balance tip toward the windshield hole. "Get off me! You're gonna make me fall!"

He climbed off and tried to sidle in next to her, between her body and the dash, but the space was too small. "Hold on," he told her, and wrapped his arms around her as if he was giving her the Heimlich maneuver. "*I'll* pull you; *you* pull her." His prosthetic leg thumped against her hip and he straddled her again.

His massive arms squeezed the breath out of her. She couldn't speak, but she didn't let go of Marina's arm. Slippery blood. Marina kept sliding. The woman muttered a prayer in Spanish. The look in her maple-brown eyes was unmistakable—the elder Valenzuela was *topped off* with fear, one-hundred-percent filled with terror.

"I'm losing her." Robin clawed for a better grip.

Underneath her, Carly couldn't stand up to get leverage, so all of the woman's weight was on Robin's arms.

The girl grunted. "Got her shirt."

Marina's hands squirted through Robin's, dropping all her weight on Carly. Unbalanced, Robin headbutted Kenway in the chin.

"*Unnh!*" he said, staggering.

Buttons raked off in a rapid-fire *pop-pop-pop-pop*. "Mama, I got you, Mama, *I got you*." The teenager's fists were balled up in the collar of Marina's shirt and her mother hung precariously, her shoulders scrunched up to her ears.

Stitches ripped. Robin crouched over Carly again, reaching for her.

When Marina put her arms up to grab at Robin's hands, it took all the torque off her armpits, and she slid right out of the sleeves, easy-peasy, leaving her daughter holding an empty shirt. They watched with stomach-turning horror as Marina Valenzuela plummeted into the canyon.

Track 17

The scene played out in slow motion, every second of it: the woman's eyes widening in realization, her mouth frozen in a shocked O. Her shriek was a saber across violin strings. Hands and feet pedaled uselessly at the air.

"No!" screamed Carly, struggling. Robin only held her tighter. *"Mama!"*

Darkness swallowed Marina.

"I'm so sorry," Robin muttered endlessly into Carly's hair, "I'm so sorry, baby, I'm so sorry."

The teenager fell silent, cold. Catatonic.

Damn. Robin pried herself away and led the girl into the RV cabin, where Kenway crawled through the busted skylight and reached back in to help Carly out. Gendreau followed her, sliding out and tumbling into the dirt.

Guilt and horror rippled through Robin's chest. She'd gotten involved, gotten involved against her better judgment, and now what? Carly's mother was *dead*. Robin had failed to keep her safe.

This thought wedged itself between her ribs like a dagger.

"Jesus God," Kenway said outside. His voice was desolate. "Goddammit."

Flicking a light switch, Robin took a moment to look for the Osdathregar and some kind of gun, combing through drifts of food that was now so much garbage.

Shotgun was nowhere to be found, but the Osdathregar lay in a tumble of boxes, jammed through a box of Cheerios and slimy with grape jam. Luckily, she'd put her MacBook away, back in the overhead compartment with some throw pillows and blankets. It would probably be all right until she could come back and properly salvage their stuff, barring some unforeseen theft or the gas tank exploding.

"Hey," Gendreau grunted. "Could you find my ring? I lost it in the crash."

"I can try."

Several taut minutes passed as she dug through drifts of what was now garbage, trying to find the curandero's relic ring, keenly aware of the passage of time. Wouldn't be long until the Wolfgang caught up with them, and she wanted to be on the move long before then.

Ah, there it is. Mystical energy wafted off of it like fog seeping out of a freezer. Hidden under the valance, behind the kitchen sink. Straddling the window, she ripped the curtain away and grabbed the ring.

As soon as she touched it, a vision crowded into her head.

Two figures stood in a strange room much like a safe-deposit-box room at the bank, but tighter, claustrophobic. Illuminated by sickly fluorescent beams on a low ceiling. Soft white static filled the air with silent snow, as if she couldn't get a good fix on the scene.

One of the drawers lay open between them, and the person on the left had taken out something that glittered red in the misty light. "Last one I want to try on you today." The magician woman, the Origo, Rook. "One of the newer relics. Not in historical terms—the organic matter is quite old—but it is a recent acquisition. May not be as powerful as the cane you had, at least right now, but with time you may find other nuances, other pathways that will help you unlock its true potential."

"It's fine," said Gendreau, the other figure, coalescing from the fog of time. "Took time to attune to the cane; I expect no less from this."

"Don't let her ruin this one," said the Origo.

"I won't," said Gendreau, slipping the ring onto his finger. "You can rest assured of that." The magician absentmindedly caressed the scar across his throat. "Okay, I guess we should give it a try."

"Remember what I taught you," said the Origo. "Close your eyes. It's like dowsing for water. Let it into your mind. Let her into your mind."

Gendreau's eyes eased shut. "I hate this part."

"I know," said the Origo, "it's like hooking into the neighborhood junction box and stealing power from the power company."

"With the potential electrocution hazard."

"Not if you're careful."

"Thanks for doing this for me, Haruko. I hate being a fuckup, and you're good at not making me feel like one."

"You're not a fuckup." A wry smile. "Now concentrate."

With a start, Robin opened her eyes and a chill coursed down her arms. *Haruko? Where have I heard that name before? Wasn't that—*

A red light glittered in the rubble. She dug it out and discovered one of the GoPros. After a moment of indecision and guilt, she strapped it to her chest. She would just raw-dog a bunch of footage and sort through it later. Assuming, of course, there would *be* a later. She felt bad about filming everything—especially after what happened to Marina—but this action was too good to let go to waste.

The show must go on.

"Do you have the shotgun?" she asked Kenway, peering through the skylight hole.

"Yeah."

She sighed. The AR-15 was useless now, the magazine spent, the few grenades that were left scattered across the Winnebago. She took the black tactical tomahawk and a katana that had miraculously managed to stay attached to the wall (which was now the ceiling). Didn't have time to look for anything else.

More shotgun shells were in a box in one of the kitchen drawers. "We got to go," she said to her boyfriend, wriggling through the hole in the roof. As soon as she got outside, she smelled gasoline. "They're gonna be right behind us."

"Don't have to tell me twice."

Gendreau pointed across the arroyo. "There's a house." On the other side of the dry river bed, a dark square loomed against the night, tall and angular. No lights. "Or something. Did you find my ring?"

"Yeah," Robin said, holding it out.

The magician reached out, but she didn't put it in his hand. Instead, she forced him to awkwardly pull it out of her fingers.

At first, he gave her a strange, almost angry look—or maybe offended, a little confused. He twisted it back onto his index finger, still staring at her with that vaguely alarmed expression, and walked away.

Kenway lifted the catatonic Carly up and carried her like a baby.

No night sounds meant the soundtrack to their flight was only the scuffing of their shoes on the dusty asphalt. Overhead, a galaxy of stars blasted a million pinholes in a beautiful black sky. They hobbled around the back of the Winnebago and up onto the nearby bridge, where, to their surprise, a motel lurked squat and dark at the bottom of the hill from the house.

Their first stop was in the office. Kenway stomp-kicked the front door open, almost falling on his ass, and they went inside.

Pitch-black darkness. Robin ran into a chair and barked her shins on a coffee table, swearing. "Here you go." A light winked on behind her, casting a stark but faint glow across the room. Gendreau had a little keychain flashlight.

"This place out of business or what?" Kenway deposited Carly on a tweed sofa, stirring up a cloud of dust.

Behind the front desk, Robin searched for keys. A corkboard on the wall was covered in yellowed, dog-eared pieces of paper. A row of nails was hammered into the bottom of the frame, but no keys on them. "I guess so." She pulled out drawers, searched through cabinets. Finally, in one of the bottom drawers, she found a shoebox full of receipts. Sliding around loose in the box were a handful of keys with plastic fobs on them. Robin took the key for suite 22 and put the box back in the drawer, kicking it shut. "Come on," she said, taking her sword and tomahawk and leading them back outside.

"Looks like the abandoned *Psycho* set or something," said Gendreau. On the sidewalk, Robin paused to listen for motorcycle engines. Nothing yet.

She led them down a short corridor between the office building and the suites. The motel was constructed in an L shape, with a big pool in the middle. A chain-link fence kept visitors out of the pool area, and a chain wrapped around the latch. Long strips of plastic had been threaded through the mesh for privacy. She expected it to be locked, but the chain pulled apart. They slipped through and she closed the gate.

Suite 22 lay on the other side. As they skirted the pool, Robin leaned over to look inside and found only dry cement and a large puddle of stinking green water. One whole side of the pool was thrown into shadow by the moon in the east.

Gendreau lingered poolside, shining his tiny flashlight into the pit. "You know, we could hide in there. They'd never think to look in the pool, you know. Besides, that crap at the bottom stinks so much, I don't think they could smell us. Smells like Los Angeles crawled in there and died."

As if on cue, the snore of a fleet of motorcycles came burring into earshot.

"Time to test your hypothesis." Kenway picked his way down the plaster stairs in the shallow end, his prosthetic leg threatening to collapse out from under him, and they followed him. He weeble-wobbled like an old robot. "Lord help," the veteran said, setting Carly down in the shade as softly as possible and dropping onto his ass in exhaustion. "I felt safer in a war zone."

She handed him the box of shells she'd salvaged from the RV. He opened them and filled his pockets with them. "Did you really dig that damn GoPro out of the Brave?"

"Yeah."

"Whatever the hell for?"

"If I'm going to go through this shit, I might as well get some useful footage out of it."

He sighed, shaking his head.

"What?"

He said nothing.

The sound of the motorcycle engines didn't seem to be getting any closer. They stopped on the other side of the bridge.

"They're checking out the RV," Gendreau muttered.

Several minutes of silence passed.

She thought she heard someone yelling, *Fuck, it's Tuco,* and further words that were too soft to make out.

Then, from a distance, a sound came ripping through the air that at first Robin mistook for a motorcycle engine starting up. Goose bumps rippled down her arms as the voice became a roar of pain and rage, a guttural, inhuman vocalization, the wail of a feral beast on the verge of madness. Could have been the same as St. George heard as he plunged his sword into the belly of the dragon; could have been Grendel as Beowulf tore off the beast's arm.

"Oh, my God, oh, my God," muttered Gendreau next to her. He trembled violently, on the verge of bolting. "He found Marina."

Robin stayed him with a hand, but she couldn't think of anything reassuring to tell him. She clutched the mute teenager to her chest, and Carly pressed her hands against her ears. A thin, breathy squeal slipped through her teeth, reminiscent of a whining dog. "I'm gonna get you out of here," Robin told her, stroking her hair, "Gonna keep you safe. Take care of you." Didn't escape the witch-hunter's notice that Carly was now in a similar position to herself: deprived of a mother, menaced by a monstrous father. Even reacting the same way Robin had as a teenager six years before. Out of her mind, mute. Closed off. Dissociated.

What bothered Robin was this question: if she hadn't told Marina to grab her hands, would it have ended the same way? Did they *ever* have a chance of saving her? For God's sake, was it Robin's fault the woman was now lying broken at the bottom of the ravine?

She sighed. She'd flagellate herself later. Right now, she had a job to do, and that job was keeping them alive. "Need you to be quiet, baby," she whispered into Carly's ear. "They're going to hear us."

To her surprise, the breathless whining stopped.

Glass smashed somewhere nearby. Kenway slowly closed the shotgun breech with a subtle *click.*

Tension wound into Robin's body, hardening her fists, her heart trying to hammer its way out of her rib cage. The others were all but invisible; their breathing was a soft, shallow susurrus. The magician sounded like he might have been trying not to sob out loud, vibrating with fear.

"WHERE ARE YOU?" snarled a cavernous voice from the pits of Hell.

Wood and steel barked as a door was smashed in. The paracord wrapped around the handle of the tomahawk creaked gently in Robin's hand. Her bladder screamed for release, the muscles in her legs taut and ready to move.

"Come out, you murdering bitch! I know you're here SOMEWHERE!"

Itchy sweat crawled down the side of Robin's face.

Doors slammed open and windows shattered across the suite

complex. The Los Cambiantes were going from room to room, looking for them. *"You can't hide! I CAN SMELL YOU!"* Santiago's voice was an earthquake with a mouth.

"God, dear God," Gendreau breathed.

Steel screamed as the gate to the pool was torn out of its frame and thrown aside. Scuffling feet and scraping claws came out onto the patio over Robin's head, rustling through the dead and naked hedges. More doors were bashed in. Windows imploded. *"I will find you! You're in one of these goddamned rooms, and it's only a matter of time!"*

Terrific booms echoed off the inside of the pool as the werewolves slung furniture around, knocking holes in the suites' walls. An old tube television came hurtling over the edge of the empty pool and slammed into the mucky puddle at the bottom, the screen shattering. Filthy water sprayed up the walls, speckling Robin's face with slime. The magician's shaking intensified into a St. Vitus' Dance of terror. *Just hold steady, man,* she thought, *stay strong, they'll give up and move on eventually. They'll start looking for us in the house up there, and when they can't find us there, they'll search up in the hills, and then—*

One of the werewolves came crawling around the edge of the pool, slow and sinuous in the dim moonlight.

She had no love for what she saw. The creature had the peaked shoulders of a hyena and jagged, twisted limbs. Patches of greasy skin glistened through its coarse black hair. Naked as a jaybird, the wolf-man turned to peer into the swimming pool with a feral, misshapen parody of a human face: teeth as long as fingers, beady black eyes, gaping nostrils, all embedded in a head like a potato. Two hoary gray ears cupped the quiet night.

No light reflected from its retinas, which told Robin it couldn't see in the dark. Still, was the moon enough it could pick them out in the shadows of the pool's bowl?

It stared for what felt like a week.

The pool stank ferociously of stagnant water. She hoped the

stench hid their scent. A nub of darkness moved in the corner of her eye and she realized Kenway was pointing the shotgun at it.

"TO ME, FUCKERS!" snarled Santiago.

The werewolf jerked its head up at the sound of their leader's voice and scuttled out of sight. Another window shattered, one last desultory act of vandalism.

"What are they doing now?" Gendreau breathed in her ear.

"No idea."

Silence dragged on forever. Angry muttering echoed from the other side of the suite complex. Then they could hear the transfigured bikers charging up the hill. The Los Cambiantes were searching the abandoned house. *"Find them,"* came a shout from the moonlit sands behind the motel. *"Kill that murdering cunt."*

"They're gone," Gendreau whispered. "They fell for it."

She pressed a fingertip to his lips and he made an effort to still himself. Carly shuddered, and put her face in her hands.

The magician wouldn't stop talking. "We should make a break for it while they're up there in the house," he hissed. "We'll run the other way, across the road, and go into the ravine. We'll hide under the bridge and—"

She interrupted him, squeezing his mouth with a hand. "Shut up," she breathed into his ear.

He nodded, chastised.

Robin took his hand and put it on Carly's shoulder, and put the girl aside so she could move freely. As carefully as possible, without grinding her shoe sole into the plaster floor, she raised up and looked over the rim of the pool.

Motionless, a shape crouched in the moonlight, staring at the suites that faced the inner courtyard.

Remnants of a red lumberjack-plaid shirt streamered from its shoulders in pennants. Werewolf's back was to her. Was he waiting for them to come out of hiding? What the hell? Confused, she hunkered down again, heart racing. Her hand ached, the tomahawk's corded handle biting into her palm.

Turning, the werewolf approached the pool's edge and stared up at the dark house on the sagebrush hill. Robin tensed, preparing to launch herself upward. The werewolf looked down into the pool, beady eyes glittering.

It snorted once, watery snot peppering her face.

A suspicious growl gathered deep in the monster's throat.

Stepping up the curve of the pool's bowl, Robin leapt up and grabbed a handful of hair at the pit of the werewolf's throat. She used her weight to pull him into the pool, and the biker landed on his shoulders with a wet, heavy slap.

Scrambling astride the creature's belly, she began to tomahawk it, but the werewolf snapped at her face with a mouth big enough to crush her skull whole, bristling with jagged yellow teeth that reeked of tobacco. Again, *snap,* again, with that vicious Ferrari-engine growl. She'd managed to wedge the axe-haft in its mouth. She swore in a panic, holding him at arm's length, bench-pressing his face.

Someone unsheathed the katana on her back and plunged it deep into the monster's guts, *splutch,* again, *splutch,* and again, *splutch.* Kenway, beside her. The growling died off into a wretched gurgle, and the thing underneath her kicked and bucked in mindless hysterics.

Bright red blood ran down the slope of the pool into the dirty water.

"Fuck you," coughed the werewolf.

Amazing. Still wasn't dead. Well, she'd solve that problem for him. Tossing the tomahawk aside, she took the katana out of her boyfriend's hands and pointed it under the beast's chin, putting her weight on it. The sword blade slid through the werewolf's throat and up into its skull.

Faint crackling echoed up the steel as she pierced eggshell bone. "Grrk." The werewolf relaxed.

Still straddling the hairy corpse, Robin tried to will her heart to settle down. Claw-wounds down her arms stung, building into an orchestra-swell of pain as more dark blood trickled into the swamp. Subtle ripples across the water made the moon dance.

"Thanks," she told Kenway.

"Yeah."

"Come on," she told them, sheathing the sword. "We can't move this big bastard, and they'll see him as soon as they come back down. We'll head out the other way while they're distracted in the house."

"Why didn't *I* think of that?" said Gendreau.

"Lead the way, Cochise." Kenway handed Robin the shotgun and lifted Carly.

The crew started down the corridor that led back to the front parking lot, but the privacy-fence gate had been torn down and lay haphazardly across the path, only traversable by walking on the noisy chain link.

At the end of the corridor, a hulking shadow lurked on the sidewalk. *Damn, they're standing guard down here,* she thought. A shape came trudging around the far corner of the L-shaped building, walking into the pool area on all fours. If he looked across the pool into the shadows under the awning. . . .

To her left yawned a black doorway. Bracing the shotgun with the haft of the tomahawk, she darted into a shabby little apartment with outdated decor.

Everything was covered in a fuzzy layer of dust. A surprisingly pristine calendar hanging on the wall said it was September the year of our Lord 2005. Probably the office manager's living quarters. Santiago's wolves had demolished the place; the sofa was upended, the kitchen cabinets ripped open. Luckily, there was no food to make a mess with.

"What is that smell?" asked Gendreau, and Robin's boot squelched on wet carpet. A pungent, sugary parody of Honey Smacks and chicken bouillon roiled up into her nostrils—wolves had pissed on the floor. She turned the deadbolt on the door that led to the front office and found it blessedly empty.

Once they were inside, Robin shut the apartment door and wedged it shut with a folding chair. Wouldn't be much help, but it was better than nothing. She joined Kenway and Gendreau behind the front counter.

The veteran grabbed her wrist and jerked her rudely to the floor.

"Ow," said Robin. "What gives?"

"Something out there." Kenway jabbed a finger toward the front entrance. "On the road. Can't get out this way. Fucking *huge*, whatever it is."

She peered over the Formica counter. Motorcycles were parked in a staggered row in front of the office. A great dark shadow lumbered back and forth on the other side of the fleet, pacing protectively in the watery moonlight. At this distance, it was the approximate size of a buffalo. Maybe bigger.

"Looks like sabotaging the bikes is out of the question," said Gendreau.

"You had that idea, too?"

Kenway shifted uneasily. "Can't go forward, can't go backward. Now what?"

Track 18

The hour stretched on as the four of them sat behind the front desk of the foreclosed motel. Kenway propped Carly against the counter, where she stared desolately at the carpet. "No way we can take them on by ourselves," muttered the veteran, only a lighter smear of gray in the darkness. "Not with just two blades and a handful of shotgun shells." His tone made it clear that this was something he wasn't used to saying: "What are we gonna do? He ain't gonna give up on finding us, not after what happened to Marina."

"We're fucked," said Gendreau.

"Hate to agree with you," said the vet, "but yeah, as much as it pains me to say, we are well and truly fucked."

Seeking some kind of solace or strategy, Robin searched the shadows for her mother's ethereal ghost, but Annie was nowhere to be found. "I don't know. I just don't. Guess we wait. Wait for them to come back down from the house, then we'll go out the back and head up there ourselves and . . . chill in the attic or something 'til morning."

The two men said nothing. She supposed they agreed with her plan. Best they had, anyway.

Moonlight fell through a small window in the door as she looked outside. Everything was rendered in shades of gray. Straight ahead, the sidewalk stretched across the front of the L-shaped suite complex. To her left gaped an empty parking lot. She leaned so she could see the fallen gate to her right.

A dark shape came loping up the pool-area corridor. It clutched the gate and gently lifted it out of the way, leaning it against the clapboard wall of the L, and the werewolf dropped back on all fours, walking up the corridor in the slow, hip-rolling saunter of a caged panther, moving up the sidewalk toward the parking lot. As she watched it move, Robin wondered where the extra mass came from when people were transfigured—Theresa's hog-monster form was easily ten times larger than her original shape. These wolf-men were twice the size of an average human, with hulking shoulders, barrel chests, towering shoulders.

"Bitch gotta be here somewhere," said a voice outside.

A shadow cut through the moonlight in the corridor window. "Can't believe they wasn't in the house. Thought for sure they'd be up there in the house, shakin' and pissin' they panties."

"Must have been Tuco that caused the crash. That weird motherfucker was down there with Marina's body."

"So it's Tuco's fault?"

"I ain't sayin—"

"Well, he's *dead,* so—" said a third.

"Don't give a damn whose fault it is. Santiago sure don't. He just wants that girl's ass, and any of her friends we can find out here. Wouldn't pay to piss him off today. He wrecked Pops, according to Javi. Said he ate Guillermo's face right off his skull. Killed him."

Kenway swore under his breath. "Gil got ganked."

"Yeah. Shit's crazy," said one of the wolves.

"Man, I kinda hate that, y'know?" someone replied. "I liked Pops."

"Getting too big for his britches. He the one that let this bitch run off with Marina. He had it coming."

"Still. . . ."

"What is going on?" asked one of the bikers.

"Whatchu mean, man?"

"Like, this werewolf shit. Feel like I'm losin' my fucking mind. This shit real? I feel like I'm not real. This is some seriously weird shit. Right? We on the same page here?"

Trying to internalize the relic's influence, Robin realized. Trying to work out their cognitive dissonance, beginning to "converge," the Dogs' term for the merging of their magic-influenced minds and non-influenced minds, the spark of understanding that—

"This shit ain't real?" asked one of the men.

—the strange phenomena they were experiencing wasn't just coincidence, or a fever-dream, or a hallucination. It was real life, these transformations and half-lucid fugue states were actually happening, and they had a source.

"Feel like I'm taking crazy pills. Found a dead cat on my porch two months ago; thought the neighbor's dog did it or something. Dreams I've been having . . . dreaming about running naked in the desert, huntin' down rabbits and shit out in the badlands. Waking up with dirty feet. Blood in my bathtub. So, it's real? All of it?"

One of the shadows shrugged.

"You too?"

"What you think's doing it? D'you think we're—"

"Real werewolves?"

"Yeah. Like, d'you think silver hurts us?"

"Don't know. Think that's just Hollywood bullshit."

They're like . . . false werewolves, thought Robin. *Ginned-up bullshit from that Transfiguration relic in Santiago's motorcycle. That movie stuff—silver bullets, full moon, none of that applies here. You can kill them with steel.* She caught Kenway's expression and had the feeling he silently agreed.

"I'd ask Santi, but—that—man, I just—he's fuckin' scary, dude.

I don't want to piss him off, you know? I mean, does he even know what it is? What's causing it?"

"If he does, he hasn't mentioned it."

"Is *he* the one doin' it?"

Someone laughed. "Man, Santi's a hard-ass and he's got chops, but he couldn't pour out a piss-pot if the instructions were on the bottom. I doubt he's into that eye-of-newt black-magic shit."

"Don't let him hear you say that."

Another voice rang out from the pool area. "Hey, Donato. What is this in the pool? Was this always here? Looks like something got trapped in here and died." A pregnant pause. Robin could still smell the musty pond-scum stink of the stagnant water; it lingered in her nostrils like a stain. "What the shit? It's José. The bitch killed José."

"Got some kind of Lady Rambo on our hands, boys," said one of them. "First grenades, now she out here cuttin' us up. Who *is* this chick?"

"Santi gonna be pissed. And you know piss runs downhill, man."

"That's why he don't need to find out."

"Find her," rumbled the beast.

"Hey, what are you guys up to?" asked another biker, joining them. Sounded like he wasn't alone, by the *plop-plop* of bare feet. "Ain't nobody in the house. Santi says we're gonna go across the road and fan out, look for 'em out in the desert. 'Hands Across America' or some shit."

"I think we should keep looking here at the motel."

"You'll do what I tell you to do," said Santiago. He sounded tired, his voice raspy, low, a breathless murmur. "And you'll do it. Unless you want what Gil got."

"Yeah, okay, man."

"Good. Goddamn, it stinks out here. Pool smells like rancid frog shit. Hidey, you go down and check the RV again—they might have doubled back on us."

"You don't think Max woulda seen 'em?"

"Just do what I told you," said Santi. "You fuckers are like herding cats, you know that?" *Snick, snick, snick,* the ignition of a lighter. Santi firing up a cigarette. "Anybody know where José went?"

"Said something about going to take a piss."

A moment of silence, and then Santi blew out smoke and said, "Why didn't he just piss on the floor? He's a dog. That's what dogs do."

More silence.

"Don't shrug at me, asshole. Go get him." Santi walked away into the parking lot. "You guys come with me. We're gonna go look out there across the road. They might have headed south and gone to ground up there in those hills. Lot of places to hide."

The other men followed him, leaving the parking lot desolately still.

"I think we should sneak up the hill and go hide in the house while they're out of the picture," muttered Gendreau, a few minutes later.

Her boyfriend scratched his beard, a dry sawing noise in the shadowy quiet.

Robin studied Carly's emotionless gaze. The girl seemed to be transfixed by something on the other side of the planet. Robin waved her hand in front of Carly's face. No reaction. She lightly patted her face, and this time Carly looked away, shifting her whole body to the side and tightening into a fetal position. *Okay, so she's not totally out of it. She's just dissociating.*

"All right," said Robin. "Let's move."

She got up and pulled the chair out from under the door handle, revealing the apartment.

Relief. No wolf-man waiting in the cramped living room to ambush her. She checked the breech on the shotgun and led them outside, preserving the silence with an index finger to her lips. The four of them slipped out the back and around the pool area.

Steps made out of cross-ties zigzagged up the hill toward the house, and tufts of chaparral bristled from the sand. Robin found herself exposed on a hillside with no tree cover, showered in frosty blue moonlight. She glanced over her shoulder and saw a constellation across the desert: Santi's ants crawling their way toward the south horizon. Flashlights and lighters twinkled in the dark.

Dread of being spotted up here on this bald slope made her pick up the pace, running with the shotgun at low-ready. The tomahawk's handle beat against her knee.

Ten or twenty years earlier, the house on the hill might have been nice, if a bit boring. Utilitarian. Puritan, even. Probably aiming at "Victorian," but there was no unnecessary ornamentation, no gingerbread scrollwork. Just no-nonsense clapboard.

Darkness gaped at the top of the steps; the doors had been torn down and thrown into the front yard. Robin raised the shotgun and pushed into the house, rolling her steps, swiveling back and forth cop-style. Stacks of old magazines, newspapers, and novels were hoarded against the baseboards in jagged stacks. Lawn chairs in various states of abuse shared space with about a dozen aquariums—which, thankfully, had been empty, because the werewolves had smashed them and strewn the floor with shards of cloudy glass. A tweed sofa was soaked in sour piss, a coffee table smashed in half. Walls were sprayed with a litany of obscene graffiti and had gaping holes smashed into them, through which Robin could see adjacent rooms.

Ranch implements were nailed up like the decorations at a fancy down-home restaurant: horse tack, a scythe, horseshoes, a two-man tree saw, frontiersman snowshoes that looked like wooden tennis rackets. Also a few car parts and rear tags: Arizona. New Jersey. North Dakota. New Mexico.

Black screws picked out a missing item about the size of a Frisbee.

Followed by an increasingly tired-looking Gendreau, Kenway stepped up onto the front porch, cradling Carly in his beefy arms.

Robin paused to look out the window.

The biker that had been ordered to go find José had returned to the pool and was dragging his shaggy werewolf corpse out of the blue pit.

Behind her, Gendreau turned his head sideways to read the titles on the weather-beaten paperback novels with his penlight. Stephen King, Nora Roberts, an assortment of nineties sword-and-sorcery.

"They're afraid of him," said Robin.

"Afraid of what he'll do if he sees them fuck up." Gendreau picked up one of the Koontz novels and tried to open it, but the pages were stuck together. He dropped it like a hot potato and wiped his hand on the wallpaper. "Hate to wonder what he did to poor Gil back there." The magician sighed and looked toward the second floor, as if beseeching the gods for guidance. "If we can get into it, I think we should hide in the attic."

Framed photographs lined the stairwell walls, depicting an older couple, both of them wearing rose-colored bifocals. None of them looked newer than 1995. Progressively older photos of two boys and a girl.

The bedrooms upstairs were completely devoid of furniture except for a gang of ratty-looking mattresses, also foul with werewolf piss. Neatly stacked collection of shoeboxes, each one full of various things: baby-food jars full of what looked like lab specimens preserved in formaldehyde, Beanie Babies, USB thumb drives, broken china. Another bedroom held a massive stockpile of clothes hangers, while another was wallpapered with pages torn from porno magazines.

As soon as Gendreau stepped into the porn room, he recoiled like he'd walked into a spiderweb and pulled his shirt over his face. "Jesus Christ."

Other than an eternity of nudity the only thing in the room was a moldy-looking cardboard box in the corner. As if beckoning them closer, a mannequin arm stuck up out of the box.

"Hell, no," said Robin, leaving.

Didn't seem to be an attic. No access ladder, at any rate. "Probably full of bullshit like the rest of the house, anyway," said the curandero.

"Hey," Robin said, mildly.

"Yes?"

"Got a question for you."

"Fire away," Gendreau said, arming sweat from his forehead.

"Don't know if it's my demon blood or what, but sometimes when I touch things—relics, or just sentimental possessions—I get a flash of insight about who handled it last. Sometimes just a sensation, a snapshot of their mental state. Sometimes it's a whole moment in time." Robin pointed at the ring glistening on Gendreau's finger. "When I touched that ring back there in the Winnebago, I saw you and Rook, standing together in a place that looked like a card catalog in a library. Think it was the day she gave it to you."

Wincing in exhaustion, the magician glanced at his finger and let his hand fall back to his side. "Weird. Kinda cool, I guess. Did you ever tell me you could do that? I don't remember you telling me you could do that."

"Didn't seem important. It's never really helped me. I mean, it's how I found out the Euchiss boys poisoned Joel Ellis last year, but it wasn't really vital information. Something different happened this time."

"Oh, yeah? What was that?"

"You called her Haruko," said Robin.

She didn't say anything else, opting to let Gendreau fill the silence.

"Now is not a great time to talk about this," he said curtly, calling her bluff, and started to walk away. Robin reached out to clutch his shoulder, and as if by instinct, he shrugged her hand away, his hand up in a guarded posture, creating distance between the magic-eating demon and his relic.

"That's Leon's wife, isn't it?" She held his stare. "Wayne's mother. They think she died of cancer. Why are you hiding her from them?"

"We'll talk about this later, when we're not running for our lives." The magician turned and marched down the stairs. "But I will tell you that we have a very good reason."

"Better be a great one."

• • •

Along the top rim of the kitchen cabinetry were about a hundred empty liquor bottles, their luster lost. The counters were a wilderness of garbage and filthy appliances. Three refrigerators stood open, each one full of a nasty ichor dried to a scummy spackle. Beer bottles and plastic wrappers jutted out of the black paste. The sour miasma floating in the humid kitchen could gag a Sasquatch.

"Basement," said Kenway, pointing at an open door. Gendreau shined his keychain light, holding his shirt over his face like a colonial fop with a lace handkerchief. A stairwell led down into black nothing.

"After you," he said, adjusting his grip on Carly.

"You first."

"You have the flashlight."

"Ugh." Gendreau plodded down them, his silhouette pushing the dim white glow down the stairs. Wooden risers complained under his expensive Italian leather shoes.

"I'll stay up here and keep an eye out," Robin told them.

Kenway's voice came from somewhere down in the dark. "I'll leave Carly down here with David Blaine and come up there with you."

"David Blaine?" asked Gendreau.

"Need you down there protecting her, babe."

Kenway's reply was muffled. *"Uhhh?"*

"Your ego will live," said Robin.

"You know me better than that, lady. I'm not leavin' you alone with Teen Wolf out there."

"Goddammit." Robin pushed past him. The stairs complained, creaking and crackling as her hand slid down the dusty, smooth wood of the baluster. Gendreau stood in the middle of the basement, shining his keychain light to and fro. "If I come down here with you, will you be satisfied?"

The light passed over a surprisingly large basement and a collection of junk: A dirty work table with nothing on it. Boxes of rags. Empty paint cans. Cold furnace. Stained mattress. Two red jerry cans that stank of gasoline. A clawfoot bathtub full of green muck that smelled like burnt plastic.

"Stinks down here," she said.

"You don't say." Gendreau stifled a cough.

"Should mask our scent the same way the stagnant swimming pool did earlier."

Gendreau shined his flashlight in Kenway's face. "Mister, I need you to explain that *David Blaine* crack. Have you ever seen me swallow a goldfish? Do I look like some kind of sleepy-eyed two-bit street busker to you?"

"Yikes. Did I hit a nerve?"

• • •

Underneath the stairs was a closet, unfinished, with naked studs, and not the good kind. Cobwebs draped in cotton bunting between the rafters, promising spiders and, thankfully, breaking that promise. They hid in this shadowy alcove and pulled the door shut, then sat, blind, to rest. And wait. And listen. Listen for the furtive movements of an investigating wolf-man, or the angry carnage of a temper tantrum elsewhere in the house.

But they heard nothing. Nothing but the howl of the wind and the subtle, restless movements of the elderly house.

"Miss Martine," murmured Gendreau.

"Yeah?"

"You should change your *Malus Domestica* show into a conversation-based podcast format. Without so much, you know . . . screaming and running, and whatnot. Just a nice chat. A nice goddamn chat. With a studio cat with a funny name. Pop filters and nice chairs and a cappuccino machine."

"You know me. I ain't the talking type. I'm a doer."

The magician sighed. "Then we need a plan."

"We do," said Kenway, a breath against her cheek. "Any ideas, Mr. Wizard?"

"Lure them into the house and burn it down," said Robin.

"Too dangerous," said Gendreau.

"More dangerous than being killed by a bunch of werewolves?"

"Too easy for things to go wrong," said Kenway. "For one of us to fall into our own trap and get stuck in the house. Go down with it. Besides, we probably wouldn't be able to get them all in here at once."

They sat in their own individual solitude for a little while. She couldn't tell how long. The darkness robbed her of her sense of time. Felt like ten minutes, might have been a half hour.

"I've been meaning to ask you something, Doc," said Robin.

"Another question, huh?"

"Good-hearted Muggles like you can use magic when you're not a witch? I thought the power was channeled from Ereshkigal herself. In that vision I saw, you said you could hear her."

"The power is user-agnostic," said the curandero, shifting his weight in the shadows. "You know how a fetus is just a wad of genetic matter until a certain point in gestation where its brain activity ramps up into something closer to a human. Teratomas are like that pre-fetal wad of tissue—too dumb to know any better. Ereshkigal doesn't know where her essence is going any more than you know where your tax dollars are going. Of course, once that teratoma reaches a certain stage and develops sentience, then all bets are off. But she knows it's going somewhere. She sends whispers. Patronage magic, from Ereshkigal in particular, comes with a price. If you use it too much, or too hard, she can drive you insane. The exchange of power opens a line of communication. Whenever a heart-road is opened, it's like calling a wrong number. The person on the other end can talk to you, but they don't know who you are."

"Like Santiago?"

"Exactly. Right now, he's acting as an unregulated warlock. We've been charged, as you well know, with taking custody of unregulated relics like his motorcycle."

"And there's no supernatural caller ID?"

"Not that I am aware of."

"Fetuses? Death-goddesses? This is not a conversation I want to have in a dark basement," said Kenway. "Especially not under an abandoned house in the middle of nowhere."

Question answered, Robin fell silent again.

"Home alone!" she said a few minutes later, startling the two men.

"What?"

"Home alone. The movie, *Home Alone.* Where Macaulay Culkin kicked the shit out of those two robbers," she explained. "All that Cracker Barrel stuff up there on the walls—think we could set up some traps with it? Get 'em as they come in through the doors?"

The veteran shook his head. "Too many points of entry. Not only do you have two, maybe three door entrances, you've also got maybe eight to ten windows, and that's not counting the second floor and the windows in the attic—"

"Witch windows."

"What?" blurted Kenway. "Seriously? Why do they call 'em witch windows?"

"They're not witch windows," said Gendreau. "Witch windows are sashed windows half-rotated to one side. They were designed crooked to confuse witches back in the colonial days, to keep them from getting into the house."

"Dormer windows?" asked Robin.

"Dormers are those little protrusions coming out of the roof slope like doghouses. You know, they have their own little roofs."

"Then what the hell are they?"

The curandero's shrug scuffed in the dark silence. "Attic windows? Vents?"

"They're windows; they have glass in 'em."

"Who the fuck cares?" asked Kenway.

"How do you know so much about home architecture?" asked Robin.

"Because I come from a family that's always lived in houses with gables and dormers and things like that?" The magician made a face. "What're you asking me for? You grew up in a Victorian gingerbread. Those things are, like, sixty-five percent gable."

"Can we get back to the plan here?" asked Kenway.

Robin leaned over him. "Whaddaya call those spinny metal thingies on the roof that look like Jiffy Pops? I saw one of those belch fire like a dragon one night after I lit a witch up in Colorado. Fuckin' top just blew off, the fire was jetting out blue and red—"

A big warm hand clapped over her mouth.

"Plan," said Kenway. "Can we get back to it? They could come back here any minute."

She nodded and he let go.

"*Home Alone*?" asked Gendreau. "Can we do it?"

"Like I said: too many entry points, not enough gear. I only saw a couple of bear traps on the wall, and there's nothing else up there in good enough shape to fashion into a trap—if any of us even knew how to make traps out of it all. Besides, can you see any of that stuff up there stopping a monster militia?"

"So . . . what?" asked Robin. "All we can do is hide? And wait?"

"Maybe. I don't know. That's why I'm trying to brainstorm here."

"Wait to die?" asked Gendreau.

"Fuck that noise," said Robin. She cracked the shotgun open, checked to make sure it was still loaded, and bullwhipped it shut again. *Click*.

• • •

After a long, unproductive discussion, they slept.

Well, all but one of them dozed off, in that fitful strange way that people do when in the helpless throes of slow panic—that way that a child can drift off to sleep buried under a blanket, confident in the existence of a slithering closet-monster lying in wait underneath their bed, and then wake up in the morning, having forgotten all about whatever had menaced them in the night.

That one who did not sleep now, Robin Martine, sat by the door, filled with crawling ants of anxiety, pressed into her boyfriend's feverish hard bulk, with her knees up and her hands clasped against her belly.

She breathed through her mouth to stay quiet. Listened for intruders. She wanted to sleep. Her eyes were grainy. But—

But—

Listen.

Smells competed in the cramped space. The musk of Kenway's sweat; the moldy quiet of the long-disused closet; the exotic tang of Gendreau's cologne; the always lurking rotten-egg-campfire stink of Robin's sulphurous demon half, forever waiting for a reason to rampage and kill. Her own personal dark side.

What would it take to trigger another transformation? Would they have to bite off her arm, the way Theresa the hog-witch had? Was there some other method of bringing that side of her out (and there her mind interjected with *turning me inside out* as if she were some kind of hand puppet lined with the velvet of heresy, which gave her gruesome mental images and the perennially horrible word *degloving*)? Would she need to touch another demon, like last time? God forbid—literally—would she have to touch her father again?

She wondered if she could control it this time.

When she'd transformed into that otherworldly thing before, that sinister, ligneous creature, it had been a slow, gradual change. She'd had time to adjust, as much as you can adjust to having a skinless snake for an arm and wood for skin.

Her skin had, indeed, been greenish wood like her demon father's, hoary with red hair like flames. The same green shade as her childhood home. Her demon-self had been constructed—or constructed itself—from the clapboard and floor planks of Wayne's dimensionally iffy nightmare house, Andras's decrepit prison, that ancient Victorian that only existed in Robin's childhood memories, 1168. Her second chance had been built from trauma. She was *made of pain*.

Was that how the demon side of her worked? Did it build itself a body out of its own environment? Did it rebuild her out of the rubble of trauma?

She sighed. Rubbed her eyes. Dug her fingernails into her face, trying to wake herself up, or at least the chewed-down nubs that were left of them. The ragged rims left fine marks.

Listen.

Wood for skin. That would be really handy right now, wouldn't it, against those terrible claws and teeth out there in the night?

"Robin."

Her head jerked as she kicked up out of the pond of sleep. She had dozed off. She scanned the darkness and heard her name again.

"Doc?"

"I'm here," said Gendreau. "You were talking in your sleep."

She pulled the Osdathregar out and gripped it in both hands. The dagger's point had chewed a hole in her jeans, and the cold cellar floor pressed its wet nose against her left ass-cheek. "What was I saying?" She shifted her weight, straightening, stretching the cramps out of her legs and hips, and laid the dagger across her thighs.

"Something about skin. Super creepy."

"Sorry."

She waited.

After a while, Gendreau murmured, "Haruko is Leon's wife, yes. We knew of her talents for artifice from her Etsy store. We approached her in the hospital and made her a deal—we'd cure her cancer, and in exchange, she would come work for the Dogs of Odysseus as a curator and custodian. But she couldn't take her family with her. As far as they were concerned, she perished of her illness."

"And I thought *I* was an asshole."

"Haruko made that choice of her own free will. All we did was open the door. She's the one that walked through it."

"Shitty choice. Submit or die, hmm?"

"Wasn't my call." His voice was barely audible in the cramped closet.

"I have half a mind to tell the Parkins she's still alive."

"Don't you think that's up to Haruko? You might want to wait and talk to her before you make such a rash call."

"That little boy deserves to have a mother."

Changing the subject, Gendreau asked, "Speaking of mothers, how did Marina and Carly end up in your Winnebago? That seems like an unlikely series of circumstances."

"I've always had a tendency to stumble into these situations, or, rather, they stumble into me," she replied. "Happened even before I went full-on demon. Andras was always there in me, I guess, even if I didn't know it, and from what I know of them, demons have a magnetic attraction to . . . lost things, hidden things, people in deep dog shit. I reckon it's how I always seem to be in the right place at the right time."

"Trouble magnet." The magician scoffed in amusement. "I suppose that's how the devil always shows up in the old stories, poof, just when people need to make a deal? Old Scratch does always seem to be right where he needs to be."

"More like 'right where he's needed.'"

She waited, but he said nothing else. Time languished, the seconds leaking under the door like a quietly welling puddle, and then the soft sound of snoring came from the magician's corner of the closet.

Robin ground her fists into her eyes.

Listen, said the black-eyed warhawk in the bathroom mirror. *Listen, girl, wake up and LISTEN. Do you need to burn yourself with hot water again?*

No noise except for breathing and the desert's night sounds. A faint insectile buzz came insistent and metallic from somewhere behind the house, and from time to time, the wind tossed handfuls of sand against the casement window by the closet. She cocked her head to the side and listened to the wheezy whistle of Kenway breathing, his side swelling and ebbing against her.

No water here in the desert.

I'll make do, said the warhawk. *I'll stick you in the leg with that dagger you got. Maybe I'll pop off a shotgun round in the ceiling and scare the shit out of everybody. That'll wake your ass up.*

No, she told the mad-eyed woman she'd seen in the motel bathroom mirror, *what that'll do is draw the wolves.*

Is that such a bad thing? Maybe they should just get their asses up here and we can get this bullshit over with. The warhawk grinned. Her eyes were green sea-lamps. *Fuck them. Fuck you. You like fighting, don't you? Then let's fuckin' fight 'em. Then you can come down off your combat high the way you used to like to do—rub one out, flick the ol' bean, then stick your feet out the van window and smoke and drink a beer. What say? It's been a while.*

They faced each other in the darkness, the daughter of a God-fearing woman and the daughter of a demon. Two luminous green points floated in the shade like two alien cigarette-cherries, unblinking, unwavering. Which was which? She couldn't tell anymore.

Not that person anymore, said Robin. *I'm not you.*

You sure about that? You think this man cured you? That you saved each other? The demon-daughter laughed. *You really are as stupid as you look.*

Eventually, the closet filled with an oppressive chill as the adrenaline seeped out of her system, draping her in a wet creeping sheet, and not even Kenway's big warm body could warm her up. She woke just long enough to realize she'd fallen asleep again, and closed her eyes.

Track 19

Then

Wind chimes tinkled somewhere nearby, joining the chorus of birds flittering about in the scratchy, stunted desert trees. Black soot stains made the place look as if a thousand pounds of firecrackers had gone off. The teenager crept quietly through buildings and crumbling concrete walls made up to resemble an Afghanistan village.

Decades ago, before the Army bought it and turned it into an abandoned MOUT range (Movement Over Urban Terrain), Hammertown had been a soundstage for a spaghetti-western movie called *The Whirlwind in the Thorn Tree,* and the buildings around her still somewhat resembled their former glory, even under all the concertina wire and Arabic signage.

When the Army built a better course in the middle of the firing ranges on Fort Hood in 1998, Killeen law enforcement started using that one and left this one to rot. Teenagers made it their clubhouse later, evidenced by all the graffiti, used condoms, and beer cans everywhere, but Heinrich had cleaned all the garbage out and moved into the largest building on the property, a four-story firefighter-training structure. The doors were all kicked in, but Heinrich replaced them with fresh new steel doors, each one with two deadbolts, and put welded rebar grilles over the windows.

Clutched in Robin's hands was a nine-millimeter Beretta. She moved cautiously with the pistol up in high ready, thumbs overlapping like Heinrich had taught her.

In a window, a wooden silhouette stood up with a creak. Crudely painted on it was a man with a furious, snarling face, his hands up as if he were going to choke you. Robin fired with an ear-splitting blast. An empty casing tinkled against the wall. The silhouette fell.

To her left, another silhouette stood up behind a road barricade. She knocked that one down, *bang*.

For some reason, he'd made her put on a bunch of armor and pads: a hockey mask on her face, hockey pads on her hands and feet, a catcher's vest that looked like it'd seen its fair share of fastballs, and her jeans and shirt sleeves were wound about with several layers of duct tape. On top of the IOTV and ankle weights, this extra stuff was making her sweat more than usual. She continued to move through the tangled MOUT course, walking down a winding, narrow street, firing nine-millimeter bullets into man-shaped wooden boards. They appeared around corners and in windows, standing up from behind the chaparral and swinging down from the undersides of balconies. Heinrich ran pell-mell back and forth through the buildings, his boots clapping hollowly in the shadows, pulling ropes.

Three more silhouettes, turn right, head down the corridor, one silhouette, and then. . . .

Getting faster, her shot placement surer. Squeezing off her shots instead of pulling them now, and practicing proper trigger discipline by taking her finger out of the trigger well when she wasn't firing. A woman with a crazed grimace slid up from behind a windowsill, eyes wide, hands clawed over her head. *Bang!* A hole appeared in her chest. The silhouette whirled out of sight.

Hot breath glued the hockey mask to her face with cold sweat. Robin stepped through a doorway into a dark corridor.

Halfway down, a silhouette stood up and she put a bullet in it. She turned left into another corridor where she raised the pistol in anticipation, but the target she expected never came up.

Reloading the Beretta, she passed through a pair of plywood sheets that hinged inward to create a door. Normally, when she got to this part, it would close in front of her and create a picture of a giant creature meant for her to empty the magazine into, but this time, when the plywood swung shut behind her and met with a clap in the middle, painted on the back was a crowd of enraged people leaping in midair and running with their fingers hooked like cat-claws. She spun and fired. *Pow, pow, pow-pow!*

Black holes appeared in their faces and chests. *Click.* The slide stayed back. Empty. She dropped the magazine, putting the Beretta on safe, and gently placed the pistol and mag on a little end table.

"I'm out." A knife lay on the table today, a wicked-looking Ka-Bar combat knife like something a Marine would have carried into Vietnam. "Mind telling me what all this crap I'm wearing today is? Gonna come out here and beat me with a stick? You leave me a knife and you're gonna get stabbed again."

Several seconds of silence passed as she waited for an answer.

"You there, old man?"

Squeaky-squeaky-squeak, pulleys in the walls labored to open the plywood door again, revealing the dark hallway inside. Something clapped open in the shadows, a brittle metallic sound like that of a birdcage. *Tick-tick-ticka-tick-tick.* Sounded like water dripping on plaster. Heavy breathing.

"Pick up the knife, kid," said Heinrich.

Something moved in the darkness beyond.

German Shepherd. Absolutely *huge*—eighty or ninety pounds

by the looks of it. White fuzz rimmed his eye sockets and lips. The dog growled, sending a thrill of fear through her.

As the growl deepened, the dog's head lowered, his ears folding back. He stared up at her from under his eyebrows.

"Pick up the knife," said Heinrich.

"I'm not stabbing a dog, asshole."

"Name's Luke. Lucky Luke, but his previous coworkers called him LT. Retired police dog. Ten years old and can't see out of one eye. Got a bit of a waddle 'cause some tweaker stuck him in the shoulder with a screwdriver. Bought him off a dogfighter that stole him out of a cop's backyard."

"You *what*?"

The dog charged at her. Robin turned and ran. Lucky Luke gave chase.

The hallway ended in a door. She shoulder-checked through without pausing, stumbling down the stairs on the other side. She found herself in a sort of plaza surrounded by building façades. Didn't make it twenty feet before she got ahead of her feet, overbalanced, and went down, skinning the heels of both hands. The dog was immediately on her, clamping sharp teeth on her padded left wrist.

"Get him off me!" Robin shrieked, pounding on Lucky Luke's face with her free hand. *"Get him!"* He was immovable, inexorable, invincible, jerking fiercely at her arm. Didn't even flinch at her blows. Each jerk was accompanied by a hideous growl like a violin being played with a hacksaw.

"Get up, stupid!" yelled Heinrich, coming outside.

Dimly thankful Luke had grabbed her wrist and not her fingers, Robin wallowed around until she could get a leg underneath her. As she got to her knees, the dog pulled and jerked and yanked on her padded glove. She braced herself with her other hand and rose to her feet.

"Punch him!" shouted Heinrich. "Punch him in the face!"

"I AM!" she screamed at him. Like a nightmare, even her hardest

of blows couldn't fend off the growling dog, as if she were underwater and her fist just wouldn't move fast enough. *"Call it OFF!"*

Something clattered across the concrete and bounced off her foot. Combat knife.

"Gonna have to do something," said Heinrich. Luke gave a hard jerk and pulled her down to one knee. "Won't stop until you're dead or he is."

"Why won't you call him off?" Robin cried in a rising panic.

"Won't be anybody to call that witch off when she latches on and starts eating you. They gone drag you down like a dog in the street and tear you limb from limb, and then they're going to fucking *eat* you! Witches eat people, Robin! They're cannibals! That's what they do! Kidnap kids, put 'em in cages and boil the meat off their bones!"

The knife was behind her at this point. Luke had succeeded in pulling her away from it. Robin pulled back, starting a deadly game of tug-of-war. Only way she was going to be able to save herself. It was going to have to be the knife.

"If I have to walk over there and put the knife in your hand myself, I'm gonna take you to Killeen and put your ass out by the side of the road!" Heinrich ranted from the top of the steps. "You can hook for your dinner for all I give a shit! *I bet that's about all you're good for anyway!*"

Heat rushed into Robin's face and she envisioned herself snatching up the knife. But instead of sticking the dog with it, she wanted to rush Heinrich. She gave a good hard jerk and gained some ground. His gums left bloodstains on the glove. The dog growled venomously, planting his feet, and Robin pounded him in the ear as hard as she could.

"Do it!" Heinrich yelled, applauding slowly. "Prove you can win, little girl!"

To her surprise, the dog let go. She dove for the knife, frantically trying to pick it up with her thick, mittened hands. *Got it.* She rolled over and the dog bit into the hockey mask.

Teeth jabbed through the eyehole and holes, jagging her across the nose and scratching her lip. She screamed, almost forgetting the knife in fear. Luke ripped the mask off her face. The nylon straps popped like gunfire, whipping her ears, and he backed away in what seemed like confusion.

Spitting the mask out, he lunged at her again.

This time she held out the knife.

The tip of the blade went in directly underneath his collar, sliding through the hard muscle of his chest all the way to the hilt.

Didn't stop him, though. Luke continued to snap at her face, slavering and growling, throwing cold ropes of saliva, absolutely apeshit, trying to bite every available appendage and surface she gave him access to. Her arms were extended out straight, elbows locked, muscles trembling. One mistake and she'd have teeth in her throat. She turtled, tucking her chin under the catcher's vest.

Abandoning her face, he latched on to her arm and growled, flexed like a dying snake, coiling, stiffening. Angry growls became higher-and higher-pitched until they were more like squeals.

He coughed through his teeth, spraying her glove with blood.

No, no, no. . . .

Tears filled Robin's eyes as the dog started losing spirit.

Heaving and panting in pain, Luke's legs buckled and he knelt next to her. Finally, he lay down in the dust and blood, and looked up at her with dark honey eyes.

Robin got up onto her knees and pried her fingers free of the knife. The Ka-Bar's handle throbbed with the beat of the dog's heart, blood streaming out from under it into a puddle.

She toppled forward onto her hands.

She cried her eyes out. Tears plopped into the dust between her bloody gloves.

She sobbed until she retched, and then she retched until she threw up acidic yellow bile. Heinrich didn't say anything, he just lit one of those coconut cigars and sat down on the stairs, smoking and watching her cry.

Stab that son of a bitch, said the lamp-eyed warhawk.

Robin wheeled on the dog and wrenched the knife out of his chest. Blood ripped out of the wound, pattering across the ground. She strode toward her cigar-smoking mentor with every intention of gutting him.

"He limps 'cause he's got osteosarcoma," said Heinrich.

Robin hesitated.

"Bone cancer. Extensive, all up in his spine and hips. He was gonna die anyway, Robin Hood. Only had a couple months, half a year at the most." Heinrich spoke out of the corner of his mouth, the cigar hanging from his lips. "You don't know it, but you did him a favor."

Sick, impotent rage built inside of her. Robin glared at him. *"What the hell kind of favor was that?"* she growled through gritted teeth. Wanted to jump on him, claw him like a monkey or a fucking chupacabra or something, bite him, bite his face, bite his nose off, bite his neck open. The rage was all-consuming. Of all the things he'd made her do in the name of her revenge, this was the worst. It was one thing to shoot at cardboard targets and let him knock her around, but. . . .

Every fiber of her being wanted to rush at him. She knew he could put her down without breaking a sweat. Probably wouldn't even have to toss his cigar. Goddamn coconuts.

"You gave him a warrior's death," said the bastard.

Robin stared in incredulity.

"FUCK YOU!" she bellowed, throwing the knife at him. Heinrich ducked and the blade went whirling over his head, clanging across the steps. "Fuck you *and* your manipulative bullshit—" She charged him, meaning to hit him in the face, but he caught her hands and twirled her in an awkward pirouette, then shoved her back the way she came. She went down face-first, stumbling to her hands and knees next to the dog.

"I can get you to do anything in the world," Heinrich said quietly, in that desolate, commanding tone of voice that told her he was done joking. "Climb any mountain, swim any sea. All I gotta do is piss you off."

"FUCK! YOU!" Robin shrieked one last epithet and stormed away.

When he'd smoked as much of the cigar as he was going to smoke, Heinrich reached up and took one last draw off the cigar, stubbing it out.

Standing up, he loped down the stairs and over to Luke, where he pulled a revolver out of his cross-draw rig. Robin was in her makeshift bedroom packing her stuff when the gunshot came rolling out to her.

Track 20

Now

Boredom finally got the better of her, and she crept out of the basement closet to explore the house. Ended up in a filthy upstairs bathroom, where she found a dusty wood-cabinet television, of all things, standing like an altar where the tub should have been, amidst thirty or forty VHS tapes.

When she plugged the TV in, Robin was amazed to realize the house still had power. She pushed a stiff button and the screen blazed to life with snowy static.

Selecting a tape, she pushed it into the VCR. The image resolved into a scene of a birthday party, distorted by bad tracking. She turned the volume up just high enough to hear it, but instead of a family singing "Happy Birthday," it sounded like a chorus of demons howling a garbled hymn. She watched it as long as she could stand it, then tried another one. The next tape was of a children's ball game, jerking and stuttering, the stands full of more howling banshees. Baseball? Tee-ball? She couldn't tell. The camera panned to the right and the screen filled with the face of the woman in the stairwell photographs. The wife. Markedly younger in the video . . . late thirties, maybe.

Robin tried to read the label on one of the tapes by the glow of the TV. WEDDING, scrawled in blue ink pen. Several others were labeled in the same manner: PARTY, FUN AT THE PARK, JOHN'S GRADUATION, one cryptically labeled "11/02/97," and one that simply said LILY'S SERVICE. As soon as she touched the one labeled LILY'S SERVICE, Robin was pierced with a sudden, sharp sensation of loss and heartache. Smelled ointment, heard the grinding swell of an electric organ. Cheap fake flowers ghosted across her fingertips.

11/02/97. This tape was the cleanest so far, with only the occasional tracking issue. The woman from the stairwell photographs gave the camera operator—most likely her husband—a tour of the motel down the hill. Very happy, spry for her age, even giving a little shimmy as he followed her down the suite sidewalk into the office. She lifted the counter leaf, her eyes sparkling—no bifocals yet—and took her position behind the ledger. Must have been the owner-operators of the motel.

Robin suddenly remembered she was wearing the GoPro. She leaned the shotgun against the bathroom wall, detached the camera from the chest harness, and held it in front of her face.

"If you're watching this," she told her YouTube audience in a voice just above a whisper, "I'm probably still alive. Hopefully, I live long enough to upload it." She pointed the camera at the TV. "We're currently hiding from werewolves in an abandoned house out in the Texas scrubland." Her face twisted in a wry way. "I know, right? *Werewolves?* As if the witches and cat-people and magicians weren't crazy enough. And Heinie himself even said there were no such thing as werewolves." She turned the camera back toward her face, feeling giddy and strung out. "Hope I got footage of that fight in the Winnebago and the part with the grenade launcher. Gnarly fucking action, right? Car chase. Exploding motorcycles. Jesus! Hope the camera in the bedroom was on."

For a few more minutes, she sat and watched the videotape until it abruptly cut off and the screen went blue. Robin replaced it with the videotape that said LILY'S SERVICE on the label.

Soon as the tape started, she regretted it. This one seemed professionally produced. Standing in front of an open casket was a young man, and surrounding him were people of a multitude of ages: cousins, siblings, grandchildren. He began a heartfelt eulogy.

She turned the volume down before he could really get going.

• • •

In the living room. She stood catty-cornered to the front window, peering around the edge of the window frame, and saw that the biker had dragged José's corpse out of the empty pool, through the back gate, and into a stand of rocks and bushes at the farthest corner of the property.

Does he think Santiago isn't going to notice that dude being gone? Robin thought, shaking her head.

Flashlights glittered in the dark distance, faraway stars in the ocean of night. Some of them had turned back, lights twinkling toward the motel. She went back through the kitchen and into a dining room, looking for a more advantageous window.

A large table had been overturned, two of the legs broken off. Chairs were smashed and strewn all over the already-filthy room.

Through a door on the other side she could see the outline of a desk in the moonlight, the blotter swept clean. A little office. Maybe something she could use in there. A small window overlooked a ten- or twelve-foot drop to the steep front yard, and would make a good vantage point for unloading some buckshot across the porch.

One of the wolf-men had overturned a china hutch in front of the door so that it lay on its side. She thought about turning it facedown so she could walk across the back of it, but decided it would make too much noise. Laying the shotgun down, she climbed on top of the hutch and sat down, swinging her legs into the little office. She took the shotgun, ducked under the lintel, and slid off into the room.

Her right foot came down on something hard and angular, *KER-CHUNK.*

White-hot silver bolts of pain as a bear trap clamped down on her shin. Undoubtedly the missing item from the Cracker Barrel bullshit nailed up in the living room. The Los Cambiantes had set up a snare—they'd funneled her right into a trap. She was no cleverer than a goddamn jackrabbit. *"Ahh! Fuck!"* Robin shouted into the silence of the abandoned house, gushing a deluge of four-letter words, and fell over. *"Motherfucker! Jesus Christ trapezoid! Fuck me and fuck my life!"*

She wedged her fingertips underneath the lips of the trap and pulled as hard as she could, but there just wasn't enough strength in her arms to pull them far enough apart. Helpless, she let the trap ease shut again, the teeth grinding into the bone and muscle.

"Fuuuuuuck!"

Footsteps came barreling up the basement stairs and into the kitchen, cutting through the dining room. As soon as he saw the overturned hutch, Kenway wrenched it to the side, out of the way. "What the shit!"

In the distance, a wolf cried a long, mournful note.

Every movement elicited another stab of intense pain. "Fuckin' bear trap." It was everything she could do not to sob.

He slipped his fingers between the trap's teeth and pulled the iron jaws apart, shaking with exertion. Pulling her foot out, Robin rolled away, and the pain didn't diminish—it only grew stronger and stronger as she lay there, her hands over her eyes. She drummed fists on the floor, throwing a tantrum of agony and rage.

Three incredible gashes encircled her shin, like she'd tried to saw off her foot. Robin swore as he helped her up. Blood ran black and thick in the darkness, soaking into her sock. "Somebody heard you." Kenway got up and thumped over to the window. Flashlights in the desert. Just a few hundred feet from the motel parking lot. "They're coming back."

"Come on, we gotta get into the basement." Tears swam in her eyes. Grabbing the shotgun, she hobbled into the kitchen behind him and Kenway opened the cellar door, ushering her in.

"No," she told him. "You first, in case I fall."

"Yeah, okay."

He went in. She slammed the door behind him. Near the top of the door was a deadbolt; she slid it home and he immediately hammered on the door from the inside. "Have you lost your mind? Open this damn door."

"Can't let you guys get hurt again." Robin rested her forehead on the door, wincing at the pain in her leg. "You and Doc have almost died because of me. You forget about the knife in your back last year? I almost lost you."

"Let me out of here. *Now.*" The veteran's old sergeant-voice came through the door like a growling Doberman. "That's—"

"—An order?" Robin straightened, holding the shotgun at low-ready. Her bowels were an acid hurricane. Blood and adrenaline surged through her. "I'm not one of your soldiers, babe. Now, get your ass down there and—"

Bang! She jumped as the door slammed loudly. He was kicking it. *Bang! Bang!*

"Open this damn door!"

A wolf howled again. Sounded like it was in the front yard, coming up the steps from the motel.

That was followed by the most terrifying, earth-shaking roar she'd ever heard and felt in her life, so heavy the texture of the sound seemed to swarm across the ceiling. Robin actually ducked. If she didn't know any better, the ground had opened up and the devil himself had come galloping out.

Maybe that'd be better. At least she was on a first-name basis with the devil.

She shook so bad, she thought she would drop the shotgun.

Robin limped into the living room, looking for a place she could hide and ambush them guerilla-style. *"Robin!"* Kenway kicked the door again, *BANG!*, jangling the deadbolt, *BANG! "Let me the hell outta here!"*

Pouring blue moonlight at her feet, the broken front door yawned in front of her. "Get your ass in that crawlspace!" she shouted over her shoulder, and went blind as the room turned black.

Blocking the moonlight, a colossal shape filled the hole where the front door had been, shoulders brushing the frame on both sides. Golden eyes glittered in the massive silhouette, embedded in a massive head. Big enough to swallow her whole, a mouth opened in a man's distorted, bearded face, revealing meat-tearing teeth as long as Robin's fingers.

The Mexican Mountain was a bear.

Half a ton of gold-eyed, pants-shitting man-bear. He roared again, filling the house with trumpeting Godzilla noise, and lumbered into the living room, standing up to his full height of what looked like eight or nine feet.

Everything from that moment to the kitchen passed in throbbing, panicked slow-motion.

One swipe of a massive claw raked the shotgun out of her hands and flung it aside. Black talons flayed the back of her forearm and hand down to the bone, but as amped up as she was, she didn't even feel it.

She turned and half-hobbled, half-ran.

Max fell forward with an incredible *SLAM!* that trampolined the floor and the behemoth gave chase. She threw herself into the first room she came to, a side bedroom off the living room, and slammed the door in Maximo's face.

Room was empty. A hole had been knocked in the wall to her left, but something was pushed in front of it from the other side. A fridge. Robin pressed her hands against it and shoved it out of the way. Max hit the door behind her and knocked it across the bedroom, barely missing her, smashing a window.

Diving through the hole in the wall, she threw herself into the kitchen. An enormous claw reached through after her, and Robin grabbed the tomahawk, hacking at him. Max growled and withdrew, and she shoved the fridge back into place.

"Gotcha, bitch," snarled someone behind her.

Werewolf in the kitchen, the back door standing wide open. She drew the katana out of its scabbard and said, "Get *this,* fuck-boy," surprising him with a tomahawk across the face.

The werewolf recoiled in pain and lunged at her, jaws gaping, arms outstretched. She stepped aside and parried his awkward charge with the katana; the sword sliced through his wrist with a sick, bony chop.

Blood pattered on linoleum. Kenway kicked the cellar door again.

The sudden *BANG* made the werewolf look up from his severed hand, and Robin took advantage of the distraction, plunging the sword into his neck. Fever-hot blood sprayed from the wound and she followed it with the tomahawk in the other hand, whacking him across the forehead, peeling his hairy scalp back.

Yelping and staggering away, the werewolf turned and ran out of the house, face-planting in the dirt.

A hulking shadow stepped over him, another werewolf taking his place.

To Robin's left, the door leading from the living room exploded into sticks and the Max-bear leered through. His patchy, sweaty half-man face was a nightmare, a swollen deathbeast with a hellmouth and dead black eyes, but the door was narrow enough that he couldn't get in. The doorframe groaned under his weight.

As she took off for the dining room, Robin ducked a swipe from the other monster coming in through the back door. Talons whistled through dusty air.

Not the good idea she hoped for. Soon as she stepped into the room, she realized the only way to go was back into the office, and that only had one other exit—the window looking out onto the front yard. This window collapsed in a crash of broken glass, a werewolf leaping through.

"Shit," said Robin, and the dining room wall caved in. Maximo pushed through the chaos, a hairy bulldozer shoving through the drywall.

Powdery sheetrock fell onto the floor in shards. Wooden studs splintered against his shoulders but refused to break, restraining him. He reached through with one massive paw, clawing wood shavings out of the floor.

The werewolf leapt out of the office at the same time the other one came in from the kitchen, pincering her inside the dining room with the bear. Maximo snapped at her with slobbery jaws and Robin did a back somersault over the tabletop, rolling off the other side.

Landing on her feet, the trap-chewed leg howling in pain, she kicked the table into the bear's face.

Snarling in a blood-rage, she turned to slash at Backdoor Wolf's mouth with the sword, then sank the tomahawk into the side of Office Wolf's head. Backdoor gargled, spitting out teeth. Office reeled from the blow to the skull and halfheartedly tried to bite her once before sprawling on his back, pulling the tomahawk out of her hand.

Wall studs crackled. Gnarly teeth clashed just a foot away. Max trying to bite her again.

Someone reached through the door to her left and fired a Roman candle of sound and fury. Buckshot tore through Maximo's face, splattering the dining room wall with blood and snot. The bear actually *gasped,* a hoarse coughing noise, and retreated into the living room. Every one of the beast's footfalls shuddered the house's frame.

Breaking open the sawed-off shotgun, Gendreau snatched out the hot casings and flung them over his shoulder.

By the look on his face, Robin could tell he was terrified. Pride roared in her chest at seeing him in the fray. "The hell are you doing? You're gonna get killed. Let *me* handle this."

He reached into a hip pocket for a shell, reloaded the shotgun, flicking it shut, *ka-chik,* then he knelt to apply some healing energy from the ring to the wound in her leg. "I was hiding in the living room. And it's a good thing, because you lost the sawed-off. Come on. You aren't the badass you think you are. That demon inside you doesn't make you invincible."

"Didn't *need* the sawed-off."

Gendreau rolled his eyes at her. She sneered at him.

Blood streaming from his face, Backdoor Wolf tried to collect himself, and Robin shanked him twice in the back, deep, the sword scraping bone. He didn't get up again.

"Be that as it may," said Gendreau, "you need to get into the cellar with us."

"*Yo!*" Santiago, outside.

Careful to stay in the moon's shadow, Robin approached the window and the magician joined her, the two of them peering through dingy curtains. Men and wolves stood together in the sagebrush, watching the house. Some of the men carried pistols.

"Send me my daughter, and I won't kill you," Santi called.

"Hard to believe," said Gendreau.

"Just trying to get the kid out so he can shoot the place up," Robin told him. "He doesn't want to send any more of his boys in. I think he's getting the picture: I'm not somebody he wants to fuck with."

Santiago shouted again. "Ain't nobody else got to die! Come on, hard-ass, let's talk this out!"

Eyeing Gendreau, Robin tried to pull the tomahawk out of the werewolf's head, but it was stuck fast, wedged deep into his skull. She abandoned it and reached behind her back for the Osdathregar tucked into the waist of her jeans. "Here," she said, handing the dagger off to Gendreau. "Get back downstairs. If I don't make it, at least this won't end up in their grubby hands."

The Maximo-bear roared from somewhere else in the house,

a resonant saurian blast. Through the hole in the wall, she saw his great hoary bulk shuffling around on the far side of the living room.

Sudden light turned the window into a fireplace.

For a brief second, Robin thought Santiago's men were throwing firebombs onto the roof, which would have been par for the course.

Screams of pain in the night. Robin and the curandero ran to the window and found a rush of heat and light as a fire-tornado billowed up from the grass. Flaming werewolves scattered into the brushland, some of them running for the cover of the house, bringing the fire with them.

"It's the cavalry!" cried Gendreau, grinning madly. He ran for the kitchen. "They came back for us! Callooh callay!"

"Callooh callay?" Robin followed him. The magician handed her the shotgun and unlocked the cellar door. But instead of sticking around or going below, Robin stormed into the living room.

"Hey, where you going?" demanded Kenway, bursting out of the cellar.

"I'm loaded for bear."

The instant she went in, Maximo swept the couch out of the way, throwing it into the fireplace, and charged her. The shotgun barked fire and buckshot into his face, but he kept coming. She rolled out of the way and Maximo slammed into the staircase. Farm implements rained down from the walls in a metallic cacophony.

Blinded, the behemoth man-bear wheeled around, raking a claw over Robin's head, and the witch-hunter countered with her own slash across his belly, the katana opening a rubbery mouth that belched a cascade of steaming intestines. Blood ran down his thighs in a waterfall of red.

Dropping the empty shotgun, she ran for the stairs.

Kicking off the wall, she leapt, pivoting, pulling the sword back, and at the last second, she thrust the blade into the side of his neck in another Superman punch, letting the heavy muscle guide the sword down into his body and into his mammoth heart.

Both of them crashed to the floor, and Maximo went *through* it, wood planks collapsing in around him. They plummeted into the cellar through a deafening apocalypse of debris and dust.

Track 21

Blood bubbled out of his jaws as Maximo struggled to breathe. One of his eyes had been punctured, fluids running down the side of his face, and the lips on that side had been blown away, teeth glinting through gore.

Robin stood over him, watching him die.

"That's what you get," she said, and spat on him.

Eyes glinted from a small closet under the cellar stairs. Carly gaped out at her, hunkered in the back with her arms around her knees.

Fire lit up the room as a bright shape came billowing through the front door upstairs, screaming and flailing. Tongues of flame flickered from the werewolf's arms, and his feet left a burning track. Fire spread to the walls, the drapes becoming a fence of flames. He stumbled right into the hole, pitching himself on top of the dying Maximo.

"Come on, baby, we got to get out of here," said Robin, running for the crawlspace.

The girl screamed, pressing herself into the corner.

"House is gonna burn down, you idiot!" shouted Robin, reaching for her.

Taking a deep breath, Carly started *shrieking* at the top of her lungs, like she was being sawed in half. The expression on the rest of her face couldn't have been anything other than absolute ice-cube-shitting terror.

Robin recoiled. "The hell is—"

"You murdered my wife," said Santiago, right behind her.

Toward them padded a monster nearly as big as Max. Orange and white hair made a Creamsicle masterpiece out of his skin. His oversized head divided in the middle to reveal twin rows of jagged white teeth. Honey eyes stared out of the ugly bulge of his face, ringed in black tiki stripes. Santiago Valenzuela looked like a kindergartener's crazed fridge-art rendition of a tiger, his face a crazy Picasso mishmash of man and monster.

No hesitation, no thought. Robin lunged for the jerry cans near the crawlspace and whipped one at Santiago's face. To her surprise, there was at least half a can of fuel in it. He batted it out of the way, *TONK!*, and it spun over his head into the fire.

"Now give me—"

The gas can exploded in a blast of light and heat, sending a shudder through the concrete floor and showering Santiago in gouts of flame. The ceiling caught fire as well. Santi screamed—*row-rowwr!*—and writhed around on his back, trying to scrub out his burning pelt. Robin had a weird moment, thinking about the Jungle Book—*Shere Khan hates man's red flower.*

Grabbing Carly's arm, she dragged her out of the crawlspace and pushed her up the stairs.

The girl stared at the tiger-thing. "Is that—"

"Not anymore," Robin said, truthfully. "Not anymore." She shoved the girl. "Get your ass out of here!"

Filthy sneakers ran up the stairs. Robin thrust the sword into the belly of the remaining jerry-can and gasoline dripped from the blade. She flourished it once to get rid of the excess (causing several more fires to erupt as she did this) and held it up in the air like a barbarian, letting the ceiling ignite it.

Fire raced down the sword's length. She held it out in both hands, a kendo pose aimed at the creature just getting to his feet. "Strike me down," she quipped, scoring an Obi-Wan Kenobi reference. Maybe she'd get the hang of this one-liner thing after all. "Whatever doesn't kill me just makes me stranger."

"Finally, the bitch that kidnapped my family." Santiago's black-ringed face warped into a bizarre grimace as he paced around her. "Smaller than I thought you would be. You look stringy."

"I didn't kidnap *anybody*. They were afraid of you." Robin backed toward the stairs, the flaming sword pointed at his face. "They ran from you and hid in my Winnebago. And I didn't *kill* anybody, either. Marina's death was your buddy Tuco's fault. *He* caused the crash. You wanna blame some—"

"MY WIFE DIED ON YOUR WATCH!"

Saliva misted her face. Santiago feinted at her and Robin thrust the burning sword at him, the flames rumbling and woofing. The handle was growing hot—she was going to have to fight or run. And soon.

As if he were being dragged, Santiago slid backward.

Talons pried up chunks of concrete. Confused, Robin looked up through the hole. The Origo Rook was upstairs, holding her Zippo lighter up like a groupie at a Grateful Dead concert.

Telekinesis.

The Gift of Manipulation relic. Pulling the tiger by his tail. "Get out of there!" cried Rook. "While I've got him!"

Didn't have to tell Robin twice. She scrambled up the stairs, the sword leaving tongues of flame along the risers, and flung herself into the kitchen, where Kenway was fighting a wolf with the tomahawk. The veteran's arms were a hash of deep scratches, blood running off his wrists. He split the werewolf's skull and the creature went down in a heap.

Robin finished it off with a flaming sword blow. "You okay?"

"Need some quality time with Doc, but otherwise I'm good," he said, surveying the nasty cuts on her arm.

Two werewolves wedged themselves into the back door, snarling and snapping, trying to claw their way into the kitchen. Carly screamed from her hiding spot in the corner. Robin grabbed her and pulled her into what was left of the living room, skirting the edge of the hole in the floor.

Fire had overwhelmed the room, blanketing the ceiling and walls in orange, and the air was thick with smoke. The man-tiger screamed downstairs.

"*Go!*" shouted Rook, waving them out the front door.

Running out onto the front porch, Robin was not thrilled to see a herd of shadows flowing up the hill toward them. Wolves bellowed from the moonlit brush. Terrified, Carly shrieked and veered to the left, sprinting into the dark desert. "No!" yelled Robin. "The hell you going?"

Navathe came around the corner of the house just in time to almost get bowled over by the girl as she ran into the night. "What's going on?" he asked in his urbanite London accent, and thrust his snow globe out, throwing jets of flame across the slope. Werewolves and greasy stands of sagebrush burst into flame, turning the desolate front yard into a wildfire.

"I'll go get her!" Gendreau ran after the kid.

The werewolves ignored them. Robin began to say something and then a hairy shape leapt out of the dark, throwing her down, tearing at her before they'd even skidded to a stop. Slash marks across her chest. Kenway pulled him off, planting the tomahawk in his ear with sick squelching noises.

Rook screamed from inside the house.

"Dammit," growled Robin, running for the porch steps, clutching the cuts on her chest. Through the front door and back into Hell.

Fire curtained from the walls of the living room, mushrooming across the ceiling. Santiago clung to the edge of the hole, suspended over the flames in the basement, and his claws were embedded in Rook's leg. The magician lay on the floor like the elderly lady from the emergency-alert commercials: *Help! I've fallen and I can't get up!*

"Got you!" Robin shouted, sliding to the edge of the hole as if it were second base.

Trails of fire licked up through the floorboards as she jabbed Santiago with the sword. The tiger-beast roared in pain and renewed his grip, Robin's blade jutting from his flesh. Talons pried up burning boards.

Embers and shards of wood slipped through the cellar's joists: the floor was coming apart under them. Kenway appeared out of the smoke to hack at Santiago's arm, trying to either get him to let go of Rook or chop the fucker's hand off, whichever one happened first. The tomahawk hit thick bone and stopped cold.

"GRAAAAH!" Santiago reached out and snagged Robin's arm, letting go of the joists, and as he fell, he dragged both women back into the basement in a cascade of burning wood.

She landed in the fire and rolled out onto cold concrete, tumbling through a blizzard of red sparks. The sword danced across the floor, singing and clanging. Floundering up onto her hands and knees, Robin slapped at the flames on her jeans.

The magician had pulled off her flaming shirt, throwing it aside.

"Get out of here, Haruko," she told Rook.

"But I can—"

"JUST GO!" bellowed Robin.

Burning timbers fell from above, battering the edge of the hole in the ceiling. "Aaugh!" Kenway said, flinging himself back.

A meteor-like shape sprang out of the inferno, screaming, claws flashing. Santiago was covered in fire, thrashing around on the cellar floor, screaming, tearing the shelves off the walls in an attempt to find something that would put him out. He set the stairs aflame, blocking their escape.

"Fuck's sake!" Rook screamed. She scrambled into the crawl space.

Robin snatched up the sword and stuck it into Santiago's back. The malformed beast let out an agonized roar and belted her across the stomach, flinging her against the cellar wall. Black meat hooks tore strips of skin from her bare belly. Before she could recover, he was on her, throwing her across the room.

Gasoline splattered all over her as Robin rolled through a puddle. *If I can just get my hands on the sword,* she thought, reaching for it as the beast hunkered over her. Teeth closed on her arm, piercing skin and muscle, and he yanked her up off the floor, throwing her ass-over-teakettle into the fire.

This time, there was no escape. The gasoline all over her instantly ignited. Robin went up like a witch, her arm hair and head hair evaporating in one crackling *whoosh!*

"Burrrn, baby, burn!" snarled Santiago, laughing.

Light enveloped her in excruciating pain, a gigantic despair that reduced her to a singular, primitive, panicking instinct—*get out of the house. Find water.* Robin crawled out of the burning debris, a figure of billowing flame, and tried to stand. *Get out of the house.* Undulations of fire rolled up and up her arms and legs in waves of stinging hornets. Her jeans were shrouds of flame. *Find water.*

"Gotta go back in. I like my murdering whores well done." Santiago shoved her into the fire, still laughing.

Ashes roiled around her in a cloud of red stars. *I've got to go. I've got to get out of here. He is going to kill me, if I'm not dead already.* She tried to scream and inhaled only torment. The insides of her lungs crisped, frying like bacon in her chest. Her tongue was jerky, shriveled in her mouth. *Find water. Find water.*

All the strength went out of her legs and she collapsed.

Crawling after Santiago, she put her hand in a puddle. A blue aurora burped across the gasoline's surface as it ignited.

"You look busy," he said, coughing as he pulled the katana out of his back and threw it away, *clang-clang,* flinging an arc of blood.

“Think I’m gonna leave you to it.” The warped tiger-creature went to the crawlspace and ripped the door away, pulling out a filthy Rook and dragging her up the stairs by her throat.

Glowing ashes rushed out of her mouth as Robin tried to rasp, “No,” and with them went the pain.

Nothing left to hurt. The burns went too deep, the skin destroyed, no nerves to feel anymore. Summoning everything she had left, Robin began her agonized via dolorosa up the stairs, following Santiago, crawling on burning hands and knees. The last scrap of her clothes fell off.

“Come on, baby, you can do it.”

Her mother’s ghost stood at the top of the stairs, waving her on, begging, sobbing, swearing. Embers floated unimpeded through Annie Martine’s translucent body. She wore the pristine sundress she’d died in. “You can do it,” screamed the ghost from her perch at the top of that tunnel of flame. “*Get out of there.* Come on.”

Closing her blistered eyes, Robin focused on climbing, the steps peeling away her palms. The soles of her feet came off in gluey strands like hot cheese. Annie continued to encourage and chide her, shrieking like a madwoman.

Blood boiled and smoked on the stairs as wolves howled triumphantly in the distance.

Track 22

Then

"Stop Me" by Natalia Kills pounded the Top Dollar Gentlemen's Club with a driving beat. Lights strobed through a bead curtain, glittering across Robin's face as her heart fluttered in her chest. This was not the kind of place where they do a background check, then blow a bunch of money on training you to pole-dance. This was the kind of place where they put a *Girls Wanted* ad in the town trading-post magazine, and if you have all your front teeth, they put you to work next week and pay you under the table.

She was beginning to regret answering that ad.

One of the other girls came dancing over with a shot glass. "Here, newbie, you're gonna need one of these," said the girl, handing it over. She was dressed like Tinkerbell, which clashed nicely with her almost-skeletal face and the sores on her arms. "You got that deer-in-the-headlights look, and Bobby ain't gonna like it if you puke on his stage."

Sniff, sniff. Smelled like pancake syrup. "What is it?"

"Good shit. Just drink it. You're on in ten."

"Ten minutes—?"

"Ten seconds."

"Well, hell," said Robin, throwing back the shot. The whiskey went down like a sweet cannonball. She coughed, covering her mouth with her wrist, and handed the glass back to the girl. "What was your name again?"

"June."

"Oh, right. Thanks, June."

"Knock 'em dead." The girl pushed her through the bead curtain.

"Stop Me" was still rolling at top volume, vibrating the floor under her feet as Robin shuffled out onto the stage. A twenty-foot catwalk led to a large round dais, where a brass pole ran up to the ceiling, all of it illuminated by red footlights, and the audience—what there was of it on a Thursday evening—exploded with noise. Between the bar and the tables, she estimated there were about thirty people.

(the exits)

They'd given her the gunslinger routine: assless chaps, a leather bikini with fringe, and a pink cowboy hat. Strapped to her hips was a pair of holsters, each of which contained a realistic cap-gun revolver. Her cowboy boots *clip-clop*ped across the mirrored platform, and every muscle in her frame locked up in stage fright.

(look for the exits)

"Damn, baby!" shouted someone in the darkness.

Alcohol made her panic rise to the surface as a strained giggle. Robin put on her best hip-rolling strut and made her way toward the pole. *Slow down. This ain't the hundred-meter dash.* She'd done this a hundred times in rehearsal, but as soon as her own face gazed up at her from the mirrored floor with that shell-shocked stare, all of it flew out the window. For a brief adrenalized instant, she thought she saw it flicker into cold fury, a dark micro-expression, revolving from the face of someone running from a serial killer, *into* the killer, and back again. Watching her mother die, Heinrich's brutal training, the years spent in the mental hospital eating creamed corn in handcuffs and explaining her delusions to bored men in neckties: it was all trying to surface.

Do it, said the warhawk inside as the fear returned to her reflection's features, *just fucking do it.*

Getting down on her hands and knees, she stretched luxuriantly, arching her ass in the air, and crawled the rest of the way, pistols waggling. The toes of her cowboy boots felt as if they were about to smash through the mirror floor. She sort of hoped they would. Goddamn, it would be satisfying, wouldn't it? She reached the pole after what felt like a humiliating six-hour crawl and pulled herself to her feet. Individual faces gazed up at her. This didn't help the anxiety at all. Robin closed her eyes and tried to focus on the pole in her hands, tried to pretend she was there by herself, all alone. "Dance like nobody's watchin'," Darlene had told her yesterday, and that was easier said than done.

An insect fluttered against her thigh. Her eyes snapped open and saw a crumpled-up dollar bill.

She went back to dancing, looking up at the ceiling, at the back wall, at her own reflection below her boots, the pole, anywhere but the faces of the men watching her. She threw her best moves into the mix, bending over to peer between her knees (luckily, her hat was pinned to her hair), sashaying in a circle around the pole, bending over backward to flash her scant cleavage.

"Take your top off!" someone shouted from the bar.

She pressed one hand against her chest and reached behind her back with the other, untying it. The strings fell through her armpits, but she held the top on.

"You heard the man," said a familiar voice from her left.

Eyes darting in that direction, she saw her erstwhile mentor sitting at a table, nursing a beer. Heinrich Hammer's eyes sparkled in the red footlights. "Give him what he wants!"

What is he *doing here?!*

"Go blow a goat," she said, shouting to be heard over the music, strutting back up the catwalk. "I'm trying to work."

All he did was light a coconut cigar and sit there in the red shadows, smoking it.

She ripped the bikini top off with a leathery whipcrack and twirled it over her head like a lasso. Her nipples were tiny and dark, hard from embarrassment and air-conditioning. She flung the top into the tables in one motion. A man in a business suit caught it. He loosened his tie, pulling it out of his collar, and hung the bikini top around his neck like a towel.

The businessman threw his tie onstage. Robin picked it up, lasciviously flossed her ass with it, and threw it back, eliciting a wild cheer from the club patrons and a sprinkling of currency. Something about gaining control dissolved her tension. If she kept this up, she'd be running the room. Hell, she could even get them to drag Heinrich out and throw him into the parking lot.

Pulling the six-shooters out of her gun belt, she went through a series of sinuous action poses, shooting at the men in the audience. Some dark splinter in her relished this part of the routine; she could feel her face darkening, her brow tightening as she put imaginary bullets in perverts' heads. She bared her teeth at them, aimed with her eye, and killed them with her heart, and they loved every minute of it. *They'd be whistling a different tune if these guns were real.* She blew imaginary smoke out of the guns' barrels and shoved them back in their holsters, then lunged for the pole and swung herself around it, throwing her legs wide.

Never ceased to amaze her that these poles weren't fixed in place; they rotated on ball bearings. *A year of this,* Robin mused, *and I'll have leather palms. Hand jobs will be like masturbating with catchers' mitts.* She thrust her pelvis at the audience and crawled toward the nearest man.

"Damn," said a red-faced bald man in a Steelers T-shirt. His breath was rank with liquor. "You are totally amazing."

She pulled a pistol and shot him in the temple. *"Powww."*

"You blow my mind, baby."

"I can blow more than that, you know," she said, sitting up. Her initial anxiety was beginning to drain away, and when she turned around and threw her feet over the edge of the stage, rhythmically flexing her ass for Baldy, she realized why. This whole display was making Heinrich uncomfortable. That fact made all the shimmy-shimmy-shake worth it. *I can get you to do anything in the world, climb any mountain, swim any sea,* he'd said that day in Hammertown, just before she'd thrown the knife at his face. *All I gotta do is piss you off.*

Well, now she was pissed off.

The gnarly witch-hunter glared at her from under his hat brim, twirling a bottle of Corona. His cigar smoldered in an ashtray.

Rumpled dollar bills danced across her bare back. A mean smile spread across her face. She got up and pinched one of the strings hanging out of the knot holding up one side of her bikini bottom, showing it to Heinrich. *Check it out, old man.* She grinned at him, biting her bottom lip suggestively. It was Go Time, take it or leave it, last train to Omaha, buddy. *You better say something if you don't want me flashing my barely legal pussy at these howler monkeys.*

Wait, did she really want to do that? Did she really want to go back to Hammertown? Back to that dusty shithole of a—

"Look, I'm sorry," growled Heinrich.

"Sorry about what?" Robin asked, letting go of the knot string. Pulling out a pistol, she put it between her legs as if it were a penis, then pantomimed jerking off, leaning back in feigned ecstasy. She pulled the trigger and it shot off a cap with a loud bang, startling her. The bar went insane with laughter.

"About Lucky Luke." Heinrich got up and knelt by the stage, looking up at her. "I'm just—well, I just wanted—I'm tryin' to train the hesitation outta you, kid," he said, taking off his black gambler hat.

"Hesitation?" She pulled the trigger, moaning, giving it her best *Sleepless in Seattle* orgasm, firing caps as if she were blowing a load over the audience's heads. *Pow!* "Ohh!" *Pow!* "Ohhhh!" *Pow! Pow! Pow!* "OHHHH GOD *YES!*" She scowled at him, trading the pistol for the other, holstering the empty one. "You trainin' the hesitation outta me, or the heart?"

"You got enough heart for both of us."

She rolled her eyes.

"I been lookin' for you for days, Robin Hood," said Heinrich, grinding his teeth. "This ain't you. You're better than this. Come back home."

"Don't start that, you old bastard."

"Hey," Heinrich protested, as Robin turned the pistol around, "who you callin' old?"

"*You*, you dried-up old bastard." She proceeded to slowly saw the cold gun barrel in and out of her crotch like a credit card that just wouldn't take. "I bet you can't even get it up at *your advanced age.*"

Hurt and anger battled on his face. Heinrich sat back down at his table and puffed on his cigar, his eyes going dead. *Maybe I went a little too far, maybe got a little weird with that one.* She gave a mental shrug. *So what? He deserves to be uncomfortable. Deserves more than that. Deserves a good ass-kicking.*

"Hey," said someone behind her. Baldy.

"Yeah?" asked Robin, crawling toward him. He had a twenty in his hand, but he wasn't holding it out to her.

"Are those scars on your legs?"

Old hashmarks shared space with fresh scabs, a dozen of them across the tops of her thighs. She'd tried to cover them with makeup, but the harsh stage lights made them stand out—along with her goose bumps—like Braille. "So what if they are?"

"Well, like," said the man, wincing sheepishly, "I just wanted to know if you were okay. Looks like you've been, I dunno, cutting yourself or something."

She turned the pistol around and pushed it into his hands. "You too? I'm showing you my tits, and you want to psychoanalyze me?"

He looked down at the pistol in his hands like she'd handed him a picture of his dead grandma.

"Thanks, Dad, but I'm fine," Robin said, climbing up the pole.

"I just care, man, you know? I give a fuck."

"Good, I could use a few." She grinned coldly. "I'm all out of those."

"Bitch," he muttered.

In lieu of another thanks, she took another jaunt around the pole, untying the bikini bottom, and laid it gently over the top of another man's head. Her pubic bush glossed in the footlights.

Laughing, she looked over at Heinrich to satisfy herself with the expression on his face, but his table was empty, his cigar stubbed out in the ashtray.

• • •

The western horizon was a slash of purple and orange by the time Robin came out of the club, a little wobbly from the liquor, counting a wad of cash. Or at least she was trying to, because the minute she stepped out of the employee entrance, her mind decompressed, her frame unlocked, and her eyes fogged up with tears.

When she looked up again, she stood at the edge of an infinite expanse of hardpan, furred with dry sagebrush and overpowered by the full majesty of the Texas sunset. It was the most beautiful thing she'd ever seen.

"Did you get it out of your system?"

Her Obi-Wan Kenobi sat on the hood of his ancient Ford Fairlane, a devil-red land yacht of a car. In his hands glittered a long, thin dagger, and his hat lay open by his right leg, as if waiting for donations.

"What are you still doing here?" she asked in a low, miserable voice.

"Thought you might like a ride back to wherever you're staying." He stared at his feet, wagging the dagger in his hands as if it were a diving board and the pavement below his feet was a swimming pool. "Where *are* you staying, if I may be so bold?"

"Nowhere right now," she replied. "I mean, I guess I have my van, but I have some money, though; I can stay in a motel room if I want."

"You bought a van with the money you stole out of my cookie jar?"

"Yeah."

"Is it down by the river?"

"If that's a joke, I don't get it."

A few moments passed as they lingered, sizing each other up, perhaps. Robin squinted at the silver dagger, gesturing at it with a handful of ones. "You told me that'll help me kill Marilyn Cutty and her coven."

"Yes, ma'am. Thought it was high time you saw it, got a look at it for yourself. Held it in your hand. No more wooden swords, no more rubber Ka-Bars."

Her feet carried her over to him. She wore the bikini again, her jacket over her shoulders like a cape, and the *algiz* tattoo stood out on her white chest like a cattle brand. She held out her hands and Heinrich put the dagger into them. Might have been her imagination, but Robin thought she felt a peculiar heat in the handle, a subliminal static charge. Or perhaps it was just the heat of Heinrich's hand.

"You sure this can kill a witch?"

"It can pin one down like a butterfly in a case, so you can burn 'em good, just like Tilda. You jab a witch with this and push it all the way through into the floor, and they'll be there until the end of days."

Hair blew across her face. She tucked it behind her ear.

"I have a headache," she said, and Heinrich said, "I'm sorry," both of them speaking at the same time.

"Got some Tylenol"—he tipped a thumb back at his car—"rolling around in there somewhere."

She stared into his weather-beaten brown face.

All I gotta do is piss you off.

"No more Lucky Lukes. No more of that shit. You can PT me until I shit my kidneys out, I'll even let you beat me up with the pugil sticks some more, but if you do that to me again—"

"Cross my heart—"

"Never again," she said a little more forcefully. "You—"

"—hope to die."

"You do that to me again and you'll be lucky if I leave again. I might just catch you asleep and use this on you." She offered him back the silver dagger, but he didn't reach for it. She thrust it out a little more. His hands went up in mild surrender. "You want me to keep it?"

"Yeah. Keep an eye on it for me, will you?"

Wispy, starry clouds glided across the flat of the blade. She nodded solemnly.

"I'll take care of it."

"Back in the day, the Persians called it the Osdathregar. Folks I ran with called it the Godsdagger. Whatever you wanna call it, you take care of it, and it'll take care of you."

Track 23

Now

Boxes were piled against the wall: Budweiser, Coors, Frito-Lay, Yuengling, Dos Equis, Miller Light, Coca-Cola, Dr. Pepper. A wide metal door in the far wall led into what was probably a walk-in freezer—for meat, maybe? Probably alcohol, too. No casement windows allowed sunlight into the room, but a pair of humming fluorescent lights hung from chains.

"How did you do what you did to me?"

Roused by the sound of an angry voice, Kenway looked around in a daze. His wrists were tied together and the rope was over a metal pipe in the ceiling. Three men wearing Los Cambiantes colors stood nearby, but they weren't paying attention to him.

Magician Rook had been tied to a chair, a bandanna around her eyes. Her shirt was gone, though she still wore her sooty bra and black jeans.

"I want to know," one of them said. "And you're going to tell me."

"Can't tell you. Just something you have to learn," Rook said exasperatedly, rote dialogue she'd probably been repeating all night. "It takes—"

A tall drink of water with salt-and-pepper Fabio hair slapped her across the face. To her credit, she didn't make a sound, even though she had apparently already been through plenty. Her nose was bleeding, she had a fat lip, and her face was livid with bruises.

"Then teach me," said Santiago. His right arm was in a sling, his chest shrouded in bandages. His skin was a livid pink, and burn scars made grotesque whorls across his face and arms. "I want to know how you did what you did. How you move things with your mind."

"Looks like Big Boy is awake," grunted a short, barrel-chested guy in a pinstripe dress shirt. The patch on his biker vest said his name was MEZA. The pencil mustache made him look like a Latin Danny DeVito.

Santiago glared at Kenway, but his scowl broke into a grin. "Good morning, sunshine. Did you sleep okay?"

"Slept in worse places," said the veteran. His mouth tasted like feet and cheese. "Where am I? What did you do with my leg?" Then he saw it dangling from Meza's hand by the ankle, pointed at the floor like a baseball bat. "Man, it would really mean a lot to me if you could put that back on."

Meza wound up and clubbed Kenway across the belly with his own prosthetic leg.

"Swing, batta-batta!" laughed Santiago.

"Urrgh." Kenway bent double, though the impact wasn't nearly as forceful or painful as he let on. He broke character and laughed, tossing his hair out of his eyes; he couldn't help it, the display was pathetic. "I'm sorry, man, you hit like a little girl. How did Little League tryouts go? Make the team yet?" If he could piss them off and divert their attention, maybe they would leave Rook alone.

Meza stared, astounded. "This motherfucker!"

A grenade went off in Kenway's sinuses as Santiago's fist pumped into his face. He rocked back, the pipe in the ceiling the only thing keeping him upright. "Now, *that's* what I'm talkin' about! Woo!" said Kenway, swaying giddily. Blood coursed from his nostrils and down the back of his throat. He spat it on the floor at their feet.

"Gimme that," Santiago snarled, ripping the prosthetic leg out of Meza's hand. He whacked Kenway in the knee with it like he was clearing brush with a bush axe.

The pipe in the ceiling creaked ominously under the big vet's weight as he dropped onto his wrists with a shout of pain. "Talk shit *now,* pendejo!" Santiago stepped over to a workbench and hammered the fake leg savagely against the edge of the countertop until it came apart in a spray of titanium and plastic.

Damn, man, Kenway thought, despair washing over him. *I'm useless on one foot.* He scanned the cellar from where he stood, searching for something he could use as a crutch. A dry mop stood in an empty bucket next to a deep sink. Maybe he could use that.

Throwing the leg across the room, Santiago scowled. "I know what you're doin'. Ain't going to work." As he turned away, he seemed to have second thoughts and came back. "Hey, you're that wife-killing bitch's boy toy, ain't you? What's it like, fuckin' a butch lesbo like that? How you even get your dick in a pussy that dry?" He laughed. "Bet you kids go through a lot of Astro-Glide. How'd you even talk her *into* it? Bet you lost that leg in the sandbox. What're you, Army? Marine? I bet you're a Marine. Semper fi, buddy—you must be a hell of a man to turn a dyke."

Kenway gripped the rope and pulled himself up, stomping Santiago right in the crotch.

Tearing out of its brackets, the pipe broke loose and dropped him on his ass. The pipe hit the floor, ringing like a church bell, and the president of the Los Cambiantes went to his knees, hunkering over as if he were praying to Mecca, cupping his balls. Kenway took advantage of the distraction and dove for the busted pipe.

Throwing himself forward like a frog, Santiago did a sort of stretching fencer's lunge, stomped Kenway's hand, mashing his fingers with a heavy, chunky-soled riding boot.

The bones in his hand ground together in excruciating pain. *"Aah! Goddammit!"* shouted the vet, grimacing. He let go.

Santiago stood, pulling his right hand out of the sling and massaging his crotch. Flying into a rage, he whacked Kenway across the back with the pipe. When the big vet rolled over with a bark of pain, the changeling biker beat on him. Iron pipe bounced off his forearms and knuckles. He turned his wrists so he caught most of the blows in the muscle. Still, it was everything he could do to keep from getting his arms broken.

Reaching for the pipe on the downswing, he tried to grab it out of Santi's hand but missed. It skittered up his knuckles and he turned his face at the last second, earning a blow across the side of the head. Luckily, he'd slowed it enough that it didn't break his jawbone, but the brain-jarring knock to the skull threw Kenway into a blind rage and he punched his assailant in the shinbone.

"Ay! Fuck you, boy!" Santiago tried another swing.

This time Kenway caught it, ripping it out of his hand. The vet sat up and swatted Santiago across the thigh with the pipe. Awkward angle and a short swing, but the biker still yelped. No doubt he was feeling the jabs Robin had given him the night before. Kenway pointed the pipe at the other men and they hesitated, but only for a second. Long enough for their new pack leader to interrupt.

"Let him stew," said Santiago. "He ain't got but one leg. He ain't goin' nowhere. Look at him. He's a crip. What's he gonna do? He's a one-legged man in an ass-kicking contest." He laughed and opened the door, ushering Meza and the other guy out. "Come on, I have to take Carly home, and then we'll come back and deal with these shitheads." He turned to Kenway, his eyes flashing gold. "You best be glad I'm runnin' on fumes, boy, or your ass would be grass."

Before he slipped out, Santiago paused and smiled. "Your girl didn't make it out, by the way."

"What?" Kenway went cold all over.

"Your little Xena Warrior Cunt Princess. Didn't make it out of the house before it went down." Santiago grinned. "Last time I saw her, she was on fire. Eyes runnin' out of her face like candle wax. She's one crispy bitch." He spat on the floor. "That's what she gets for messin' with me and mine. Mess with my family, you get dead."

Tears pooled in Kenway's eyes and ran into his beard. Sudden deep despair took his voice away. The sound his gritting teeth made in his head reminded him of the creaking of the timbers settling as the house burned above him, and that only drove the knife deeper.

"Maybe I'll go back up there and piss on her ashes," said Santiago.

Kenway threw himself forward and swung the pipe in rage, but came up short. The tip banged against the cement floor, ringing loudly.

"*Tsk tsk.*" Santiago wagged a finger.

"I'm going to kill you," Kenway said coldly, breathlessly, and meant it. His heart was gone, and in the middle of his chest was a deep dark hole.

"I believe it."

"I'm going to rip you apart."

"Keep ahold of that anger. It's all you got left. Now if you'll excuse me, I got things to do. Peace out, white boy." Santi flashed a V sign in farewell. "Ring the front desk if you get hungry."

The door clicked shut, and keys rattled on the other side as someone locked it. Heavy door, probably solid oak. Considering the deadbolt was shot into a brick wall and it opened into the cellar, he'd never be able to kick it open even if he had two legs.

The only other door was the walk-in cooler across the room. He had no delusions they'd be able to escape that way.

Kenway dragged himself over to Rook. "You okay?"

Blood leaked from her nose, dripping into her bra. "Yes . . . yes, I suppose I am. They're going to kill me, though. When that man realizes he's not going to get what he wants, he's going to kill me." Her mouth drew into a deep, hopeless frown, and she hunkered down, her shoulders bunching up. Quiet tears ran out from under the bandanna, cutting tracks in the blood. "I don't want to die, Mr. Griffin. I'm not ready to go yet."

"They're not going to kill you," said Kenway. He peeled off the Origo's blindfold to reveal haunted eyes. "We're going to get out of here."

"We're not. We're not getting out of here. This was a mistake, wasn't it, coming down to Texas?" The longer Rook spoke, the more frantic she became. "Andy warned me about this, about getting mixed up with Martine. I should have listened."

"We are." His fingers worked at the knots behind Rook's back, trying to untie her hands. "We are getting out of here."

"What is that stink?" she asked, glancing back at him over her shoulder. "The pipe you tore down, was that a natural gas line?" Just faintly, at the end of the broken pipe where it jutted out of a hole in the joists, he could make out the ripple of distortion where gas spewed silently out into the air. "Hurry up," said Rook. "We need to get out of here before it reaches the pilot light in the furnace. Or we suffocate, whichever one happens first."

"I'm trying. Knot's too tight and I don't have anything to cut it with."

"In my pocket—the lighter. My lighter. Take it out, please. Get it."

"Busy trying to untie you."

"Get the lighter, then go back to what you were doing," said Rook. "I want you to have it in case we don't get out of here before they get back. In case you escape and I don't. I need someone to carry the relic out of here so this evil bastard doesn't get his hands on it."

Slipping his fingertips into her pocket, he dug around in the soft lining until he discovered the steel rectangle of her Zippo nestled against the curve of her thigh. "How do you use it?" he asked. "Maybe we can unlock the door with it."

"That would be a good idea, if the room wasn't filling up with flammable gas. I have to ignite it to use it. Power conduit, you have to use it to make it work. Use it in here, we both go up in a fireball."

"Shit." He coughed. The room was beginning to spin.

"Now put that in your pocket and get back to untying me. Hurry!"

Over in the corner, the furnace was a massive metal obelisk with a Rheem badge on the front. From where he sat, he couldn't see a pilot light, and he didn't hear any sound coming from it. "That thing even running?" He frantically picked at the knotted rope behind the magician's back. "I mean, it's summer; I wouldn't imagine they'd need heat anyway."

"No idea. Don't want to find out the hard way. Hurry up!"

Track 24

A shabby pile of rags sat up with a start, awakened by some furtive noise. Gendreau's pearlescent blond hair flew around his head in the early-morning breeze, now gray and cottony with soot.

Under the bridge, it was still dark. The magician sat in a pebbly scree next to one of the struts, opposite the crashed Winnebago. Wind blew smoke in his face. Squeezed in his slender hands was the Osdathregar, the witch-killer dagger. She'd handed it to him before he ran after the girl.

The girl . . .

At the bottom of the ravine he could see the dried blood where Marina Valenzuela had fallen. A vulture perched on a rock next to it, inspecting the tacky red splatter, looking for carrion to salvage. Tuco's grotesque lizard torso was still down there, a pile of green and black, and the vulture picked at the tangle of gore hanging out of his severed waist.

The biker gang must have taken Marina's body.

Yellow lizard eyes stared lifelessly up at him as the carrion-eater pulled at Tuco's guts. Gendreau hefted a baseball-sized rock and threw it. The bird took off, heavy wings beating the air.

"Ah, God. Aaahhhh. . . ." He sat back and pressed fists against his eyes.

Such a fucking coward.

Memories loaded into his head in chunks and starts like computer programs: the previous night's battle, running after Carly, fleeing into the darkness.

"Wait! Come back!"

Running, the girl running, cutting through the motel pool area.

"Stop!"

Werewolves chasing them. Two. Three of the slavering, laughing, capering beasts, chasing them through the motel.

Had to hide. Carly broke for the bridge. The magician didn't know what she had in mind—fleeting thoughts of seeking safety in the Winnebago, or perhaps some deluded need to go down into the ravine and find her mother—but he had the idea to hide under the bridge. Some part of his mind told him that it was a futile endeavor—no doubt they would find him under there—but it was the only cover he could see. He overtook her, sprinting, his Italian leather shoes clapping, outpacing her, and ran for the bridge guardrail.

"Down here!" he called to her, skidding down the wash. Rocks tumbled around him. But he was alone.

The girl did not follow.

Footsteps overhead. She had continued on, running across the bridge. He was about to shout, "Down here!" but the sound of panting and of toenails clicking across asphalt made him hold his tongue.

"No!" screamed Carly, as the wolves caught her. "NO!"

Rooted to the spot, heart pounding, shaking like a tuning fork, Gendreau prepared himself for her screams as the wolf-men shredded her, but there was only struggling and swearing.

"Let me go!" she screamed. They were carrying her away.

Panic laced his fingers behind his head, and Gendreau withdrew into the shadows under the bridge, crouching at the top of the ravine's slope like a gargoyle, trembling, listening to his heart thunder in his chest until he was sure the werewolves had gone away, and then he cried in utter fear and shame.

Engine. Getting closer. Louder.

The magician opened his eyes. A vehicle squealed across the bridge, grumbled down the long, sandy highway, and screeched to a stop in front of the motel. The *clap* of a door slamming shut.

Scrambling out from under the bridge and over the edge of the ravine, the magician stood and beheld a pitiful sight: the house behind the motel was only a pile of embers, a tumble of black pikes pointing haphazardly at the gray sky. Smoke loomed over the scene like a tornado, rising into the sky, drifting into the east. In the front yard, someone was on his knees in front of a woman in a jean jacket. From here it looked like Navathe. The woman pointed a hunting rifle at his face. Navathe was wounded, holding his side, a vivid patch of blood soaking into his Batman T-shirt.

"Hey!" Gendreau shouted from the bridge.

Both man and woman looked at him. The woman swiveled and aimed the rifle down the hill, shouldering the stock. *POCK!* A bullet whirred in and clanged off the guardrail next to him. Gendreau screamed, ducking.

No second shot followed.

Still prostrate, he peered through his filthy hair at the top of the hill. Navathe was talking to the woman and she had lowered the rifle.

Tucking the Osdathregar into the back of his belt, Gendreau walked up the hill with his hands up, his expensive shoes digging troughs in the loose soil. Great swaths of the hillside were scorched, the grass seared and black, crunching under his shoe soles. Roasted wolf corpses littered the property, at least twenty or thirty of them, smoking in the morning air. To his horror, it smelled like pulled pork.

When he got to the top, he went straight to Navathe and held out his relic healing ring, starting on the wound in the pyromancer's side. "Thank you so much," said Navathe, teetering forward onto his hands in the soot and dirt.

"Thank God it's not another gunshot wound."

"What do you mean, *magicians*?" the woman asked. She looked natural running around with a hunting rifle, black-haired and plain, Latina, slim and fit, wearing all denim and sensible combat boots. She looked like a survivor from a zombie movie.

"Just what I said, lady," said Navathe. "*Unnngh!* Magicians, as in, *people that do magic*."

"That what you're doing?" she asked, gesturing with her elbow. "Magic?"

Hummingbirds of red light flickered between the curandero's ring and the claw marks in Navathe's side. As they watched, the ragged skin slowly knitted itself together. "That's what I do, ma'am," said Gendreau. "I do magic."

A ringtone cut through the morning, startling all three of them with a tiny voice yelling in Spanish. Still staring at the two men in suspicion, the woman tucked the rifle into her armpit and took out a cell phone, answering it in the same language, and giving the two men a suspicious sidelong look as she did so.

"Andy," said Navathe.

"What?"

Navathe rubbed his face exasperatedly and hesitated, as if the words were cold, hard diamonds embedded deep into the coal of his mind and he had to chip them free. "I don't think she made it." All of his cheeky confidence had fled, and his hands shook. "She was in the house when it came down."

No need to ask who "she" was, the *she* in the house.

Gendreau's face and hands went cold, and his guts turned to water, his heart becoming heavy stone and sinking into his bowels. He stood up without saying a word and walked on numb stilts toward the tumble of still-smoking ruins.

Most of the front porch had survived the fire, except for a trail of black going up the front steps. The roof had collapsed, though, dropping a pile of embers on top of it.

Burnt paint and filth made a foul horror of the air. The only sounds were the subtle crackle of hidden fires, the hollow breath of the wind, and his shoes in the dirt. Gendreau stumbled around the side of the house, trying to find entry through the debris. The house had fallen in, creating what looked like the remains of a gigantic campfire, a pile of gothic black spikes. "She's a demon, she's a demon," he muttered endlessly to himself, eyes searching the black angles of the house. "She's a demon, she's a *demon*. Of course she survived. They *live* in fire, don't they? They're filled with fire. They're *all about* fire. Fire is all they know, right?"

The back wall of the kitchen was mostly intact—an eight-foot shark's tooth of clapboard—but had fallen in, creating a sort of archway where he crawled through on his hands and knees onto a mangled treasure map of linoleum.

To his right, a slope of blackened wood planks led up to empty space where the second floor had been. Gendreau peered through a gap by the fridge and saw where the living room ceiling had collapsed into the basement. "Robin?" he asked, or at least he tried. His voice caught in his throat. Standing in the destroyed kitchen, clutching the Osdathregar against his chest, he tried again. "Robin? Are you in here?" His chest seized in a hot, hard anguish as his eyes darted over the ruins. "Come on, Miss Martine, Robin, you're okay. You've got to be. You've *got* to be."

Navathe slipped under the kitchen wall. "Hey," he said gently.

"What?"

The pyromancer pointed at the bottom of the pile of wood where the ceiling had caved in on the cellar stairs. He didn't say anything, and he didn't have to.

Pins and needles raced up and down Gendreau's body and he turned away, pacing in what was left of the kitchen. A sob forced its way out of the pit of his stomach. A carbonized hand protruded from underneath the fallen ceiling, gnarled into a black, claw-like fist.

Tucking the dagger behind his belt again, the curandero reluctantly joined Navathe as he started trying to lift it off of the hand's owner, and together they hauled the burned wood up, dumping ashes all over the floor, and turned it aside with a crash. Smoke and soot roiled up as it broke. Underneath was a figure coiled into a fetal position, a charcoal ghost.

Faint orange light traced veins across her embrous skin where tissue still smoldered inside. Her teeth were white pearls in a black mouth.

Tears streamed out of Gendreau's eyes. "No, no, no, no, no."

"I'm so sorry, mate," mumbled Navathe.

All they could do was stare in despair and disbelief. "I don't know, I just *don't,* how could this happen?" Gendreau raked his arm across his face to wipe away the tears and left a war-paint stripe of gray. "I don't know how demons work, but damn. Damn, man. How could this be? I don't get it." His brain was a tangle of disconnected thoughts, all fighting for attention. "She grew her fucking *arm* back. This shouldn't have been—"

His hands started to hurt. Gendreau looked down.

"Ow." The silver Osdathregar in his fists. "Ow! Shit!" Getting hot, as if it had been heated over a fire. In seconds, the heat was unbearable. He fumbled the dagger on the floor.

Thin blue smoke—like the oil smoke coming out of a model train's smokestack—whispered up from the linoleum underneath it, as if it were eating a hole through.

"What in the world?" asked Navathe.

Crack.

Navathe twitched and took a step backward. "Oh, my, God. Oh my sweet Jesus God, Andy."

The corpse moved.

Track 25

She heard them coming into the house, heard their shoes scuffing on the charred boards. "Robin? Robin? Are you in here? Come on, Miss Martine, Robin, you're okay. You've got to be. You've *got* to be."

"I'm in here," she wanted to say, but her mouth didn't want to work right; her jaw had been tied shut like Marley's ghost, and she couldn't draw breath to speak. How unfair—they hadn't even left a coin on her tongue for the ferryman.

The morning's wind, even slipping meekly through the cracks in the wood, was as icy as an Antarctic gust. If she thought she could, she would have shivered. The fire. Had she fallen asleep? Had she *died*? Was this how death went? Your soul doesn't actually go anywhere, you just sit in your corpse, unable to communicate, watching the world pass you by until there's nothing but dust, nothing for what's left of you to cling to?

Where do you go after that?

Soft sunlight fell across Robin as the two men lifted the wood off of her and pushed it aside with a crash.

"No, no, no, no, no."

"I'm so sorry, mate."

Their voices were muffled and hollow, distant, as if heard through an air vent in a drafty old mansion. She listened to them talk, listened to them stand there and stare. She wanted to console the magician, to give him a hug around the neck and tell him that—

(that they would be better off without her? The world would? No. That's defeat talking. That's the Blackfield psych ward talking)

—that everything would be okay.

Am I still dead if I can give myself a pep talk?

"You're not dead, my love," said a warm third voice.

Mama?

"Yes, I'm here."

Mama, I didn't make it. Look at me. Santiago kicked my ass fair and square.

Visions of Annie passed across the surface of Robin's mind: the two of them sitting in the kitchen of 1168, Robin just five years old, tears rolling down her face. Annie knelt in front of her, pulling a Band-Aid across an ugly scrape on her knee. "You'll live, it's not that bad," she said, and made her daughter a glass of chocolate milk and a peanut butter and honey sandwich, and lo and behold, she did indeed live.

This is a bit worse than falling off the front porch, Mama.

"Did you forget what you are?" asked Annie's ghost. Her lisp had disappeared again. "*Who* you are?" A hand pressed itself against Robin's shoulder, and it was like being caressed through an astronaut suit. She was encased in unfeeling death, a roasted husk.

(demon demon demon crooked cambion)

How could I forget?

"Then get up. Get up, you little hellion." Annie challenged her and berated her like a drill sergeant. "Get up. Walk it off. Ain't no daughter of mine gonna get beat that easy."

What is that noise? It sounds like

(bacon cooking, ain't nothin good bacon can't make better)

flies buzzing.

"Ow!" shouted Gendreau, and he dropped something on the floor, something heavy, something metallic.

A cold, hard light materialized in front of her, like a distant star. She peered through stiff eyelids and saw the Osdathregar lying at the magician's feet, almost within reach. The dagger burned with an intense white fire, slag sizzling out of the sun's reflection like a welder's torch.

"I think it likes you," said Annie.

Can I keep it?

Annie, 1999, laughing as five-year-old Robin holds up a beat-up-looking cat for her mother's approval. "Yes, if you promise to—"

—Feed it.

Yes, it's hungry, isn't it?

Who do you really belong to, Mr. Knife?

Track 26

Crack. Crackle. Crumbs of charcoal dribbled from its arm as the cinder-corpse slowly, glacially slowly, reached for the dagger. Black fingers uncurled and hooked uselessly against the warped linoleum.

"Oh, fuck *me,*" said Navathe.

He stumbled outside to retch in the weeds.

Crackle. One of Robin's legs rose up and she planted a foot on the cellar door frame, pushing herself weakly across the floor. More charcoal fell off with a soft clatter. Almost imperceptible, barely audible under the wind, a dry rattle slipped out through her pearly grimace.

Anguish and terror mixed into a ball of acid in Gendreau's throat. His legs buckled and he fell on his ass, pushing himself in the other direction until his back met the wall. The Osdathregar was now a strange firebrand, glowing an angry propane-blue against the dark linoleum, piercing his ears with a tinnitus whine.

A black film spread outward from the dagger, radiating like

mold across the floor. "What the hell is *happening*?" Gendreau said in a shell-shocked whisper.

One carbon claw reached for the Osdathregar.

"Do you want this?" he asked the girl, or what remained of her.

Coal-encrusted fingers flexed for the dagger's handle.

The magician stuck a foot out to push it closer to the Robin-shape. Turned out to be more of a kick, knocking it past her outstretched hand and next to her face. The seared hand retreated, folding around the dagger's blade. Her mouth opened with a gruesome *crack* and she screamed feebly, a baby-bird squeak, exhaling a gnat-cloud of red embers. Her roasted skin turned as black as pig iron, and her hand and arm seemed to plump and regain their original shape, filling out.

My God, thought the curandero, *my God, I can't even imagine . . .*

Sliding one burned arm under her, Robin pushed herself to a sitting position. Her face was a gaunt parody of human features, frozen in a toothy yawn, eyes shriveled. Gendreau watched in a state of stunned horror. *She looks like a stop-motion skeleton in a Ray Harryhausen movie.*

She opened her eyes, like jade lit from within, green traffic lights in the pits of her eye sockets.

Demon eyes.

The darkness seeping out of the Osdathregar ran down her wrist, encroaching on one of those veins of deep, smoldering red. A cloud of steam spewed out of the crack as the dagger's coldness battled the heat of the fire under her skin. Gendreau crawled through the gap under the wall, stumbling down the back steps and out into the sand, where he turned to regard the house and the steam billowing up out of it.

The coal figure lurched through the back door and down the stairs in hesitant, stiff, mummy-like steps. Her arms, still drawn tight against her body in rigored knots, had turned smooth shadow-black, matte-black, as if she'd been spray-painted. Robin paused on the steps, unsteady, and Gendreau came forward to help her, but she jerked away, almost falling.

"No," she whispered, glancing at him with incandescent eyes.

Three of them. Three eyes.

A third eye had opened in the middle of her forehead.

No, Jesus, there were *five* of them! Two other eyes opened in her temples. All of them focused on Gendreau's face and a sublime chill vibrated through him. Hair on the back of his neck stood on end.

"The hell is going on?" Navathe, astonished, crouching in the weeds.

Gendreau shrugged helplessly back at him.

"Don't know," Robin wheezed through her lipless teeth. "I think it's happening again." Pieces of charcoal fell away as the burned husk peeled off to exhibit beet-red muscle, only to be replaced by a strange shell, as though the dagger was recreating her flesh out of black leather. The Osdathregar's influence spread across her chest and up her neck, trickling down the xylophone of her chest.

"Demonization?" Navathe stared in amazed fear. "Is this what it looks like?"

"Does it hurt?" asked Gendreau.

"It did. Oh God, it did." Her voice was an elevator full of people all whispering at the same time, and when she spoke, her mouth didn't move, a grim reaper's grin, white teeth set in flawless obsidian, fossils stuck in a tar pit. "Not anymore." Liquid shadow continued up her neck and down her belly in fractal Mandelbrot splotches, spreading, ossifying, covering. Slipped over her chin and poured itself up her jaw, becoming a soot-and-bone mask.

Two black horns thrust into the air from the crown of her skull, becoming a thorny rack of antlers, as the charcoal shell slid over her forehead. Intricate lines etched themselves down the edge of her jaw, tracing chevrons down her throat and a thousand scrolling curlicues along the contours of her chest, as if some invisible artist were putting the final touches on a suit of medieval armor.

Robin looked like Persephone brought to life. As the demon came down the back steps of the house, her five eyes twinkled green emeralds in the watery dawn sun. "Mama says I got promoted," she said, her voice strange and multitiered, two people talking in unison: Robin, and a deeper, darker thrum, like a violin and a bass in harmony.

"Oh, my God," said the Latina woman with the rifle. She'd put away the cell phone and now stood behind the magicians, her mouth wide open.

"Promoted into *what,* love?" Navathe asked, staring with terrified eyes, his mouth hanging open. "And why isn't the Sanctification killing her or expelling her?" he asked Gendreau. "She's not in Hell, not in some pocket dimension or otherworld. She's right here on Earth, in front of us. She should be evaporating, or being sucked down into a hole in the ground or something."

Candle flames licked up from the corners of her mouth as Robin studied her black-gauntleted hands. "He was right. He was right—the Godsdagger, it *did* take care of me."

"What the fuck are you?" asked the woman, pointing the rifle at her.

"I'm a demon. Please don't shoot me."

"Yeah, that's not very reassuring. I'm going to shoot you now."

"No!" cried Gendreau, stepping between them, his hands up. "It's okay! I know she looks like she eats babies, but she's a good guy! I swear to God."

Robin recoiled. "*What—*"

"Okay." The magician clasped his hands as if he were begging. "Okay, all right, square one: what's your name, ma'am?"

"Elisa."

"Elisa . . . ?"

"Elisa Valenzuela." She gestured with the rifle barrel. "Who are you? Why did you kidnap my brother's wife and my niece?"

"You're Santiago's sister? I, we—ahh—we didn't. We didn't kidnap anyone. We found them hiding in our Winnebago and we were going to take them to a battered women's shelter back home. Marina told us everything."

Elisa stared at Robin, still unwilling to lower the rifle.

"Who were you talking to on the phone just now?" asked Gendreau.

"My brother."

"Santiago?"

"No, the other one, Alfie—Alvaro. Our older brother. He called to tell me Santi rolled into their clubhouse with Carly, some Asian woman, and the one-legged blond guy."

"Rook and Kenway," said the five-eyed shadow-demon.

"What the hell are all these dead animals?" Elisa threw a hand at the carnage behind her. "Looks like a bunch of clowns burned down a rodeo out here."

"Werewolves. Your friends Los Cambiantes."

"*Werewolves?*" Elisa was incredulous.

"Santiago's motorcycle. It's got a—" Gendreau cut himself off. "Hard to explain. Let's just say it's got black magic in it and he's been using it to turn him and his friends into—"

"Werewolves."

Reluctantly, Gendreau nodded. "Among other things."

"You're telling me this thing is one of Santi's asshole buddies?"

"Yes. Sounds like you don't believe me, but you've been anticipating this for a while, judging by the rifle in your hands."

"I just knew Santi and his gang were up to no good. Went to the bar outside Almudena, and my friend said they found Gil's body in a house down the street. Alfie thinks Santiago's finally gone off the deep end. When they followed you out here, Alfie stayed behind and called the police in Lockwood. There's a warrant out for Santi now and every L-C member that came out here."

"If Alfie called the police, why are you running around with a rifle? That's a good way to get shot, I think. If the Los Cambiantes didn't get you, the cops probably would."

"My brother's hurt a lot of people, Mr. Magician. Wish I could tell you I came here to hurt him back, but I think I'm just doing what I've always done when it comes to Santiago."

"What's that?"

"Deal with the aftermath. Help the people he's hurt. Pick up after him." Elisa sighed. "I've always picked up after him."

"Maybe it's time to stop."

"That's what I thought—that it needs to stop. He's turned the Los Cambiantes into his own personal army." She held up the rifle. "Maybe that's why I brought this. I wanted an equalizer. People tend to stop what they're doing and listen to what you have to say when they see a gun in your hands. Also, apparently, there are demons here now, so I'm glad I brought it."

"What is he going to do with my friends?" asked Robin.

Elisa renewed her aim, and the demon put up her hands. "If shit has gone south like I think it has, and they're all on the warpath, it can't be good." She locked eyes with the curandero, and hers narrowed in resigned determination. "My brother is not a nice man."

"Neither am I," said Robin.

Elisa tightened her grip on the rifle. "I believe it."

Track 27

"We need to go," said Robin, heading toward Elisa's truck. "We need to save my boy, *now,* and we need to save Marina's little girl. I made a promise."

"Hold up," said Gendreau. "You were a bacon sculpture not ten minutes ago. Don't you think you should take a breather before you head out to fight tigers and possessed motorcycles and God knows what else?"

Wind combed through her bizarre antlers. "Do I *look* like I need a breather?"

"No, I d-don't suppose you do," Gendreau stammered as those five green lamplight eyes focused on him.

Once they were on the road, Robin found herself at a loss for something to do that didn't involve staring at her own hands like a stoner. Couple of hours at least before they arrived at the Los Cambiantes' clubhouse. According to Elisa, it was on the outskirts of Keyhole Hills near the east gate of the abandoned air base, heading out of town toward Almudena. They'd driven right past it leaving town in the Winnebago, and none of them had a clue.

"So, what do you think *this* is?" asked Gendreau, gesturing in a general way.

"Guess I'm full-on demon again." The words came out of her mouth, but they sounded as if someone else were speaking them.

Strange hunger lay in the pit of her stomach, boiling on an element of rage. Only word she could find for the feeling was *hangry,* that term for when you're angry because you're hungry, but whatever was lurking inside of her at the moment transcended mere "hangriness" and blew past the intersection of *rage* and *starvation.* She wanted to rip and tear with her teeth, like wolves setting on a caribou carcass; she wanted to rampage and devour.

What the hell was the portmanteau for it, then? *Starge? Ravation? Hurious?*

Whatever it was, it was familiar. Same feeling she'd experienced that day in Hammertown, that furious urge to jump on Heinrich and rip his face off, only ramped up into the stratosphere. She looked at her friends and suddenly they seemed quite delicate, *so delicate,* and she could imagine her jaws closing on their faces, like biting into a hollow chocolate Easter bunny.

There I am, said the glow-eyed warhawk. Her demon side. *The power was inside you all along. The real treasure was the faces we ate along the way.*

Robin looked away, mortified and terrified.

"I mean, we knew you were part demon," said Gendreau, oblivious, "but I'm hard-pressed to say this is anything like your previous sublimation at all. I distinctly remember *that*—you looked like somebody had taken apart a wicker chair and a handful of wire clothes hangers and made a human sculpture out of them. This?" Gendreau made an inclusive gesture at Robin. "This looks like a Power Ranger invented by Clive Barker. You have five glowing eyes and antlers, for Christ's sake. That's not normal."

"I think the demon side re-creates me out of whatever killed me. Or the place where I died. Or something? Whatever, I . . . M-maybe it's my built-in second chance. Maybe I'm like a cat with nine lives."

"Maybe you didn't die," said Navathe. "Maybe the demon part of you keeps you alive regardless of what happens to your body."

"My demon heart?"

They couldn't think of any better aphorisms, so they all just sat there, wobbling with the road, trying to avoid eye contact. The fire magician picked up an empty soda can and pretended to be enthralled by the ingredient list. A broom lay in the bed of the pickup truck, the old-school kind with a wooden shaft and sorghum bristles. Robin brushed the palm of her hand across the wood and contemplated the weight of it, the strength—and the irony of finding something so iconic, so entwined with her lifelong enemy, in this place, in this condition. She could make use of this.

"Just hope we can reverse it," said Robin, interrupting their reverie. The Osdathregar had stopped casting that fierce light, but it still thrummed with potential, pulsating darkly. "Gonna make it hard to get a new driver's license to replace the one that was in my wallet."

"Hope we can, too," said Gendreau.

They rode on for a while in wary silence.

Eventually, it dawned on her that she needed to hear their voices, needed their company just then. Maybe she needed to be reminded of her own humanity. To be grounded. To help drown out her own inner monologue, to keep it from filling the quiet with anxiety. The silence had an alluring, scary edge, a soundless siren call drawing her toward some deep and sinister part of herself.

The devil on her shoulder, trying to talk her into some heinous shit—that was what she needed to be distracted from. The warhawk.

"They said I could be anything," she told them, breaking the quiet, "so I became a rotisserie chicken."

Stifled laughter.

"You said you got promoted," said Navathe. "What does that mean? Do you think it has anything to do with why the Sanctification isn't blasting you to smithereens right now?"

Just the same as it had been when she'd reached out from her father Andras's Hell-prison and touched the mortal world through the painting in Kenway's studio, the air was intensely cold. The Sanctification made Earth inhospitable for her, like trying to step naked onto the skin-crystallizing surface of the distant planet Neptune.

Or at least it had been last October. This time, it was more like a casual dip into a cold mountain river. Wasn't sure what kept her from shivering uncontrollably, but she wasn't dead and she hadn't been ejected into Hell, so—points for that, perhaps.

"I don't know," she said. "What do you graduate to from a demon?"

"An angel?"

Gendreau reached out to touch her and his fingertips came away sooty. Carbon? She looked at him, her antlers thumping the ceiling. "Does this *look* like an angel to you?" she asked.

"Perhaps," said the curandero. "They're supposed to be frightening. The chubby-cheeked cherubs in classical art aren't actually angels—they're called something else, but I can't remember what."

"What if demons *aren't* fallen angels?" Robin asked. "What if it's the other way around? What if angels are ascended demons? What if they all start out that way? Like, demons are a *one* and angels are a *ten*? Maybe I leveled up to a five." Made sense to her. "Aren't angels supposed to have wings?"

"Multiple sets, from what I understand. Flaming, covered in eyes. At least, that's how classic religious literature describes them. Cherubim and seraphim. Among others."

"Wings would be cool," Robin said, picking up the broom. "Could do without the covered-in-eyes part. But I'll be straight-up honest, real talk here, I don't think I'm an angel. I think I'm back in demon mode. I got a real bad itch to fuck shit up, and not in a good way. I'm having a hard time controlling it."

Navathe blanched.

"So," said Gendreau, "the Sanctification isn't destroying you like it would have if you'd stepped foot outside of Weaver's deconjuration pocket in your demon form. If you're still a demon, that means you must have earned your right to be here in this form, Miss Martine." They stared at her again as he spoke. She felt the urge to hide her face. "You died in that fire, right?" he asked.

Her answer was just above a breath. "I don't know," she said. "I guess I did. Never died before. Don't really have a frame of reference, you know?"

"You sacrificed yourself trying to beat Santiago and save Rook," said the curandero. "You traded your life for hers. For *all* of our lives. You earned this." He punctuated each point with a jab of his finger at her, his curative ring glinting in the light. "Whatever you are now, demon, angel, para-fucking-legal, you *earned* your right to be here. You passed your supernatural bar exam. The Sanctification doesn't apply to you anymore because of what you did. You've been absolved of 'the sins of your father.'" Blinking in surprise, he added, "Putto!"

"What'd you just call me?"

"No, *putto,* that's what those angel-babies are called. They're not cherubs, they're called 'putto.' Well, *putti,* in plural. Italian. Took some art classes when I graduated high school, back before I knew about my grandfather, Frank, and his secret society."

"You didn't *always* know about the Dogs of Odysseus?"

"No." Gendreau looked like he'd been through hell—dirty, covered in bruises, fancy white shirt splattered in blood, face nicked and scratched. The scar across his throat was shiny pink in the light filtering through the window. "He came and got me out of college and talked me into joining the Dogs because he wanted someone in the family to be part of it and he didn't think my father could handle it. He didn't find out that I was assigned female at birth until almost a year after inducting me. Didn't take *that* too kindly. But by then it was too late, and he had to make do with me. Wouldn't have been fair to throw me out, and honestly I don't know if he would have even possessed the capability to do so—I was already well entrenched by then and had developed powerful friends who would have stood up for me, like the Jötunn."

Taking the broom in both hands, Robin snapped it over her armored knee, right above the bristles, leaving her with a four-foot section of wooden broom handle. She pressed the Osdathregar to the broken end and wound duct tape around it, lashing the dagger to the end of the broom handle until she had a makeshift spear.

"What'd you do that for?" asked Gendreau.

"Probably not going to get close enough to stab him with the dagger," she said. "Gonna have to needle him. Wear him down from afar."

"Why not shoot him? Got to be somewhere we can pick up some firepower in Almudena."

Testing it, she was satisfied to see the spear point didn't budge. "I cut him multiple times with the katana. Burned him. He just shrugged it off. I don't feel like guns are going to do the trick. I need something supernatural." The freshly crafted spear frothed with ghostly smoke like frozen nitrogen. The Osdathregar's influence leeched slowly down the broom handle, turning it all black. "Think I have a better chance of bringing him down if I go after him like a Roman foot soldier with the Osdathregar. With a spear, I'll have better reach."

Track 28

Then

A teenager and an old man staggered through dusty Las Vegas alleys littered with trash. Behind them burned the Oracle of the Sands Casino. Howls of cat-people—witches' familiars, men and women driven insane by arcane energies—made a siren that roller-coastered up and down, washing over them in shrill alien waves.

They'd walked into a trap. The two witch-hunters had launched an assault on Gail Symes in her casino on the outskirts of Vegas. Unfortunately, they didn't know she kept a Schrödinger box on the premises—a cat-bomb, basically, a kill switch designed to sacrifice a shit-ton of cats and send their little cat-spirits into any nearby unmarked bystanders. In just a few seconds, the entire casino was flooded with raving maniacs. They'd assassinated the eponymous oracle Gail Symes herself and barely escaped with their lives, but they'd managed to set up several firebombs throughout the building before a member of Symes's security team caught them.

Flames roared out of the casino's windows. The giant neon

Illuminati sign out front was on fire. "Gotta get you to a hospital," said Robin, blood streaming down the side of her face. Heinrich hobbled alongside her, one arm thrown over her shoulder for support. He clutched his chest where one of the security men had put a bullet in him.

Apparently, in Heinrich's world, when a 220-pound slab of beef with a Glock tells you to stop what you're doing, you forget how to English.

"No, kiddo, no hospital. Ain't got no insurance anyways."

Fire-engine sirens overcame the howling of the familiars as they wandered through the demolished front doors, shrouded in fire, and collapsed in the street. Robin carried Heinrich down a side alley bordered by restaurant kitchen doors and fire escapes, emerging into a vacant lot where her Conlin Plumbing van waited.

Vibrating with adrenaline, she helped him into his seat and closed the door on him, then threw herself into the driver's seat and fumbled her keys out of her pocket to turn the engine over. Beside her, Heinrich looked like death warmed over, a heap of crumpled man sitting in her passenger seat. His respiration was a series of wet, ragged sighs.

"Man," he grunted, his hands full of blood, "sure wish that Andy kid was here."

"Who?"

"Never mind. Just get us out of here."

"You *need* to go to a hospital," said Robin, pulling her seat belt on. "You're fucking bleeding all over the place."

"I'll be fine. Just get us home."

"Hammertown is hours away. It's in *another state,* Heinie. You're going to die if I don't—"

Even in his decimated state, her mentor could still burn a hole through a bank safe with his eyes. "Then we'll get outta town and get another motel room! The goddamn cops are going to be all over this part of town, lookin' for whoever blew that place to shit, and if we don't get out of here, we're gonna get the first degree."

“The third degree?”

“Who cares what degree? *Just drive!* And don’t”—*cough, cough*—“don’t call me Heinie!”

• • •

A car alarm chirped next to the van, *oy-oy,* wrenching Robin out of sleep. She sat up with a start and rubbed her eyes.

The van was frigid with the night cold of the desert. She’d driven all evening and into the night, ten hours, stopping in Las Cruces, New Mexico, when she couldn’t stay awake anymore. Heinrich told her it was okay to stop, she remembered. She pulled into a Walmart, a big gray Supercenter, parked in the shadows, and passed out almost immediately.

Her eyes flicked over to the passenger seat. He was gone.

Jesus Christ, blood *everywhere.*

Robin peered through the windshield but saw only a squad of frat-boys coming around the corner of the building, pushing a cart full of junk food, beer, and Gatorade. The one leading wore a hoodie with their university logo.

In the back. She twisted in the seat.

Lying on the air mattress between the racks, under a pile of blankets, with his hat over his face. Heinrich was motionless.

She shook him. “Hey, Heinie, you awake?”

No answer.

“You okay, man? Wake up.”

Still no answer.

“Oh, my God. You better not be dead, Heinrich Hammer. You better not be dead.” Bilious panic rose in her throat and suddenly she couldn’t catch her breath. Tears welled in her eyes. “Don’t leave me here all alone, you asshole. You’re all I got. Wake your Black ass up, please.” She shook him again and his hat fell off.

To her relief, his eyes were shut. But his mouth was open.

She got up on her knees and lowered her ear to his lips to listen for his breathing. Maybe? She couldn’t tell with the frat assholes laughing and screwing around next to the van making so much noise.

Pressing her fingertips to his neck, she searched for a pulse, but he was so leathery, she couldn't be sure.

"*Damn,* baby," said one of the frat boys, his alcohol-slurred voice muffled by the window. Jock type with a military haircut. "That is a *magnificent* ass. Please don't be a dude when you turn around." Robin looked over her shoulder and realized her jeans-clad rear end was up against the steering wheel.

Two guys were staring at it through the windshield. "Oh, hell yeah. This chick looks like she knows how to party. Check out that Mohawk."

"Hey, you wanna ride with us?" asked Army-Jock.

"We're on our way to Mexico, and we got *plenty* of weed."

She glanced at the motionless Heinrich and back at the frat boys. "Fuck off, please. I'm in the middle of something."

Both boys recoiled in surprise.

"*Fuck off,* she says," said the one on the right, a heavy-browed kid that could have been a stunt double for a caveman. "Man, you believe the mouth on this chick?"

"I got something she can use it for."

The third guy came around the front of their car, the one in the uni hoodie. "What are you two retards jabbering about over here?" he asked, but then he spotted Robin still bent over in the van. "Oh, my God, this punk chick is hot as fuck."

Someone pulled the van's driver door open, and turning around, Robin found herself face-to-face with Army-Jock. "What's wrong?" he asked, his breath reeking of vodka. "You swing the other way?"

"Get out of my van," Robin said, pushing him out.

Not far enough, though, and she couldn't get the door shut before he was on her again. "Bitch, I'm trying to talk to you. Just settle your ass down and gimme a few minutes to get to know you. I'm not such a bad guy."

"I don't have time for this. You're all drunk and you're not thinking straight. You need to just get in your car and leave." She shoved him and tried to close the door on him again, but he slapped the door out of her hand and thrust himself into the van, almost head-butting her. He was so drunk, he was sweaty and his eyes seemed to have trouble pointing in the same direction, drifting around like a chameleon on quaaludes. "God, I hope you're not driving."

"Why don't you step out here and get some fresh air?" he asked, grabbing the lapels of her jacket and hauling her out of the front seat. "Stinks in there." Army-Jock pressed against her.

"Stinks out here, too," said Robin.

The man kissed her.

His mouth was like making out with an ashtray full of Everclear and he needed a shave—his face could take the paint off of a car. *I can get you to do anything,* Heinrich echoed from her subconscious. *All I gotta do is piss you off.* All of the fear and shock in her popped like a bad bulb (later, she would swear she actually *heard* it pop) and turned into rage.

Biting into the soft meat of his upper lip, Robin latched on as fiercely as a snapping turtle.

The man screamed into her mouth. She didn't let go when he reeled back, and the two of them did an awkward *West Side Story* dance there in the parking lot. *"YOU CRAZY VITCH!"* he shouted, grabbing her head, and he pressed his thumbs into her eyes, squeezing stars out of her brain. Robin released her grip and slipped out of his hands, trying to see through a haze of black spots.

His friends came around the car and surrounded her.

"Who do you think you are, Mike Tyson?" asked Hoodie, pushing up his sleeves. "Who bites a dude in the mouth? He just wanted a little sugar."

"Tyson didn't bite Holyfield in the mouth; he bit him on the ear."

"To hell with sugar, man," said Army-Jock, talking through his fingers. He was cupping his bloody mouth. "Kinda just want to kick the shit out of her now."

Robin's heart pounded in her neck. Her hands shook as she methodically took out her earrings and put them in her Army jacket's pockets. Then she shrugged her jacket off and tossed it under the back bumper of the plumbing van, out of the way.

"Oh!" said Caveman Stunt Double. "She *does* want to play!"

"Think she likes it. Check *that* shit out." Hoodie pointed at her chest. The desert chill made her nipples stand up under her Florence + the Machine T-shirt.

No. I just get off on making you hurt.

The ulna bone in your forearm is one of the hardest and most impact-resistant in the human body, and what they didn't know was that she'd spent the last year or so chicken-winging a kick bag and letting Heinrich whack her across the elbows with a leather belt and then a broomstick. The little phalangeal bones in the back of your fist can break with a punch—commonly known as a "boxer's break"—but that bone running from your wrist to your elbow is like a baseball bat made of concrete.

Hoodie reached for her. She grabbed his wrist, whacking him across the face with the bony front of her elbow, and his nose crunched. He stumbled backward against the back of her van, coughing in pain. Then she turned and kicked Army-Jock's knee out from under him, driving him to the pavement with an elbow to the ear.

Stunt-Double just watched in disbelief. She didn't give him a chance to jump in, turning on him with a haymaker to the chin that twitched his head around. Pain resonated through her fist, those phalangeal bones thrumming like a tuning fork.

"Good one," he said, punching her in the stomach.

All the oxygen immediately rushed out of her—*"UUHHRRRR!"*—and she went to her knees, doubling over with a ball of molten iron in her guts. Stunt-Double grabbed her Mohawk and lifted her head so that it was even with his crotch.

"Perfect height."

"Grrrr*rrraaAAAAH*," she bellowed, punching him in the dick as hard as humanly possible.

Stunt-Double collapsed in a heap, both hands over his crotch, and lay in the fetal position, rolling back and forth. "Aaaaah!" he cried, his face turning red. Drool ran out of his mouth onto the asphalt. "*Aaaaaahh!* Christ almighty! One of my balls is gone!"

"You're done," said Army-Jock, getting up, one hand on his ear. He checked his fingers and saw blood. "That's all you get." He charged, meaning to spike her into the parking lot like a quarterback. Robin was waiting. In a flash of movement, she reached for his shirt—a plaid button-up—and turned on one heel, kneeling, and thrust her hip into his stomach, pulling him over and dropping him on the top of his head.

This was something Heinrich was more than familiar with. Robin had aikido-tossed him dozens of times.

"You brog by fuggin dose," said Hoodie, still leaning against the back of the plumbing van. Blood streamed from his nostrils, plastering his mouth in red and running down the front of his uni hoodie. He stood up straight and reached into his pocket. Unfolding a little buck knife, he brandished it at her. Light trickled down the blade. "Dow id's *by* turn."

The back doors of the van flew open and Heinrich kicked him in the ass.

As Hoodie went sprawling at Robin's feet, the blood-soaked witch-hunter stepped down out of the van. His white shirt had turned completely red.

He racked a shotgun. *Ka-chak!*

"Y'all motherfuckers got five seconds."

Army-Jock scrambled up and resumed loading their "groceries" into their trunk, hunched over like a kicked puppy. Glass beer bottles clinked and tinkled as he worked. Stunt-Double started helping him.

"DID I SAY GET YOUR SHIT?!"

All three boys threw themselves into the car—"Go go go go!"—and peeled out, backing into their own shopping cart and knocking it over. Hundreds of dollars of alcohol and bags and boxes of junk food spilled out in a cornucopia pile. *SKRRT!* The car spun out again and the frat boys drove away, the rear driver tire popping a bag of Funyuns.

Opening one of the few bottles of beer that wasn't broken, Robin took a swig and sat next to Heinrich on the back bumper of the van. She handed him another one.

"You look pretty good for a guy I thought was dead about five minutes ago," Robin said, taking a pull of Sam Adams.

He opened the Coors with a wince and downed half of it in one go, his other hand holding his ribs. "Wasn't as bad as it looked. He just dinged me. Told you all I needed was a good night's sleep."

"You bled a hell of a lot for just a 'ding.'"

He shrugged and pulled himself to his feet, limping over to the splay of food, treading in a puddle of beer. Bending over, he picked up a box of Fiddle Faddle and threw it to Robin. "Here, let's pick this shit up. Maybe it'll last us 'til we get back to Texas."

Track 29

Now

“We’re here,” said Gendreau, waking her.

The nap had done more than rejuvenate her; she felt whole again, twice as good—incredible, even. But what nibbled on the edge of her nerves was that the nap had done nothing to quell the hangriness. A ravenous hunger, a carnivorous fury. A walking appetite, armed with a nuclear temper. Felt like a black hole—massive, ominous, insatiable.

She carried Hell inside her, and it threatened to burn its way out.

The look on the curandero’s face did nothing to assuage her. Robin sat up, careful not to bang her antlers on the ceiling. “Still creepy, huh?”

“Yeah. I’m sorry.”

“It’s okay, I feel a hell of a lot better. Think the armor healed me.”

“Been working on you, too.” He held up his ring.

"Thanks."

The back door of the camper shell flipped up and the tailgate creaked open. Elisa peered in at them as Robin slid out, taking the makeshift spear with her. "Where did you get *that*?"

"Made it on the way here." The spear had turned completely black and the broom handle now seemed to be coated in the same sort of opalescent black material as her body. "Sorry about your broom. I'll buy you another one."

At the end of a short gravel driveway stood the Los Cambiantes clubhouse. Looked like a place Patrick Swayze could have called home, a sprawling ranch house with beer-brand neons and a bachelor's distinct lack of landscaping. The only vehicles in attendance were an antediluvian Buick and a bunch of Harleys.

What designated this place as belonging to the gang was the blue wolf head painted on the front door. Otherwise, it could have been any roadhouse in the south.

"This is where Kenway and Rook are?" Robin asked Elisa.

"Alvaro said they were here."

She started for the front entrance, carrying the Osdathregar spear under her armpit like General Patton with his swagger stick. The door was made of dark glass and steel, but she could see the sign inside had been flipped and read CLOSED.

Tried the handle. Locked.

She crashed the door open with one powerful kick, tearing the deadbolt out of the frame and stuffing the entire door itself into the bar beyond. The glass exploded, spraying all over the hardwood floor inside.

"You guys stay out here," she growled over her shoulder, and Robin marched into the Blue Wolf.

• • •

Inside was a spacious mead hall reminiscent of ye olde Viking taverns, with tall, airy ceilings, exposed wood beams and rafters, and a well-polished bar that ran the width of the room. Tin-sheet posters, neon signs, and nudie-mag centerfolds littered the walls, advertising seven different kinds of beer and motorcycle brands and depicting five or six busty women in tiny bikinis.

Bikers sat at tables to her left and right, while the rest of them leaned against the barstools, staring in half-amused astonishment. A radio on the bar was playing nineties hits.

Faint tongues of flame licked from the corners of her mouth. Standing on top of the ruined front door, Robin looked around at the men, her five green eyes blinking independently of each other. The antlers protruding from her forehead felt heavy and potent in a masculine, almost sexual way.

"What the hell is *that*?" said a man, getting up from what looked like an early lunch of a hamburger and fries. He smirked. "Is it Halloween already?"

The bartender, a big, bald, cornfed piece of shit in a 5.11 T-shirt, had leveled a shotgun over the bar. "I don't know, but they're paying for that fucking door."

No one said or did anything, just stood in place, stupid confused smiles on their faces, brows slowly darkening.

So, she hefted the Osdathregar spear and whipped it like a javelin. The point passed through the bartender's chest as easily as you please and lifted him off of his feet, shoving him backward and pinning him to the wall. The mirror behind him shattered and the shelves collapsed, spilling thousands of dollars of liquor bottles in a hellacious crash. *KA-BOOM,* the shotgun discharged into the ceiling, setting a deer-antler chandelier to jangling.

"Buhhhhh," groaned the bartender. Crimson slowly soaked through his white shirt. He relaxed, and the shotgun slipped out of his hands, clattering to the floor at his feet.

"Fuck that guy in particular," said the witch-hunter.

"Santi ain't here, and neither is his magic motorcycle," said Hamburger Guy, hands up, eyes searching their faces. "So, we ain't gonna be able to pull our *Dog Soldiers* trick. Now, I don't know about *you* guys, but I got shit to do today, and it don't involve having my—" He looked at Robin.

"Asshole pulled over your face like a ski mask."

"Yeah, that. Good luck, y'all." Hamburger Guy edged around her, stepped over the demolished front door, and ran outside. Echoes of a gunshot filtered through the open door as he was gunned down in the parking lot.

"Sorry," said Robin, "Should have mentioned the lady outside with the rifle."

A short, chubby guy with a John Waters mustache snatched up the bartender's shotgun and ran out the back through a door behind the bar.

Another biker picked up a pool cue and ran at her. Robin threw out an arm, blocked the stick with her elbow—*CRACK!*—then snatched it out of his hands and spun on her heel, launching it like a tomahawk across the room at someone that turned out to be "Wacky" Joaquin Oropeda. Joaquin ducked and the pool stick embedded itself in the drywall behind him.

He pulled it out and wielded it in both hands like a pike. "That puta from the vets' bar that tried to choke me out in the parking lot," he said. "It's got to be. Same voice."

"In case you forgot, she's also the bitch with the grenade launcher," said one of the men.

"She ain't got one *now,* does she?"

"Why's she look like that?" asked someone else.

"Maybe she's got that juju like Santi got."

"Nah, bruh, that's something different," said Joaquin. "That look like some devil shit."

"Where is the Japanese woman and the big blond guy?" asked Robin, eyeing them. She flexed her fingers in anticipation. "I'm only going to ask once. Does this place have a downstairs?"

"Fuck you," said Joaquin, gold tooth flashing. "I don't care *why* you look like that; I'm gonna beat your spooky ass." The radio segued into Rage Against The Machine's seminal anticapitalist mosh-fuel hit "Maggie's Farm," and the room exploded into movement.

Track 30

Finally, the knot slipped loose and Kenway relaxed a bit, pulling the rope free. Grinding the heels of his hands into gritty eyes, he lay on his back. "Okay, now what?"

Gas still poured from the broken pipe in the basement ceiling, distorting the air. "Now we figure out a way to unlock that door from this side without blowing ourselves up. Starting to feel sick." The Origo staggered to her feet and went to the door, turning the handle. "Just a deadbolt. Why is there a deadbolt on a cellar door, anyway?"

"Probably to keep people out of the stock room. And I'm guessing this probably ain't the first time they've had somebody down here." Kenway dragged himself toward the walk-in cooler door in the far wall. "Our best bet is to hide in there. We'll be better off cold than dead. Come help me open this door."

"Look, guy," Rook made her way to the door and opened it, kicking a box of Yuengling beer in front of it to prop it open. "I have to tell you something, in case we can't get out."

“Don’t know what you could possibly need to tell me, considering you barely know me, but right now, our top priority is getting away from this gas before we die.”

“I need to tell you my real name.”

Gripping the shoulders of Kenway’s shirt, she started dragging him toward the cooler. Between the two of them, they managed to inchworm him across the cellar. “Your real name?” he asked, low-crawling the last several feet over the cooler threshold. The freezer floor was searingly cold, burning his arms. “Rumpelstiltskin?”

“Haruko.”

That was familiar. “Leon Parkin’s wife? Thought you were dead.”

“Only on the inside.”

The cellar door slammed open and a man charged in, eyes wide in panic. Meza, the short guy with the pencil mustache, and he carried a shotgun, a fancy country-club double-barrel with a wooden stock. Kind of thing a bartender in a biker dive might keep behind the bar. “Hey, the fuck you doing?” he asked, marching toward them, just in time for Rook to slam the freezer door in his face.

Meza grabbed the handle and tried to open it, but Kenway was holding the handle on the other side. Peering through a tiny window, they could see the top of the biker’s head bobbing below. “You know what, asshole?” Meza asked, raising the shotgun and racking the pump, “I got a key right here.” He backed up and leveled the shotgun at the door handle.

“NO!” Rook and Kenway shouted in unison.

Track 31

Someone grabbed her from behind and Robin reversed the man into the pool table, pinning him against the rail. Joaquin ran in and smashed the pool cue across her chest. Felt like he'd whacked her with a foam pool noodle. She kicked him in the belly, somersaulting him into a table, scattering Hamburger Guy's lunch all over the floor.

Someone slammed a pool ball into the back of her head and she barely registered the thing as it bounced off the carbon shell-helmet.

Wheeling on him, she lowered her head and plunged the antlers into his belly, pitchforking him off his feet and on top of the pool table. He screamed as she pulled out, the prongs festooned with stinking streamers of intestine. Blood ran down her face.

Scrambling to his feet, Joaquin wrenched the Osdathregar spear out of the bartender, climbing on top of the bar.

Fists and chairs came at her from either side. She took hold of a man's belt with both hands and bicep-curled him straight up into the ceiling, where his skull collided with an exposed timber, eliciting a singular coconut *bonk*. She flung him into his friends and then a man screamed—a strangled, high-pitched banshee shriek, Robin couldn't tell if it was terror, or bloodlust, or agony. She turned to look.

Raising the Osdathregar spear, Joaquin leapt at her like a crazed Spartan warrior from a movie, preparing to pin her to the clubhouse floor.

Even as he came down, Robin saw the spear burning his hands, frost-smoke shooting from between his fingers. She reached up and grabbed the haft of the weapon, pole-vaulting him into the crowd headfirst.

Before she could react, men were all over her, slugging her in the face and ribs with what felt like a thousand punches, a cloud of fists. Robin pugil-sticked them with the Osdathregar, bone and teeth snapping under the butt of the spear, the dagger point tearing through skin and fabric.

Another hard object collided with her head and Robin stumbled to her hands and knees. Chair, it felt like. Pieces of wood clattered all over the floor.

One of the antlers protruding from her skull broke off.

Lying on the floor, it resembled some kind of chitinous alien creature, a big black stick insect. A leather boot banged into her face, snapping her head back. Two teeth clicked on the hardwood, knocked free. Spitting a gout of blood, she managed to get one foot under her, and an attacker clubbed her across the back with a barstool, knocking the wind out of her.

"UHHHRRR-hrrrr," she bellowed at the forest of blue-jean legs around her. Pain flowered in her side. Broken rib. A man spat on her back, then another.

"My hands!" Joaquin's palms were black with frostbite. *"My fuckin' hands!"*

"You're done now, maldita puta," a man said, standing over her. "I'm gonna make sure you're dead this time if I have to cut you into fuckin' chorizo with a chain saw and mail each piece to everybody in the phone book." He stomped on her wrist and pried the spear out of her grasp. "Let's see if—*aaaAAAAHHHH!*" he started to scream, as the demon spear burned his hands with supernatural ice, and then he was interrupted by the Apocalypse.

With the loudest sound she had ever heard, the floor *bulged* up and outward, and a violent eruption of wood and fire blew Robin Martine upside down through the front window. Men were engulfed and pulverized by the detonation. Levitating sideways like a magic carpet doing a fighter-jet maneuver, the pool table smashed the dead man into the wall.

Even as armored as she was, Robin was almost knocked unconscious by the blast. Broken glass rattled against her face and chest as she landed on her back outside and slid seventeen feet. Pieces of flaming wood sailed out of a storm cloud of fire four stories tall.

Dazed, she stared up at the fireball and then, disbelieving, at the crater where the clubhouse used to be.

All four exterior walls had blown out, scattering debris in every direction, and everything was burning, even the trees at the edge of the parking lot. All the motorcycles had been knocked down and the explosion had blown the gravel back, exposing the dirt under the parking lot. A geyser of blue flame jetted up from the center of the ruins, producing the venomous, whistling roar of a jet turbine.

A shotgun fell out of the sky, twisted into a helix.

"Baby? *Kenway?*" Robin asked, dizzy. She got up and tried to march into the fire, but the debris was an impenetrable tangle of flames and fallen timbers. The heat was intense, the hard, angry radiation of a lava flow. *"Fuuuuck!"* she wailed, pacing around the corner of the building. "No, no, *nooo,* baby, *goddammit*!"

Blood trickling down their faces from shrapnel, a limping Gendreau and Navathe joined her, the former supported by the latter. Elisa Valenzuela came after, clutching her rifle.

"Why did it *explode*?" screamed Robin. Her swamp-light eyes focused on Elisa. "Are you *sure* they were here? Your brother got it right?"

"Yes, Alfie—"

Frustration and despair fed the hunger-anger inside her, stoking hellish flames. The air stank of sulfur, a pungent brimstone, even over the high acrid smell of the natural gas fire. Robin rushed at the flames, trying to get into the building again, but the wall was an impregnable mess of bricks and fire.

Strange black frost emanated from the Osdathregar. She got an idea. "Flame off!" She thrust the spear point into the fire several times, but the supernatural chill didn't seem to extinguish anything. "Flame *off*, dammit!"

She went back to Elisa. "Did he say where Santiago went?"

"Left to take Carly home."

A maniacal scream echoed out of the fire and a burning shape came staggering out of the clubhouse.

At first, Robin thought it might have been Kenway and went running to his side, but at the last moment, she realized it was one of the bikers, wreathed in flame. The man stumbled, collapsing into the gravel, where he rolled around in a gibbering frenzy, and Robin shanked him through the flames like a spear-fisher.

Smoking blood leaked out in a puddle, filtering through the rocks, and "Wacky" Joaquin lay still.

He smelled like barbecue, sweet and thick.

Robin felt her stomach tense up. She wanted to find the biggest rock she could lift and smash him into the ground with it until he was a smear in the gravel. The demon in her also wanted to eat the man, to dig her pearly fangs into the charred meat and tear it away in strips, choke them down.

Fuck. Fuck. I have to get out of here. I'm losing control. Just like Frank Gendreau thought I would. The magicians were right.

They were right, they were right, sang the warhawk.

"Where is their house?" she growled over her shoulder.

"Single-wide trailer out in the Alderman Street subdivision in

Keyhole Hills," said Elisa. "Past the Conoco. You'll know it by the motorcycle in the driveway."

Speaking of a motorcycle . . . Robin went over to the dead Hamburger Guy and dug his keys out of his pocket. A few minutes' search found his motorcycle and she pulled it upright, jumping on the kickstarter. The engine erupted to life. She only hoped she could drive the next several miles to town without laying the bike down—or getting attacked by a terrified state trooper. She didn't need a warrant out for her arrest for killing and eating a cop.

"Get my niece out of there, lady," said Elisa, eyes locked on Robin. "Bring Carly to me, and I will take care of her."

"I will."

"My brother's gone too far. Running guns, selling drugs . . . now he's killing people and, and . . . turning into a freak. *It's the motorcycle.* I know it is. You don't have to kill *him* if you can destroy La Reina. Destroy the Enfield. That will stop it."

Alien rage still hummed in Robin's bones. *It's not the bike,* Marina had told them. *He was always like this.* The midday sun glinted on her obsidian skin like oil on asphalt, black and faintly iridescent. *The bike just brought it back.* Mutated it. Mutated *him.* She caught Gendreau's eyes and saw terror there,

BITETEARKILL

and it was all she could do not to run away, to get as far as she could get from him. Flaming intestines dangled from her remaining antler. She ripped them down and threw them away. *They were right,* the warhawk said in her ear, laughing.

"I can't promise you—"

"Not in front of Carly," said Elisa. "I still think he can be saved, but if it has to happen, don't do it front of her."

"Take me with you." Gendreau came toward the bike.

"No. You've been in enough danger. You stay here." Robin pushed the spear into a shotgun scabbard between the saddlebag and the rear fender so that it stood up behind her. "I need to do this alone. I'm already going to have one liability with Carly being there."

Wordlessly, she heeled up the kickstand before the curandero could protest and peeled out of the parking lot, spraying gravel. Annie's remonstrations rang in her mind as she squealed into the eastbound lane: *Get up, dragonfly. Get up. Walk it off. Ain't no daughter of mine gonna get beat that easy.* Wind coursed over her sleek, strange body. She thought back to all the times she'd burned herself with hot water and cigarettes, trying to psych herself back up for the Great Hunt, trying to fury away all the fear. *I can get you to do anything I want,* said the Heinrich in her head, *climb any mountain, swim any sea. All I gotta do is piss you off.*

If only she'd known back then what she was, what she was capable of doing, of becoming . . .

You're gonna do it, ain't you, said the warhawk in the mirror, said the teenager hiding in the bathroom, fighting off a panic attack with scalding water. *Don't run, coward. Are you going to run?*

"No."

She overtook a tractor-trailer and darted between two cars. Highway reeled out behind her in a long roaring ribbon.

ARE YOU GOING TO RUN?

The warhawk's voice deepened, became demonic. In her mind, in her memories, the face in the bathroom mirror burst into flames.

Light sizzled between her teeth, and coals burned in her eyes. Robin revved the bike, ice-wind breaking over her like the tide, and she realized she was looking at her real face, her now-face, in the motorcycle's mirror. Fire licked from the corners of her mouth.

NO, said the reflection.

Green light crackled in her eyes.

Track 32

Santiago sat in the hallway of their trailer, his back against the bedroom door. Behind him, his daughter sobbed quietly, all the rage wrung out of her. The place still stank like pepper spray, leaving a spicy funk in the air like bad takeout.

The girl had fought like a wildcat at the motel, punching, kicking, screaming, cursing, calling him every name in the book, threatening him with death and castration, blaming him and his motorcycle for everything from her mother's fall to the fucking moon landing.

One good slap to the mouth ended that. She rode home with one of the other boys—no room on La Reina with Marina's body, wrapped in a bedsheet from the motel, slung over the back like a bandito on the back of John Wayne's horse. He brought his dead wife straight home from the clubhouse, taking every back road he could find to stay off the highway, and scooped everything off the coffee table onto the floor, depositing her carefully and neatly on top of it.

There she lay in state, a primitive, Viking-like sort of viewing. Santi sat on the couch and prayed over the blood-splotched cocoon, crying silently into his hands until he heard a knock at the door.

Javier Barela with his daughter, one hand locked around her upper arm.

La Reina scrawled an insidious fingerbone down the inside of Santi's skull as he stood there trying to recognize them. *Scrrrrr-ratch.* "Put her in the bedroom." Santi plodded back to the couch to sit down.

As soon as Carly saw her mother lying on the coffee table, shrouded in a bloody bedsheet, her legs buckled and she crumpled on the floor in a heap, covering her face with her hands. A thin, whistling cry slipped through her fingers and Barela stood over her, an exasperated man with a Mohican haircut and a red face.

"Put her in the bedroom," Santi murmured again.

"Yeah, okay." Barela stood Carly up and half-carried her into the master suite. She immediately balled into the fetal position on top of the covers and he respectfully backed out, shutting the door and locking it.

With a wary glance at Santi, he left.

Now the patriarch of the ruined Valenzuela family sat in the hallway, trying to ignore the sound of La Reina scratching that hideous nerve in his head that sent pulsing waves of heat and color across his eyes. A red heat-strobe, a firetruck light in his head. "I'm sorry, baby," he said over his shoulder, hoping his rusty voice would carry through the bedroom door. "I'm real sorry this had to happen. I'm sorry it had to happen to you. And your mother. And me. But if you hadn't run off . . ."

He let the accusation linger.

Santi got up and went into the kitchen, hesitated, and passed through the kitchen to the living room, where he stood at the end of the coffee table and looked down at the shrouded corpse. Something squirmed restlessly inside of him, a giant grub-worm made of grief and rage and despair. He wanted to ask, "Why did you leave me?" but he knew the answer. It was because Marina was stupid, she was *weak,* she had no idea how to be a

(queen?)

good wife to a good man. She had no faith in herself and had no—what's the word?—*oomph,* she had no testicular fortitude, and she at least was lucid enough to understand that, and to try to take herself out of the picture, to take the burden off of her husband. But she made a vow to him the day he put that ring on her finger, and marriage, oh boy, marriage, 'round these parts, that's written in stone, you can't just throw in the towel on Catholic marriage. You sign your name on the dotted line and them's the breaks, man, you're in it for life, for richer or poorer, for good times and in bad.

Wind hooted through the broken window in the kitchen.

Been a long time since you received the Eucharist, isn't it? asked Mother Mary.

"Yeah. Hell, been a while since I went to church at all."

Earlier this year.

"Yeah. February, maybe. No recuerdo por qué fuimos."

After a fight. You broke one of Marina's ribs.

Santiago reached out and felt for her side through the bedsheet. His knuckles brushed the swell of her left breast. "Ah, yeah."

You asked her to go with you because you wanted her to see you suffer. You wanted her to see you grovel and beg for forgiveness. You came out of that confessional booth a free man, and you wanted her to see you absolved of your transgressions, out of . . . what? Guilt?

"Pity?"

Control. You wanted her to see how the worst you could do to her would be washed away as if it were nothing more than dirt on your hide. That you could do whatever you wanted to her and God would forgive you. And God's forgiveness made you omnipotent. A moral phoenix. Like a murderer getting out of prison on a technicality. Only, the technicality was permanent and reusable.

Santi stared down at the bundle laid across the table and swallowed heavily. With shaking hands, he peeled back the sheet covering Marina's face.

I forgive you, Santiago, said the voice. *I am the only god that matters now. I am the only god that has ever mattered. I am your god and mistress now, and as I am in you, so too are you a god. I live through you, living god, and thus I do my works through you. You must seek forgiveness from no one as long as I am in you.*

Most of the damage from the fall had been sustained to the skull and upper body. Broke her neck on impact, judging by the grotesque jag of vertebrae straining against the left side of her neck, and her left temple was caved in from the eyebrow to the crown of her skull. Luckily, this was all hidden under her hair, a blood-plaster of black and brown. Her eyes had rolled toward the top of her head so that she peered beatifically skyward, like people looking at God in old paintings.

Her mostly white eyes were nauseating and somehow terrifying to look at. He wanted to apologize to her like he'd apologized to Carly, but he couldn't find a reason in his heart to do so. He'd had no hand in this—it had been solely Marina's idea to run away, hadn't it?

Probably bought the pepper spray, too.

"No," he said, tears spilling out of his eyes. Droplets turned blue on the white sheets piled at his feet. "No, yo la amaba. La amo."

She can't run off now, huh?

He shook his head and ducked, as if the sob that came out of him was a thing that could be dodged.

Or can she?

"No, she's dead. Esta muerta. Gracias a esa perra punk que murió en el incendio. She can't go anywhere now."

She'll start to deteriorate eventually, Santiago.

"No."

Yes. She will leave you in the end, Santiago, she will leave you, and she will take everything with her, leaving you with nothing but dust and bones. It is inevitable.

"No."

Do you want her to stay with you forever?

"Yes."

Then you know what you have to do.

Slowly at first, he shook his head, and then hard enough to give himself a headache. His chest felt as if it were imploding, collapsing in on itself as if he were drowning in the hot-cold darkness at the bottom of the deepest oceanic trench. "No. No, no, no, I don't want to do that. Don't make me do that."

Been a long time since you received the Eucharist, isn't it?

"Shut the fuck up," Santiago mumbled, beating on his forehead with the heels of his fists. "You shut the fuck *up*."

Communion.

Pain raked coals down the bones of his arms. As if in a dream, he turned his hands and saw that orange shag running down the edges of his forearms again.

"No, goddammit," he said, his teeth growing out of his gums.

Drool and blood spattered where his tears had fallen. He watched in the dead television's gray reflection as his lips stretched across yellow fangs, his nostrils gaped, and his eyes bled and bulged out of his face. White whiskers sprouted from his chin and cheeks, his jawbone widening into an awkward moon-face.

Communion.

"No," he sobbed, the black talons sliding along underneath the skin of his thickening fingers, materializing in his palms, thin daggers gliding up and out of his fingertips, where the skin split open and the obsidian hooks came curling out from under his nails. Blood ran into his upturned palms. Breath came out of him in ragged, horselike wheezes. The giant dazzling head of a jungle phantom gazed back at him from the dark television screen.

"Dios mio, verdaderamente soy un monstruo," he said in hoarse Spanish, feeling his face. *El Tigre. El Tigre.* Santiago hooked his claws into the bedsheet, drawing it away, uncovering Marina's broken corpse. Then he leaned forward, opened his massive jaws, and closed his mouth on the corpse's flank.

Brittle ribs cracked under his teeth. Cold blood welled over his tongue as the president of Los Cambiantes devoured his dead wife.

Track 33

Took some riding around, but Robin eventually found the Valenzuelas' house in an obscure corner of the rearmost subdivision, at the top of Keyhole Hills' gentle slope. Mountains loomed over her, the properties here climbing into hilly scrubland that reminded her of that old television show *M*A*S*H*.

Santiago's motorcycle was parked in the driveway. Army-green Royal Enfield—admirable, almost cute. Hard to believe that this run-down-looking machine was what had caused all this mess. She parked the Harley by the side of the road next to the mailbox and dismounted, plucking the makeshift spear from the bike's shotgun scabbard. The spear was heavier than she remembered.

Standing next to the bike, she listened for Santiago.

Wind howled lightly off the desert, a few birds out in the scrub, and the barking of some dog a block away.

If she could destroy the relic before Santiago even knew she was there, she could avoid a battle altogether. She crept toward the motorcycle and paced slowly around it, trying to guess where the teratoma was inside the bike. Did someone mix witch-blood into the paint? No, that wouldn't make any sense. Maybe hair? Teratomatic hair? She knelt close and studied the paint-job. No, that wasn't it, either.

Searched the saddlebags. Nothing.

Maybe hair or bones inside the engine somewhere. She went into the shed out back to look at Santiago's tools. Wasn't much—hammer, C-clamp, a box with a socket wrench and a bunch of mismatched attachments.

Hanging on the wall was a hacksaw. She took it.

Back in the driveway, Robin grasped La Reina's handlebars and rested the toothy, rusty blade on the steel bar.

KA-BOOM, the side of the trailer exploded outward like a can of biscuit dough, shredding the air with aluminum chaff. Some enormous shape rocketed through the storm of metal and collided with her, and the two of them plowed through the fence in a tangle of limbs, knocking wood across the street. The Valenzuelas' mailbox somersaulted into their neighbor's yard, spilling unpaid bills on the dead lawn.

In the clear daylight, Santiago was a terrifying, confusing sight, even bigger than Robin remembered. Full-on Beast Mode, a hulking creature striped in black-and-orange shag, his head massive and asymmetrical. A thousand teeth jostled for space in a pit of gray-pink flesh, all of it swimming in blood. Too many muscles, too many joints, whipping-beating appendages that ended in maces bristling with a dozen claws. An elephantine cock dangled between his hind legs, spiky and purple like some kind of deep-sea anemone.

He was a living siege engine.

"LEAVE HER ALONE!" Santiago roared, pounding Robin's head into the dirt.

Darkness danced in the corners of her eyes. His fists were sledgehammers wrapped in mink. She wasn't going to be able to take much more, even in her strange state.

Reaching up, Robin caught his fists and pushed. To her surprise, she was able to stop the onslaught. Santi leaned forward, pressing his weight. Her knuckles slammed against the ground and the tiger-thing lunged at her face, his mouth cavernous and fleshy. Teeth scraped her armored cheek as antler-points jabbed his gums, and hot blood drizzled into her eyes.

Snarling in pain, he lifted Robin over his head, flinging her toward the shed in the back yard. Fragile wood shattered under the impact. The entire structure collapsed on top of her: tools, joists, dust, and dead wasp-nests.

Before she could even get her bearings, the monster was already digging her out of the wreckage, flinging wood and shingles aside.

"KILL YOU," he snarled, uncovering her.

"You tried that already." Robin cracked him in the eye with the back end of a claw hammer. Santi recoiled and the claw hooked in his eye socket, wrenching it out of her hand. Robin clambered out of the remains of his toolshed as he writhed on the ground, screaming.

Red gore hung from the tool's head like hot cheese. Santi threw it aside and rolled over, struggling to his feet. Blood ran down his warped muzzle.

As she walked past, circling him on her way to get her hands on the Osdathregar, he seemed to be growing larger. His chest deepened, arms lengthened and swelled. Wriggling black tentacles sprouted from his jaw, pushing teeth out into the dirt. Streaks of dark color marbled his shoulders and forehead: patches of wolf hair and pebbled lizard hide. He was becoming something more than just a man-tiger: some kind of Lovecraftian animal-god, a taxidermy nightmare, a walking evolutionary chimera.

A new eye pushed its way through the gory eye socket, this one a greasy marble orb with a crocodile's slim pupil.

"I spy, with my little eye," laughed the multibeast.

Holy shit. Robin dove for the spear and Santiago rushed her at the same time, thundering across the ground with that tripartite William Tell *thump-thump-thump.* She combat-rolled

(This time she was ready.)

and the Osdathregar's freezing spear point met Santiago's cobbly flesh and fur,

(The dog jumped on the knife.)

penetrating skin and muscle, driving deep into his throat. Supernatural frost chilled the blood as it erupted from the wound, splashing Robin's face, crystallizing in midair like a jackpot of cough drops. With a scream, Santiago flinched away, rolling in the dirt, clutching his wound.

Ice formed around the gash in his neck. Santi charged at her and she prepared to stab him again, but he bulled past and slammed into the Royal Enfield. He dragged it out into the street as if it were a dead antelope, where he worked his claws into the engine and pried it apart. Metal squealed deep inside. La Reina's gas tank broke off, spraying gasoline all over the pavement.

Wait, he's destroying the bike himself?

The jumbled shoggoth lifted it up—when had he grown a third arm?—and galloped down the street, fleeing west.

So, that's where the teratoma was. Gas tank.

Robin stood there in the front yard, head aching, dripping with blood and shaking in fear and shock and pain, suddenly grateful that nearly every homeowner in sight was gone to work. She climbed into Santiago's trailer, pulling herself up through the colossal hole and into a blood-smeared kitchen. She stood the spear on end and looked around.

Fridge. Inside was a half-jug of iced tea. Milo's. She gulped some of it and set it down, panting, leaning on the counter. Bloody handprints marked everything she touched. Carnage and offal were strewn all over the carpet. Robin recognized Marina's shoes and she retched, her stomach lurched, threatened to disgorge all the tea she'd just drank.

"Oh, my God," she murmured. "He was eating her body."

No, not lurched, she realized in disgust. *Growled.* She and Santi were more alike than she wanted to admit. The rage-hunger came in waves, like birthing contractions. One minute, she was a dark, cold void, empty and desolate, and the next, a bonfire surged inside of her, starving for something to burn.

In the window-reflection over the kitchen sink, a very human Robin grinned demonically, green eyes alight.

They were right, said the warhawk.

"No," said Robin, wrenching the curtain over the other-Robin's face. "I'm in control. I've got this."

"Go away!" Carly screamed from the back bedroom.

"It's me, kid, it's me." Robin went down the hallway and spoke through the door, clutching her side. She leaned against the wall, gritting her teeth, her eyes shut tight against the twisting of the hot screw in her guts. "Don't come out. Keep hiding, okay? If my friends show up, go with them. But otherwise, stay hidden."

The teenager said something, but she was crying and whatever it was, it was too hoarse to make out.

"What?"

"Daddy's crazy," said Carly. "He turned into something."

"I know."

"What *is* he?"

"I don't know. And I don't know if he's going to be able to make it out of this alive." Robin sighed. "Gonna be him or me. He killed my boyfriend and almost killed me." Her voice shook. The hand she was leaning against the wall with curled into a fist against the cheap wood paneling. "I can't let that go."

Carly said nothing.

"I told you I was going to take care of you when this is over. And when I say I'm going to do something, I mean it." Her other fist tightened around the spear. "Your aunt Elisa wants you. She's gonna—"

"Just go," said Carly, her tone flat, dead.

Robin hesitated, her heart sinking. "I told you this would be a bad idea. It always ends badly."

Because I'm a bad person. I fucking suck.

"I'm sorry," she said.

"I don't want your sorries," Carly said through the door. "I'm tired of sorries. That's all I've ever heard from everybody, especially my dad. Sorry about this, sorry about that. Sorry I broke your phone. Sorry I hurt your mother. Sorry I hurt you. Sorry I couldn't stand up to your father. Well, I'm done hearing it."

"Okay—Okay, well, I have to go end this. Somebody other than you is going to stand up to him today."

Robin paused awkwardly, then walked away, and paused again at the edge of the hole in the trailer wall. "You knew I was going to have to kill him from the minute you asked me for help. You both knew what I do." She sighed. "He ain't gonna let me destroy the relic in his motorcycle. Gonna have to go through him to get to it."

"Do what you have to do, lady," Carly said forlornly. "Just stop apologizing for it."

• • •

Gasoline made a splattery trail all the way down the street. Ah, good. Tracking him would be easy. Robin hopped astride the Harley and kickstarted it with one jump, roaring away with the spear tucked under her arm and braced between the handlebars as if she were on her way to a jousting tournament.

Following the trail of spilled fuel, she followed Santiago's path of destruction across the back end of Keyhole Hills, the "cheap seats" part of the town's slope. Back there, the streets weren't paved worth a damn, with great scribbly tar-patches and gaping potholes. She slalomed slowly between the holes, passing through neighborhoods of mimosa trees and jacarandas, stirring up devils of yellow leaves and petals. Warehouses and run-down shacks, shabby apartments and mobile homes accompanied her as she made her way deep into the town's twilight zone. *How many of these people were Santi's wolf-boys?* she thought, scrutinizing the empty-looking apartments. Only saw a handful of cars and occupied houses since she rode into town not even twenty minutes before, and those were all out on the surface streets and the highway.

A spindly man in a giant white shirt came out of a house as she ambled past, carrying his baby daughter. Squinting in the sun, they watched Robin pass. The little girl was crying, and her father looked like he'd seen a ghost.

Did he have his claws sunk into that many of these folks?

The gasoline trail petered out, becoming little more than a series of increasingly spaced-out dots. Drying up, too, fading almost before she could find the next spot. Eventually, she came to a stop sign and lost the trail.

"Where did you go?" she asked the wind.

Two fenced lawns flanked her on either side, as dry and dirty as any other property in the Hole, and another faced her across the street. To her right, two houses down, divots had been carved up out of the alkali, like the rut marks of tires, except the ruts had claw marks in them.

What looked like a stampede's worth of feet had churned up the homeowner's patchy lawn, kicking up deep whorls and crescents. She eased out into the next street and turned the corner, driving across the oncoming lane and up onto the sidewalk to get a better look. Their roof was damaged, shingles raked off onto the ground, a hole punched in the boards.

Dismounting the motorcycle, Robin moved onto the property and into the narrow space between the houses.

On the other side, a wooden fence had once separated the backyard from one of the many scrubby, rocky foothills leading into the mountains. Santiago had busted right through it, leaving a tumble of sticks. She marched through the gap and over the hill.

At the bottom ran a one-lane access road, unkempt and buckling. Thirsty, rough-looking pine trees made a scabby fence, following the road into the distance. "Give it up," she whispered, jogging along the lonely road with the spear in one hand. She felt like a bushman on the hunt, or like Hector of Troy heading out to fight Achilles. "Give it up, man. Make this easy."

Rounding a curve, she found a tollbooth. "What the hell?"

It stood on a median, forging through the asphalt river of the road with a triangle of dead landscaping. The tollbooth gate had been smashed and lay in shards all over the road. A sign was mounted to the top of the tollhouse that read EAST GATE, and another one below that revealed what lay beyond: the decommissioned Air Force base, Fort Bostock.

As she passed into the old fort, the hardy little desert trees stopped growing, replaced by weeds that burst through the road in brown tufts. None of the Hole's few indigenous birds sang out there, though she saw a few crows that coughed and gobbled. Legions of ramshackle buildings still stood here, mostly long single-story clapboard barracks that looked like turn-of-the-century train depots, some of them gutted by fire.

A coyote trotted past some hundred yards distant, watching her warily, and disappeared into the brush.

"Abandon all hope," she said to herself.

"—Ye who enter here," said Annie.

Robin's luminous eyes cut over to the ghost. "Hey, Mama."

Annie smiled. "Hey, baby."

"Where have you been?"

"Saving up for another ticket to come visit you."

Sunlight faded as white cloud cover filtered in from the east. The two of them strode purposefully into the depths of the abandoned base, following a runway that seemed to go on forever. Huge flat concrete rectangles stretched across the desert in branching patterns, the former floors of disassembled Quonset huts.

"Mama," Robin said quietly, "are you a figment of my imagination?"

Annie said nothing for a long moment.

"What makes you ask such a thing, hon?"

"Sometimes, I wonder if I really am crazy." Robin sighed and swung her arms, stretching her shoulders. The black armor clung to her musculature as tightly as her old skin had. She wondered if it *was* her skin now, and if she would ever be—or at least *look*—human again. "Maybe this is all just a fever dream. Werewolves burned me alive. Now I'm a demon again, walking around in the sunlight, talking to my dead mother, fighting the urge to kill and eat everybody I see. None of this makes a bit of fucking sense. Maybe I had a psychotic break. Maybe I'm still cooped up in that psych ward, doped up on Thorazine or whatever they were giving me, and—"

"I don't think so—"

"—maybe I've just dreamt the last several years. Only rational explanation I can come up with."

"Surely not."

"You don't think so?"

"I can't speak for the rest of it all . . . The time you spent with that fella in Texas. All them witches you fought." Annie's smile was bright enough to make up for the cloud-hidden sun. "Kenway . . . oh, I love Kenway so much, baby. I really do. Good man, and I'm glad he's with you. But me? Does it really matter if I'm a delusion?"

"What do you mean?"

"Which is better, a hallucination of a good thing that makes you happy, or nothing at all?"

"Even if she's just around to tell me what I want to hear?"

A wry smirk flickered across Annie's translucent face. "I tell you what you *need* to hear."

Behind her mother's spirit stood a village of decrepit office buildings, two-story structures made to look like old Spanish mission houses. Dozens of them, tall and slender, the windows busted out. Looked a lot like Hammertown—so much so that she almost expected to see painted wooden silhouettes popping up in the windows.

The buildings were decorated with scrawls of graffiti. She was relieved to not see any witch runes. "Don't remember you being this cheesy when you were alive, Mama."

"When you're dead, you have a lot of free time to think up cheesy stuff. You should hear my material. If there are any comedy clubs in Heaven, they may kick me out."

"Well, wait up for me," said Robin, kicking through sagebrush. "This guy may tear me to pieces. I might be coming with you."

"Doubt it. My daughter is a grade-A badass."

"Love you, Mama."

"Love you too, tough-stuff."

By now, Annie had almost completely disappeared. The only thing left that Robin could see was her face, like a kindly Cheshire Cat.

"Oh!" cried Robin.

"Yes, baby."

"Forgot to ask you—is Marina with you? Is she okay?"

"Yes," said Annie's disembodied voice. "She's here, somewhere. The others, they're hard to see, hard to find. She made it here in one piece, so to speak. Let little Carlita know she's okay, spiritually speaking."

"Tell her I'm sorry about what happened."

"She understands," said the wind, pushing a leaf across the road. "She doesn't blame you."

"Good. I don't need another ghost up my ass. One's enough."

The wind chuckled, tumbling the leaf into the dry culvert. Robin continued walking, heading into the maze of buildings. "You never really answered my question," she said, glancing at the now-overcast sky. "Are you real or not?"

Sunlight glimmered briefly through a gap in the clouds, and her shadow leapt from her feet, disappearing as quietly as it came.

Track 34

"Are you real or not?" Her voice carried to him from the other end of the building. Santiago sat in the corner of a dark room. Sunlight fell across his legs from a nearby window and it was not warm—indeed, the colorless quality lent it a singular, desperate, cold look, like something out of one of those World War II movies he used to watch with Guillermo in the days before Marina, before he was road captain.

Am I real? he thought, staring at the walls-ceiling-floor-sky, clutching the wound in his side and trying not to vomit. His vision was all over the place, split between half a hundred eyeballs, like watching an entire panel of surveillance cameras all looking at the same room from different angles, some of them monochrome gray, some of them in vivid blue-and-orange thermal, some so gritty with motion blur that it made him nauseous. He wasn't hungry but he knew he had to kill, every one of him had to kill because someone wanted him, a hunter bent on ending his life, and he had to keep on going. He had to keep going for Carrie—or was it Charlie?—and he had to keep going for Mother Mary.

La Reina. His hotline to the divine. He would put her back together. The gas tank . . . he could reattach it. Make her good as new. But first, he had to get to safety. Had to be safe. Then he could fix her.

Santi.

Somehow, the gas tank seemed to have migrated into his body as his other selves emerged, sitting in the middle of him like a giant chrome liver. The shapes made him less solid, more fluid, and the big metal tank had passed through him and into him like a sperm forces its way into an egg.

Santiago.

Crouching there in this cramped room, he managed to keep himself silent, though it seemed a thousand mouths all wanted to bleat-roar-scream at once. Keeping himself together and quiet was like trying to talk flies into a jar.

SANTIAGO!

The voice made him twitch. Santiago looked out the window, but no one was there. "What," he tried to say, but his mouths wouldn't cooperate.

She's out there. She's here for you. No time to rest. You need to fight.

Fight who? The wound the girl had given him throbbed in agony. Wasn't deep, or even that serious, but goddamn, did it ever hurt. Like being shanked with a knife that'd been heated over a fire until it was orange-hot, brand-hot, hot as the sun. Creeping frostbite spread outward from the gash.

Why are you hurting me? Isn't this *your* power? Didn't this come from you, the same place this power I have came from?

No, this is something different. This is not mine.

Whose?

Them.

Who is "them"?

Doesn't matter. What matters is that you fight, Santiago. You fight for your life. Our life. You fight for both of us today. Don't let her kill me, Santiago. Don't let her kill me again.

Who is she?

Robin, said Mother Mary, *the one who burned me in the trenches and the one you burned in the house in the desert. The one with the blade of the purifying light, the blade that was broken from its spear so long ago, the spear that killed—*

The girl I burned? The one they call Robin? She survived?

Yes.

What the hell is wrong with her? The black skin, the horns . . .

She's one of them, those creatures from the void where I remain. The Dökkálfar, the Se'irim, the Rabisu. I float in their world of black nothingness, their desert of anguish, always seeking safety. They surround me, scenting me like sharks. They chase me with insolent eyes and audacious teeth, seeking to eat me alive, drain me of life. I have hidden from them for so long. Who hunts a queen? Who hunts a goddess? And now they even hunt me in the world of the living. No realm is safe.

How did she survive?

When they die protecting innocent people, offering their own life in place of another, these vermin are given free rein in the sanctified world and the chance to serve the White. She is the first Rabisu in two thousand years to ascend. The last to ascend was the Christ himself, that clever cambion, who sacrificed himself in the name of all of humanity to establish the Sanctification and forever close the door on us. He gave his life to diminish the bond between your world and mine and, in doing so, made himself part of the White.

Our plans are fucked now, ain't they?

Yes, I'm afraid so. My resurrection must somehow continue without your protection. They will find me, I'm sure; they'll find me and cut me out of your daughter and crush me unless you can end them. Kill them, Santiago. Kill the half-darkling Robin and then kill them all, all those thieving magicians, before they find me and rip me out like they've ripped me out so many other times out of so many other innocent women.

Soon, Carly will be able to protect herself, but until then, I need your word. I need your protection. She needs your protection.

Don't let them find me.

Kill them.

Yes, my love. Yes, Mother Mary. Yes, my heart and my fire. We will kill them. We will tear the hunter open and strew her guts across a hundred miles of sand. Robin Martine will pass into your domain screaming.

Track 35

Buildings loomed over her, the walls of a canyon, and the darkening sky sapped the day of light, leaving Robin in an abyssal environment, as if the ruins of Fort Bostock were at the bottom of the ocean.

Black windows gaped blindly like eye sockets in gargantuan skulls, some of them filmed by glass cataracts. She walked slowly, gripping the spear.

Took everything in her mind and heart to control the demon's anger-hunger, to make herself focus on the task at hand instead of hiking back to town. Every step tugged at a rope tied to her insides, pulling her toward civilization. The glow in the sky where Keyhole Hills and Lockwood sent their evening light into the dusk—she could see it, and she wanted to go there and tear it down. She'd told the Dogs of Odysseus there was no danger of her losing control, because at the time, there *wasn't* . . . but if her grasp on her humanity was weakened even more by her next transformation—assuming there would be another, somehow—then there would be no guarantees. Every time it happened, she was becoming more and more naturalized . . . more feral.

Can't let that happen. Broken window-eyes leered down at her. *This has to be the last time. No more Nancy Drew shit, no more Dexter-for-hire shit, no more helping strangers get rid of their stalkers and abusive husbands and pervert uncles. No more sacrifices. No more martyrdom for the downtrodden. Keep letting this go on, and one day, you're either going to come back as an uncontrollable monster, or you won't come back at all.* She felt as if she were abandoning everyone, but she had to think of herself for a change.

Had to get as far away from her friends as possible. As far away from *everybody* as possible. She couldn't save Kenway anymore—he was past saving now, thanks to this mutant son of a bitch—but she could save the Dogs of Odysseus and the Parkins and Joel and everybody in Blackfield from the demon inside of her.

Baby steps. You can't save everybody from each other, but you can save them from yourself. Do what you can with what you got.

She sighed. *Dude, fuck the supernatural. It sucks.*

"Give me the relic, Santi," she called, but her voice, exasperated and hollow, barely seemed to carry ten feet in front of her. "Let me end this. Your daughter is still alive."

"No." Santiago's voice sounded like a crowd of mouths. She could have sworn people spoke to her from every one of the windows around her. "I have to kill you, or they're going to kill her."

"Who?" Robin turned in a circle, looking for eyeshine. "Who's going to kill who?"

"You. And your friends. You're going to kill my daughter like you killed my wife."

"What? I agreed to this to *save* her."

"My wife." Santi's voice was a crowd of conspiratorial whispers. "She's dead. Did you promise to save *her*?"

Robin's heart rumbled anxiously in her chest. She wondered if it was a charge of pure light, a sizzling star, like it had been when she was the demon in the Darkhouse last year, or if it was a real heart this time. "No!" she told him, fists clenched. "Marina died because we were attacked by your friend Tuco, and he caused the RV to run off the road. Marina went through the—"

"Lies. You *lie* to me. You threw her into the gutter to get to me. You let my wife die just to hurt me."

"I'm telling the truth."

"You say anything to save your own skin," growled Santiago in a thousand raspy tongues. "Leave my daughter alone, and I will let you live. She stays with me."

"Why did you eat Marina?"

"Because I couldn't allow her to leave me again."

Then, to Robin's surprise and disgust and despair, Marina Valenzuela's voice came from the ruins around her, a forlorn city of voices. "Now I'm part of him," said the dead woman, "forever . . . and ever."

"You're sick, Santi."

Santiago's rusty laugh reverberated throughout the maze of buildings. "Took you this long to figure that out?"

"Give me the gas tank, and we'll leave."

Silence.

Thought she heard the rasping of scales from the windows to her right, but it could have been nothing but the sighing of the damp breeze. Rain was on the way. *Gonna have to end this before then, or my visibility is going to go to shit.*

"Don't make me come find you," Robin called out.

Still no answer. She headed for the nearest door and kicked it open, smashing the deadbolt in a cloud of dust.

"When I was a little boy," said Santiago's voice from somewhere in another room, "the person I used to be was convinced a monster lived under his bed."

Inside was a dark foyer with a splintery hardwood floor.

"He lived in a trailer, his grandmother and he."

The armor running down Robin's legs had hardened into weird biomechanical shoes that protected her from the splinters—hard black exoskeleton, like the chitinous carapace of a beetle, a segmented Gigerian cross between cowboy boots and bare feet. She didn't know what this new development was, but it had saved her ass back there in Santiago's driveway. Hard as SWAT armor, leathery but tough, sturdier than anything Heinrich Hammer had ever given her to wear. Condensation or something collected on it, giving it a shiny look like a wet car.

Armored in a panoply of ashes and shadow.

"His father, he . . ." Santiago paused. "Well, to cut a long story short, his father decided it would be best if the boy lived with his abuelita."

Robin moved through the office building, armored feet crunching on long-neglected floors, pushing open doors with the butt of the spear, buzzing with anticipation of an ambush.

"They lived in a trailer, in a trailer park, and the boy I once was slept in a bunk bed, in a bedroom just wide enough to contain it. His brother slept on the top bunk."

"Where are you?" Robin called out, looking out a window at a two-story drop.

"In the middle of the night," said Santiago, ignoring her, "the boy was terrified to get out of bed. His brother used to lie in his bunk and tell the boy the most horrible stories about boogeymen and chupacabra and demons."

Summoning her courage, Robin vaulted the windowsill and threw herself onto the dirt below, rolling to her feet. She picked up the spear and went to the building across the street.

"Ay! Then he would lie awake for hours, even if he had to piss, thinking about those monsters," continued Santiago. "He could just see them, in his mind, lying right under his mattress, inches from his back. Sometimes, the boy thought it was Freddy Krueger, the man with the hat and the claw, because of those movies his dad liked to watch when he was high."

This door was chained and padlocked shut but no match for the spear. She pushed the Osdathregar's blade into a steel link and shoved the spear into the gap, neatly breaking it in two. The chain slithered out of the door handles.

"Candygram," she called, pulling the door open.

No answer. Robin walked into another dark lobby. "Then one night, he realized something," Santiago said from deeper in the building, his voice a hollow echo. "Since his brother's bed was over his own, the boy was under a bed himself—"

A goat bleated from behind the double door in front of her, and she thought she heard hoofbeats.

This was followed by a gravelly, leonine snarl.

Robin made a face. "The hell?"

". . . SO THAT MADE *HIM* A MONSTER TOO!"

Flinging itself wide open, the door disgorged a flood of hot bodies into the room, a stampede of screaming shapes that slammed into her and pushed her back through the front door, knocking it off of its hinges. Robin hit the ground rolling, the spear cartwheeling alongside her.

When she found her feet, she saw one of the strangest things she'd ever witnessed in her life.

It's said that when sewer rats hibernate, they gather together in a cluster for warmth, and because they're so filthy, their tails can become intertwined and permanently stuck together, creating a collective organism called a "rat king," an ambulatory knot of rats all tied together at the tail. That's a pretty good analogy for what Robin Martine saw that day in the ruins of Fort Bostock as Santiago Valenzuela came pouring out of that Tex-Mex pueblo, except instead of rats, it was a multitude of creatures all molded like Play-Doh into one singular shape.

The Santiago-beast's face had an immense Chinese-lion grin, a mouth bristling with saurian teeth, and his shaggy head was covered in multicolored eyes of a thousand shapes and sizes. Fur ran down his fat, sleek sides in striations of orange, red, and gold, shredded by stripes of waxy white scales.

Thousands of legs marched underneath him, hoofs and claws

clattering across the sandy macadam. Santiago surrounded her in a coil of his body as if he were circling the wagons, then lunged inward at her.

She rolled aside as his jaws thundered shut inches behind her, and jabbed him in the ribs—or at least what she thought were his ribs—with the spear. The abomination roared, flinching. The hair around the wound rippled like a blast wave, flickering from soft brown horsehair to the stripes of a zebra, and then to the rich russet of a fox.

Before she could jump back, the wall of muscle and hair swung forward and slammed her to the ground. An eagle foot as big as a chair came out of the living tumult and pinned her legs. "Aaugh!"

It's inside him.

Coming into contact with Santiago had given her some sort of visceral insight—she could *feel* Ereshkigal's power thrumming from deep inside him.

The relic is inside his body.

Darkness overcame her as Santiago's mouth closed on her upper body.

Pebbly-scratchy tongue caressed her back and two teeth slid between plates of armor, plunging pain into her abdomen like a giant barbecue fork. Tentacles slid under her crotch, trying to lift the rest of her into his jaws. She shrieked down his throat and grabbed two other teeth in either hand, wrenching them loose. Santiago choked off a scream, spitting her out.

Blood flowed from the bite wounds in her waist, running in a sheet down her legs. Now she had teeth as big as mattock-heads in her hands, but the Osdathregar spear was still stuck in Santiago's side, waggling up and down. She jumped, trying to knock it loose, but Santiago corkscrewed as he crawled, pulling it out of reach.

Agonizing heat built in her stomach where he'd bitten her. Was he venomous now? "Nice try," Robin said, brandishing his own teeth at him like a knife fighter. She leapt at his flank and jammed the right tooth into his flesh, creating a handhold.

That great maw came at her again and she juked back, letting the teeth snap together in front of her face.

She planted her foot on his cheek and used it to kick herself farther up, where she stabbed him with the left fang. Santiago roared and lunged again, this time biting down on her legs. Another tooth went through her hip with a *crunch* and he dragged her away, lifting her into the air.

No doubt he meant to hoist her up and swallow her like a shark. Robin curled under with a scream of pain, doing an upside-down sit-up, stabbing both teeth into the soft underside of his throat.

The beast howled, choking, and flung her away.

Whipping across the street, Robin slammed against a wall and fell on her head. Her other antler snapped off with a noise like a gunshot and clattered across the pavement, a broken branch of shrike thorns.

The Santiago-chimera writhed and flailed around in the street, trying to get the fangs out of his throat, the ground vibrating under him, a tremendous zoological foam, as if God had put the entire animal kingdom on to boil. Lions, squids, and bears roiled out of his flesh and dissipated back into it. Blood sprayed out of his wounds, misting the air, painting streaks and puddles all over the asphalt in crazy graffiti whorls.

"Gonna cut that thing out of you, Santi." Robin limped around him, holding her bleeding side, to where she could see the spear lying in the road.

As soon as she got her hands on it, the thing snapped at her again. Luckily, this time none of his teeth got through her armor, but he threw back his head and flung her the other way.

Glass shattered across her shoulders as she hurtled through a window into some second-floor room.

Exhausted, she got up, grabbed up the spear and took off running, that whole three seconds reeling out in slow motion, her feet *thump* . . . *thump* . . . *thump*ing across the dry parquet and back through the window. She tucked her knees to clear the windowsill. Cool sunlight fell across her.

He was waiting, jaws open, striking at her in midair . . .

. . . But she had the spear up and ready like Zeus' lightning bolt. Driving it into his mouth, Robin rode him down into the dirt and pinned his tongue to the ground with the Osdathregar.

Her antler lay in the street. She picked it up and hobbled toward Santiago, clutching her belly.

He thrashed around, flopping and body-slamming himself trying to get out from under the dagger's spearpoint, a piece of paper under a paperweight, helpless and immobile, a gargantuan blob the size of his own mobile home, with dozens of legs—padded lion feet, hooved horse legs, lizard claws. Just as many wings had sprouted from his back: leathery bat wings, iridescent bird pinions, veiny insectile paddles. They cut the air incessantly as she got close, whooping and flapping.

His head was a massive confusion of skins and parts, constantly glitching through thousands of eyes and horns and teeth. Transformations rolled backward from his face as if he were swimming through the concept of evolution itself.

"Let's open 'er up," growled Robin, jamming the antler into his side. Santiago roared in pain and fright. "See what we got." Pulling it free, she thrust the antler into him again, and again, carving a hole in the wall of his belly as if she were hoeing garden soil, driving the spikes into his skin, over and over, twisting them until her arm ached. Soon, she had a ragged pit punched in him the size of a watermelon. She threw down the antler and shoved a fist inside, entering the gaping laceration all the way to her shoulder.

Meat gave way under her knuckles, gliding and squirting sinuously over her elbow. She had the sensation of being in the nastiest porn video ever taped. "Come on, buddy, give it to me," Robin told him, groping around for the gas tank. Could feel it down deep, the relic's dark resonance like the angry rattling of a snake. Her hand bumped into something more solid than bone, a rod with a right angle to it: a piece of the motorcycle's frame.

As fast as lightning, a hooved foot popped out and mule-kicked her in the side.

"Ungh!" One second, she was standing next to him; the next, she was sprawled on her back, splattered in Santiago's blood and her own blood, all the oxygen driven out of her. Black spots and stars wormed through the white sky as she fought sleep.

"Get up, Robin!"

"Mama?"

"GET UP!" shrieked Annie Martine's ghost from somewhere behind her. *"Get up and get it! You're almost there!"*

"Almost there," she wheezed.

Rolling over, Robin got to her feet and staggered back toward the multiformed gorgon, a maimed St. George facing down the dragon. She reared back and threw a haymaker into the bleeding gore, shoving her hand deep inside, and grabbed the gas tank strut again.

"Got you." She pushed the other hand inside, pressing her cheek against Santiago's rippling flank. Both hands had it.

The horse foot lashed out again, kicking her in the leg. If not for the armor, it would have shattered her femur. As it was, the blow buckled her knee and knelt her in the dust. Another kick bashed her under the arm, refreshing the agony of the rib the bikers had broken at the Blue Wolf.

Robin fought for breath. "*Uhhhrr*-hrr-hrrrgh!"

All right, chick, she thought, planting one foot on the wall of shivering skin. *It's go time.* She found another foothold and pulled with everything she had on the blood-slicked steel.

Another kick, this time in the ass. Burning cramps rolled down her leg. Another kick glanced off her thigh.

Can't take too many more of these.

Another kick nearly brained her, bouncing off the side of her head. Reality narrowed to a fine point. Sound streamed out of a hole in the blackness, thin and high, the distant thundering of Santiago beating the shit out of her a thousand miles away. Unconsciousness slowly put its hand over her face.

What woke her up was the squeeze of a huge eagle claw slipping around her waist. Air wheezed out of her. Santiago pulled, but she was stuck as fast as a tick. Even as slick as her hands were, she wasn't letting go. He had her pulled straight out, legs kicking, arms extended, a flying Superman.

Slurp. Crunch. It was coming loose.

Fibrous muscle ripped out of the way, popping like rubber bands as the gas tank slid toward the surface. Santiago screamed in pain and indignation. *Can't tell if he's doing it on purpose or not, but he's helping me.* Cold sunlight glinted on the white star. *Almost there! Just a little fa—*

The gas tank popped out and hit her in the face.

This was immediately followed by an overwhelming gush of hot fluid, cascading all over her, a geyser of steaming black gore. Gallons and gallons of black slime poured out of the monster that used to be Santiago Valenzuela, piling all over the road in thick, tarry puddles that smelled like black licorice and smoldering plastic and rotten ham and infection. The eagle claw threw her aside and turned into an octopus tentacle covered in warthog hair and porcupine needles, slapping around in a frenzy.

Something rattled inside the tank.

Yahtzee! Robin struggled to her feet in the slippery gore, unscrewing the tank's gear-shaped cap. She held the tank upside down and shook it. Something tiny fell out, and at first, she thought it was a green bean.

Finger bone. Dyed green from years soaking in gasoline.

"Cuttin' you off, you Mesopotamian motherfucker!" Robin tossed the gas tank aside and picked up the bone. Pinching it between her armored fingers, she snapped the brittle thing in half.

The goddess of death howled in outrage from the nothing beyond the wall of the world, and the sky shook.

Glowing vapors spewed between Robin's fingers as if she were holding a supernatural smelling-salt capsule. She inhaled the glittering fog, sucking it through her bloody teeth, and the heart-road's ectoplasm snaked down her throat, filling her with heat like a belly full of vodka on a cold winter night, stoking some black fire deep inside her.

In seconds, the finger bone was just that—a broken bone in her hands, a bit of fractured calcium without meaning or purpose. She collapsed on her back, waves of white-hot euphoria snapping through her, a tectonic iron core at her center, churning and burning, stones and iron grating against each other.

This was different. She'd absorbed heart-roads before, but this was definitely something else—far more intense, more than a simple internalizing of energies. Before, drawing a heart-road into herself had been like . . . a cigarette after a session of good sex. This, *this,* was a blood transfusion from the center of the universe, a cosmic orgasm searing her insides with light, reawakening some dark and strange part of her.

As the euphoria drained from her body, it left her empty, a vessel full of starving fire. Clawing in the dirt, she turned onto her belly. Blood made black mud of the earth underneath her as she pulled herself along the ground, trying to get away from the collapsing mess that used to be Santiago.

Dear God, the hunger, she tried to think through a whirlwind of mental fragments.

Only, it was no longer so simple as "hunger"; it was that satanic need to devour and destroy again, but this time it stood over her: enormous, steel-hard, unavoidable. No resisting it. No longer at the eye of the hurricane, she *was* the hurricane, swelling, howling, gorging, massive, monstrous.

With every grasp of rock and dirt, tiny pinprick spiders trickled out from under her armored hands, scuttling into the dust. They were oil-black, with *Tron*-like red racing stripes.

Hello, world, said the warhawk Robin from the surface of a puddle. Her labored breath was deep, metallic, reverberating like a thousand-foot robot. She could feel herself fading away and the demon taking over. *Let it flow through you; let Calgon carry you away. That's right.*

This was what her need to fight had always been, hadn't it?

The bloodlust, the warhawk in the bathroom mirror. The demon half of her trying to come through, come out and drown the human in darkness.

"The Transfiguration," said her mother Annie, the ghost's face underlit by the hellfire licking out of Robin's mouth. "You're going feral, baby. Losing control. You gotta slap a lid on this while you're still lucid, or you're gonna go off the rails and the magicians will have to rein you in."

Tell her to fuck off, said the warhawk.

"No," Robin croaked with a buzz-saw voice. She breathed deep, reaching for air, and what came out was that same drowned-engine sound she'd heard in that nightmare house last year: *Grrrrrruru-ruhuhuhuh.*

"You don't want that," said Annie. "It's you or them if that happens. So, you gotta fight for me, okay? Stay with me. Stay here."

Her daughter stared at her with eyes that emitted gaseous, luminescent plasma. "I got this," Robin said, and turned inward, searching for La Reina's Transfiguration heart-road. It was there, hidden, coiled in the pit of her throat like a sort of rope-chakra, and she drew it out. Slowly, methodically, as if trying to tailor a dress in a hurricane, she applied the Transfiguration to her body, sewing it into her limbs, restoring her humanity piece by piece.

A lizard wriggled toward her, drawn to the warmth.

The demon pounded it flat with a fist and she fed it to herself as if throwing meat to a lion, tore it apart with her teeth. Cool blood squirted down her chin and immediately burned into sweet smoke.

"Fight it," said Annie.

Carbon plating over her face cracked, spiderwebbing like fine china. Robin threw the remains of the lizard aside and clawed the armor away, crushing coal in her fist, revealing new, pink skin. Green light still emanated from her eyes, but her face was human again. She peeled the shell away from her skull, and her hair flagged in the desert wind, wet and dark and new.

Tightening her fist, Robin broke the carbon mask with a sharp *snap!*, letting the pieces tumble through her fingers.

Track 36

They found her lying on Fort Bostock's desolate runway in the middle of nowhere. Blood left a trail of smears and droplets into the distance. Elisa screeched to a stop and everybody piled out of her truck into a misty drizzle of cold rain. As she got out, she pulled her rifle from behind the seat and opened the bolt, checking the chamber.

"Help me out!" said a frantic voice from inside the camper shell. "I gotta, gotta be there—see her—*fuckin' help me!*"

Navathe and Gendreau ran to the tailgate as a very sooty Kenway slid out and stood up on his one leg. Looked like he had the world's worst sunburn, butter-yellow blisters developing on his face, but he was otherwise intact. The two mages helped him over to the strange figure lying on the ground.

The Osdathregar spear lay by her side, thrumming softly.

Between the protection of the supernatural armor (carbon? Brimstone? They weren't sure) and Doc G's ministrations, the face peeking out was fresh, whole, healthy. Everything was human again except for Robin's left arm and torso . . . and the horns. Her antlers were broken off, leaving two diabolical goat-horns jutting from her pale forehead, the right one a couple inches longer than the left, just below the hairline.

But they saw a strange, wild, unfamiliar thing in her eyes that made them hesitate. Ragged breath hissed through her teeth like a wounded animal, and even though her face was human, her eyes were still a luminous radium green.

"Looks like she's having a hard time staying human," said Navathe. "Is it a good idea to be this close to her?"

Gendreau gave him a sideways look. "We've been with her this far. If she was going to go off the deep end, she would have done it back at the hoarder house." He studied her face as her eyes rolled, focusing on them for just a moment before drifting up to the sky. "Besides, even if she *was* on the verge of losing her mind, she's too messed up to be dangerous. She should be in the ER, not lying on a tarmac in the rain. And my God, man, we're her *friends.* We can't abandon her."

The pyromancer seemed chastised. He got up and paced behind them, glancing over with concern at the girl-creature writhing at their feet. Ironically enough, the demon looked possessed, clawing slowly at the asphalt, eyes wandering.

"What is she wearing?" asked Kenway. "Is that some kind of armor?"

Three terrifyingly nasty stab wounds in her abdomen and chest were still leaking vivid red blood, thick like paint. Thin curds of yellow fat were visible inside, torn muscle fibers, dirt, bits of grass. "Calm your tits. I got this," Robin told him with a voice like icebergs grinding together: deep, metallic, sibilant. "I can control this. This is nothing, okay? Nothing. *Uggghhrrr* . . . got this in the fucking bag. Trust me."

"I don't know if she's wearing the armor or if it *is* her." Gendreau squirted a bottle of water into the wounds to wash the debris out, then began the laborious task of closing the holes. A vicious sparkler of red light burst out of his ring, the motes of energy swirling into her wounds like fireflies going down a drain. “Try not to finish Transfiguring yourself right now. You might not survive with these wounds as a full-on human.”

“My devil-girl,” Kenway cradled her head. “I’m so glad you’re alive.”

“I could say the same thing.” Her gleaming green eyes narrowed, studying his dirty face. “What happened? Clubhouse exploded. They said you were inside. Thought you were dead.”

Kenway’s clothes were blackened, with scorched holes over blistered skin, and his eyebrows were gone. “Gas leak in the basement where we were locked up, and the guy with the shotgun ignited it, but we were hiding in a walk-in freezer when it happened. Rook used her telekinesis relic to get us out of there by pushing the debris away from the door.”

“Got a bit of a heavy-duty tan.” Rook joined them, her face as black as a chimney-sweep’s. “But the freezer door took the brunt of the blast.” She forced a smile, rubbing her eyes on her filthy sleeves.

The warhawk paced behind them, eyes glowing, separate from glass and water, a strange ugly Faces of Meth version of Robin Martine, cigarette burns littering her skin, teeth filed to points. The warhawk reflection reached over Navathe’s shoulder and held a finger-gun to his temple. He did not react, and neither did anyone else. First time Robin had ever seen her outside of a mirror, freely inhabiting the real world, and to be honest, if she weren’t on the verge of death, it might have been existentially terrifying.

You’re dying, it said, grinning. *He got you, chick. This is it.*

Gendreau’s relic ring was a blowtorch of hissing light. He thrust the gush of energy into her wounds, concentrating on knitting the flesh and arteries back together, but the blood was pumping out of the wound too fast to contain.

“Stay with me, Miss Martine,” he said, frantic. “I’m gonna get you through this, I just need you to fight.”

She wheezed through a mouthful of red blood and smoke that

stung her lips and tongue. Robin thrashed in pain, spitting, coughing, choking, roaring in that terrifying silver voice. Her black left hand ended in a rake of talons, and she clutched at her friends in fear and fury, tearing the rags of Kenway's burned shirt. Felt like she was drowning in fire, magma erupting from her belly and pouring out of her face, and sudden panic gave her the strength to grab at every handhold she could see, trying to pull herself out of the flames. But she wasn't slipping into it; it was *coming out of her.* No escape. She was dying, her guts and lungs and skin were roasting again, and she was dying, and after the second time in two days, it was horrifying beyond all rational thought.

"The fire is coming out of her heart," cried Gendreau. "Santiago hit her in the heart; I can see it! That's where her birthright hid itself away from the Sanctification all along, isn't it? My God, a heart full of hellfire! *That's* why you smell like brimstone when you're angry!"

The pain was monumental, Biblical, impossible, as if she were being dismantled at the subatomic level by a steel machine made of infinite white-hot needles.

That's your weakness, demon, said the warhawk, looming invisibly over her friends. Rain hissed and evaporated against her black armor, as if striking a hot griddle. *Burn you. Stab you. Beat you. Cut you. You're unstoppable. Only thing that can kill you is to pierce your heart and let the hellfire out.*

Remember that.

"Hold her down," said Rook, grabbing Robin's arm and pinning it with her knees. "Before she hurts herself—or one of us."

The curandero fought sobs. "It's not working."

"What?" said Kenway.

"I'm not fast enough. The hellfire is burning her insides."

"No, no, no." Kenway cradled Robin in his lap. "Is there not another way? Is there a way these two can, I don't know, supercharge you somehow?"

"It's okay," Robin told him in her grinding steel voice, her eyes unfocusing and going dark as her body gave up on her. "I love you."

Each heartbeat was a slow, soft stamping of a wooden staff in her chest.

"I love you."

The hellfire quietened and quelled, extinguishing with a hiss.

Track 37

When the fire went out, it left her adrift in the deepest darkness she had ever known. After a time, she realized that she was lying not on a rainy tarmac but on a dry parquet floor, fuzzy with dust. Extending into the distance was a narrow sort of wooden catwalk in black space.

Shapes loomed at her from the void, drifting toward the parquet catwalk like raised sails, slow and monumental. Great shards of wood and plaster, accompanied by smaller, jagged pieces and stony red bricks. The bricks assembled themselves in piecemeal columns and crags like a jigsaw puzzle, and the tongue-and-groove wood slid into place around it, forming walls. Plaster spread itself over the wood like white peanut butter, hardening instantly. Wallpaper gift-wrapped the structures in damask the red of wine.

Some sort of otherworldly house was building itself around her.

A light came on, blinding her. An electric lantern hung from the ceiling, a fragile-looking china globe in a brass fixture, encircled with painted blue flowers. Robin got the feeling this place existed only when it needed to.

Big dark rectangles gaped in the walls. Doorways. Panels eased into place from the abyss, coalescing from the dark—doors, red doors, with brass knobs and glossy paint. Brass peepholes appeared in the doors, tiny glass lenses glinting.

None of the doors had numbers, just peepholes. Robin got to her feet and went to the nearest door.

Light streamed from the lens; she held up her hand to catch the light and an image appeared like the screen of a movie theater. In her palm was a beach, windy and rocky, and the sun shone in a cloudless sky. Distant cries of a seagull. Lethargic waves pushed endlessly onto the shore.

A woman sat on the beach, her back to the door. She turned to glance back as if she'd sensed someone watching her, then once again to the ocean. Whoever she was, she didn't seem unhappy. The woman stood and walked away, moving along the shoreline, once stooping to pick up a stone, and an expression of disappointment briefly crossed her face. She chucked it into the ocean.

Robin closed her hand and the image disappeared, and then she gave a short, sharp gasp.

Half-glimpsed in the lantern-light, a figure towered down the hallway, a goliath dressed in mourning black robes that hung open in the front to reveal a pair of enormous breasts and a bell-shaped belly. She was tall and mountainous, her velvet-black arms bulbous with muscle, and she was barefoot. Her head was a cow's head, black and silky, with guileless black eyes and moon-white horns.

Suspended in the air between those horns was what appeared to be a miniature representation of the Milky Way, a spiderweb of light stretching from horn tip to horn tip. Starry pinpricks migrated throughout the galaxy as it revolved, a subtle but dazzling spindle.

The cow-headed woman glanced at her and walked away into the dark.

Robin followed her.

As they made their way down this hallway, the electric china globes overhead blinked to life, illuminating their progress. Always, the cow-headed woman faded into the dark just as soon as the next light came on, walking ahead of them as if she didn't need it to see, or she knew where she was going with or without it. Which definitely might have been the case, as the miniature Milky Way threw a faint light on the walls around her like a flashlight shining through clenched fingers.

"Who are you?" asked Robin.

No answer, only the constant and deliberate *clunk . . . clunk . . . clunk* of the cow-woman's boots—or perhaps they were hooves—reverberating on the wooden floor.

"Where are we going?"

"Your mother awaits," said a voice that was surprisingly soft and maternal, in a thick accent Robin didn't recognize. The cow's mouth did not move; the voice just seemed to *be heard* as if someone had narrated it over a movie scene, and was also faintly muffled, as if she were speaking through a thick blanket. "Welcome to Cosmotelluria."

"This is the afterlife?" said Robin. "Not quite what I pictured."

"The afterlife is not what you picture. It's how the afterlife pictures you."

"Soviet Russia, huh?"

"No," said the cow-god. "It is called Cosmotelluria."

"So, Cosmopolitan thinks I'm an old house on the inside?"

"You might say so."

"Why?"

No answer. Just as well; Robin had the feeling she wouldn't have liked the answer.

"Could have been worse. At least I'm not a vape shop on the inside."

They walked.

"What do I do? Feel like I've been here way too long already. By now, I should be lying in the back of an ambulance as paramedics electrocute my chest with shock paddles or something."

The cow-woman paid no attention.

Robin followed her down the corridor, several times through intersections and around corners, passing dozens or perhaps hundreds of red doors whose peepholes sprayed light from private worlds. She paused once to put her hand into one of the cones and the image in her palm was one of a bespectacled man sitting quietly in a massive library, reading from a stack of books as the sun streamed down on him from a tremendous Gothic window.

"These are people's personal Heavens, aren't they?" Robin asked the cow-woman.

"These rooms contain whatever you are in want of," said the figure, whose back was always turned to Robin as she trundled through the mysterious house. "But they do not always contain what you want."

"Who are you?"

At this, the cow-woman glanced over her broad shoulder, the galaxy turning with her horns. "I do not often hear that question. Most of you are more concerned with where you are and where you are going than who I am or why I am taking you there."

"Welp," said Robin, her bare feet padding across the parquet, "I'm asking it now."

"Some call me the Mistress of the West," said the cow-woman. "Some call me the House of the Rising Sun. Yet others call me the Mother of Rivers. I am also known as the Lady of Joy. But above all, I am the custodian of this place."

"House of the Rising Sun, huh? Groovy. Was your mother a tailor?"

"I have no mother. None that I remember."

"So, you don't have a *name*-name?"

"If I ever chose for myself a name, I do not remember it. Only what I have been given." She held her hand up to a peephole light and Robin glimpsed a woman strolling down a forest path in the sun. She was startled to recognize a twenty-years-younger Marina Valenzuela, all the gray gone from her hair, the wrinkles erased, her eyes bright and clear.

"You said you're taking me to my mom?"

"You will not be here long," said the Mother of Rivers. "The power of the Queen of the Earth is going to send you back soon. I have taken it upon myself to bring you to your mother while you are here, because it is going to be a long time before you return."

"The Queen of the Earth?" asked Robin, stopping in the hallway.

"You know her as the goddess of death Ereshkigal. To the Greeks she is known as Hecate."

"Oh."

Robin eyed the door, the one that led to Marina's personal afterlife. "Is there any way I can take this one back to Earth with me?"

"No," said the Mother of Rivers.

"Why not?"

Instead of answering, the cow-headed goddess turned and walked deeper into the maze. Reluctantly, Robin tore herself away from Marina's door and followed. "Why not?" she tried again. "She's got a daughter she needs to take care of. She's got unfinished business. Ain't that why ghosts always get stuck on Earth?"

No answer.

"I mean, not that I want her to be a ghost—she needs a body and shit."

Nothing.

"You sure we can't swing it, just this once?"

They moved on. The god's obstinance irked Robin significantly, but what was she going to do, challenge a deity? That didn't sound like it would end well.

Still. . . .

"So, Western Sizzlin', what does *Queen of the Earth* mean? Does Ereshkigal actually rule the world?"

"Once," the god said, "a long time ago, when I was young. A beautiful queen of the ancients, a half-god with immense powers gifted to her by the Father of the Moon. But she was exiled to the Desert of Anguish for murdering her sister, and there she has been ever since, scheming to return to her kingdom."

"And that's where my knowledge begins. Thanks for the backstory."

The Mother of Rivers stopped in the middle of the hallway. Even when she was standing still, the floor groaned and complained as if it were about to come apart under her feet. The ceiling was at least twelve or thirteen feet tall, and the cow-horns protruding from her skull often came very close to upsetting the china lanterns. "We are here," she said. No expectation in her black bovine eyes or, really, any emotion at all. All of her personality was in her voice. She was monumental, immovable, stoic.

"Lady of Joy, huh?"

Approaching the door nearest the Mother of Rivers, Robin held her hand in front of the peephole.

In the palm of her hand were two faint smudges of light—a little portable television, and sitting in front of it, the recliner where Robin spent her childhood watching Saturday cartoons. Her skin crawled with recognition.

Sitting in the recliner was a very familiar woman.

"Mom," said Robin.

The Mother of Rivers said nothing, but the nothing sounded like agreement.

"Why is it so dark in there?" Robin peered at the picture in her hand. "Not much of a Heaven. That ain't her personal Hell, is it? To sit in the dark for all eternity?"

"I told you what these rooms contain."

"You did."

"If you could see what is on that television, you would know what your mother is in want of."

Suddenly, Robin very much wanted to open that door and walk through it.

So, she did.

• • •

Warm summer breezes came wafting through the window-screen, carrying the soft chirp of crickets. She was in the Winnebago—hers, the Brave that was supposed to be smashed into a guardrail somewhere in the Texas scrublands—but the thing was in pristine condition and it was nighttime outside. The little kitchen booth was removed, replaced by the recliner, and the weapons Robin had bracketed onto the walls were now ceramic figurines of foxes and fox Beanie Babies. Her mother loved foxes.

On the little black-and-white television, Kenway and the others were kneeling beside her lifeless half-demon body on Fort Bostock's rain-soaked tarmac. Robin and Annie watched her friends mourn or perhaps wait patiently for something to happen. Elisa had gone to the truck to comfort Carly, but Kenway and the magicians were still kneeling in a huddle around Robin's corpse.

"Hi, Mama."

"Hey, baby."

"Where do you go when I can't see you?" she asked. "When you're not around—where are you? Here?"

Annie seemed to mull it over. "Yes, I'm here. When I run out of steam and I can't hold on to the real world anymore, I snap back here. Not a bad place. Warm. Quiet. A damn sight better than Marilyn Cutty's tree. Little bit like a phone going back on the charger. I can still see what's going on with you, but it feels far away, like you're a TV show and I'm watching you on a little portable television." She pointed at the tiny Magnavox. "This one. Like the kind we used to have when you were little."

"The one we took camping." Robin took a deep breath and let it out in a sigh, surveying the facsimile of her now-destroyed RV. "Pretty nice, actually. I could use a little peace and quiet."

"Oh . . . no, honey, not yet," said Annie.

"What do you mean?"

"It's not your time."

A childish petulance Robin hadn't experienced for a long time came over her just then. "Why not? Why can't I stay here with you? Why do I have to go back?" The petulance evolved into a panicky knot in the middle of her chest. "If I ever had a debt in my life, fuck, *fuck*, I've repaid it a thousand times over. The notches on my gun, those horrible people I took out—the pedophile in Florida, the rapist in Louisiana, the serial killer in Oregon—and God, all the witches. All those fucking witches. I've been shot at, bitten, stabbed, cut, burned up. I'm like fucking Rasputin over here." She just stared at her friends on the little TV, shaking her head. "I died yesterday and now I'm dying again today. How many times do I have to die before I make up for those child molesters, rapists, killers? I'm ready to pay off this loan and stick a fork in it. Yeah, I hurt them, ran them out of town, got them arrested. Killed them. Hey, the state does it. All I'm doing is cutting out the middleman." The more she spoke, the faster the words tumbled out. "If I didn't stop them, they'd just keep on hurting people. The system is bullshit. The system doesn't work. I—"

"Baby."

"I'm not Batman!" Robin continued trying to rationalize. "Killing these assholes doesn't make me as bad as they are! Doesn't make me a monster! There's a line and they cross it! They're not innocent, and *I'm not a monster!*"

"Baby," said Annie, touching Robin's arm, trying to calm her.

Robin flinched from her mother's hand—not in horror, but in surprise. She'd visualized her mother regularly since last Halloween, but Annie had never been tangible before.

"You touched me!"

"Come here," said Annie, reaching out to her daughter.

The sounds of sobbing came from the people gathered around her body. Kenway was on his knees, his forehead on Robin's lifeless chest, and he was crying his eyes out.

"Damn," said Robin, sighing in defeat. "Damn."

She wrapped her arms around Annie and gave her mother the biggest hug she thought she'd ever given anybody.

"You're not being punished, honey," Annie said over Robin's shoulder. "I know you think you are because you've dealt with so much these past few years. This is just part of being a hero. Most of the time, the good guy gets the shit end of the stick. Know what I mean? We can't win 'em all, but we can keep fighting. That's the point, isn't it? Winning isn't what makes you a hero; it's continuing when you lose. And as a hero, you're helping good people. You're keeping them safe. What's that quote? 'We sleep soundly in our beds because rough men stand ready in the night to visit violence on those who would do us harm.' And who said you had to be a man to be rough?"

Her daughter only clutched her tighter.

"Being bad means doing the easy thing. Being good means doing the hardest thing. You're not an easy woman. That's not how I, or Heinrich, bless his rotten heart, raised you."

"Don't leave me again," she said into Annie's shoulder, squeezing.

"I never did." Annie freed herself from Robin's desperate embrace. "All right. Time to go." She smiled, holding the girl's shoulders. "Kick it in the ass, kiddo. Nobody is gonna beat my daughter. I meant what I said—you're a rough woman. Go out there and do your work."

Same feeling of patronized relief came over Robin as those halcyon days of skinned knees and emergency cookies. "How am I supposed to get back?" Robin stared at the TV version of herself, sprawled on the ground, covered in blood. "Look at me—I'm dead as hell."

Strange knowledge twinkled in her mother's eye. "Go find Marina, daughter of mine. My little hellion."

"Marina?" Robin asked, confused. "I saw her Heaven door, but—"

"Trust me," Annie said, smiling. "Get out of here. Go find

Marina. Ereshkigal, she knows you're here; she's looking for you. She's coming."

"I don't understand. What am—"

"Did you forget what I am?" Rising from her chair, Annie turned off the camp television. "I am inseparably linked to Ereshkigal through my heart-road, even without a flesh body." Something about hearing her mother mention having a heart-road—a term she'd been associating with witches, these raving, shark-toothed hags that had chased her screaming down dark alleyways and slashed at her arms with dirty fingernails—caught Robin mid-stride, gave her a cold, hollow feeling, as if she'd been scooped empty and refilled with a breeze from a cellar door. "I'm like a Marine; just because I'm dead doesn't mean I stop being a witch." She led Robin to the RV's door. "Go find Marina. Take her back with you; take her back to the living world. For Carly."

"How?"

"You'll figure it out, little demon."

The blunt way her mother said *demon* took Robin by surprise, leaving her further disoriented and maybe a little offended. She gave Annie a strange look, as if seeing a new facet of her for the first time. "Even if I could, *Mom,* I don't think the rules say I can do that." She pointed at the door. "Becky Buttermilk out there said no. I already asked."

"Since when have you let a little thing like *no* stop you?" Annie peered into Robin's eyes, fists on her hips. "What's she gonna do, throw you out?" She opened the RV door. "Go. I'll be right behind you," she said, and shoved Robin through it.

Track 38

Back in the celestial hallways of Cosmotelluria, Robin tried to gain her bearings. To her relief, the Mother of Rivers wasn't waiting to ambush her. "How now, brown cow?" Robin murmured to herself, taking off at a power-walk pace, eyes dancing over the doors and their luminary peepholes. Wandering through the maze of corridors, she tried to backtrack to where she thought she remembered seeing Marina's heaven in the palm of her hand. "How the hell am I supposed to get you past the Lady of Joy and Cheese?" A beam of light across her fingers. A small woman in thick glasses perused the stacks in a huge library, accompanied by a tall, thin dog.

Behind the next door, a man rode a golf cart through what looked like an abandoned Walmart.

The door after that yielded a woman sitting at a table in a crowded coffee shop, happily sipping a foamy latte, watching customers come and go. "Where are you, Marina?" she asked the darkness. The lamps did not ignite for her the way they did for the cow-god, so Robin crept through cloistered hallways illuminated only by the soft cones of light.

Holding up another hand, she inspected the image. A man sitting on a stool overlooking a desolate beach, painting the landscape on a huge easel.

Behind her, the floor creaked. Lamp glow gave shape to the doorframes.

Looking over her shoulder, Robin saw the familiar bulk of the Mother of Rivers striding toward her, the galaxy between her horns a distant smear of light in the darkness. The lamps came to life as she walked, extinguishing in her wake.

"No," said the witch-hunter, pointing. "I'm doing this, Elsie. You can't stop me. I'm taking her home."

The cow-god followed, inexorable, ponderous, each peephole-light flashing bucolic scenes across her chest and face as she passed. Her massive, sloping shoulders cut an ominous silhouette. She said nothing, but Robin had the idea that, for a god, elaborating on *no* was probably unnecessary. Gods had no need to rationalize their edicts and decisions. This was *her* domain.

Another peepshow. A man riding a roller coaster. A woman sitting in a window nook, watching rain fall onto a gleaming gray city. A woman in a mid-century modern living room, covered in a horde of puppies.

Robin began to panic. "Where are you, Marina? We need to go."

Over her shoulder: the Mother of Rivers was right behind her, no more than twenty feet away. Robin held up her hand to another light. "Come on, come on." A man eating a huge sandwich in a New York bodega. "Come on, where are you?" A woman climbing a mountain in the badlands.

The third peephole made Robin's breath catch in her throat. Marina Valenzuela strolled through idyllic storybook woods. "Jackpot," she said, and a fist like steel closed on the lank curls of her hair.

She wrenched around to face the Mother of Rivers.

"You were warned," the god said imperiously, sternly, but not evilly. Not meanly. "Marina Valenzuela cannot go back with you. Death—*real* death—takes something from those who pass beyond its walls. It exacts a toll."

"What's that something?"

The cow-god did not answer.

"Part of her soul? Is that what it takes? Like it's some kind of spiritual currency, or train ticket?"

Her hair was still gripped in the Mother's immense fist, holding her fast. Robin realized that the god wasn't entirely cow, just her head and shoulders—the rest of her was human, familiar, if gargantuan in frame and musculature. The Mother of Rivers was truly enormous, she saw now. The galaxy between her horns spiraled silently, glittering in the dark like the finest tinsel.

Robin waited for further elaboration. "That all you got?"

The cow-god said nothing else.

"Then peace out, Steak 'n Shake. I don't have time for these games, and at this point, I'm willing to take the risk," said Robin, and she put her foot on the cow-god's thigh and twisted. Hair ripped free of her scalp with a brief stab of pain, leaving the Mother holding a clump of chestnut locks.

"She won't remember," said the Mother of Rivers, tossing the hair on the floor. "That is the toll, witch-hunter. When you pass into your after, you are freed of your memories, for good or ill. Freed of your regrets and pain. You give up your broken heart. That's what Heaven is."

"Sublime contentment," said Robin, the doorknob warm in her hand.

"And Hell," said the cow-god, "is sublime regret."

"That's the joke," said Robin.

"That's the joke," the cow-god replied, presenting the first bit of levity she'd seen out of that terrifying face since she'd set foot in this weird labyrinth.

"You give up your broken heart."

"Yes."

"Why would I ever want to do that? My broken heart is what makes me who I am. It's my best feature."

"If you go in there after the woman," said the Mother of Rivers, "Hell is going to come looking for you. It seeks those who do not belong, the lost ones, the trespassers. It is the Great Corrector. And it will punish you."

Robin opened the door.

"Fuckin' bring it," she said, and stepped through.

• • •

Gilded sunlight filtered through emerald treetops, shattering softly across feathery grass. The air was kind with strong, sweet honeysuckle. Robin found herself following an earthen path. She blinked, taking it all in, and screwed her fists into her eyes—something about this was strangely romantic, all the colors were a little too saturated, the details a little too blurry, as if she were looking at it through a lens smeared with Vaseline, like old Hollywood used to do for Ingrid Bergman and Rita Hayworth. But it felt fake, like painted scenery on a stage.

She hated it.

"Marina?" she asked the stillness.

No answer but birdsong that had the canned quality of a recording being played on a public address system.

"Okay," she said, pushing her hands through what hair she had left, "enough screwing around. I need to find Marina and get out of here." Cupping her hands around her mouth, she began to yell. "Marina! *MARRIIIINAAAA! Where are you?*"

Cresting a small hill, she slipped through a tangle of supple pine branches and found herself looking down at a crystalline lake of a pale, tired aquamarine blue. Sunlight glittered across its surface. Jutting out into the brilliance was a long wooden dock, and sitting at the end were two people holding fishing poles.

"Marina?" she called. "Is that you?"

Coming closer, she realized that one of them had goat horns not unlike her own broken antlers. The horned figure turned to admonish her, and Robin saw that he had no shirt on, or really any clothes at all, except for a red scarf. What she'd thought were pants were actually a coarse, woolly coat of hair. He wasn't a devil; he was some kind of goat-man.

"Not so loudly!" he said, "You'll scare away all the fish."

"What the fuck?"

The horned figure scowled. "Don't be a boor, ma'am." Marina cast an annoyed glance over her shoulder and went back to fishing.

"Who the hell are *you*?"

"I am a faun from the banks of Glasswater Creek," said the horned man, in a soft, airy English accent. "My name is Aegeus, and this is my friend Marina, and we are here fishing. If you don't mind, I'd be greatly appreciative if—"

"Where are we?"

"Narnia, of course," said Aegeus.

"Narnia? As in *The Lion, the Witch, and the Wardrobe?* That Narnia?"

"How many Narnias have you heard of, miss?"

"Just the one?"

"Then by your own admission, wouldn't this be the only Narnia?" He squinted up at her horns, then down at her feet. "What happened to your legs, miss? Aren't you a faun like me?" He looked up, his face falling. "Were you cursed by a witch?"

Robin stared at the faun.

"I don't have time for this," she said, placing a hand on Marina's shoulder. "Hon, we need to go. You have a daughter to get back to."

"Daughter?" asked Marina.

"Yeah, a little girl named Carly. D'you remember?"

"Carly?"

"Yeah."

"I told you, witch-hunter—she would not remember," said the

cow-god behind them. The Mother of Rivers stood at the head of the dock, ebony-black human feet planted in the technicolor-green grass. Against the verdant color, her robes were the darkest sable. "She has been stripped of all her pain. Her after—her contentment—is what you see before you."

"A book?"

"When Marina Valenzuela and her mother Gloria crossed the border into California under cover of night in December 1986 and were given sanctuary, she discovered a copy of *The Lion, the Witch, and the Wardrobe* on the bookshelf in Alexandra Martinez's house."

Reeling her line out of the water, Marina flicked the hook over her head and sent it deep into the lake.

"For the next six years, she would treasure that book," continued the Mother. "It was her only solace in a turbulent childhood, moving from home to home, avoiding the authorities, and it was how she learned to read and write English. Narnia is brightest in her mind of all the places her heart has ever called home."

For a moment, she thought she saw a shadow in the water, a whale-shadow perhaps, but it might have been a trick of the sun. Robin sighed, looking back and forth between the shadow and Marina. "That's sweet and all, but we need to—"

The galaxy inside the cow-god's horns was barely visible in the sunshine, a spiderweb frosted with dew. As she spoke, the stars burned brightly for a second, a spiral of blue gas-flame. "The after will fight to keep her. Hell will fight to claim you. And you cannot fight Hell. Not even I can."

"If you're not a faun," said Aegeus, "then you must be a devil." He set down his fishing pole and stood to confront Robin. His face took on a scratchy, soulful definition and she realized that the riot of color around her had begun to darken and desaturate. Details were sharpening, filling in. The sun cowered in the sky and pulled a protective veil of clouds across its face. A sinister grit came over the lake, and the whale-shadow she thought she'd seen a moment before once again coalesced beneath their feet. Just beyond the dock, the water sank, bending downward into a bowl of dark glass.

"Carlita," Robin told Marina, "your daughter. Your gorgeous, smart, brave little girl. She pepper-sprayed your asshole husband trying to save your life."

Finally, the woman peered over her shoulder. "Carlita?"

"Yeah."

"I have a daughter?"

At the end of Marina's fishing line, the lake sank into a glassy cavern, becoming a pit of darkness as if some great mouth had opened just below the surface. Wind blew down the beach—a soft breeze at first, but it soon grew into a gale, threatening to push them into the widening gyre. Robin shifted her weight, her hair whipping.

"Yes," shouted a familiar voice. "And she's waiting for you."

Power welled from Annie Martine's eyes, distorting the air in a glassy funnel, as she used her Gift, her memory-powers, to put the missing pieces back into Marina's mind like some kind of jigsaw puzzle. She stood on the bank next to the Mother of Rivers, weight forward, leaning into her power, almost trembling with the effort.

"You're lying," the gritty, gray, high-definition faun shouted back. "You just want to take my friend; that's what you want to do. I know your kind! You'll say anything you want to get your way! You lie, and you cheat, and you—"

Interrupting his diatribe, Robin punched the goat-man square in the face.

One full-strength jab in the upper lip, and he toppled backward into the lake, where he swirled down the vortex as if it were a bathtub drain.

"Rude," said the cow-god.

Boards peeled loose from the dock, nails jutting, bobbling in the wind like wooden piano-keys. The water crawled backward, unveiling a slimy, muddy shore, uprooting water plants as it went, and crayfish were unscrewed from the mud and pulled into the hellhole. Robin squinted into the wind, reaching for Marina's hand. "I can explain later. Right now, we need to get out of here."

The woman's hands wrung themselves in indecision. A mental image flashed in Robin's mind of this same woman suspended by those hands over a yawning void after the RV crash, and some frustrated steel inside of her said she would not fail Marina again, not this time, not ever, and she bent down and took one of those hands by force. "I told you I would help you and your daughter, and when I make a promise, I keep that shit to the end and beyond. Do you comprende?"

Marina's face darkened—not in rage, but in determination. "Yes . . . you made me a promise. I remember that. I *remember*."

"I died keeping it. Twice."

A dock board broke free and whirled past them, missing Robin by inches.

Rounding on the hellhole, she flipped it the bird with both hands. "I have shit to do, Hell," she bellowed into the darkness, *"so pack it in and piss off!"* and she pulled Marina up from the dock.

The abandoned fishing poles whipped into the now-vast gulf before them, a churning tornado below the lake. Deep inside the mad whirl, the craggy bottom was visible, with its mucky green waterplants and thick, sloppy mud. Beyond that, the fabric of Narnia seemed to come apart, and inside the shatter was nothing—a dead TV channel, a speechless mouth, a thrumming absence.

Then, suddenly, a world-shaking shriek came from the abyss.

A voice she'd heard before. Last year.

The half-birthed thing on the floor of Kenway's apartment, plumbed by a thousand silver filaments like interdimensional leeches. Something stirred at the bottom of the pit. A pale figure crawled toward them, caped in a brilliant web of shimmering white light. A cluster of red-rimmed eyes stared up at them, feral and terrifying. Its face was contorted by rage into an alien grimace, a white mask stretched thin over strange bones.

Ereshkigal.

"You," breathed Robin. "Let's pop smoke, lady."

Rumor has it there's one for resurrection—

One that can manipulate time, a phantom Gendreau said in the back of her mind. *One that can kill with a glance. But I've never seen them. They're all kept in a big warded vault in our place in Michigan.*

She grabbed Marina's hand and raised her other toward Ereshkigal as if to stop her, but instead, a filament of wriggling paranormal plasma burst out of the witch-goddess, threading itself through Robin's palm, down her arm, and into her heart.

"*Uh-n-n-n-n-n-nh,*" Robin stuttered, trying to focus on the power, trying to bend it to her will, force it to suit her needs. Her eyes were snapping flashbulbs, her throat a sizzling light socket. She was pulling a heart-road straight from the source, and it was like taking hold of a bare powerline. Her bones turned to lightning; her heart raged in her chest. Her brain lit up like every inch of neon in Las Vegas.

Resurrection.

She searched through the energies surging through her, tasting each of the goddess's powers as if sampling a soup buffet hooked into a 220-volt junction box. Candle flames ignited themselves in the grass at her feet. The grass itself parched, curled, and died, turning nicotine-brown.

"Run if you like, demon," Ereshkigal hissed, as she clambered over the end of the dock, reeling herself in on Robin's energy-filament like a fish on a line. "I'll follow you to the ends of Creation."

Rumor has it, said Gendreau.

"You got this, baby," said Annie somewhere behind her.

There's one for resurrection.

Power—green and warm and alive. She let it in and was suffused with the warmth of sudden life. The Narnia around her burst with vibrant, vital color once again, even with the howling hellhole punching through the middle of it, and Robin knew she'd found the right heart-road.

Fighting like hell to exclude all the others, she breathed deeply of the power until it filled every crevice of her soul.

Before the death-goddess could reach them, light strobed between Marina's and Robin's interlaced fingers and they exploded like a nuclear bomb, shunting the dock straight down and jamming the support poles fifteen feet into the earth of False Narnia.

Ereshkigal, the dock, the shore, her mother, and the cow-god all scattered into dust, and Cosmotelluria itself evaporated in a vast white light.

And then . . .

And then everything hurt.

Track 39

Robin gasped and sat up, almost jabbing Kenway with a horn. Gendreau managed to sob and laugh at the same time, and Navathe quietly threw his fists into the air as if she'd scored a game-winning touchdown. Kenway gathered her up into a hug so tight, it made her neck hurt. "Oh, my God, oh, my God," he jabbered, her face mashed into the sweaty pit of his shoulder.

She held him, reveling in the woodsmoke-and-musk smell of his body. The demon rage was completely gone, leaving only a bone-deep exhaustion, and the real world was a fog reeking of real-world smells. Petrichor, sweat, burnt paint, wet soot. She hadn't realized how *clean* the afterlife felt until this moment.

"Sorry about that," she said. "I died, but I got better."

Kenway chuffed hoarse laughter.

Robin gasped. "Where's Marina?"

"What?" he asked. "You know—"

"No! *No!* I saw her! In there! *I saw her;* she was in Middle-Earth or some shit, with a goat-man. I saved her. Ereshkigal found us and

I used her power against her to bring us back to life. The cow told me not to do it, but I did it. I guess in Heaven it's illegal to steal magic."

"The *cow* told you?" asked Gendreau.

Body screaming, bones aching, she rolled to her hands and knees and stood, scanning the tarmac. "Where is she? Please tell me she made it back."

To their credit, every single person there looked around.

"I don't—" Elisa began. "She's not here."

Oh, no, thought Robin, her heart dropping in despair. After all that, she didn't make it. "I didn't do it right." Balling her fists against her eyes, she fought dual urges to shriek and weep. She'd wasted her only golden ticket.

A chunk of stone lay nearby, dislodged from the tarmac.

Snatching it up, she pitched it across the wasteland and loosed a singular, throat-shredding scream of rage.

• • •

Loading Robin into the back of Elisa's truck, they drove up the runway to look for whatever remained of Santiago's transfigured form. "Stop here," she said through the back window as they neared the street where the battle had taken place. She could already smell the bitter, sour stench that accompanied the grotesque tar gushing out of Santiago's wounds, a foul reek somewhere between burnt hair and long-spoiled food.

"Why are we stopping?" asked Carly. "Where's my dad?"

"Don't know what we're going to find, and you deserve to remember him the way he was," said Robin, moving stiffly. Her injuries had been mended by the resurrection, but she was still a mass of aches and pains. Having a human form, even partially, wasn't all it was cracked up to be. "The relic in his motorcycle really changed him, and it wasn't a good change. Things got a little crazy at the end. There *is* no Santiago, not anything that you would recognize."

The teenager met Elisa's worried eyes.

"Might be a good idea, hon," said Elisa, digging around behind the seat. She came up with a flashlight, a heavy police skull-cracker. "Stay here in the truck, and I'll go check it out."

Rain continued to fall as Robin, Elisa, and Navathe got out and trudged down a dark, narrow alleyway, blurring Robin's eyes and turning the truck's headlights into clusters of white circles. She examined her belly as she walked. The gashes where she'd been gored had sealed over; unfortunately, the demonic carapace over the wound didn't re-form, leaving a hole in the armor over her chest about the breadth of her finger, surrounded by hairline cracks. *So, that's how it works,* she thought. *My heart. That's my kryptonite.* She made a mental note to buy a bulletproof vest. *Adapt and overcome, indeed. Man, Fish, you didn't know just how right you were.*

When they emerged from the alley, Navathe clapped a hand over his mouth and made a hoarse gagging noise. The pyromancer just managed to stagger over the sidewalk before he vomited into the scraggly landscaping.

Foul-smelling black slime heaped in the middle of the street like blood pudding. Swimming in it were monstrous tangles of shaggy limbs and bones, scraps of matted fur, mounds of ropy gray innards. Dozens of misshapen skulls floated in the ooze, some of them sporting three eyes or split palates.

"What the hell?" said Elisa, her voice shaking. "Looks like a tannery's been using this place as a dump."

"In the end, he couldn't figure out what animal to Transfigure into," said Robin. "So, he became all of them."

"*This* is what's left of my brother?"

"I'm sorry."

At first, she couldn't figure out the watermelon-sized object lying at the edge of the scene.

La Reina's gas tank.

Since removing the teratoma—and thus Ereshkigal's power—from inside it, the tank had become a corroded shell, as if some giant cicada had shed its husk and left it there. No doubt the rest of the motorcycle had followed suit as well; by the time they made it back to town, the Enfield would just be a pile of rusty parts and bald tires.

"Never shot anybody before today," Elisa said forlornly, looking up at them. She panned the flashlight back and forth over the grisly remains. The undercast gave her a ghastly, stricken appearance. "Ain't like the movies, is it?"

"No," said Robin. "It isn't."

As soon as the words left her mouth, a hand reached out of the slime and clutched Navathe's ankle.

He gave a shrill scream and jumped straight up in the air, doing an uncoordinated bicycle kick, and ran in the opposite direction, shoving his way through a barracks door, swearing the entire time.

Peering down at the muck, Robin and Elisa were shocked to find a human body, covered in blood and slime.

The figure drew ragged breath.

"Marina?" gasped Elisa, flinging the rifle into the weeds. She knelt to grab the woman's hands, Robin took Marina by the arm, and together they pulled her away from the swamp-smelling carnage, depositing her on her back. She was completely naked, her modesty preserved only by a thick sludge of gore.

As the worsening rain washed her face, Carly's mother gazed up at the sky. "Where—where am I?"

"Texas," said Robin.

Marina blinked, as Elisa helped her to her feet and took off her own jacket, wrapping it around the newly reincarnated woman.

"I think I'd rather have gone to Hell," she said, matter-of-factly.

• • •

As soon as Elisa pulled into the driveway, her girlfriend Isabella came charging out of the kitchen door, shouting obscenities in Spanish. "Where the hell have you been?" Her black eye had turned a jaundiced yellow-green. "Christ, I've been worried sick!"

As Robin climbed out of the back of Elisa's truck, Isabella went quiet, her eyes widening.

"Buenos días!" said the horned, blood-slimed witch-hunter.

"Uhh, buenos días."

Isabella pulled her house robe tighter.

"Mi nombre es Robin, y estoy en una biblioteca." One corner of Robin's mouth quirked up in a half-smile. "Sorry, my Spanish is a little rusty."

Isabella's eyebrows shot straight up. "Uh . . . *huh,*" she said, and turned to Elisa as she and Navathe got out of the truck. Robin and Rook helped a one-legged Kenway out of the back. "What is going on? Who *are* these people?"

"They're . . ." Elisa searched their faces. "New friends, I guess."

Isabella stared at Robin's jet-black left hand and the horns jutting from her forehead. "What is she wearing?"

"Long story," said the witch-hunter. "If you got some coffee on and a bottle of Extra Strength Tylenol, I can tell it to you."

Track 40

Despite the coffee, Robin dozed off in the middle of her story about the battle with Santiago and the ensuing visit to the bizarre in-between land called Cosmotelluria, and slept for three and a half days.

Track 41

She woke up voraciously hungry and thirsty on the afternoon of the fourth day. Kenway sat in a wheelchair by her side the entire time, administering what liquids he could manage, which mostly consisted of squeezing a water-soaked rag into her mouth. Being a registered nurse, Isabella dug up a packet of saline solution and was gearing up to hydrate her with an IV when Robin opened her eyes.

She was hungry, but she was relieved by how *normal* it was. How *human.* The kind of hunger that begs for burritos, chicken chow mein, hamburgers, pizza, not entire civilizations. That demonic need to destroy and devour was gone.

"Afternoon, Rip Van Winkle," said Kenway, smiling.

Behind him, the TV was on and women were yelling at each other in hushed volumes. Robin lay on the sofa, and they had pushed the coffee table against the entertainment center to make room for Kenway's wheelchair.

"Afternoon?" She blinked. "How long did I sleep?"

"Almost four days."

"Wow."

She examined herself. No change in her appearance in the intervening time; the only parts of her that were fully human were her legs, right arm, right shoulder, and head; her left arm and torso were still sheathed in the chitinous black exoskeleton.

"Damn." Her stomach growled.

"What?"

"Had hoped all this would be gone," she said, tapping the thumb and fingers of her left hand together like castanets, producing a solid knocking sound. Her left hand was a wicked-looking gauntlet, with segmented fingers. A ridge of crags crossed her knuckles.

"We'll fix it," said Kenway. "We'll fix it, baby. We'll find another Transfiguration relic and you can pick up where you left off."

"I guess."

"Now that you're up, I don't guess you need this after all," said Isabella, holding up the IV needle and saline packet. "Sounds like you're hungry. Lunch should still be warm, if you want some."

"Yes, please."

"Good thing you woke up," said Kenway. "She couldn't find a vein on you, so I was going to have to administer the saline . . . the other way."

"Up my nose with a rubber hose?"

"Anal. Uhh, anally."

"You were going to squirt saltwater up my ass?"

"Last-ditch hydration technique. They teach it to every combat medic from here to Timbuktu. If it's stupid and it works," he said, turning his wheelchair around, "it's not stupid."

"Talk about a way to end a long, hard day. Kick back with a nice ocean colonic." Robin raised up into a cloud of dizziness and sat there with her forehead in her hands, listening to the *telenovela*, only understanding every third word. The carbon spikes jutting out of her forehead were still there, between her fingers.

"Got a hangover?" asked Kenway.

"A little bit."

Even though the only light was the sun filtering through a set of venetian blinds, the room seemed too bright. Elisa and Isabella's living room was cozy, with wood paneling and lots of cutesy figurines and religious paraphernalia. "Ah, shit," she said, staring at a dazzlingly busy portrait of the Virgin Mary. "What do these folks think about having a demon with horns sleeping on their couch?"

"Elisa hasn't been here much. She's been helping Navathe, Gendreau, and Rook get our stuff out of the Winnebago. I'm going to have it towed to Jake's garage and sell it to him for parts and scrap. Now, *Isabella,* she . . . she's cordial enough, I guess, but she doesn't seem to want to get near you. She wanted *me* to stick you."

"So sorry your RV got fucked up."

"*Our* RV." Kenway squeezed her left hand. She could barely feel it through the carbon armor.

"Yeah, but you bought it for me."

He shrugged. "Shit happens."

"It does." She rubbed her face, wringing her mouth. "It happens to me a lot. And now that we're a thing, it's going to happen to you a lot, too." Robin's eyes met his. "You almost died back there. In the clubhouse. Because of me."

"But I didn't."

"You almost did. I *thought* you did."

"But I didn't."

She sighed in exasperation, staring into his eyes.

"Shit happens," he reiterated.

Standing up, she unfolded her stiff limbs and stretched, her back crackling in satisfaction. "Have you eaten yet?" she asked, pulling Kenway backward and turning him into the kitchen.

"No, not yet today."

Pulling a chair out from under the kitchen table, Robin eased his wheelchair up under the edge and sat across the corner from him. Her armored back clattered against the wooden chair, and

Isabella flinched subtly at the noise but didn't say anything as she put plates of lukewarm spaghetti and garlic bread in front of them.

"Thank you," Robin told her. "For everything." She picked at her food. "For letting me crash here for almost a week. For not . . . for not being upset at me over what happened with Santiago."

"You don't have to be worried about me," said Isabella, pointing to the yellow ring around her eye where her erstwhile brother-in-law had punched her in the face. "He was an asshole. Don't know if he deserved to *die,* but he was due for an ass-beating, at least. Things played out how they played out, though." The hard expression on her face softened. "What happened out there?"

"The thing in his motorcycle twisted him into something that wasn't human anymore," said Robin. "Dunno that he would have ever been human again after that. He already had a screw loose, I think, but La Reina took *all* his screws out and then put his batteries in backwards."

"Elisa," Isabella said, "she might be a different story. He was her brother by blood. I don't know how she feels."

Robin's heart sank.

"Haven't seen much of Carly. She went back to school the next day, though I didn't think it was a good idea. Doesn't come home after. Doesn't go to the mall with the other kids. I think she doesn't like the mall; she associates it with her father, maybe. Marina running away to the mall with her, y'know, when Santiago—" Isabella cut herself off, going to the fridge. "What do you like to drink? I have Sprite, tea, Dr. Pepper . . ."

"I'll take a Dr. Pepper," said Robin, twirling spaghetti around her fork.

As soon as the food hit her tongue, that was all she wrote. Wolfed it down like it was her last day on death row, fork in one hand, garlic bread in the other. Isabella sat across from them and ate a bowl of ice cream.

Looked like fudge ripple. From time to time, Robin caught her looking at the horns.

"How is she?"

"Marina?" Isabella sighed. "Quiet. Serene, you might say, oddly enough."

"She knows what's on the other side now."

"So you say. She hasn't said much. Said it was nice. Says she's not afraid of death anymore." Isabella stopped eating, staring down into the bowl. "It's a bit scary, to be honest."

"She doesn't mean she wants to die," said Robin.

"I know."

A car pulled into the driveway, crunching across gravel. A few minutes later, Gendreau, Navathe, Rook, and Elisa came in through the carport door.

"Miss Martine!" cried the curandero, hugging Robin. "You're awake!"

"I'm awake." She squeezed him with her human arm.

"Got just about everything out of the Winnebago," said Navathe, holding up Walmart bags full of what looked like camera gear and toiletries. "State trooper came along as we were cleaning it out and gave us a hand. We gave him the canned food that wasn't ruined so he could take it down to the homeless shelter in Lockwood. Jake's going to tow the Winnebago to his garage and scrap it."

"What'd he say about the mess Tuco left on the front of the RV? The blood and guts."

"Told him we hit a deer."

"What'd he say about that?"

"'Musta been a hell of a deer!'"

"Luckily, he didn't ask where the deer went," said Kenway.

"No, we had already gotten the swords and gun stuff out and put it away the day before," said Gendreau. "Some of that might not have been one hundred percent legal, I think."

The carport door opened again and Carly stepped in, her book-bag slung over her shoulder. As soon as she saw them all gathered around the kitchen table, she paused. Her eyes danced across their faces.

"What?" she asked coldly.

Elisa glanced at the clock on the wall. "It's a quarter to two, honey. School doesn't let out 'til three. What are you doing home so early?"

"I got sick."

"Sick?" Alarm lit up Elisa's face. "Are you okay?"

"Not that any of *you* would give a fuck," said Carly, giving them all one last smoldering glare.

"Carlita!" blurted Isabella.

The teenager marched out of the room. A few seconds later, the guest bedroom door slammed shut.

Everybody stood stock-still, searching each other's faces for quiet answers, or perhaps permission to speak again. "She's upset about her parents," said Robin, her stomach settling heavy.

"I don't know what I'm going to do." Elisa fidgeted with the wax fruit in the centerpiece of Isabella's table. "I don't know shit about teenagers, much less one that just lost one of her parents, and the other parent is on the verge of joining a convent."

"Especially when the one that killed her father is sitting in the kitchen, eating spaghetti," said Robin. The food in her mouth, as much as she wanted it, had lost all taste. She got up. "Where is she?"

"Marina?" asked Isabella.

Robin nodded.

"Out back."

• • •

Toasted grass and hardpan dirt crunched under Robin's feet as she slipped out the back and eased the screen door shut. Isabella's back lawn wasn't big, but with nothing in it and the merciless Texas sun beating down, it seemed a mile wide. Desiccated sticks jutted out of a brick-lined garden off to one side.

In the shade of a desert willow, Marina Valenzuela sat in a rickety lawn chair. Half a glass of lemonade sweated in one hand. She squinted in the sun, bereft of sunglasses.

"Hey," said Robin, approaching.

"Buen día," said Marina.

"Hot day."

No response. Carly's mother stared at the back of the house, or maybe nothing at all. Robin sat next to her, plopping down on the spiky brown grass. Occasionally, Marina would clear her throat, or sigh, or close her eyes for a moment, but for the most part, she just focused on the middle distance.

To Robin, it looked like shell shock. "You doing okay?"

"Sure," Marina said, a bit listlessly.

"I'm sorry."

"For what?"

This time, Robin had no response.

"You did what you thought you needed to do," said Marina. "You were right. You made a promise, to me and my daughter. Bringing me back here was the only way to honor that promise."

"She—"

"Yes." Marina sipped at the lemonade. Ice tinkled against glass. "She needs me. I know. That is why I'm here."

Definitely something missing, thought Robin, giving her a sidelong look. She couldn't help but experience a guilty sort of regret as she watched the woman space out. Had it really been necessary to drag her out of the Matrix-pod of her own personal paradise and force her back into this hot, stupid, unfair world?

Yes. It had been. Marina had been lost before her time. She still had money on her meter, so to speak. Now, if she'd died of old age . . . that would have been different, right?

Right?

"Is this what it's like?" asked Marina. "For, como se dice, near-death experience? To see heaven, and to experience it, and come back to the real world?"

A lone cricket chirped somewhere in the bushes.

"I feel like—" Marina peered into her lemonade as if the words she needed were in there. "I feel like I won the lottery and then I had to give it all back, every penny."

Robin winced.

"And now I am a ghost."

Welcome to the club.

"I am La Llorona, come to life. I am a heartbroken spirit forced to wander the earth, crying for something she cannot have."

Some fire in Robin's chest ignited—adrenaline, not hellfire—and she got stiffly to her feet, standing over the other woman. "No. You're not going to do this. I didn't drag you back here, in the face of Hell and defiance of two gods, so you could mope around and wait to die again."

Marina looked up, vaguely startled.

"You are in the prime of your life, Marina. Live it the best you can," Robin continued. "I got that albatross Santiago off your neck; now make sure I didn't waste my time, and go out there and make something of the time you have left. And take care of your little girl while you're at it. She still needs you—she'll always need you. Now you know what's waiting for you when you get to that finish line, but for right now, you need to get your fucking feet on the ground and stop pining for the fucking fjords. Live fearlessly if that's your jam, but *live*. Or do I need to kick your ass, too?"

Sitting straighter in her ancient lawn chair, Marina poured the remnants of her lemonade on the ground and held the glass in both hands. Seemed as if she were hugging herself. With suddenly haunted eyes, she said, "That thing at the bottom of the whirlpool."

"The supernatural asswipe in charge of all the witches I've been hunting down," said Robin. "She wants to drag me into Hell. And my demon daddy is probably down there waiting for me."

Marina went back to staring into space.

For a moment, Robin was afraid she'd retreated into herself again, but then she produced a pair of big Jackie Onassis sunglasses and slipped them onto her face. "If that terrible creature down there is what waits for bad people—I am going to live my life so that I never have to go to Hell and see her again." Marina took a deep breath through her nose, held it, let it out, and stood from the chair. "I shall not die of a cold, my son. I shall die of having lived."

"Lovely," said Robin. "Is that a quote?"

"Willa Cather, in her book *Death Comes for the Archbishop.*"

"Had no idea you were so literary."

"Never really went to church. Disculpame pero, God never did much for me. But books, they can save you in ways religion can't. They can give you strength, teach you, give you a place to go when the world is too much. I wanted Carly to have that refuge too, so I always made sure she could go to the library and that our home always had books."

"I've read a lot of books," Robin noted, as they walked across the dead lawn to the house. "Reference books. History books, occult stuff. Never really did it for fun. Not since I was a kid."

"Maybe this is the time to start."

She thought about it, holding the door open for Marina.

"Their rock was an idea of God," said the woman with a wan smile, quoting Willa Cather again. "The only thing their conquerors could not take from them."

Track 42

"We'll be back later today," Kenway said, crutching out the door of their motel room six days later. It was the day of his VA appointment to get fitted for a new prosthetic leg. Gendreau had elected to go with him in Robin's place, since she didn't exactly want to sit in a clinic waiting room, decked out like a demonic Stormtrooper. "Try not to get in a fight with a gang of vampires while I'm gone."

A pale blue dawn settled over their heads, making the world cold and watery and weak. Robin's "tactically acquired" Harley-Davidson stood in the parking lot next to the magicians' car. Robin wore a light jacket, T-shirt, and jeans over her armor carapace. Part of her wished she'd gotten rid of the horns while she had a chance, but hindsight's twenty-twenty, ain't it?

"Vampires aren't real."

"Neither were werewolves."

"Don't worry," she told him with a kiss. "Just going to sit in the room. Watch movies and eat. When you get back, I'll be in a food coma." She helped him into the car and slipped his crutch into the back seat. Shutting the door, she gave him a kiss. "Love you."

"Love you too, babe."

She rested her hands on the windowsill and looked him in the eyes. "I love you very, *very* much, Kenway Griffin," she said as sincerely as possible. "You know that?"

His smirk turned to puzzlement. "I love you very, *very* much too."

"Be back as soon as we can," said Gendreau. The magician started the car and the radio came on, droning some nameless country song. As the car backed away, she blew Kenway another kiss, and his eyebrows furrowed.

Then the moment was gone. Gendreau drove up to the highway, put on his blinker, and pulled into morning traffic. Robin sighed and went back inside, where she sat and finished her breakfast as Rook lay on the bed reading the news on her phone.

The MacBook had sustained visible damage in the Winnebago crash; the bottom plate was warped and the screen was loose, but otherwise, it still worked. As she gathered all the equipment she thought she could fit into her saddlebags, she made a mental note to stop by an Apple store somewhere.

As for the Osdathregar, Robin had cut the twine binding the spear head to the broomstick, making it a simple dagger once again, so that it would fit in the Harley's bags. Belatedly, she kicked herself for not thinking to ask the cow-god if she knew anything about the weird dagger-spear-thing, the supernatural ice, and the fact that it turned her into a monster.

Rook looked up from her phone. "What are you doing?"

"Packing my stuff." She thought about adding a smart-ass remark, but thought better of it.

"Are you leaving?"

"Yes."

"Without us? Without *Kenny*?"

"Yes."

Rook stood up from the bed and dragged the bag Robin was packing out of her hands, clutching it against her thighs, looking uncharacteristically vulnerable. "What for?" she asked, staring into Robin's face. One arm was pinned to her chest with a sling; the explosion under the Blue Wolf had torn her rotator cuff.

"Thinking of taking Doc G's advice. Ending the YouTube videos and starting up a podcast. With a cat and a Keurig. Wanna be my co-host?"

"That's not what I asked you."

Reclaiming her bag, Robin sighed and focused on rolling up clothes. "He almost died because of me. Because he's *with* me. And then back there on that runway . . ." She looked up, her throat tightening. "The pain on that man's face, Rook. His heart wasn't just broken; it was shattered." Her eyes burned, threatening tears. "I don't *ever* want to see that again. It will kill me so hard, nothing will be able to bring me back."

Tears spilled out anyway, tracing the curves of her cheeks. She redoubled her efforts, folding shirts even tighter. "You can't go," said Rook. "If you're gone when he gets back, it's going to break his heart anyway."

"I can and I am."

"Listen—"

"I would rather him be a little bit hurt than a whole lot of hurt . . . or *dead*, goddammit." Robin thrust a hand into her bag and showed the other woman her little GoPro camera. "I'm going to keep making my *Malus Domestica* videos. Or the podcast, or whatever. He can keep an eye on me that way if he wants. But I'm not putting him in danger again."

She coughed into her gauntlet fist and put the camera away again. "I forgot to thank you."

"For what?"

"Saving his life."

"Oh, hell," said Rook. "Anyone else would have done the same, had they the power I do."

"All the same." Robin continued packing, shoving things into the bag as if they'd done her wrong. The blue guitar she'd bought at the pawn shop a billion years ago lay on the bed between them. "You know, Haruko," she said, looking up from her violent packing method, "you should let your family know the truth."

Rook froze. She let the statement linger for a difficult beat.

"How did you know?"

"When I touch things—mostly relics, but sometimes mundane objects with a lot of sentimental value—I get a mental flash of moments, memories. Insights of its previous owners. It's like I'm supernaturally tasting them, like I'm licking everything I touch. I don't do it on purpose." She glanced at her fingertips, as if she would see taste buds sprouting from them, and then down at the guitar that used to belong to a teenage girl. Robin wondered where that girl was now, and if she still wanted to be in a rock band. "I'm some kind of demon fly-person, I guess. I'm a demonic Jeff Goldblum."

"I see."

"But I picked up Andy's ring just after the Winnebago crash, and saw a sliver of time—the moment, standing in whatever repository you keep relics in, that you gave him the ring. He called you Haruko. I'd been suspicious of you before then, both me and Kenway had, but that's when I knew."

Gently shaking her head, Rook crossed the room and stood at the window, staring outside. "I can't. There are just too many strings in the mix to undo what's happened."

"If that's a metaphor or something, I don't get it."

"My name isn't Haruko anymore," said Rook, turning to regard her. "It's Rook. It's whatever it needs to be. *I'm* whatever I need to be, whatever *Frank* needs me to be. Haruko *is* dead. All that's left is an Origo, a magician, and I live a dangerous life. One I don't want Leon and Wayne involved in."

"Why you?" Robin sat on the edge of the bed, leaning back on her elbows. "Andy told me they found you through your Etsy shop or whatever. Why did they pick you? Why did they make you fake your death and abandon your family?"

Hurt flickered across Rook's face.

"Hey, I'm sorry, but facts is facts, man," said Robin. "You know Leon's drinking got really bad after they lost you, right? Got so bad that Wayne basically raised himself. And nursed his own father back from the brink on his own."

Guilt warred with hurt as Rook's eyes sank to the floor and she turned back to the window. "No matter what I chose, they would be mourning me. It was either die of cancer—*for real*—or let the Dogs cure my cancer and then I'm obligated to pay them back by working for them."

"You could have refused. Told them to eat shit and kick rocks."

"Agreeing to work for them was a condition of treating me from the get-go. If I hadn't agreed, I'd—"

"Yeah, I wouldn't be talking to you right now."

"Exactly."

The two women languished in the silence, one of them wrestling an old ghost of guilt, the other fighting to choke down her irritation. "Man, what a shitty dilemma to put on you like that. Throw away your family or die. Remind me to give Frank Gendreau a piece of my mind."

"It's not so bad," said Rook, shrugging. "I get to put my skills to work to help people. They didn't know it when they came to recruit me, but it turns out I'm the most naturally gifted Origo the organization has ever seen. I'm really good at it, and I finally get to stretch my legs for real now, doing real good. Found my purpose. You know Frank sends his healers—me, Andy, a few others—out to hospitals to cure people of terminal illnesses? In secret, of course. Unlike you, we can't make the newspapers or put videos up on YouTube. Just doesn't work like that."

"So, what, are you like, the Men in Black or something? The CIA of magic?"

"No," Rook said with a wistful smile, "just a few friends trying to make the world a little less shitty without inviting trouble to our doorstep." The magician sat next to her, folding her arms. "You know, you're being real hypocritical right now."

"How so?"

"I don't want to contact my family because I want to keep them safe. You're leaving Kenway because you want to keep him safe. What's good for the goose is good for the gander, you know. If you can't walk the walk, don't talk the talk."

"Fine, don't talk to them," Robin said with a scowl, "but because of those rings you gave them, your husband and son are mixed up in this shit anyway, you know that, right? And they still *have* those rings, lady."

"Well, I didn't expect them to move into your childhood home. And I didn't expect the rings to react to the wards your mother put on that house, either."

"The sentimentality of objects and the energies of magic go hand in hand," said Robin. "Magic is about connotations. You of all people should know that. Better than me, probably." She went back to packing her bag. The last thing in the satchel was the GoPro. Turned off, for now. She stared into its dead, unseeing cyclopean eye, and a tiny reflection of her face stared back, broken hematite spikes jutting from her forehead. Looking up at the mirror over the motel room desk, she studied them from afar—one of them, the right horn, was longer than the left at about four inches. The other, a little under three inches, was almost hidden by her bangs. Using the Transfiguration relic to regain her human form had resulted in her undercut growing out, so that she had a full head of hair again.

"Why did you keep the horns?" asked Rook.

"Can't seem to get rid of them." Robin reached up to touch the left horn. "They wouldn't go away."

Rook stared at her wryly until she relented.

"Okay, yeah. I wanted to keep them. They're cool. Happy?"

"No problem!" Rook put her hands up. "Your prerogative. Might make it hard to find a job, and the TSA will probably find them problematic, but otherwise, they're pretty stylish. I'm sure Wayne would say they look badass."

"Thanks. Think I'll keep them for a while."

Soft knocking came from the suite door.

Both women glanced at each other and then at the door. Whoever it was knocked again.

"Who's there?" called Rook.

"Me."

"Carly?" said Robin, face scrunching in surprise. She opened the door to find a teenage version of herself standing on the sidewalk.

Since her outburst at Elisa's house, Carly had dyed her hair purple and dressed all in black—black band T-shirt, black skinny jeans, black Converse, spiky punk bracelets, a studded dog-collar belt, a lacy black choker. Black lipstick. Against her rich Latina skin, goth was more fetching than it had any right to be.

Lord have mercy, Robin thought.

"Nice," she said, taking it all in. "You look like a Hot Topic mannequin gained sentience and ran away."

"What is Hot Topic?"

"What are you, like, six? Is there a diaper in those jeans?"

"I'm only a few years younger than you," said Carly. "What kind of six-year-olds you know wear diapers?"

"These are the jokes; take 'em or leave 'em."

"Whatever, look, I want to go with you."

"What?"

"I want to go *with you,*" Carly reiterated slowly, as if talking to an idiot. "I want to help you get rid of all the magic things and witches out there fucking up peoples' lives like they fucked up mine. I want—I *need*—to keep what happened to me from happening to anybody else. There are women and little girls out there staying silent because they're afraid they're going to get their freakin' teeth knocked out." Carly threw her arms wide for emphasis. "I know what you do. What you've seen, the things you do. The people you help. I want to do that. And I want to be like these guys," she said, throwing a hand toward Rook. "They can use magic! They throw fire! They—they make things move with their mind! I mean, seriously, that's *amazing*!"

"Are you crazy?" asked Robin, going back to packing. "You're not coming with me."

"Why not?"

"Because I already let one person into my life and it almost got him killed. Twice. Your mother died, and almost you and Andy. Do you hear me? I already have enough death on my hands."

"I can take care of myself," said Carly.

"You have demonstrated that admirably well."

Carly fumed. "I saved Mom from Dad when he was hurting her. I stopped him from—"

"Well, that didn't help—" Robin started to say, alluding to the fact that Marina Valenzuela did not survive this week's major fiasco, but Carly clenched her fists.

"Don't you even go there, lady."

Robin shook her head sadly. "You're already at my throat. Just goes to show you that this would never work out." She zipped her bag shut and passed Carly, walking out the door with it. "Besides, there ain't but one seat on my motorcycle, and I'm no cradle-robber."

Rook cackled, then said, "Ew," and covered her mouth.

"You're leaving?" Carly followed her outside. "By yourself?"

"Yes."

"What about your hot boyfriend with the one leg?"

"Kenway is safer without me. Everybody is. Navathe, Gendreau, Rook. You. You're all better off without me." Robin opened a motorcycle saddlebag and took out a wad of the previous owner's dirty gym clothes, making a face. A little glass pipe fell out and broke on the pavement.

"Is that a hash pipe?"

"I think so."

"Gross." Carly folded her arms. "Take me with you. I can be your sidekick."

"Don't *need* a sidekick." Robin buckled the saddlebag shut and rounded on Carly. That's when she noticed the rectangle pressing against the inside of the girl's hip pocket. Man, Elisa and Isabella both would kill her if they knew she was smoking. She pointed at the cigarettes. "When I started doing this, I was just a couple years older than you. Smoked a lot back then. My nerves were shot from fighting these crazy undead witch-bitches and their *28 Days Later* cat-zombies. Hate to sound like a cliché, but I've seen some shit. Seen bugs come out of my skin. Children cooked in ovens like brisket. Fucking arm was bitten off by a hog the size of a UPS truck, and I got so pissed off, it grew back." Lifting the blue guitar, she ducked through the strap and let it lay across her back. "Used to cut myself and scald myself with hot water and burn the insides of my thighs with cigarettes to psych myself up and push the pain and the PTSD and fear out. Just to keep going. That's how scary this gig is. I've gone up against things that would make Dracula piss the bed."

Carly remained where she stood, her arms still folded.

"*Can* vampires piss?" Robin asked.

Slowly, Carly's fists sank down to her sides. "If *you* won't take me, then I'll go with the magicians."

Throwing a leg over the motorcycle, Robin sat down and stood the Harley up, folding the kickstand back. "That's up to them." She walked the bike backward out of the parking spot and stood there straddling it in the middle of the access.

"Maybe after you've graduated high school," said Rook, in a humoring tone. "I'll have to talk to the others, and Frank, first. Frank runs our operation. He's got final say on who comes and goes."

"There you go, then," said Robin. "That's sorted out. Your mom would probably rather see you go to college or something, but hey—a job's a job, right?" She shrugged. "Why don't you go to school and be a social worker?"

"Why didn't *you*?"

"Because I didn't choose what I do. It was chosen for me. What I do is a cold river. I was thrown in and it was sink or swim. Actually, I was more Houdini chained up and thrown into a river. And I'm only just now getting out of those chains and clawing my way back to the surface." Hopping off the seat, Robin came down on the kickstarter and the engine let out one hideous gunshot backfire, growling to life in that farty Harley way.

"What do I tell him?" Rook shouted over the roar.

Robin revved the motorcycle once and squinted into the morning sun, burning their faces into her memory. "Tell him not to come find me. Once I've burned and slashed my way through all the witches, monsters, and devils, and there's nobody left to hurt him, I'll come back. He's still got his debit card for my account, and there's more in there than I could possibly need all by myself. He can get another RV. Or, hell, get his own apartment. I don't care. Long as he's safe."

"Wait," said the Origo. She threw her hands up in exasperation and wrung them. "What else can I say to convince you to stick around?"

This anguish was more agonizing than any injury she'd weathered thus far. Burning up in the hoarder house, losing her arm, seeing Marina fall, being gored by Santiago . . . none of it held a candle to what she was feeling just then. Took every single bit of her willpower not to walk the bike back into the parking spot and turn it off.

I have to keep them safe.

"Be good, Wednesday Addams. The world needs more good people."

"Oh, jam it up your ass. I hope you wreck." Carly's voice was the warm burr of a newbie smoker.

"Thanks, you too."

With a last salute, the witch-hunter roared away.

Track 43

As so often that summer, the old house was quiet and solitary, a hollow edifice of air and shine, catching dust and spinning time. Its current occupants spent most of their days elsewhere—the elder, at work and hanging out with his new colleagues; the younger, running around town with his friends, and—

—in other places, strange and distant places.

But today, the boy was just getting home from school. Footsteps thumped across the front porch, and a key rattled in a deadbolt lock.

As the front door opened, the phone rang.

Now several inches taller and a dozen pounds heavier, Wayne Parkin walked into the Victorian and dropped his bookbag in the foyer. Making a beeline for the kitchen, he grabbed the handset phone and pressed his ear to the earpiece. As he did so, the sunlight streaming in through the kitchen window glinted on the curve of the wedding band around his index finger. An identical gold ring glistened on the index finger of the other hand.

"Hello?" he asked, out of breath.

He stood there, listening to the voice on the other end of the line.

Goose bumps crawled up his arms. He attempted to speak, but only a choked sob came out. When he tried again, he could only manage one word at first. He removed his glasses, scrubbed his eyes with his sleeve, and put them back on.

They spoke at length, both of them crying.

When they finished, he hung up the phone and twisted the rings off of his fingers, holding them up like a pair of binoculars.

A soft shaft of light appeared inside the hoop of the one in his left hand, pointing into the dusty stillness of the house. He turned. The light grew stronger still, becoming a ghostly dagger blade. He followed it up the stairs and into his father's room, where it became a shining white blowtorch. He held the right-hand ring to his eye and looked around the room.

To his left, between a big armoire and the closet, was a door. But it was unlike any of the other doors in this house; instead, it was a steel fire door, the kind you see in department stores and government buildings. He pushed it open, and on the other side was a weedy backlot, a stretch of pavement overlooking a rusty chain-link fence and, behind that, what appeared to be an apartment complex.

Seagulls called from beyond the doorway, mewing, a sound so alien in rural Georgia that his heart pounded in his chest.

Only took him a few minutes to empty his bookbag of everything inside and replace it with a few provisions—a twenty-dollar bill, the rest of the granola bars, a half-box of Cheez-Its, a thermal bottle full of water. Giving it a second thought, he put his homework back in.

Back upstairs, he shouldered the backpack and pushed the rings onto his forefingers. The light vanished, but the door did not.

"I'm coming, Mom," said Wayne, and walked through.

Track 44

Three Months Later

She was almost out the food court door when the mall security guard caught her. Adrenaline blasted through Carly's system, making her heart pound in her fingers. "Where d'you think you're going?"

She rounded on him with dark eyes. "Home. Do you mind letting go of me?"

"Thought you was bein' slick, didn't you?" Tall, beer-bellied man with wet lips and steel gray in his temples. His uniform was a simple white polo shirt and black slacks, and he wore a patrol belt with a radio and a flashlight on it.

Carly stepped back inside, letting the door ease shut on a cool autumn breeze. "What do you mean?"

Still hadn't grown out of her sudden goth phase. If anything, she had gone even deeper: tiny miniskirt, combat boots over a pair of thigh-highs, denim jacket over a band T-shirt. Every stitch of clothing: black. She'd dyed her hair Irish-rose red. Robin was right. She looked like the nineties had taken on a life of its own and was trying to hook on the street, but she liked it—Marina had always dressed her like some dowdy goody-two-shoes teen queen from a family TV show. Felt good to buck Mom's authority and slum it as hard as possible.

But the guard kept ogling her ass when he thought she wasn't looking, and as he spoke to her, his eyes would occasionally flick down to her tits. Maybe there was a point to Mom's mom jeans, utilitarian granny panties, conservative shirts.

No, said the Robin in her head. *Stop. This asshole's behavior is not your fault. It is not your responsibility to protect every man-child on the street from his own libido.*

"You was waiting for someone else to leave the shop, to walk through the radio tag gate with you," he said, "so you could skip out with the stuff you shoplifted and leave the other customer 'holding the bag,' so to speak. You realize we got cameras, right? You was in deep shit before you even walked out the door."

"Don't know what you mean," said Carly, pulling. His liver-spotted mitt was clamped around her wrist.

"Come on."

Tugging her away from the exit, the man walked her through the food court and toward the arcade. Between Fong's Fun Palace and a pretzel shop was a narrow hallway, and hanging from the ceiling in the mouth of the hallway was a sign: MALL SECURITY. Carly briefly entertained the thought of dropping all her weight on the floor, just throwing herself down and bucking like a maniac, screaming she was being kidnapped or raped or something, but couldn't bring herself to do it. She might have done it two or three years before, but in the intervening time, she seemed to have developed a sense of embarrassment. Besides—and this was the worst part—a strange numbness had overtaken her, and she had frozen, letting herself be led by the hand.

Motion-detector fluorescents came on with a twee electric *blink-ink* sound, filling a long corridor with bright light. Five doorways led into other offices: RECORDS, BRIEFING, HUMAN RESOURCES, EMPLOYEE BREAK ROOM, UTILITY, SECURITY MANAGER, CCTV. The mall cop took her into the room marked BRIEFING and left her there by herself. Carly sat at a cold cafeteria table, in one of twelve cold metal folding chairs, and stared at her hands.

One wall was occupied by a pair of whiteboards, and while one of them was wiped blank, the other one had a litany of names. A moment's contemplation told her it was the various shops in the mall and who their general managers were. Fire evacuation chart. Shift schedules. Lists of shift duties, radio frequencies, codes. Timeclock with an ID swipe. USERRA poster reminding military veterans of their rights. OSHA papers and other displays droning on and on about safety precautions and procedures.

She raised her middle finger to the organization chart. Then she raised her other middle finger and panned them both around the room.

"Fuck everything in here," she said to herself, twisting in her chair. "Fuck that poster. Fuck that clock. Fuck this inbox. Fuck that outbox. Fuck that fire extinguisher. Fuck whatever that is. Fuck this whole room and everything in it."

Yes . . .

Someone whispering over the PA system. Carly almost leapt out of her chair in surprise, banging her knee on the underside of the table.

Her chest tightened as if there were a python under her skin, slithering between her ribs and squeezing them together. She massaged her chest, wincing. What the hell *was* that? Her eyes shot up to the ceiling and darted around, searching the corners where the dim lights left cottony shadow, but there were no speakers.

Startling her out of her reverie, the door opened and the security guard came in. "Thanks for, uhh, playing nicely."

Does this look like a game to you? thought Carly.

He sat down in a chair across from her and interlaced his fingers. Carly looked into his face and saw an utter lack of self-awareness in his bovine brown eyes. The corners of his mouth glistened with saliva. "Ma'am, we're going to sit here and have a nice little talk about what you did today."

"Goody-goody gumdrops." Her heart surged with fear and indignation.

"You'll be happy to know since this is your first offense, the manager ain't goin' to press charges as long as you give back what you shoplifted. You'd be surprised how many little girls like yourself do this kind of thing in an average year. If they tried to press charges, they'd be up to their eyeballs in nonstop bullshit." He fetched a deep, deep sigh as if he was the most tired, jaded man on the planet, and gestured toward Carly's purse with his thumbs. "Anywho, I'd like to ask you right about now to voluntarily cough up the stuff you stole so I can return it. If you're not willing, *that* is when I'm obligated to contact the police and—"

"Okay! Okay," said Carly, pulling her purse up onto the table. "Okay. Here." It was actually more of a messenger bag, a black canvas tote with a red medic cross on the cover flap. She upended its contents onto the table.

"Thank you for choosing the easy way instead of the hard way," said the mall cop, staring at the array of crap in her bag:

- her cell phone
- a pack of fruity chewing gum
- a GameStop lanyard with keys on it (a key to her school locker, a key to Elisa's front door, a copy of the key for Isabella's Kia they didn't know Carly had, the key to Mom and Dad's now nonexistent mobile home, a key to the security gate at GameStop, two other mystery keys, and last but not least, somehow she'd ended up with the key to Dad's old bike La Reina)
- three wrappered tampons
- two condoms
- a half a bag of Skittles

- black lipstick
- a makeup case
- her wallet (her learner's permit, library card, school ID, a photobooth strip of her mother and herself at the county fair three years earlier, a ten-dollar bill, and a handful of quarters, nickels, and dimes)
- a pack of Camels (only two left)
- a pair of stolen designer blue jeans
- a bottle of stolen aromatic lotion
- a fistful of shitty stolen jewelry

Carly snatched up one of the tampons and offered it to the security guard. "Here. You could use this."

"Don't appreciate the attitude," he said coldly.

"I'm sorry," she replied, before she even knew what she was saying. "For . . . for stealing the stuff." Not for the remark, of course. But for the stuff, yes. Carly pushed the expensive jeans, the gaudy hippie jewelry, and the little bottle of lime-bamboo Seashore Dreams lotion toward him, then scraped the rest of it back into her bag and dropped it on the floor beside her chair.

The mall cop put the jewelry and the lotion on top of the jeans and folded it into a wad, pushing it aside. "Thanks, kid. You did the right thing. Well, technically, you did the *wrong* thing, but then you made up for it. Kinda. Anyway—"

"That mean I can go?"

"Anyway," he went on, and licked his lips, stopping to woolgather for a second. "As I was about to say, still got to do something about all this, and in situations like this where the shop manager decides not to press charges and leaves the matter in *our* hands, the usual course of action is to ban the shoplifter from the mall for a certain period of time. Usually three to six months. If you're seen on the premises—"

"What?" Carly stared, mouth open. *"Banned?"*

"Now, it's what we usually—"

"No, you don't understand," said Carly, reaching into her bag and dragging out the lanyard full of keys, holding up the GameStop barrier key, and as she spoke, she became progressively louder and louder. "You can't ban me from the mall; I freaking work here! I work at the GameStop now! You can't do that! I've only been there for six weeks! I'm closing tomorrow!"

"Now, it's— You should—" Mall Cop got flustered, trying to cut in.

But she was on a roll. "They're going to fire me! My aunt is going to kill me! Took months to get that job! They're the only people that would give me an interview! You can't ban me from the mall! I *have* to come back! I work here!"

"Should have thought about that before you decided to shoplift a hundred-and-fifty-dollar pair of blue jeans, honey."

Honey. Carly fought the urge to punch him.

"I *need* that money." An embarrassed anger rose up in her so fierce, it caused tears to spring to her eyes. She wanted to flip the table on top of him, stab him in the throat with her keys, kick him in the balls. "I need it. It's the only money I have." The last word faded into huskiness as her emotions took over and she dropped her face into her hands, sobbing.

"You should have thought about that. I'm sure you can find something else. Department stores are going to be hiring for the Christmas rush pretty soon."

She hated this man so much in this moment, she could wish him dead.

So she did.

Her hands clenched into tight fists and she leaned toward him, staring into his face. Wishing with everything she had the man would drop dead right here and now, she growled "Fuck you," as venomously as possible.

"Now, that's not a very nice thing to say." The mall cop's expression turned from remorse into a wry smirk. No doubt she had just proved him right in his mind: she would be banned from the premises, and for *six* months, not three, because, well, because—

"—You're an asshole. You're such an asshole."

He seemed to think about it and said, "Yeah, guess my ex-wife would probably agree with you. Look, you're gettin' off real lucky here, kid. You could be leavin' in the back of a cop car, but I'm lettin' you off with a temporary ban and a warning."

Carly grimaced, her lips drawing tight and white over her teeth. "I hope you die."

She glared into his face, trying to visualize his brain behind it, and imagined crushing his head with her bare hands like a clay pot full of wet sand. Could almost feel the shards of his skull and the cauliflower form of his gray matter squishing through her fingers.

The mall cop sat back, visibly disturbed.

"Think it's high time I called your mother and escorted you and your smart-ass mouth to the parking lot to wait for her to pick you up, to pick you up." He gathered up the stolen goods and seemed as if he were about to stand up, but he hesitated, still seated, staring down at the bundle in his hands as if he'd forgotten what he was about to do. "You were vrr irresponsibrrr today. You should . . ."

A drop of blood hit the table.

Looking up, the mall cop twitched, and one eye squinted briefly as if to dislodge an annoying fly.

Blood trickled out of his left nostril, where it filtered into the coarse hairs of his mustache. His head twitched as if he were trying to look to the right but his neck didn't want to behave, and he kept talking, but what he said was some kind of tongue-tied pig Latin. To Carly's amazed horror, he sat back in his chair and the entire right side of his face went slack.

Both upper and lower eyelid sagged, revealing the red and watery flesh underneath his eyeball, and the right side of his mouth sagged in a deep frown. "Whass duss," he said, mushy and thick. A syrupy string of pink drool slipped out of his mouth and fell on his polo shirt. "Muffa gooba dum."

Slowly, gradually, the mall cop leaned to his right and fell over. The chair squirted out from under him with a loud clatter and he hit the floor on his side, the radio popping out of his belt with a squelch of static.

Carly's face and hands went as numb as if they'd been shot full of Novocain. She got up and crept around the end of the table. "Are you okay?"

He lay on his side, his head wobbling weakly on his unsteady neck like an infant. His gaze wandered the underside of the table and the tiles under his cheek, and then his face turned toward Carly and one of his eyes fixed on her, stunned and unrecognizing. The other pointed sideways at the floor.

Blood pooled on his tongue and welled in his ear. "Grrhhm-maangh."

"Oh, my God." She recoiled.

She stared at him as he continued to writhe sluggishly on the floor like a dying octopus, his dry lips sticking together, his eyes rolling.

Did I do this?

Something was in her hand. She raised it. Between her thumb and forefinger was the key to her father's Royal Enfield.

Did some of that rub off on me? Is there still something in this key?

"Hebbb," said the mall cop, gagging on the words. "Hebm. Whzzz."

Her eyes rose up from the key and fell on the man lying on the floor. Even if she *did* do this, what the hell did she do? Did she *really* want him to die? *Was* he dying? What the hell was wrong with him? Tightness in her chest only grew closer and harder—felt as if a brick sat between her lungs. Her hands tingled like she'd been sitting on them.

She wrenched the door open and looked out into the hallway.

"Hello?" she called, looking back and forth. "Hello? Anybody out here? I think this guy is having a heart attack or something."

None of the other doors opened.

Alone with a dying man. She ducked back into the briefing

room, where her new acquaintance still lay under the table. "I don't know what to do," she told him, wringing her hands. Panic made them shake, and the only way she could think of to make them stop was to twine them together.

The radio keyed and produced a young man's high, tinny voice. "Hey, chief—I'm gonna grab a late lunch."

"Aight," said an older man with a deep, dusky timbre. "Let me know when you come back."

"Roger."

Carly picked up the walkie-talkie and keyed it. Tried to think of what to say. Let go of the button. Keyed it again. "Hey, listen, somebody, there's a man—one of you guys—he's in the mall-cop room with the sign that says BRIEFING, and I think he's having a seizure or a heart attack or some shit." Searching the front of his shirt for a name, she found only LOCKWOOD MALL AUTHORITY embroidered over his heart.

"Who is this?" asked the man called Chief.

"A concerned citizen," said Carly, blurting out the first thing that came to mind.

"This some kind of joke?"

"No joke. He's a tall guy with a mustache and dark silver hair. Pot belly. Mister, he's really ffff—*messed* up. He's lying on the floor, bleeding out of his nose and ears. You might wanna get in here."

"All right," said the Chief. "Sounds like Deakins. Briefing room, you said? Mall security area?"

"Yes, sir."

His voice jiggled as if he were running. "Okay. Stay right where you are, I'll be there as soon as I can. Don't touch him or move him. Collins—"

"Yeah," said the guy on his lunch break.

"Got your phone on you? Call 911 for me."

"Roger. Already did it."

"Good boy."

About twenty seconds before these guys came barreling in

there, and she had a decision to make. Carly shot to her feet, dropping the radio, and eyed the shoplifted stuff on the table. Two decisions, actually.

Should I stay or should I go?

Grab the stuff and run, or leave it?

She picked up the bundle of stolen clothes but held it at arm's length in both hands like a dirty diaper. *Should I stay or should I go?* She even heard the guitar licks in her head: *Dun-dun-dun-dun-dun-dun-dun-dun. Plink?*

"Shit."

She tossed the stuff back on the table.

Breathlessly, she threw up a bird finger at the incapacitated Deakins, backing away. "Sorry, mister." She opened the door again. "I have to beat feet. But hey, I may have just saved your life, and I left that stuff I took, so let's just call it even-stevens, okay?"

Across the corridor and back out into the food court. As soon as she reached the end of the little access hallway, Carly did a U-turn into Fong's Fun Palace and jammed herself between two little boys, grabbing the sticks of a *Street Fighter* cabinet and rattling them.

A couple seconds later, keys jingled right behind her as "Chief" came running down the access hallway into the security area.

"What are you doing?" asked one of the boys.

Carly rounded on him. "Shut your face."

"Why do you smell like a skunk?"

Turning on a heel, she stalked out of the arcade and through the food court, heading outside.

"Weirdo!" called one of the boys.

Carly pushed open the door and charged into a cool, dry Texas evening, where the sunset was a murky pile of reds, purples, and oranges. She tossed her hood up over her head and jammed her hands into her jacket pockets, heading down the sidewalk, ignoring the people walking by, trying to be nonchalant, trying to pretend she wasn't just standing over a man she may or may not have injured by force of will alone.

Sunlight brushed her bare shoulders and her fists finally unclenched.

Oblivious to the black cats coming out of the shadows to follow her, the witch walked home.

Hidden Track

Rolling over, the witch-hunter opened her eyes and stared at the red numbers for several seconds before she could decipher them. Three in the morning.

Some pungent smell hung in the air, heady, smoky.

Deep, hideous thrumming right next to her face. Robin snatched her pillow out of the way to reveal the Osdathregar hidden underneath, reaching over to flick on the bedside lamp.

Subtle electricity crackled along the blade. Bone-shaking yet almost inaudible bass emanated from the dagger, rippling throughout the room, causing the headboard to buzz softly against the wall. She turned the pillow over. A cruciform burn-mark was seared through the back of the pillowcase.

As she inspected the damage, the Osdathregar burst into flames.

"Jesus please us!" she shouted, running into the bathroom with it before it could ignite the bedclothes. Bare feet on cold floor. She thrust the flaming sword into the shower and turned it on, dousing the fire, and though it flickered at first, it continued to burn even as it was sprayed with ice-cold water.

Wait—*sword?*

She laid it down in the bathtub and sat on the toilet, shaking with adrenaline.

Yeah, you read that right. Somehow it had become a *sword,* a broadsword with a thin hilt like one of those kung-fu swords you'd see in movies like Crouching Tiger, Hidden Dragon.

Hello there, said a voice.

Robin sat up and scanned the dark bathroom. "Mom?"

Pleased to make your acquaintance, Keymaster, the voice said again, creeping-crawling into her brain from the edges, a snake out of time. *It's been such a long time since I've had someone to talk to. No, I'm afraid I'm not your mother. Or your father. I'm someone much older.*

"Ereshkigal?" she asked the sword as it guttered in a puddle of water.

Wrong again, love. A sinister sound with just enough heft to register as a laugh. Genderless, it seemed to encompass the full range of tone and pitch, a beam of hundreds of voices all tied together in a sheaf of sound. *You get one more try, and then you have to go home with nothing. Would you like to buy a vowel?*

She got up and stared at her face in the mirror. Her face was puffy, her eyes red and starey.

No, you're not going crazy, said the voice. *You're not being attacked by an Illusion witch. I'm real. Real as that pizza in your guts currently threatening to boil over into the toilet behind you.*

Chills racked her body.

Go ahead and pick up the sword. It won't hurt you. The Osdathregar suddenly extinguished itself. *Here's your hint, kid. Pick it up and look at it really carefully. And I mean right up close.*

Taking the sword, Robin carried it into the motel suite proper, where the bedside lamp glittered along its edge. "What am I looking for?" she asked, sitting on the edge of the bed. Until now, she hadn't realized she was covered in a sheen of sweat. The sheets were soaked.

Hold it up to the light. You'll know it when you see it.

She raised it until the steel was just under the lampshade, looking for an etching or some other mark. *Turn it, just here—there you go.*

Reflected in the mirrorlike surface of the blade was the opposite end of the motel room: the front door, the television, the window and the ugly brown blackout curtains. *This sword is actually the point of a very, very old spear. You might say the oldest. You call it the Ozdathregar, but when it was mine, I called it Heosphoros the Dawnbringer.*

Over her shoulder, she could perceive a silhouette in the corner focusing, sharpening, filling out.

Standing behind her was a black horned figure.

At first, she thought it might have been the Mother of Rivers, but an overwhelming thrill of fear shot through her as the figure opened its eyes to reveal two orbs of green light, and opened a mouth full of emerald hellfire, and the horns curled into two ram spirals. It was the warhawk, the demon version of herself that had been goading her and terrorizing her the whole time from window-glass reflections and bathroom mirrors, the dark doppelgänger that stood over her dying body on the Fort Bostock airfield. But she was taller, brawnier, meaner-looking.

This spear is the weapon that killed God and got me cast down from Heaven, trapped inside this blade, said the warhawk. *It's been wandering the earth ever since, traded and sold and stolen and thrown away by a thousand warriors, merchants, thieves, and fools. Once, I almost got the cambion Jesus himself to take it.*

Finally, it's ended up in your hands.

"Oh, my God," breathed Robin.

Quite the opposite, said her shadow-twin. *Please allow me to introduce myself.* Flames licked from the warhawk's lips. *I'm a man of wealth and taste. I was the first demon to earn their harp and halo. I am the son of Aurora, the king of Babylon, the deposed prince of Heaven, and the exiled master of Hell. I am the Sword of the Morning. I have a thousand and one names in just as many lands.*

And, dear cambion, I'd like to have my Dawnbringer back.

I want a ticket back to the land of the living, my weapon back in my possession, and . . . You want to stay out of Hell, right? Awful lot of evil men down there thanks to you, you vicious little monster.

So. . . .

. . . let's make a deal.

She stood there in her underwear for several seconds, staring at the sword and the expectant silhouette darkening the silver blade with black-and-green Maleficent fire.

Opening the fridge, she took out the racks and stood the sword inside next to the last two bottles of a six-pack of breakfast stout and half of a burrito. Then she turned the cooler dial as high as it would go.

Wait! No!

"Not today, Satan," she said, closed the door, and went back to bed.